ORIGINATOR

ALSO BY JOEL SHEPHERD

Cassandra Kresnov novels

Crossover
Breakaway
Killswitch
23 Years on Fire
Operation Shield

A Trial of Blood and Steel novels

Sasha
Petrodor
Tracato
Haven

ORIGINATOR

A CASSANDRA KRESNOV NOVEL

JOEL SHEPHERD

an imprint of Prometheus Books
Amherst, NY

Published 2015 by Pyr®, an imprint of Prometheus Books

Cover image © Stephan Martiniere
Cover design Jackie Nasso Cooke

Inquiries should be addressed to
Pyr
59 John Glenn Drive
Amherst, New York 14228
VOICE: 716–691–0133
FAX: 716–691–0137
WWW.PYRSF.COM

19 18 17 16 15   5 4 3 2 1

Library of Congress Cataloging-in-Publication Data

Shepherd, Joel, 1974-
　　Originator : a Cassandra Kresnov novel / Joel Shepherd.
　　　　pages ; cm
　　ISBN 978-1-61614-992-5 (pbk.) -- ISBN 978-1-61614-993-2 (ebook)
　　1. Life on other planets--Fiction. 2. Androids—Fiction. I. Title.

PR9619.4.S54O75 2015
823'.92—dc23

2014027255

Printed in the United States of America

CHAPTER ONE

The play was something inspired by the Ramayana, Sandy thought. She sat with Danya and Svetlana in the pretty garden auditorium on this early Thursday evening, amidst about two hundred other parents and family of Canas School, and watched as eagerly as any parent for the next bit with Kiril in it. And here he came, a chariot driver in a golden tunic, with a toy trident wrapped in foil, running out with other chariot drivers as the older students' drum section beat a rapid rhythm. There were even some lights and sound effects, thunder and flashing lightning, as the kids ran around on stage and yelled like an army going to war.

And here came the boy playing Hanuman, jumping around with his monkey tail and staff, whooping and dancing. He was really very good, Sandy thought.

"Kiril should have played Hanuman," Svetlana opined. She was leaning on Sandy's shoulder, mostly so she could talk through the show. Today that was fun, but Svetlana was terrible to watch movies with. Danya liked to tell her that if the director had wanted her commentary, he'd have put it on the soundtrack.

"I think this boy's very good," Sandy said diplomatically. And really, Kiril wasn't quite demonstrative enough to be a monkey god.

"Why are all the warriors boys?" Svetlana wondered. They weren't bothering anyone talking; the kids and drums and sound effects made a racket, and half the audience were laughing or clapping anyhow.

"Because three thousand years ago they probably all were," said Sandy. Here went Hanuman, leading his army off to battle. Kiril tried to look ferocious with his paper trishul, but the toy horse dangling on the little chariot arm kind of spoiled the effect.

"It's supposed to be a modern interpretation," Svetlana objected. At which, a line of little girls ran onto the stage, all in pretty dancing costumes— the wives seeing their husbands off to battle.

"Well, this is grim," Danya remarked on Sandy's other side, as the audience all laughed and cheered to see their respective little girls dancing.

"It is a bit warlike," Sandy admitted. Surprising, given recent events. She knew Danya's opinion of the school's hopeless political correctness. "But hard to do anything on the Ramayana without wars."

"Why are all the dancers girls?" Svetlana continued her theme.

"Because it's Tanusha, Svet," Danya replied. "And good girls know their place." Svetlana grinned, always enjoying Danya's cynicism. Sandy liked that Danya was now almost leaning on her shoulder too. He still never cuddled, but he would do this casual, relaxed and happy thing that a tough teenage boy might do, and lean or place an arm carelessly. Sandy had learned she could get away with a semi-cuddle if she disguised it well enough. Most mothers couldn't get away with that, but she wasn't most mothers.

The kids had been on Callay fifteen months now. Danya was fourteen, Svetlana eleven, Kiril seven. A year older, taller and healthier. A year more well-adjusted, thank god. This was home now, and home for good. For Kiril in particular, Droze was just memories. For Svetlana and Danya, far more than that, but the rawness of that life had faded. They were Tanushan kids but tougher and wiser than most of their schoolmates by whole orders of magnitude. And still, for all the improvements, more troubled. That was a part of them too, forever. But in that respect, Sandy made four.

A lead dancing role was filled by a very cute little girl in her sparkling sari, who danced and danced in circles while the other boys and girls clapped a rhythm.

"She's very good for a Chinese girl, isn't she?" an Indian lady remarked loudly nearby.

Danya nodded sagely at his sister. "Yes, there's no sexism or racism in Tanusha," he said, as though imitating something his teachers had told him. "Very important to remember that."

"Hush, Danya," said Sandy, as the Indian woman overheard and turned to *look* at him. Danya looked back, with unapologetic calm. The woman saw who it was and looked quickly away. "I get into enough trouble from Svet and Kiri without you doing it too."

"Well, thanks," said Svetlana, and whacked her arm. "Hey look, demons!"

The chariot army confronted some kids wearing fearsome red masks and horns. More dancing, to a change of rhythm.

"The choreography's good," Svetlana offered.

An uplink blinked on Sandy's inner vision—FSA HQ. She was technically supposed to be working, but her hours right now were more flexible, and she'd been planning to eat with the kids after Kiril's show, then go back to work after she'd seen Kiril to bed. The audio pause that followed suggested a group announcement, something live. Svetlana asked her something else, and Sandy tapped behind her ear, indicating she was uplinked. Svetlana knew she'd only do that during Kiril's play if it was important.

"*Okay*," came Assistant Director Hando's voice, a little distracted, as everyone registered on the net. "*We're receiving something from an inbound freighter, could be important. It's going to take a while to make sense of it, nothing's chronological. I'll need everyone to stay on this channel for updates.*"

"What is it?" Danya asked when Sandy returned full attention to the play.

Sandy shrugged. "Don't know yet, we're on hold."

Rather than show actual violence, the kids drew big scarlet drapes before the action and waved them wildly while drums hammered, and there was a lot of yelling and crashing thunder.

"That's actually pretty cool," said Svetlana.

Then the drapes fell, and only the chariot kids were visible, led by Hanuman. No demons, and certainly no little demon bodies. Two years ago Sandy wouldn't have really understood that sensitivity—it was just a fun kiddies' play, after all. But now she got it completely. The chariot warriors saw they held the field and yelled in triumph, waving trishuls and bows in the air. The audience cheered with them, and the dancing girls reappeared for the celebration.

"*Still there everyone?*" Hando resumed as the play reached its triumphant conclusion. "*Okay, what we're getting appears to be a series of log records from Cresta administration. That's a moon in the League's Hope System. No idea why it's coming in the freighter's mail, but it's been tagged priority, so we're taking precautions.*"

Cresta. Sandy recalled a station, boring like all stations in the war, dull steel and nothing to do. The inhabited places below they'd not been allowed to visit, League combat GIs not being allowed to mix with the general population.

"*Now we're getting a feed here of some traffic approach data . . . looks like a big anomaly . . . just another day on a League mining colony, looks like quite a few military transports, have to get Boyle to look at that. . . .*" Pause. Then a gasp of horror. Sandy couldn't recall ever having heard Hando make a noise like it. "*Oh no. Oh my fucking god. Jesus Christ . . . Marchi! Marchi, this is going out planet wide, the media will have this any minute. Everyone, we are on full alert, condition red!*"

Then something inaudible, multiple questions coming in. Sandy sat where she was amidst sustained applause, people on their feet for the kids, who were smiling and waving. Danya and Svetlana were on their feet too, shouting to Kiril.

"*What . . . ? Hang on . . . ? Director? Director Ibrahim, are you online? Director, someone just killed Cresta. Yes, all of it. It's just gone, it looks like a V-strike. Oh, I'm not sure sir . . . I think about two hundred, maybe two fifty thousand people. Big orbital facilities too, tens of thousands more, I don't think they'd have survived either. . . .*"

"*This is Ibrahim,*" came the Director's voice for the first time, cutting in on a new audio channel. "*Everybody in, right now.*"

Sandy watched ten things at once on the way into Headquarters. Tacnet was arranged in a two-tier setup, the first level tracking her own spec-ops forces, the other showing broader units across Tanusha, alert levels, general deployments. No one really knew what would happen next; it was unprecedented.

On top of that, her own monitor programs were watching net traffic, thousands of conversations and data streams babbling at once. Mostly she watched for spikes, anything alarming from the usual sources. The media were of course going crazy, demanding to know more, they hadn't deciphered all the incoming encryption yet, but they had access to private assets who were as good as anything the FSA had, so it wouldn't take them long. They knew Cresta was gone but didn't know how.

"*Sandy,*" came Delphia on uplink, "*can you tell me any more about Cresta?*"

"Just what's on file," Sandy replied, steering the cruiser along a skylane between brightening towers as night fell. An approaching storm lit the horizon with blue flashes. "I was there a few times, only ever on the main station, it had maybe a twenty-thousand-capacity, C-class station, nothing special."

"*Local politics?*" Delphia asked hopefully. She worked in League Affairs, under Boyle.

"I was a very dumb grunt back then, and I wasn't allowed to mingle anyway. Couldn't tell you more beyond what you've got."

"*Well, that's the problem, we've got nothing on Cresta, Sandy. It's a mining base, the whole Hope System is industrial, and half the population's only been there since the war, no indigenous identity or political stuff to speak of. Why would anyone want to kill it?*"

"I suppose we'll find out."

She had ideas. Ideas like revolution, like uprising. Like PRIDE, like the revivalists, like all sorts of crazy stuff going on in the League right now. Given what they knew of the neuroscience behind the sociological breakdown, the best estimates for major blowups had still given them another year or two. Sandy hadn't been so optimistic.

She would have expected a message from Ari by now, so she dropped him a line, just to see if he was available. Click. "*Sandy?*"

"You need some help bringing this one in?"

"*Not yet. You going to HQ?*"

"Yeah."

"*Sandy, Rumplestiltskin is going to try and lock you down. You might want to go autistic for a little while.*"

Sandy frowned, processing multiple tacnets and net sweeps on internal vision, her real eyes watching the dash screen as a new Cresta Station feed came in from HQ. "Why will Ranaprasana lock me down?"

"Just will. Watch the blind side, girl." Click, disconnected. The blind side was the bureaucracy, Sandy's worst weak spot in Tanusha. Ranaprasana was the former Chief Justice of old India itself, loaned by far away Earth to the Grand Commission, as they were calling it, trying to sort out the governance mess the Federation had gotten itself into over the last year.

Vanessa connected. "*You think we'll get deployed?*"

"Hell," said Sandy, "if League's about to fall apart, the smartest thing might be to pick the biggest bit remaining and join with them to crush everyone else. At least then we have a fast winner; the worst option is to let this shit drag on."

"*Yeah.*" Worriedly. "*Dammit, I was supposed to get another two years.*"

"Wouldn't worry about it, Ricey," Sandy said with considerable satisfaction. "If we get deployed, you're not going." Silence. "I am *not* deploying a mother with three-month-old twins. So save yourself the trouble and get used to it now."

"*Yeah. Yeah, I know. . . .*"

Vision on the screen showed a bright flash. Station feed, the crescent horizon of a big moon in space. Cresta, light methane atmosphere, lifeless save for the pressurised colonies. The flash looked like a new sun being born. Then shockwaves, Cresta's atmosphere literally peeling away, rippling concussion blasts like waves across a pond, as the station feed darkened dramatically against the impossible glare. Behind it, waves of fractured molten rock, liquefied at those pressures. Then the shockwave hit the station, and the feed went blank.

Sandy had seen a lot of horrible things in her life. This was a scale beyond imagination. V-strike, only theorised until now. Everyone knew how to do it, but despite several wars in the age of ultimate annihilation, it had never been used. Until now. Probably a rock, little more than the size of a house, propelled by FTL jump engines to a speed perhaps three, perhaps four percent the speed of light. The energy involved was on the scale of stars. Against a larger world, it would devastate the atmosphere and kill all life in a few hours. A smaller moon like Cresta would be permanently reshaped, cratered on the near side, bulged on the far, and stripped of all atmosphere forever. Beneath such a force, the entire moon would temporarily liquefy, cities and people included. Against a bigger world, it wouldn't just kill people; it would kill everything, down to the microbes.

"I'm glad I just hugged my kids," Sandy said quietly.

"*Well, give them a hug from me when you see them too,*" said Vanessa, similarly quiet.

"Vanessa," said Sandy, instinctively knowing her friend's mind. "It wasn't a mistake to have kids. You picked the perfect time. If you'd waited longer you might never have done it."

"*Yeah, let's hope* that *wasn't the better option.*"

"*Sandy,*" Amirah cut in on a narrow link, "*FedInt special transmission, we've got it straight from Chief Shin.*" Sandy scanned the com display graphic that came with Amirah's link, saw FedInt command structures, barriers that should not be so easily penetrated . . . only Ami was running what spec ops called the "weather forecast," which involved spying on the Federation's leading spy agency from the inside, using their own codes against them.

"Yeah, that looks like he's moving," Sandy agreed, as the cruiser's nav comp locked into FSA airspace controls ahead. FSA airspace was a part of Grand Council airspace; failure to sync would these days result in immediate destruction. "Call Ari."

"He's patched in. . . . Ari, you sure you don't need a hand?"

"While we're still asking nicely," Sandy added.

"Um . . ." said Ari. *"Actually yeah, League won't miss that many agents coming our way. Help could be nice."*

"I'm on it," said Sandy, locking a new course into the nav comp and swerving out of FSA airspace to a new heading. Someone would see that, but Grand Council airspace was a mess, ambassadors, reps, admirals, everyone inbound, and traffic control doing somersaults to try to squeeze them all in without forcing an extra circuit.

Ari was in Santiello, where she'd first lived in Tanusha upon arrival, with Vanessa. God, so many years ago now. Ari was tailing the mysterious figure who'd been detected in various covert communications around Tanusha, and watched from that point on. Subject A, in typically imaginative intel speak. Everyone was pretty sure that Subject A was an operative with one of the League splinters, those anti-League separatists that League didn't like to admit to. Which one, no one quite knew. There was no point in arresting him until more had been discovered through observation, but problematically, FedInt were watching Subject A as well. It now seemed Chief Shin of FedInt had given the order to take Subject A in. Spec ops, Sandy and Vanessa's unit, were not on good terms with FedInt and now saw fit to intervene.

FedInt were one complication. The League infiltration team which had also been shadowing Subject A, and various other "subjects" these past weeks, were another. Ari was right, they wouldn't miss Shin's move, and now this game of sneak and observe was over. If it was League security, it would certainly be GIs, and they'd be under instruction to not allow Subject A to fall into Federation hands, not FedInt and especially not Spec Ops.

Sandy established a new tacnet frame and let it propagate. It would automatically integrate every spec ops agent in direct FSA contact. And these days, the League weren't the only ones with GIs.

A new connection, heavily encrypted. *"Commander, Chief Shin."*

"Chief, this is Kresnov, go ahead."

"I have assets moving to acquire a target in Santiello. I believe you have eyes-on; request you leave this one to us."

"Can you handle the League infiltration team we estimate is on route to eliminate your target as soon as you move?"

Pause. Surely he knew about it? Little got by Shin. *"Estimates?"*

"Front six, four sweepers, mid-to-high designation."

"Sitrep?"

She couldn't very well deny him; they were all on the same team. Theoretically. "We have them netfixed, eyes-on is too dangerous with high-des GIs. Our estimate could be off."

"So you don't have a firm fix?"

"By the sound of it, more than you."

"Request we go joint. FedInt acquires target, spec ops covers against League infiltrators."

"Our respective units do not possess that degree of interoperability. As you well know." He certainly did. Lately FedInt and spec ops hadn't agreed on much. Sandy tried to keep it civil, without compromising a damn thing.

"Surely you can improvise?"

"We certainly can. Unfortunately, I'm fairly sure FedInt can't, as we've seen demonstrated. I'm calling jurisdiction."

"That is a mistake, Commander. A grave mistake."

"Lodge a protest. Tell your people that getting in our way could be fatal. I've made the official call, spec ops jurisdiction is clear, League GIs makes this ours, it can't be clearer."

"FedInt will lodge official protest with Ranaprasana."

"You do that." Click.

Ranaprasana's Grand Commission was far more concerned with actual governance than security; the FSA had rewritten most of the security protocols for Callay concerning Federal actions and local-federal overlaps, and there wasn't actually a committee or statutory body anywhere in the Federation with the authority to override them. Sometimes Sandy wondered if Ibrahim had been counting on the events of last year to grant him the power to do that. The FSA Chief played chess across a span of months and years, moving pawns while opponents were distracted or asleep. Most opponents did not even realise they were in the game. Sadly, Shin was one who did.

"Ari, fix me." He gave her the fix; his own setup had massive local complexity very few regular humans could handle. He was seated high at the far end of the huge Santiello Stadium, capacity a hundred thousand plus. A quarter of the way around the ground, on the lower tier, sat two men, one African, the other Indian. The African, Sandy would have bet was ex-special-something; his arms were ripped with lean muscle, he just had the look. The Indian was more nondescript, wide face, smiling eyes, and sort of . . . bland. Average Tanushan height, average Tanushan skin tone, average Tanushan everything. That raised suspicions too. "You got interface feeds?"

Those came through, and Ari didn't bother giving her a briefing—at the speeds her brain worked, his words were superfluous. It flashed over her, a construct the size of a stadium, one hundred thousand mostly uplinked people, plus all the newsfeeds from the game, the live coverage options blinking on and off, automated bots scrambling to coordinate feeds and match profitable advertising lines. . . . And here were her two men, watching the game, hooked into the system. Sandy broke through ID codings; the African was plugged into game stats and commentary, the Indian was more coded . . . she broke it down further, automated tracers racing in a hundred directions to trace the relays his protective systems were bouncing it off. . . .

"This guy's a player," she said, highlighting the man. "Real netpro." Above, she was seeing Vanessa's tacnet structure fitting into place, like some manic spider spinning webs of light. "Vanessa, you watch the League and FedInt, I'm on Subject A and his friend."

"*Gotcha,*" said Vanessa. "*More worried about FedInt than League GIs, myself.*"

"Yep." She locked the cruiser into a wide circle around Santiello, not wanting to go in personally unless she was sure this was the place to commit. "Ari, I can't get a fix on this guy. Clearly a GI, you think?"

"*Oh yeah,*" Ari agreed. "*I have a couple of folks here, we could go and say hello.*"

"And start a fight in a crowd, with GIs. No thanks, let's just watch."

"*Odd thing,*" said Ari. "*Some in the crowd are hearing about Cresta. I'm sifting general traffic and they're talking about it. But this guy, nothing. You'd think he'd be more interested."*

Because Subject A, the African guy, was a League splinter and probably involved with the people who'd done it. The Indian guy, they had no idea about but didn't want to bust in and end this meeting until they knew his background, who he was uplinked with, who else might be listening in on this conversation and anything else about him. Who would a League militant leader be meeting with in Tanusha, at a football game, at the time news came through of Cresta's demise?

"Subianto security is too good to allow GIs in here with weapons," came Kriplani's voice from a temporary stop atop a stadium carpark roof. *"They're not reading anything. If the League team are here, they're hanging back and waiting."*

Like us, thought Sandy.

"Bet they have eyes-on too," said Vanessa as she thought it. *"Bet they're wondering who the guy with Subject A is, just like we are."*

"And if they do, FedInt does," Sandy added. "This is no way to bake a cake. If shit goes down, it could get very messy." She opened priority back to HQ. "I want everything we've got on standby, in the air. CSA support would be nice too, if they can spare some."

"Copy, Snowcat," HQ replied. Sandy completed another circuit of the stadium, blazing in the night with white electricity. *"Snowcat, the Director wishes you to know that the Provisional Grand Council has taken an interest in proceedings. Be careful."*

Great. Ibrahim wouldn't tell her unless it was important. The apparatus that selected Grand Council reps for the various Federation worlds had launched what was effectively a coup last year, when the prospect of a new war against the League had them sufficiently spooked. Now she was hunting the representative of an organisation that might have just sparked a civil war in the League . . . if one hadn't already existed.

Yet still the target and his friend just sat here, in plain view. That didn't make sense. Unless . . .

She called up Tanusha Central, which was what the FSA had taken to calling her newest creation. It was a multigrid, linking some of the FSA's most powerful processors and supplementing them with outside boosters to make a grid matrix several orders of magnitude more powerful than anything else in the city could string together. Experimental institutions had made grids more powerful but hadn't been able to apply them to anything before the inherent instabilities brought them crashing down.

Ari saw what she was doing. *"Whoa. You think . . . ?"*

"Just hold a moment," she said, as tacnet informed her of known FedInt cruisers heading on suspicious courses near Subianto. "Hello, Cody, could you and a few friends stabilise this for me? It's very important."

"Of course, Cassandra," replied the AI. Cody was an old friend—not an FSA employee, but willing to help and possibly the only entity on Callay who could stabilise a grid this big. And it violated several standing regulations, the FSA not liking AIs in security matters because their loyalty was impossible to psych-profile. "Do you think this might be related to the Talee?"

"I think that's quite possible, Cody," she said. He was fascinated by Talee. Who wasn't? "Let's have a look."

She set the parameters and activated the trace-and-map . . . it was insane, far too much information even for her, but the processing power was there at least. Probably the Tanushan power grid would register a slight uptick on consumption, just from this matrix alone. She hoped they didn't blow a fuse. To cross-reference every real-time visual feed onto Subianto Stadium with facial recognition on the two men sitting in section M, seats 81 and 82, and loop it through FSA tacnet's interface while juggling multiple simultaneous encryptions. . . .

It had taken her nearly a year to design the thing, little tinkerings in her few quiet moments. A year ago, her own uplinks couldn't have processed even this much monitoring capability. But for now, she saw a simplified grid unfolding, three-dimensional, sprawling, and moving in every direction at once . . . and that was nearly too much to handle.

Finally an answer. And when she matched timelines . . . they were off. Time was the hardest thing to simulate, and according to multiple cross-referenced constructs, these two had been sitting in the stadium for .0002 of a second longer than real-time cameras recorded. Net time moving more slowly than real time, as it would with ultra-large constructs. But it took crazy large processing capability to find the mismatch.

"Ari," she said, "send in your guys." Shutting down the program to patient mode.

"*Copy*," said Ari. "*What do you see?*"

"They're not there," said Sandy, with more thinking curiosity than frustration. "It's a mass illusion. I think the security systems might be the only ones not to see the empty seats. We're being hacked."

"*Fuck*," said Ari succinctly. "*Cai's back.*"

"Or his friends."

On the visual feed, she could see Ari's agents moving down the aisles between seats in the crowd, approaching Subject A and his friend. Stopping alongside, then placing a hand on the African man's shoulder . . . the hand went straight through. Then both men flickered and disappeared. None of the surrounding crowd reacted. So this was an FSA-specific hack. And whoever else was watching, no doubt.

Almost immediately, Director Ibrahim was in her ear. "*Cassandra, I take it this means Subject A was meeting with a representative of the Talee?*"

"Certainly looks that way." Hell of a time, Cai, she thought to herself. Better hope the media didn't get a lead on this. "Sir, if that's the case, he just helped our person-of-interest to escape surveillance. I know we all agree the Talee are self-interested and not hostile, but we can't just let it go because we're scared of pissing them off. There has to be a price to pissing us off, even for the Talee."

"*Agreed*," said Ibrahim. "*I want Subject A brought in, however necessary.*" And disconnected. If you have to break rules to do it, that meant, I don't want to know about it.

"*Well, they were real when they came in,*" said Ari. "*We followed Subject A here, he met the other guy—who we're presuming is Cai until proven otherwise—then they must have gotten up and left at some point, which we couldn't see. Subianto security shows . . . hang on . . . Cai bought that ticket three hours ago, that was just before the game began.*"

"Be nice to backtrack their communications," Sandy added.

"*Yeah*," said Ari through gritted teeth. "*Wouldn't it.*" Don't hold your breath, that meant. If that V-strike on Cresta was not a lone event, if it was just the prelude to many, and now the representative-of-some-sort of the people who'd done it was here . . . she put the thought away. It would not help her here.

The shot hit her cruiser without warning, then more, cracking off the rear gens. Sandy cut thrust and fell, got it back with a wobbly recovery, her panels red with alarms and aware she had a fresh breeze on her face that shouldn't be there.

"Yeah, I'm fine," she replied to the warning shouts, zooming and triangulating fast on tacnet's auto sniper-track for the source . . . three possible cruisers, and dear god, fifteen possible rooftops, so much for narrowing it down. "Anyone get that? Tacnet won't give me a fix."

"Sandy, you're listing," Vanessa observed. *"Better ditch that thing."*

Sure enough, the cruiser was dropping its left side, generators struggling to match output, nothing a few corrections could fix. "Copy, just get beneath me."

She was on the farther side from the stadium now, away from the point of attack—if it came from a tower, she was now out of range, and none of the three possible cruisers were following. Of course it could be a coordinated hit, but that had to involve cruisers, setting up a sniper crossfire around the stadium was crazy difficult on such short notice. FSA vehicles were now streaking in pursuit of the three cruisers, and checking out those towertops . . . but they didn't have the numbers. Where was the CSA help?

She stopped tracking the situation long enough to pop the door as Vanessa steered her cruiser underneath and to one side. Wind blew in, not much, she was nearly hovering . . . she leaned to recover her bigger weapon from under the rear seat, locked the cruiser's course on auto, then stepped out. She fell five meters onto Vanessa's rooftop, then swung over the edge through the window Vanessa had opened for her.

"Hey babe," said Vanessa, closing the window and powering the cruiser in the direction of those redlit towers on tacnet, quite used to such unorthodox means of entry by now. "Just dropping in?" She was chewing gum, her habit when the tension came up.

"That was League," said Sandy, quickly loading and prepping her rifle in the passenger seat. On tacnet, her own cruiser was making an emergency landing at a nearby transition zone. "That shot cluster was from over a K, GIs for sure."

"Disable or kill?" Vanessa asked grimly.

"Probably kill," Sandy admitted. "Too far out for that against a moving target, even with GIs. But they try any closer than that, good chance tacnet will pinpoint them even if they're accurate."

"Which means they think they know where Subject A is, and they're warning us off."

"Or leading us astray." They approached one tower fast, keeping below the soaring rooftop. Wind still blasted the interior, Vanessa keeping the window half-down in case Sandy needed to shoot out of it. Neither they, nor the cruiser's scanners, saw anything preparing to shoot at them. Vanessa orbited, a fast circle about the tower. "Why hit us if we don't have any leads?"

"They didn't hit us," said Vanessa. "They hit *you*."

"Without a clear chance of getting me," Sandy retorted. "It's counterproductive."

"Unless . . ."

"*Shots*," said someone. "*Main city grid, Petersham District.*"

Sandy looked and zoomed on the site . . . some street sensor had picked that up, software somehow translating random background noise into gunfire. Five Ks away.

She didn't need to tell Vanessa, Vanessa was already heading that way. "Watch the ambush," Sandy warned all vehicles. "*Firebird*, get in there first and cover." *Firebird* was an FSA flyer, a gunship with countermeasures enough to survive most portable missiles, and weapons enough to make red mist of whoever fired them. It would mean a thirty-second delay though, waiting for Firebird to get into position.

"What?" Sandy asked Vanessa, catching that sideways look. "You want to be first over target with GI infiltration teams shooting at us?"

"Cautious in your old age," Vanessa remarked.

"Thirty seconds won't kill us," said Sandy. "Impatience might."

The target area was suburban, low-rise two-storey houses hidden amidst a sea of trees, the occasional mid-rise apartment block breaking the regularity. Vanessa did a circuit rather than rushing in, as other FSA vehicles also held off, or spread on separate leads, or continued checking towers or the three possible flyers.

"*Hello, Sandy,*" came Amirah's voice. "*This is your hourly weather forecast—stormclouds gathering. Lots of downdrafts.*"

"Thank you, Ami," said Sandy, and disconnected.

"Downdrafts?" Vanessa asked.

"Chief Shin's giving a lot of orders," Sandy translated.

"Damn," said Vanessa. "Where the hell does Amirah have her forecasters anyway?" Sandy only raised an eyebrow. Vanessa saw. "Oh. You bugged him. I should have guessed. You bugged the top spy in the Federation."

"'Bugged' is a little unsophisticated." The gunship was roaring in now, underside weapon racks protruding all kinds of lethality, sensors sweeping the neighbourhood. "And it wasn't just me. Let's go."

"Does Shin know?" Vanessa asked, steering them in.

"I'm sure he does, and I'm sure the bugging's mutual." Sandy highlighted a rooftop several houses away from the target house. "Right here, please."

Vanessa dropped altitude, coming in fast over trees and houses, then flaring as they approached the point . . . no less than a hundred kph, knowing Sandy's capabilities better than most. The door cracked, and again Sandy stepped out. Fell, for several seconds, arm out to protect her rifle from impact, then crashed a knee through the rooftiles. Another bill for Federal Security.

She drew no fire and saw no activity, so she came up from cover behind the roof apex, then leapt to the next rooftop, seeing Hong drop to a similar rooftop opposite her, and Kristi to her right. Operating with GIs in Tanusha felt odd but good, and transformed capabilities considerably. Rather than make the leap directly, she dropped to the rear yard beside a swimming pool and crashed through the brick wall with a kick that sent dust and fragments blasting.

Rifle in one hand, she went fast up the side of the house, fishing her headset from a pocket and hooking it over one ear—not strictly necessary but a comfort she'd acquired since League days, particularly the rear-view camera behind her ear. She flashed a glance through a window as she ducked beneath it, then spun around a door corner and smacked it open with a flat hand that broke the lock.

Fast up the hall beyond, as Hong and Kristi came in simultaneously through other entrances, without even a word spoken to coordinate. It took barely six seconds for the three of them to clear the ground floor; no one cleared interiors like GIs. Hong and Kristi flashed upstairs to repeat the process there, leaving Sandy to consider the mess in the kitchen.

It had been a man, only now the head was missing, and plastered largely over a wall and benches. Three very-large-caliber holes in one wall showed cause. Sandy scanned them, the feed going straight to tacnet, which immediately analysed the nature and direction of the holes and began figuring trajectories and origins.

"*They had a good fix to make that shot,*" Vanessa observed from somewhere above. There were no windows in the kitchen offering a view from outside, she meant. "*If Cai was with him, it couldn't have been a net-fix. Maybe they had him bugged?*"

Stranger and stranger. Tacnet's add-on functions were identifying the body on the ground as Subject A, ninety-three percent probability. He'd been sitting with Cai (they presumed it was Cai) in the football stadium; Cai hacked the eyes of everyone watching to sneak them out and get them here . . . where he was killed by League GIs? That made sense, League wanted nothing less than their splinter group leaders to spill everything to *anyone* who wasn't League. Cai even less . . . though given the League undoubtedly knew more about the Talee than Federation did, it was unlikely the Talee could learn as much from Subject A as the Federation could. Or could they?

League-versus-Talee games that the Federation had only seen vaguely hinted at? What if the likes of Cai had played this game before with League operatives? And that wave was only now hitting Federation shores?

"*Ten bucks says FedInt fired that shot,*" said Ari, from . . . wherever Ari was now. Chasing leads even Sandy had no access to, no doubt. "*Let's keep the options open.*"

Stormclouds, Amirah said. Dammit. She hated three-sided contests, and this one was fast turning into four sides.

"*Sandy,*" said Hong from upstairs. His feed showed a woman on the ground, a GI to judge by the lack of blood from the recent hole in the back of her head. She lay on the ground beside a bed. A camera pan showed the window broken, glass on the carpet and bed covers—an entry then. No further signs of fight. League GIs would put up more of a fight . . . but the shot was to the *back* of the head.

"Cai was here," Sandy confirmed. "Or someone of similar capabilities. That GI was netlocked, then tapped in the head. They came in after him."

"*Or tried to sweep up the mess FedInt left,*" Ari corrected. "*Don't jump to conclusions.*"

Either way, it looked like a Talee-made GI had killed a League GI. Talee had killed League military personnel before, in full view of millions. It shouldn't have been such a surprise. But for one to do it *here* . . .

Figure Cai was under orders to eliminate threats as necessary. Obviously that included League GIs. What about Federation GIs? Or Federation-anyone? This was why the Talee had been so worried about intervention in human affairs in the first place—the unavoidable autonomy granted its agents, and the unpredictable nature of events, meant mission creep was inevitable, especially with this much on the line. Probably Cai had now gone further than most Talee had wanted . . . but without violating the conditions of his deployment. It happened. Had happened to her quite recently on Pantala. So now that the precedents were falling, how far would a Talee-made and loyal GI be prepared to go?

"Okay," she announced on tacnet, with careful pronunciation to be sure everyone heard, "from this point Cai, or whoever he is, will be considered a neutral hostile. I repeat, that's a neutral hostile." Approach with caution, that meant, and apprehend with force if necessary . . . but no deadly force unless left with absolutely no other choice. How the hell you *used* deadly force against someone who could hack your uplinks to disappear before your eyes was another question.

CHAPTER TWO

Ari brought the cruiser down on the roadside transition zone amidst the wall-to-wall bright lights and holographics of Sushil Square. The midnight crowds did not notice one more cruiser in the seething sky, spilling on the pavements in their crazy fashions and were far too preoccupied to glance up. A sea of humanity that would not fade until four in the morning, then picked back up at five with the early risers.

"Oh look," said Rhian from the rear seat, "Persian Princess is on!" Sure enough, the holographics a block down were showing highlights from yet another song-and-dance number, projected across the entire street, five to twenty storeys up. "I must take the girls."

"I resent the implication that only you girls would like that . . . all singing, all dancing, all fancy gowns and frilly knickers period bullshit," said Ari.

"Well, I'm not sure it's exactly Sandy's thing," Rhian admitted, as they descended past streetlights. Either ignoring or completely failing to detect Ari's sarcasm—with Rhian one was never entirely sure. "But you know Sandy, she loves a spectacle. And the music's great, I've been hearing it everywhere and Vanessa loves a rhythm."

They touched in the VIP spot beside the Grand Tanushan Hotel, and almost immediately there was a big bruiser in a tuxedo rapping on the window. Ari popped the door.

"Hey buddy!" shouted the bruiser above the din of street noise, "I don't know how you hacked the fucking TZ, but this is hotel VIPs only! You think just anyone can land here?"

"Hey *buddy*," said the woman appearing at his side, "take it elsewhere." Shoving her police badge under his nose and climbing in.

"Nice try, pork chop," Ari told the bruiser, sealing the door after Raylee and powering the engines. "Sorry to bust your dinner, babe. Got a job for the TPD."

"I'm *not* the Tanushan Police Department," his girlfriend retorted, belting in with a glance over her shoulder. "Hi, Rhi, shouldn't you be home with the kids?"

"After midnight," said Rhian, tapping her temple with a meaningful glance at Ari. "Clever time to have a crisis. Nice work, Ari. Kids all asleep."

"Husband asleep too," said Ari. "That's the best bit."

Rhian grinned. She'd been home on rotation, spending all her R&R with the family, in their house, something she complained she never got to do enough. Even Cresta's destruction hadn't revoked R&R privileges yet. "You got food?"

Raylee Sinta opened the bag on her lap as they gained altitude amidst the dancing, flashing towers and produced several boxes of Chinese takeaway. "Rhi, sweet and sour pork, wasn't it?" Handing her the box.

"Oh, I like this girlfriend, Ari," Rhian said approvingly. "She remembers."

"Yeah, well . . ." Raylee deposited Ari's food on his lap, "dinner was a bust anyway, but the food was excellent, stupid to let it go to waste."

Ari let the cruiser accelerate toward the departure lane on auto to attend to his meal. "Dinner was no good?" Raylee shook her head. "Two dozen potbellied cops giving drunken speeches in a Chinese restaurant? How can't that be fun?"

"Hey *buddy*, if I get a potbelly any time soon, we'll have an issue." Ari's mouth was too conveniently full of noodles to reply. She looked amazing, as always, leather jacket and hair in a bun at the back. Even after a year, she still favoured the right arm slightly, if you knew what to look for. "Just usual interdepartmental bullshit politics. Too boring to go into. Where are we going, and will I need extra guns?"

Ari blinked. "Babe, no, look . . . just because I ask you somewhere in the middle of the night, doesn't mean you're going to be shot at."

"And the fact that you guys are chasing someone to do with whoever blew up that moon in the League's got nothing to do with it?" Her half-lidded South Asian eyes were so nice when she looked at him like that. Ari hadn't yet seen an expression he didn't like. Well . . . maybe that one time . . . "And that you went out of your way to grab poor Rhian out of her bed?"

"I wasn't actually in bed," Rhian volunteered. "More like the bath."

Raylee gave him the Indian-head-waggle-of-accusation, with the glare of it's-all-your-fault.

"Well, I find that GIs are like handkerchiefs," said Ari. "It's always useful to have one in your pocket if you need one." Rhian whacked him on the back of the head. "Ow."

"You're right, Ray," Rhian said around a mouthful, "this is delicious."

It broke Raylee's facade, and she giggled. "You asshole," she said. "Where are we going?"

"You'll see in a minute," said Ari, eating with one hand, rubbing the back of his skull with the other. "Rhi? Spare guns are under your seat."

They came in at rooftop level across a bend of river, the water ablaze with reflected light from the surrounding towers.

"This one?" asked Rhian, highlighting the penthouse on their modified tacnet.

"Yeah," said Ari, handing his half-empty noodles for Rhian to stow. "I guess if you're going to have a safehouse, have it somewhere nice."

"What if he's home?" asked Raylee.

"It's a safehouse, babe, he's not home."

"This might be exactly the time a top FedInt spy would use his safe-house," she persisted.

"It's not."

Raylee looked at him as Ari brought them in to a landing pattern on the roof. "If you're so sure where he is, why do you need to hit his safehouse?"

"'Cause I'm not looking for *him*, I'm looking for whoever he's looking for. FedInt's been tailing someone for weeks now, it's super classified, so I'm not even sure how many people it is. But something's out there, and FedInt wants it."

"Someone other than this . . . Cai person?" Raylee was up to speed on some very classified things now and had uplink security and augments to match. Ari had told her to put her money where her mouth was, stop complaining about how FSA/CSA got paid more than cops, and make the leap. But Detective Raylee Sinta was a homicide investigator, her dream job since childhood, and wasn't about to give that up for money. And it wasn't a bad thing—cops were better at a lot of things, Ari was discovering, and new interoperability protocols made it possible for good cops to be borrowed by FSA at need.

"Looks like . . . Rhi, you got this?"

"Sure," said Rhian, and Ari popped the door. He paused the cruiser on its descent just above the penthouse balcony. Ten meters up, Rhian jumped out.

"Shit," said Raylee, peering out the window to look down, just in time to see Rhian land with nonchalant precision on the balcony, punch a hole in the glass, and enter. "Wow. I'm still not used to that. She's such a normal girl, then she goes and does that."

"Sandy's not a normal girl?" Ari abandoned the landing, bringing them into a slow orbit about the riverside towers. "You've seen her do crazy stuff too."

"It's less surprising when Sandy does it. She's . . . well, she's a bit scary."

"She's not scary."

"You know what I mean." Ari shrugged. He did. "Wait . . . you haven't disabled the security system? Rhi will be seen."

"Can't be helped," said Ari. He was watching scans as they circled, half expecting something to attack them. Not that he thought FedInt and FSA were about to start shooting at each other just yet. "FedInt don't share with us, we'll take instead."

"How does Shin get away with this? FedInt's supposed to be a department of the FSA, instead they're acting like an independent authority. A *hostile* independent authority."

"Not hostile," Ari disagreed. "Just independent. Everything just gets so damn big in the Federation . . . the problem with democracies is everyone gets power from local power bases, and that's all fine when those bases are in the one spot, everyone still agrees their common loyalty is to the nation, the state, the world, whatever. Spread those power bases over a few hundred light-years, and you start to lose that. And FedInt outdate the FSA; they were the tentacles of the squid under the old FIA, then the FIA died and was replaced by the FSA . . . but we're just the head of the squid, the squid's body is much bigger and retains all this institutional memory. We can tell it what to do— whether it listens is a whole other deal."

"Sounds like us and Special Investigations Bureau."

"Oh hell, everyone hates SIB. Here's Rhian. That was quick." Ari popped the door once more and manoeuvred out from the tower face, giving Rhian a forty-five-degree ascent. Raylee watched with amazement as Rhian climbed on the railing, gave a simple spring . . . and hit the open cruiser doorway eight meters above. She swung inside as Ari closed the door and powered them into a climbing turn.

"It's in," said Rhian.

"What's in?" Raylee asked.

"Our FedInt buddy is running his tacnet through that safehouse," Ari explained. "Easier to break in physically."

"But he'll see that now?" said Raylee, puzzled.

"Sure. So he has to stop using that tacnet setup if he doesn't want us seeing everything he does."

"Forcing him onto the main network, where we can monitor him anyway," Raylee concluded as she got it. "So where is he?"

A rough trace on the FedInt agent's location led them to a wedding. Like any good Tanushan wedding, festivities were beginning to spill from the upper podium floors of the Madison Hotel and onto the street below. Kotam District midtown showed no sign of quieting after two in the morning, firecrackers bursting over bustling streets, food kiosks parked by the pavement with nav lights flashing, small crowds of revellers, hotel guests and passersby clustering for a late-night dosa.

"So when's the TPD finally going to stop the fireworks?" Ari wondered, as crackers burst amidst passing cars. The automated traffic never flinched.

"It's harmless," said Raylee, walking beside him through the crowds. "This chemlab stuff packs no punch, you ban it and people just make their own."

"So varying degrees of illegality are now acceptable in Tanusha? And who makes that judgement?"

"Oh, shut up," said Raylee, tired of this argument but smiling. "Rhian? Is she there, I can't fix . . ."

"*He's in the podium, top tier,*" said Rhian, from wherever Rhian was. They were off tacnet; Raylee couldn't integrate it well, and with FedInt watching, tacnet wasn't always secure. "*Mind the horse.*"

"You get that?" Ari asked Raylee.

"Yeah." She looked disconcerted though. Raylee didn't just have a new right arm; she had new uplinks and sensory augments, right up to FSA standard. A year later she was still, in layman's terms, a noob. "It's like I'm getting a visual vibration when she talks. Is that normal?"

"No, you're going insane." Raylee scowled. "Where's the horse, Rhi?" Amidst a cluster of instrument playing, dancing people ahead, a white horse emerged from behind a parked van. The groom had long departed inside, and now the horse handler was struggling to control the unhappy animal, which tossed its head and stamped. "Oh, there's the horse."

"They have a permit for that, you think?" Raylee wondered.

"That's what I like about you cops, all the earth-shaking questions."

He led her up hotel steps past the dancing crowds, the photographers, the garland givers and Namastes—some hotel security thought about checking them but thought better of it. Raylee nearly walked into the glass door; Ari had to haul her around the edge by her arm.

"What the hell are you . . . ?"

"Asma Cohen!" Raylee announced, dazed and a little triumphant. "That's who's getting married, I was checking the cop database for wedding permits. . . ."

"Ah, nice Jewish wedding, then." Walking through the sea of saris and turbans in the main lobby.

"She runs a catering business, she's marrying Aditya Gaur, real estate broker. Two weddings, the Jewish one's next weekend."

Ari overrode an elevator and they got on, Raylee flashing her badge to stop several others joining them. It got some odd looks.

"Nice do for a catering business and a real estate broker," Ari suggested as the car took them up.

Raylee checked further, eyes unfocused. "Her turnover was a hundred mil last year, and his last sale was the Bradbury Tower."

"Ah."

"It's not going to work, though."

Ari glanced sideways. "Uplinks tell you that, too?"

"You know, Jews and Indians. Couldn't work." Flashing him a return sideways look.

"Of course it works," said Ari. "Judaism's just another weird little Hindu sect, your uncle said so." Raylee sighed. "You'll just absorb and assimilate

Callayan Judaism into cultural annihilation like you have every other group, and soon we'll all be happy little Indians together."

"If my family were like *those* Indians, how do you think I got a name like Raylee?"

"It's a plot," said Ari. Raylee laughed. "It's all a plot."

The elevator let them out on the upper podium, beneath the main hotel towers. Here were swimming pools, gardens and multiple DJs, entertaining what looked like a thousand guests, all flashing lights, dancing, fancy clothes, food and drink.

"Just so you know," said Ari, as they walked into it, "I can't afford this."

"*Legally* you can't afford this," said Raylee.

"Don't start." Even here, people looked at Raylee, men and women both. Even in practical clothes she stood out. "You'd be useless under cover."

"Don't start." Raylee Sinta had heard it all before. "Where is he?"

"This way." There were ceremonies going on in different places, some with priests and priestesses, others with garlanded statues of various gods, different gatherings for different family members, even a cool area for kids older than six who in the Tanushan way of things would *not* be in bed if the party was big enough.

Some tent awnings between palm trees made a new ambiance. Ari pushed in and indicated a man in a white vest and turban, conversing with several guests.

"That's him," said Ari. "You do it. They freak when it's me."

Raylee walked to him and pulled her badge. "Excuse me, Kamal Moily? Detective Sinta, TPD. Can I take a moment?"

"Of course." Moily was youngish, smooth, and completely unbothered by the approach. He went with Raylee to a slightly less crowded corner beside a table of drinks, *so* unbothered Ari knew it was all an act. A genuine innocent would be at least a little concerned, approached by the police at a wedding.

"Do you know this man?" Raylee reversed her badge to show the image— Subject A, back when his head was still intact.

Moily frowned at it. "That's Mr Rowan. He and I have done some business. Is he in some kind of trouble?"

"He's dead, Mr Moily." Very predictable surprise. "We have reason to believe that Mr Rowan, as you call him, was from the League. We think that he was killed in relation to the same business that you were doing with him. We also think there's a large possibility that the same people who killed him might also attempt to kill you."

It was remarkable how fast a man's studied calm could disappear when confronted with something that made his previous act seem unimportant. Fear and fast thinking. All these Tanushan hucksters and hustlers, Ari thought tiredly. Meet some League operative, hear some story of fast profits, and never a thought to the morbidly high mortality rate with anyone who dealt with League operatives lately. They always thought they could handle it.

"Oh my god," Moily murmured, eyes wide. "That moon that . . . this doesn't have anything to do with that, does it?"

Raylee studied him. "What exactly do you do, Mr Moily?"

"I . . . we don't have time for this, you have to protect me!"

"Well, I can't really protect you unless I know what you're into. What do you *do*, Mr Moily?" Damn, she was good, thought Ari.

"I'm . . . I'm a zodiac readjustment therapist."

Raylee frowned. Turned and looked at Ari, then back. "You're a *what*?"

"Star signs, zodiac signs, it's all so important at Indian weddings." Raylee's very Indian features showed fading patience. "And people want their prospective matches' personalities to match also. Only sometimes they don't, sometimes the Aries aren't so stubborn, and the Capricorns aren't so disciplined . . . and it doesn't make a good match. So I run them on a personality readjustment program, you know, tape teach, VR and meditation sessions to get the new couple's personalities to match up just like on the star charts. . . ."

"*All bullshit*," Ari formulated. "*Only the super-rich are stupid enough to fall for it.*"

"And what business did Mr Rowan do with you?" Raylee persisted.

"I . . . introduced him to some friends of mine." Evasively, eyes darting.

"Please describe these friends."

Real fear on Moily's face. These people scared him. Scared him worse than League operatives, by the look of it. Personality readjustment, bullshit as it was . . . and now League splinter group agents fishing for contacts. . . .

"Excuse me," said Ari, leaning in with his own badge, "Mr Moily, could you tell me if any of these faces are familiar?" He flashed his badge, uploading links onto the reverse display . . . a series of faces flashed across it. The facial-recognition software would have caught Moily's response, but Ari didn't need it.

Raylee saw it too. "*Pyeongwha*," Ari formulated to her. "*Neural Cluster Technology, wonderful. Subject A was talking to the Pyeongwha-nians about NCT.*"

Raylee wasn't good enough with internal formulation to bother with replying. "I think we'd better get you into custody real fast," she told Moily drily. "Come with us, please."

All the lights, save the independent candles and ambience gas burners, flicked off. Then the emergency services–mandated voice began, warning of a fire alarm. All wedding guests stopped what they were doing and stared at each other in disbelief.

"Not good," Ari said grimly. "Let's move." He pulled his pistol and moved fast, indicating for Raylee to bring Moily. Ari paused at the tent rear exit, then strode quickly about the rim of a pool, past milling guests in no real haste to move to the exit . . . and Ari recalled an action memo from somewhere that Tanushans in a fire drill would never move fast, being unable to conceive of an actual fire in Tanushan-designed buildings. About which they were of course correct; Tanushan buildings wouldn't catch fire unless deliberately set alight—and thus his alarm.

Something zipped in the air. Ari spun and saw a hotel waiter fall to the ground.

"*That was me*," came Rhian's voice before he could yell warning. "*Gun, left hand, he was drawing.*" Amidst fallen drinks, Ari saw the gun, the "waiter" shot neatly through the shoulder. Raylee paused from dragging Moily to stare back across the road, figuring where Rhian must be. . . .

"Move!" Ari snapped. They made fast for the rear stairwell, then down, shouldering past reluctantly moving guests, then quickly outpaced all guests as the stairs descended along the rear glass wall of the entertainment, convention, and ballroom levels . . .

. . . and suddenly the glass wall lit them up, bright lights glaring as Ari's vision augments struggled to adjust. Shots hit the stairs as glass broke, concussion blasts and gas.

"Go go!" Ari yelled, shoving Raylee and Moily ahead of him down the stairs, following as they reached the next floor ahead. Armoured figures crashed in, a well-trained combat entry, rolling amidst the shattering glass.

Raylee hauled Moily away from the stairs and, diving for cover behind potted plants in the adjoining hall, Ari struggling to follow as the armoured figures came up kneeling and aimed. . . .

And were hit from behind, a new entry through shattered glass, landing amongst them and firing all ways at once. Leg-swept one, spin-kicked another into a wall with bone-crushing force, then aimed behind her out the window to plaster the hovering cruiser there with fire. The glaring light vanished, then Sandy—because it could only be her—leaped at Ari as grenades hit behind and pinned him onto the ground by a wall as they exploded.

"*Rhi*," she formulated calmly even as Ari struggled to get his head back into order, heart pounding and lungs choking with the smoke, "*trace the cruiser, would you? It's silent but I put holes in it. I'm not allowed to shoot it down over people.*"

Satisfied that the threat had passed, she lifted Ari to his feet, as effortless as a child lifting a teddy bear. "You hurt?" she asked. Ari managed a shake of the head. Sandy smiled, kissed him on the lips, and strolled past Raylee with a wink, reloading pistols.

Raylee stared at Ari in disbelief. "You're fucking kidding me," she said.

"Yeah," Ari conceded, gasping. "I know, right?"

Raylee emerged from interrogation two hours later, blinkingly tired.

"Nice work," said the FSA lead interrogator, Sriharan, and walked to his own debrief, to which she was *not* invited. Leaning against a wall opposite was Kresnov. Watching her. Raylee still found that disconcerting. Something about Kresnov—*Sandy*, Ari always insisted she should call her—was so effortless. Calm, in a way normal humans were never calm. Interrogating her would be a nightmare.

"It was good work," Sandy affirmed.

"You were watching?" Sandy tapped her ear. She'd been watching real time in her head, then. Ari could do that too. Raylee tried sometimes, but it gave her a headache and sometimes made her nauseous. "Right."

"You want a coffee?"

The coffee machine was in a hall by big windows, surrounding offices still quite busy despite it being two hours from dawn. Sandy took hers strong, milk, no sugar. Raylee, even stronger.

"You're not attending debrief?" Raylee wondered.

Sitting opposite, elbows on knees, Sandy shook her head. "I get the summary. Nice thing with being the kinetic asset, I get to stay a few degrees separate from all the talking. Form my own opinions."

"Sounds more like you're the overview than just the kinetic asset." Sandy shrugged. Raylee couldn't deny that it made her edgy. So much power this woman had acquired. At this range, she looked astonishingly normal, shortish hair, wide features, strong figure. She had a power about her, a poise, like the gym junkies Raylee had known who walked and sat with rippling muscle, never a slouch or an awkward pose. Ari swore by her, this killer with the blood of hundreds on her hands, as though she'd never had an evil thought. Surely that wasn't possible, given what she was, and what she'd done.

But her three victims from two hours ago, she'd been astonished to learn, were all still alive. And the one Rhian had shot.

"So, what do you think?" Sandy asked with a jerk of her head back to the interrogation room.

"Well, he was the go-between," Raylee summarized. "Between your Subject A and some of the Pyeongwha radicals you haven't caught yet."

"Quite a few of those, sadly," Sandy said into her coffee. "The question is, what does a League splinter group guy want with Pyeongwha radicals?"

"Well, Mr Moily's no help there. But they're all into mind alteration, aren't they? Moily's just a low-grade hack, but he's interested in personality change, technologically induced psychology. Which is pretty interesting, when it comes to Pyeongwha."

Two years ago, the FSA had ended the regime of the planet Pyeongwha. Consensus was that Pyeongwha's brand of uplink technology, called Neural Cluster Technology, was causing radical sociological extremism, leading to a paranoid regime sabre-rattling at its neighbours, and massacring its own noncompliant citizens by the tens of thousands. NCT caused humans to go mad in groups. Now, word was, the entire League had caught a similar disease.

"Seems pretty strange that the representative of a group that just murdered an entire moon would be seeking out a group even more radical than his own," said Sandy. "They've no other connection. Pyeongwha's never had direct League contacts, they were xenophobic about other *Federation* worlds, let alone League worlds."

"Seems logical that a group that's going insane might want to find out more about the condition," Raylee reasoned.

"Can ideology recognise its own extremes as insanity? Most of humanity's genocides have been carried out by lucid and rational individuals."

"You think?"

"It's not an opinion, it's basic psych analysis. Radical politics is a natural function of human society. Pyeongwha's condition isn't something new, it's just *created* by something new. The condition itself has been observed thousands of times before in human history, statistically frequent enough to be considered normal."

And this was disconcerting too. Kresnov was crazy smart. Even Ari thought so, and Ari was so smart it sometimes made Raylee's head hurt. Why these two had ever left each other, she didn't know. They seemed a perfect match.

"Those guys who tried to kill us," said Raylee. "Ari thinks they're FedInt."

"Well, Ari would." Sandy sipped coffee. "They're underworld, scary well equipped, and they're not talking."

"Employed by FedInt. Ari insists. He says they do that sometimes, to hide their tracks."

"Which raises the question, why would FedInt want Mr Moily so badly? On his own, he's nothing."

"Same reason they killed Subject A," Raylee said tiredly. "To cover up some kind of connection between FedInt and the people who just killed Cresta. Ari says."

"You believe everything Ari says?"

"Hell, I don't know," Raylee said tiredly, rubbing her eyes. "He's a spook, I'm just a cop."

"So you keep insisting." Raylee just looked at her, sipping coffee, waiting for that remark to be explained. "You thought you turned down this offer of employment, didn't you?"

"I did turn down this offer of employment."

"And yet here you are." With mild amusement. "Again."

Raylee blinked. "Well, Ari asked, and . . ."

"And you keep saying yes. You do realise how this works? You accepted FSA-standard augments and uplinks, now you're accepting FSA jobs that require FSA-level secrecy. Soon you'll barely be able to talk to your old police friends because you can't share any of this with them. And you get this deeply entwined with FSA investigations, we'll just put you on permanent attachment." Gazing at her, with those deep-blue eyes. "But you said no."

Raylee sighed and stared at the floor. Of course she knew. Dammit. "Thanks for the warning," she said.

"Oh, it's not a warning. It's an observation. And if you don't like the people who are doing it to you, then I'm your worst enemy." She got up. "I have to go, apparently there's someone I have to meet."

"Why'd you kiss him?" Raylee blurted. Silly thing to ask, but she was tired, and it was on her mind.

"Because I can," said Sandy.

"You can do a lot of things."

"So can Ari," Sandy replied. "But apparently, he'd rather do them with you." Raylee gazed at her, frowning. And was astonished when Sandy kissed *her* on the forehead and left.

CHAPTER THREE

They sat in the briefing room, the most secure place in all FSA HQ. Director Ibrahim, Sandy, Assistant Director Hando, Ari. There could have been many more, but Ibrahim was determined to keep the numbers down to the absolute minimum. Chief Shin was reportedly frantic that he had no asset in the room and was making all kinds of calls and threats. Soon Fleet would be as well, no doubt. Then others.

Hando poured tea. Their guest took it politely, no milk or sugar. Hando passed around to others. Coffee for the Director, always.

"So, Cai," said Sandy. Lead, Ibrahim had told her. She had had previous contact and was also a GI. Ari had had more direct previous contact, but Ari was not "strategic." In the scheme of things, Sandy was somewhat superior. "How are you?"

"I'm very well," Cai said mildly. "How are you and the children?"

"Wonderful," said Sandy. "They're adjusting very well."

"I'm pleased to hear it."

"And your friends?" Sandy asked, sipping her own tea as it came to her.

Cai smiled. "My friends are doing very well also."

It was quite absurd. Pleasantries and euphemisms were fine, but Cai's "friends" were the Talee, the only other intelligent race in the galaxy, at least that humans knew of. Not only did he work for them, they'd made him, using the same technology that the League had borrowed to make the first human GIs, then called their own. The same technology, only a far more advanced version.

"I hope I have not upset anyone by being here," Cai added. "That was not my intention."

Sandy glanced at Ibrahim. Cai had just turned up, thirty minutes ago, on their doorstep. And had apologised to everyone for inadvertently getting in their way just now.

"Not at all," said Ibrahim. "In fact, we're quite pleased to see you. I'm sure you're aware of my personal desire, and the desire of many in the security apparatus here, to make communications links between our peoples more permanent."

Cai nodded. "I'm aware. But you are likewise aware that my . . . people . . . are not so sanguine."

"Can you explain why not?" Ibrahim pressed.

"No. Revealing the nature of their concerns could reveal the nature of broader circumstances. Circumstances that the Talee would rather not share."

It was paranoid in the extreme. Some analysts familiar with it expressed frustration. Sandy, for her part, thought it quite prudent, now in particular. Events at Cresta demonstrated that humans were capable of extreme action, exacerbated now in the League by an evolving crisis that was at least as much psychological as it was technological. A truly intelligent race might want to watch its step with such unstable aliens. And a peaceful intelligent race might just, in keeping their distance, be expressing a more genuine concern for human well-being than the more emotionally satisfying embrace that some humans appeared to desire.

"Cai," Sandy resumed, "you were talking to a League splinter group agent at a football game. Why?"

"I'm afraid I can't say."

"Okay," said Sandy. "If it's going to go this way, I'm not going to waste any more time asking what you're doing here and trying to connect those answers back to Talee strategic intentions. Obviously that's not going to get us anywhere."

Cai inclined his head slightly, and sipped tea.

"Let's move this to another level," said Sandy. "You chose to reveal yourself to us. You did not need to, you could have stayed quiet and none of us would be the wiser. Why?"

"There are things I would like to discuss with you," said Cai. "With all of you."

"Good," said Sandy, somewhat relieved. "Because if there's not, I'd really rather be home with my kids." Hando gave her a warning look. Ibrahim might have smiled, very faintly.

"Cresta," said Cai. "You are all in great danger."

"Who is? Us in this room? Callay? The Federation?"

"Humanity," said Cai. Silence in the room. "Cresta was a V-strike. Two percent light, quite deliberate. It came out of jump within the system shields, no defensive system could have stopped it."

"Wait," said Hando, "we don't know that detail yet. How do you . . . ?"

"Their ships jump faster," said Ari. Leaning back in his chair, dark hair, long face, leather jacket. Normally those hands fidgeted, scratched an imaginary itch, played with a stylus. Now, they held a mug of tea, unmoving, like his gaze. "He already knows. Could have known a week ago. And then went and talked to a League splinter group agent. An agent who didn't know Cresta was dead. You couldn't tell him that." The corner of his mouth twitched. "You were profiling, weren't you? Psych profile? Some kind of parameter matrix?"

Cai sipped tea. Not looking at Ari, not avoiding, not denying. Just waiting.

"You're scared League's going nuts," Sandy summarised. "You're scared the uplink technology they've been using is accelerating sociological disorder faster than anyone anticipated. I'll bet you were doing more than just psych-profiling, you were finding out what he knew; you can uplink-hack anyone you like. If you have some information pertaining to the imminent destruction of other human worlds, we'd certainly like to know."

"Nothing I can talk about." Sandy pushed back in her chair with exasperation. Hando looked at her with concern, worried she pushed too hard. Ibrahim just watched. "But I did come here with one thing I have been authorised to speak of."

"One thing," Sandy repeated. "Better than nothing, I suppose."

Cai looked down in his cup. A handsome face, like all GIs were handsome. Wide features, firm. Young but not youthful. Perhaps natural mid-twenties . . . like herself. Sandy wondered how the Talee had chosen this form as their template. No shortage of human bodies floating in space during the war, well preserved. Exact features could be randomised, so he wouldn't look exactly like someone deceased—and attract attention that way—in human company.

"The Talee," said Cai, with calm deliberation, "are a post-extinction-level-event species. Self-inflicted."

Boom. And just sat there and watched the humans all stare at each other. All except Ari, who muttered with possibly inappropriate triumph, "I fucking knew it!" And stared at Cai. "About three thousand years ago, right?"

Cai nodded.

"Big" didn't describe the revelation. Humanity had waited centuries for more news on the Talee. Possibly someone already knew, possibly League already had figured it out, their space directly adjoining the Talee's as Federation space did not. But this was the first time the Talee, even through a synthetic representative, had chosen to reveal something this large about themselves. Talee motivations had eluded scientists, strategists, sentience-modellers, and thinkers for generations. Now, finally, came the tantalising sense of long-awaited answers slipping into place.

"So you understand why Cresta might cause us some alarm," said Cai.

"How much alarm?" Ibrahim asked.

Cai fixed him with a sombre, lidded stare. "It changes things. Not dramatically, and not quickly, as nothing changes quickly with the Talee. But you might notice, I am here. Revealing things."

Ibrahim nodded, as deadly serious and intent as Sandy had ever seen him. "Please, continue."

Cai took a breath. "It took Talee civilisation perhaps a thousand years to recover. Most of the population was dead, on most worlds. On the homeworld, none remained. Only on colonies did some survive. It was clear to surviving generations what had happened; historical memory shifts and changes but cannot be entirely erased when the ruins of old civilisation remain all around. All of the new Talee race were all too clear on what had come before and been destroyed.

"Eventually those survivors built up their civilisation enough to reclaim their technological heritage, and then to reclaim the stars. They rejoined with other surviving Talee civilisations, on other colonies, and those moments are amongst the most powerful and emotive of all Talee history. If you can imagine."

"I'm not certain that we can," Ibrahim said quietly.

"The homeworld was resettled," Cai continued. "Biological engineering began to try to put things back as they were, to restore ecosystems still unrecovered after all those centuries. That work continues today. Good progress has been made, but there remains more to be done. Talee have a word for the extinction-level-event, perhaps the best and most obvious translation is "catastrophe." Catastrophe studies are prominent in Talee centres of learning. What you would call historians pore over it. Scientists examine it. Geologists look for traces in rocks, and biologists in water and plant matter. Conversation cannot avoid it. It is everywhere."

He looked around at them all. The humans stared back. Indeed, at times in the recent past, Sandy had wondered just how human she actually was, given that the origins of the technology that made her were in fact Talee. But now, confronted with this mesmerising horror, these multiple lost millennia, these untold billions of lives erased, an entire species' future and present abruptly shattered and nearly lost forever . . . she had never felt more human than now. Thank God this was not *her* race being described. Thank God. And with that thought came fear.

"I say this to make you understand—the Talee are concerned, now more than ever. This concern does not come from greed, or from hostile design, or from the desire to interfere for other selfish reasons in human concerns. The concern comes because we fear we may be seeing the fate that once befell ourselves now befalling you."

Abruptly, Ari leant forward on the table. "Can you prove that it was an uplink-related sociological dysfunction that caused your catastrophe?"

"No," said Cai. "But it fits the time frame well. And let us say, multiple circumstantial evidence, which I am not at liberty to share, further supports that conclusion."

"Talee psychology is different," Ari pressed. "If some of the theories are true, very different. Can you be sure that mass psychological dysfunction will result from the same technological phenomenon, whether the user of the uplinks is Talee or human?"

Here, Sandy expected evasion. Cai's answer stunned her. "Current Talee thinking suspects humans are less susceptible," he said. "But I might add my own observation—Talee can be . . . how should I say? Pessimistic, about themselves, where the catastrophe is concerned. Self-confidence is lacking, and judgement may be coloured. But yes, the patterns currently observed in the League are broadly similar with what Talee researchers might expect in a Talee population . . . with obvious adjustments to baseline psychological norms."

"So you're saying that while our species are not psychologically alike, our level of deviance produced by this phenomenon is approximate?"

Cai nodded. "I believe so, yes."

"Right," said Ari with hard determination. "Can you stop it?" Cai gazed at him. "In your own species, at least?"

Here again, the evasion. "I cannot say."

"Cannot? You mean you aren't allowed to, or you don't know?"

"Either," said Cai.

"That's not good enough," said Sandy. "You tell your friends that we'll put up with a lot from them, partly because we have no technological choice, and partly because we're genuinely convinced that Talee intentions are not hostile. But if the Talee can see what's unfolding in the League right now, and have even the smallest insights to share about how it might be possible to address it, on a technological level, then they have an absolute moral obligation to share!"

"Cassandra," said Hando with a faint wince, "please, this is an alien species, morality as we understand it is a very human concept. . . ."

"Talee have morality," Cai interrupted. "Different, as you say, Assistant Director, but the concept is as fundamental to Talee as to humans. But considerations are different. Reasoning is different. Value structures, prioritisation . . . please, you must understand how difficult this is for Talee to judge. . . ."

"Difficult for Talee?" Sandy replied. Not raising her voice, not yet. "We might be about to lose a good portion of our species. Or worse. And Talee morality says it's difficult for *Talee*?"

Cai stared at the tabletop, lips pressed thin. "Cassandra," he said then, "this is a dangerous simplification, but I feel that I must. Talee are very hard to convince, on this matter, that they will not simply make things worse."

"Worse?" asked Sandy. "How could it be worse?"

"Cassandra, when the Talee began to resettle their devastated homeworld, their researchers and scientists began to notice odd little things. Little discoveries, signs of civilisation in a different style or with the wrong timestamp. For a long time these oddities were overlooked. Understand that the catastrophe is the overarching mythology, the legend around which all Talee thought and culture is founded. To challenge the basic presumptions of that myth can be very hard, for even the most advanced mind.

"But finally the patterns of discovery became too compelling, and researchers from various fields found too many commonalities in their own discoveries for those patterns to be ignored. They began to get together and compare notes, secretly at first, but then with greater and greater confidence. Finally they presented their findings, only when they were certain that the truth could not be refuted.

"What they found was an earlier, previous civilisation, hidden beneath the ruins of the primary, more recent ruins. A Talee civilisation, much like the one they were supposed to be studying, but different in many ways. A lower threshold of technology, belonging to an earlier era. And evidence of sudden, violent, simultaneous, thermonuclear destruction. Perhaps three thousand years before the previous near-extinction event."

This time no one at the table even breathed. It was too awful to contemplate. And far too frightening.

"This previous Talee civilisation must have been aware of *their* catastrophe, just as this present Talee civilisation is aware of their own," Cai continued in quiet, sombre tones. "But somehow, in the second catastrophe, with the complete elimination of life on the homeworld, all memory of the first event was lost. Talee returned to their homeworld more than a thousand years later, thinking that this was a once-and-once-only event and never again could anything like it occur. But painstaking investigation finally revealed to us the truth.

"Talee destroyed themselves *twice*. The second time, in full knowledge of what had happened the first time, and all in the psychological and cultural aftermath of that first event, and all the 'never agains' that accompanied it. Now you know why the Talee will not talk to you, nor meet with you, nor trade with you. Talee live in constant fear of disturbance, of disequilibrium, of politics, of even emotion itself. They fear themselves, they fear others, and they fear greatly the consequences of every single action they take. They deliberate endlessly, and for the most part, do nothing. They are a people without faith in themselves, and they cannot believe that any contribution they could make to your current circumstances could possibly be an improvement. Humanity, in this current matter, is on its own."

"We think it's here," said Fleet Captain Reichardt, pointing to a spot on the holographic star chart above the table. "The Talee homeworld, C-492 on our charts. No doubt the Talee call it something more interesting."

The chart showed League space, a faint shade of red, and Federation space in blue. And here, several hundred light-years beyond the League's farthest reach, a collection of stars that might stretch, if these hypothetical models were real, as far as Federation and League combined.

"This is as far as you think Talee outposts reached in the second age?" Ari asked, pointing to the farthest expanse of that colourless territory, hovering between the projection paddles.

"It's all guesswork," said Reichardt. "But given what we're pretty sure the Talee ships can do, which is in turn based on some pretty nifty physics equations that remain purely theoretical for us but appears to be completely practical with them . . . yes. This is as far as we think they got. And now, thanks to our friend Cai, we have a timeline, and the timeline appears to match."

Now they were in Operations, the *other* most secure room in FSA HQ. About them was a semicircle of seats for interactive presentations, big screens on the wall behind, and a projection table here, in the middle. All the semicircle chairs were empty, but the seats around the projection table were full—the same people as previously but now including Reichardt and also Chief Boyle, Head of League Affairs. Still no Chief Shin. It surprised Sandy a little; Ibrahim was usually more consensual in interdepartmental matters. Matters with FedInt must be bad then.

Reichardt was the FSA's favourite Fleet Captain, and Sandy's in particular. He was a Federation loyalist and a pragmatist, meaning that he'd repeatedly demonstrated a commitment to the *idea* of the Federation, with all its constituent parts equal, and not just some parts above the others. Given recent turmoil in Federal governance, Fleet command had found itself without Grand Council guidance, thanks to the counter-coup the FSA had pulled to dispose of the previous Council by force, after that Council had used Operation Shield to frame-and-remove the FSA's newly acquired teeth to solve a dispute over the Federal Constitution.

Operation Shield had been implemented with Fleet help, hardly the first time Fleet had been found meddling in Federation governance to achieve outcomes some Fleet Captains desired. Post-coup, the FSA had gone after those captains hard. Several had surrendered and were in custody. One had suicided. Others remained in service, Fleet command refusing further action, but with trials ongoing. And a few more, most embarrassingly for Fleet Command, were OWO—Operating Without Orders—with ships and crew.

With chain of command inoperable, Reichardt had moved his carrier *Mekong* to immediate Callayan defensive orbit and declared himself at the FSA's disposal until a more traditional chain of command had been reestablished. Two more carrier captains had followed suit, and a number of smaller vessels. The Federation media were calling it The Emergency, the temporary suspension of democracy in the Federation, until Ranaprasana's Grand Committee found a mutually agreeable way to put it all back together again. Reichardt was now called by many the FSA's pet carrier captain. Sandy knew that the opposite was true, that far from being anyone's pet, Reichardt was probably the most free-thinking senior captain in the Fleet. Naturally Fleet had therefore not seen fit to promote him to Admiral, despite his obvious qualifications. The FSA had needed a means of enforcement against powerful Fleet Captains in their even more powerful warships, and Reichardt had volunteered himself and his carrier. He didn't care what it cost him, he was in Fleet to do the things that needed to be done, and took all personal satisfaction from that. Unsurprisingly he and Ibrahim, while not always in agreement, got along perfectly.

"Self-inflicted E.L.E. has been a theory in Fleet for a while," Reichardt continued, "but I don't think it's ever been a favourite theory. Having it confirmed changes the picture quite a bit. Certainly it explains Pantala, the old Talee stations there, where League picked up their biological replication technology. Small outposts like that could have abandoned as soon as it started and headed home. Records that the outpost ever existed were then probably lost."

"And League has found several more of these outposts," Ibrahim added. Ari gave Ibrahim a particularly long and hard look. He'd phrased it as a statement, not a question. So he'd known for a while, probably in that secret file every new FSA Director got immediately upon appointment and was then forbidden to share with anyone else.

"Yes," said Reichardt. Fleet, of course, was an information world unto itself. Like a secret society, sharing with almost no one. All that time out in the cold convinced them that no one else understood these matters like Fleet did or could be trusted with the knowledge. True or not, the belief had spawned a dangerous elitism. "We think at least two. Though we're unclear on what if any technology was harvested at these points. Pantala appears to be the primary source of GI technology."

"We're looking at a very wide area of space," said Hando, gazing at the projection. Holographic light gleamed off his bald head. "Talee were probably even more advanced at their second E.L.E. than we are now. So they'd have mining colonies, exploration colonies, research outposts. They'd be scattered all over, even more than we are. Yet still the E.L.E. managed to kill most of them, nearly all of them."

Ibrahim frowned. "Explain."

"No no no, he's right," said Ari with more typically Ari-animation. "There are projection studies done to simulate a mass-extinction war between League and Federation, a mass V-strike conflict. It's pretty horrific stuff, but though most of the major worlds get wiped out, there's always small colonies and outposts surviving, too far off the beaten track for anyone to bother destroying.

"Then you run the simulation forward . . . you think about it, it only takes a few of those survivors to rebuild a civilisation. They have the technology, or at least the records to rebuild most of the tech that's been lost, they live in space so they wait until the worlds that have been hit recover habitable climates . . . some of them never do, but most are okay within a few decades, maybe longer, the bigger ones anyway. Civilisation's massively reduced in scale, but the technological level remains the same . . . all that remains is to build scale back up; reproduction technology makes that pretty easy, cloning, birth tanks, no need to wait for women to get pregnant, you could double a population in size every few years if you wanted. Do that often enough, it doesn't take too long in the scheme of things to turn a few hundred thousand people into tens of millions, and tens of millions into hundreds and even billions."

"Recent experience tells me," Sandy said drily, "that childcare for all those kids would be more of a problem than you make out."

Laughter around the table. It was more of a humorous reaction than Sandy had expected or intended. Confronting this kind of problem for real, and not merely in the hypothetical, was stressful. People needed to laugh.

"Sure," said Ari, smile fading. "Great big mess, of course. But the point is that recovery happens quite fast, all things considered. But Cai said the Talee took a thousand years." He looked around the table, watching that sink in.

"So they lost all their technology," Ibrahim murmured. "That implies the destruction was systemic."

"Worse than systemic," Ari said. "Genocidal." Deathly silence. The air felt very cold, all previous humour forgotten. "They didn't just try to win a conflict. They . . . whatever constitutes a 'side' for the Talee, racial, religious, ideological, I doubt Cai will enlighten us . . . they tried to exterminate each other, right down to the last individual, to the last functioning microcircuit. Every outpost, every mining colony."

"Technology survived on Pantala," Hando countered. "For League to find."

"Pantala shouldn't have habitable atmosphere anyway," Ari replied, "there's so little vegetation. Federation's never had a chance to study it, what if it used to be more habitable? What if the Talee never left? What if it got hit, maybe not a V-strike, maybe biological, chemical . . . who knows what other advanced nastiness the Talee have? All traces of life gone, including much of the native stuff, but the old habitations remain?"

"Shit," Chief Boyle murmured, rubbing his forehead. "League would know, they've had Pantala for over a hundred years. Something like that, they'd know. Which means they've known the Talee are a post-E.L.E. species for a long time."

"Speculation at this point," Reichardt cautioned them. "But worthwhile."

"Whatever." Ari cut them off with an impatient gesture. "The point is that if the Talee wiped themselves out as part of some psychological condition, they had it *real* bad. So the question then becomes, was this *just* the technology that made them crazy? Or is it something native to Talee psychology? Because if it's the latter, we might be okay here. If it's the former . . ."

Sandy shook her head. "I don't think it's that simple. I know it's dangerous to speculate given how little we've seen of the Talee . . . but their recent behaviour doesn't suggest an aggressive or violent species at all. Quite the contrary. And they made Cai, and if it's possible to judge a people by their creations, Cai's nature speaks very well of them."

Ibrahim nodded a little, stroking his short beard. It was as good as a comment from him, when his people were talking. He liked to sit, and think, and absorb.

"But certain psychological types are reactive," Sandy continued. "Compulsive Narrative Syndrome proves that the human addiction to narrative patterns is not a matter of violence. Very nice and apparently nonviolent people have become so convinced in the rightness of a particular narrative that they end up doing terrible, violent things. Predisposition to violence is not a factor in a person's predisposition to fanatical belief.

"The Talee could quite easily be a very kind and gentle people, but if there's something in their psychology that predisposes them toward exponential, catastrophic pattern-recognition cascades, then introduce the wrong sort of uplink technology into that and there's no telling how it could blow up. The real thing we have to be worried about is the degree of interaction between the uplink technology and the psychology. League are using Talee tech, far more than they ever admitted, because of course they never admitted they borrowed Talee tech in the first place. Whether that technology will interact worse with human psychology, or better, or whatever, is the real question."

"Whoever's in charge of Pantala research would know," Reichardt said solemnly.

"That might be hard," said Sandy. "I'd rather take a run at Margaritte Karavitis, Renaldo Takewashi's woman on the inside of that operation."

"Or Takewashi himself," Ari added. "He might even cooperate."

"And then," said Ibrahim, "we do have an example in our hands of some of the most advanced Talee uplink technology, in the head of a human subject."

Everyone looked at Ibrahim. Then at Sandy. Sandy nodded slowly, heart beginning to thump in dull panic.

"Sir," she said, "I know you're not suggesting it. But just so we're clear— if it's a choice between me subjecting my little boy to invasive testing or the entire human race dying, then the human race dies. I'm sorry, I'm completely unreasonable about his well-being. Completely."

No one challenged her on the logical contradiction that if the human race died, so did Kiril. She made her point. Everyone stayed quiet.

Except Ibrahim. "I understand your position completely. However, surely there must be some medium?" Sandy's heart thumped harder. She blinked hard, fighting the redness that threatened to descend. About the table, everyone watched cautiously.

"Perhaps," she admitted with difficulty.

"I cannot tell you what that medium is, Cassandra," said Ibrahim. "We all know there should be further tests, not merely aimed at his well-being, as previous tests have been, but at truly understanding what is going on in his head. But the decision must be yours. And his, of course, small boys have rights too. If he refuses, then that's that. But I'm quite sure he won't refuse if you tell him it's safe."

"But it's not safe." Her words didn't quite come out right. They caught in her throat. Reichardt looked away, great discomfort on his face. "It's never safe."

"There is risk in all things," Ibrahim said quietly. "But you must decide. And, if tests are to be done, you must approve them and set your own limits. It would be completely inappropriate for any institution to attempt to impose them on you. But please, consider the stakes here. In Kiril's mind may rest the clue to how long we have left to act."

CHAPTER FOUR

Sandy got home in the morning. It was Saturday, so Kiril was watching kids' shows with Svetlana, eating a breakfast they'd made together.

"Pancakes?" Sandy exclaimed, looking at the bowl of mixture in the kitchen.

"It's healthy!" Svetlana insisted from the sofa.

"What's healthy about pancakes?" Sandy retorted, turning on the hot plate to make herself some.

"We had some fruit, too! Didn't we, Kiri?"

"Uh-huh." Kiril was too lost in his show to comment further.

"Danya's out running?" Sandy asked, pouring mixture. The hot pan sizzled.

"Yep. He left half an hour ago, should be back soon."

"I bet *he* didn't eat pancakes."

"No, but he told us to save him some for when he got back. So don't eat all of it, okay?"

"Shush!" Kiril complained. "I'm trying to watch!"

"Come on, Kiri," Sandy told him, "talking with family's more important than TV. If you can't hear, use your earplugs." But he never did. Sandy suspected it was one of those subconscious defence mechanisms that her kids had. They liked to see and hear each other, as reassurance. And then complained about the noise.

She settled on the sofa between them with pancakes and juice, and watched TV with them. The show was a nice little thing about kids growing up as explorers on some new colonial world. All animated in kiddie style, with cool aliens, wonderful landscapes, and nice moral lessons. She wasn't always so happy with the stuff she found them watching, but it was hard to tell a kid

51

who'd grown up around daily brutality that a few images on a screen would do psychological damage. Often she was astonished at how well they'd turned out, that they hadn't just aped all the awful things they'd seen other people do. It suggested something good about fundamental human nature, in some people at least.

Danya got back just as the show was ending, sweaty and breathing hard. "Pancakes?" he announced in disbelief, entering the kitchen. "Sandy, I can't believe you're eating pancakes. You'll get fat."

"GIs," said Sandy around a mouthful of her third pancake, "do not get fat."

"You don't get old either," said Svetlana. "You're so lucky."

"Crap, I get old." They'd had this discussion many times before. Sandy thought Svetlana had a narrow interpretation of the concept. "I just won't look it. Come to that, the way the age treatments are moving, neither will any of you."

Danya had a shower, cooked his own pancakes, and joined them. The next show was an action thing with superheroes. Sandy didn't like that so much, but she was hardly sitting here for the TV. Kiril cuddled up, and Svetlana and Danya fired all kinds of questions at him about who the cool superheroes were, and why, and found his answers extremely amusing as only older siblings could.

"Can you do that, Sandy?" Svetlana asked, as one of the characters on the screen shot lightning bolts out of his eyes.

"'Course I can," said Sandy. "You saw it last week when you got dirt on the stairs." Danya, she sensed, wanted to talk to her about Cresta but saw that she didn't and left it alone. "Kiri, I forgot to say how much I liked your play yesterday. I thought you were terrific."

"Yeah, it was fun," Kiril admitted. "Mrs Shula was really happy. And then, after you left? We did all kind of photos and stuff, and . . . and Mishi Roberts got poked in the eye."

"Poked in the eye? With what, was she okay?"

"Just a trident."

Sandy nearly grinned and stopped herself. "You mean a paper trident." Kiril nodded.

"Just as well it was just a paper trident, Kiri!" said Svetlana, never missing a theatrical opportunity. "Otherwise she'd have become like that one-eyed monster in your book! GRRR!" With her face all screwed-up, one eye closed. Kiril laughed.

"Now come on," Sandy told them, "don't laugh at someone who had their eye poked out."

"It wasn't poked out," Kiril reassured her. "She just cried a lot."

Svetlana rolled her eyes. "Yeah, gosh, what a baby." On some things, her kids were always going to be judgemental. Last month Svetlana had given herself a genuinely nasty cut with a kitchen knife, lots of blood, and had nonchalantly said it was nothing, she'd had much worse. Because she had. Sandy had seen the fading scars, had listened to Danya's horrifying account of pulling the rusty nail that had gone right through her arm, then another of nursing her through bad concussion after she'd fallen from a wall. And had listened to Svetlana's account of how Danya had gotten that scar on his leg, and how she'd had to sew skin and flesh back together from the razor-wire cut. And other equally horrible tales that had nearly made her cry to hear. The thought of that happening to her kids was unbearable . . . and yet, those experiences had made them who they were, for better and worse. Kiril, thankfully, they'd managed to keep relatively safe, and as the baby of the trio had been kept away from risky adventures.

"I'm sorry I had to leave, Kiri," said Sandy. "I really wanted to stay, but it was an emergency."

"That's okay," said Kiril. "I told Mrs Shula that you were a superhero, and sometimes you had to go and save the world and stuff."

Sandy grinned, arm around him. "Yeah, well. I wish I could put that on my tax forms." And then she noticed that Svetlana was looking through her wallet. Sandy felt in her pocket. Nothing. Svetlana grinned at her. Sandy gaped. "You didn't! When did you . . . ?"

"I'm not telling! It's a trade secret." She tossed the wallet back. Sandy caught and looked through it suspiciously. "I didn't take anything!" Svetlana laughed.

"Wow, Svet, that's amazing. First time." She'd tried before, but it was nearly impossible to pick a high-designation GI's pocket.

"She's been practising *so* hard," said Danya. "She's met this guy on a VR forum—it's okay, Ari checked him out, says he's fine. Professional pickpocket, has a big stage act on Ramprakash Road, says Svet's got talent, showed her some tricks."

"He's amazing though," said Svetlana. "He invites people on stage and steals their clothes while they're wearing them, and they don't even notice."

"Well, that's great, Svet," said Sandy. "But don't get carried away, because this is my safe zone, and my guard is *so* down at home with you guys."

"I know," said Svetlana. "It's actually more about minds than hands. You need good hands, but mostly you need to know what the other person's thinking, and what they're paying attention to. It's all a mind trick. I think it works better on you because I know you so well."

"So you can pick your friends' pockets," Danya remarked, "but not your enemies'?"

Svetlana gave him a look of feigned innocence. "You say that like it wouldn't come in handy?"

"Sure," said Danya, repressing a smile that hinted at many in-jokes and old stories between them. "Depending on whose side you're on."

Svetlana made an amused-but-not-entirely face at him. Danya's return expression suggested an older brother's amused-but-skeptical judgement. He held it long enough for Svetlana to get annoyed and stick her tongue out at him. Danya rolled his eyes just a little. Svetlana jerked her head back at the TV screen in a "shut up and watch" motion. A few seconds, a few facial expressions, Danya and Svetlana could have entire conversations without speaking a word.

The next show was familiar, *Rinni and Pasha*, a Tanushan institution. They were best friends in school, a boy and a girl, who liked being proper best friends so much they resisted becoming boyfriend and girlfriend . . . but obviously that wasn't going to last, even if they were the only ones who couldn't see it. Even Danya had to admit it was a good show, lots of laughs and some genuinely thoughtful stuff about how people related to each other. Sandy found it sad, because it reminded her of two GIs she'd barely known as friends and had lost immediately upon meeting. This had been their favourite show too. Eduardo and Anya, also a boy and a girl. Best friends in their short lives, but born to die, for the League's desperate uplink experiments on Pantala.

When it finished, Danya muted the TV. "You going back to work, Sandy?"

Sandy nodded. From the others' lack of surprise, she guessed he'd already told them she would be. "Yeah. It's a bit crazy at the moment. I just wanted to come back for breakfast." She took a deep breath. "Kiri? I have to ask you something."

She surfed net activity on her way back to HQ, as was her habit. Tanusha was still Tanusha; there was still more interest in football scores and celebrity gossip than in the violent death of a League moon. But those sources that were covering it were doing a surprisingly sober job. Sandy supposed there weren't many ways you could sensationalise the death of Cresta. An entire moon had been destroyed, or as good as. It was already too sensational, on a level that wasn't any fun.

She played the latest HQ official briefing over the top of her other surfing, watching five things at once as the weather turned bad, and a morning storm buffeted the cruiser with sheets of rain across the windshield. Amirah took it, of course—she was the official face of the FSA these days, and she was brilliant at it.

"Can you give us any idea of who killed Cresta?" one of the journalists in the press room was asking her.

"No," said Amirah.

"Can you at least tell us if you yourselves are aware of who killed Cresta?"

"No," said Amirah. *"Look, this is just too serious for anyone to be making off-the-cuff remarks right now. I know the media in Tanusha has a lot of very good sources who know the League quite well, and I can only suggest that you ask most of your questions of those people. Our job, in this building, is Federal Security. We're not a media information service."*

If she'd said something like that, Sandy thought, people would have grumbled about insensitivity to the people's right to know and made accusations of her supposed "authoritarian streak," followed by mutterings of "fascist tendencies." But Amirah was just too cute. Some sections of the public refused to believe she was a GI, let alone a combat GI. She was slim with a hooked nose and a cheeky grin, and had turned down a combat job in preference for administration. Sandy thought a lot of the public reaction was just shock that so many GIs were female. Tanusha's gender roles were more traditional, and despite physical augmentation, women typically did not make up more than twenty percent of FSA/CSA roles, and less still at the sharp end. But the League produced GIs on a fifty-fifty split, and defectors to the Federation were more like sixty-forty, in favour of women. A lot of Tanushans, many women among them, found that disconcerting.

"Is there any suggestion of a threat to Federation worlds?"

"*Again, I know you all have your sources on system security throughout the Federation. Those questions are best directed at Fleet, who I'm sure will tell you that Federation defences against V-strike or any other kind of strike are extremely strong, far stronger than we think Cresta's were, given the relatively poor condition of the League Fleet right now. Obviously League is facing some very severe internal security threats at present, but again, it's not something we're prepared to give a running commentary on.*"

"*With all respect,*" another journalist said, "*it really is your responsibility, because the FSA assumed government powers on Callay when it launched its coup.*"

"*Counter-coup,*" Amirah corrected, with a hint of that crooked smile.

"*Yes . . . but you are the government now.*"

"*No, we're the oversight,*" said Amirah. "*We appointed a government and it sits in the Grand Council today and governs.*"

"*An unelected government.*"

Shrug. "*Very much so, but a government nonetheless.*"

"*And you retain the power to remove that unelected government whenever you want. So that makes you the ultimate authority in the Federation right now, which means you are the government. And the government has responsibilities to answer the media's questions in a way that the Federal Security Agency, in its normal role, would not.*"

"*No,*" said Amirah quite calmly and perhaps faintly amused. The press hated that about her, but grudgingly respected it too. "*The government is the government. That's why they're called the government. Don't ask me questions about what they do, I speak for the Federal Security Agency, I'm not that smart. We appointed them because they are.*" The infectious, creeping smile. "*As the spokesperson for the Federal Security Agency, I can tell you that the FSA never comment at length about ongoing security issues. The current government in the Grand Council has an Intelligence Committee and a Security Committee, and they make decisions on these matters just like an elected government. The FSA don't tell them what to do or how to do it, so long as they do it well. Now if you'd like to go and ask them those questions, the building's five hundred meters in that direction,*" pointing, "*and we'll even lay on a car so you don't have to walk.*"

Sandy smiled as the cruiser rocked in crosswinds and rain cut visibility to a few tens of meters. Again, if she'd said that, someone would have taken it as a threat. But with Amirah, many of them were actually smiling. Amirah cheerfully selected another questioner.

Approaching FSA HQ she couldn't even see the huge Grand Council building, hidden behind the grey fog of the downpour. Automated approach brought her in to a transition zone beside green gardens, already with puddles turning into lakes on the grass, sea birds standing in blissful disregard, looking for snails. Above her, she could barely make out through the windshield the looming shapes of construction gantries, as the upper levels of HQ underwent the final stages of reconstruction following last year's bombardment. Ibrahim had used the opportunity to build an entire new wing, and several other floors to perform new tasks the FSA had not originally been envisaged undertaking.

"*Sandy*," said Captain Reichardt as soon as she'd entered the doors, "*you have a moment?*"

"*No*," Sandy formulated her response, "*but I can make one if it's important. Come meet me in the bay, I've got press rounds.*" Nodding and waving hi to several people in the halls and offices as she passed.

"*No, you come meet me. Better keep it away from the press.*"

"*I'm not coming to meet you,*" Sandy retorted. "*That's a whole five floors out of my way.*"

"*I see 'gratitude' isn't part of your programming,*" the Fleet Captain said drily. Sandy smiled and headed for the nearest stairwell. He was referring to the number of times he'd saved her neck, at considerable risk to his own. For that, she'd let the gratuitous synth-phobic remark about programming slide.

She found him in his FSA temporary office, with a one-way view of gardens and rain, surrounded by holoscreens on his big semicircle table. Lew and Bursteimer were also there, also Captains, who'd taken Reichardt's side in recognising the new FSA-appointed Grand Council government in the interim. Lew was slim, Asian, and commanded a mil-freighter, a massive thing that made even Reichardt's carrier look small. Bursteimer was squat, broad, and frequently amused, a Runner Captain with a war record even more impressive than Reichardt's.

"Hey, it's the hot girl," said Bursteimer, popping dried fruit. "How's it going, hot girl?"

"So what warrants me climbing a whole five floors?" Sandy asked them, little more than an eyebrow raised at Bursteimer. At times, Bursteimer gave a very convincing impression of a fourteen-year-old boy. Or other people's fourteen-year-old boys, certainly not *hers*.

Reichardt triple-sized the system-graphic on the holodisplay, and Sandy found herself looking at the Callayan System, Callay in orbit about its sun, the various planets, stations, facilities, la grange defence points, and current Fleet positions. Sandy was no expert, but she'd been involved in enough Fleet operations to know what she was looking at, and what all the symbols, lines, and accompanying algebra meant.

"Looks good," she said. "That all?"

"Friendly, isn't she?" said Bursteimer.

"You know what all this is worth if the Talee came after us?" Reichardt asked her. "Jack shit."

"You think the Talee are coming after us?" Sandy asked.

"The Talee," said Reichardt, his Texas drawl even more relaxed than his lanky frame in the chair, "have wiped themselves out twice in around six thousand years. Now Cai don't need to tell us that. We think it's friendly advice, we think 'gosh, ain't that sweet? He's concerned for us.' What if that wasn't just friendly concern? What if that was a warning?"

"A warning about what?"

"Don't fuck with us, we've been known to wipe out entire species."

Sandy looked at the holographics. As she understood such things, the defensive grid was solid. The physics of jump made it impossible for ships to enter a system too close to the center of a gravity well, they had to come in farther out, which gave them more time to be intercepted, whatever their residual speed. Moons like Cresta were harder to defend because Cresta orbited a gas giant, itself farther out from the system's center of mass—its sun. So whatever hit Cresta came in real close and gave very little reaction time. Callay didn't have that problem. Against *human* ships.

"Can Talee push that entry point down the gravity slope?" she asked.

"Hell, you were on Pantala, you saw what they did there."

"I was occupied at the time," she reminded him. "But I saw the replay. Few folks I spoke to aren't sure that Talee came in from any farther out than you did, it's just their stealth is so much better and we can't see them."

"Maybe," said Reichardt. Sandy got the distinct impression he wasn't telling her everything.

"You've seen more than Pantala, haven't you," Sandy said flatly. Ran her gaze across the three Captains. Lew and Bursteimer looked at each other, then at Reichardt. "Talee ships doing things even crazier than that."

Reichardt pointed to the holograph once more. "Jack shit," he repeated. "That's all I'll say."

Sandy folded her arms. "Why tell me? Not like I couldn't guess."

"You've got advanced uplinks, descended from Talee tech. I figure if anyone can work out how Talee think, it's you."

Sandy frowned. "I'm not an alien, Arron."

"Thing is," Reichardt continued, "as I see it, someone at the heart of this whole goddamn mess should be taking it into account. Talee psychology. If they want us dead, we're dead. Probably most of humanity. I'm telling you, no human Fleet can defend it, not League, not Federation."

"So now you seriously think they're a *threat*? What about their behaviour the past century or so has been so threatening?"

"Sandy," Reichardt said with a dead-level stare. "They're alien. We don't understand them. They seem to like it that way. They're prone to explosive, rapid self-destruction. They get scared easily, Cai just admitted it. And it's my job to spend time worrying about this kind of shit."

Sandy exhaled hard. Looking at the holographics, thinking. Bursteimer held out his packet of dried fruit. Sandy took one and munched.

"You want me to look at this?" Sandy asked them. "Seriously?"

"Seriously would be preferable," said Reichardt.

"Then you get me the psych modeling Fleet's done on Talee," said Sandy. No expression from Reichardt. "Don't know what you're talking about."

"Well, then clearly you're not taking it seriously," said Sandy. "I know Fleet's done psych modeling on what they know of Talee psychology. No chance at all I can do anything with this until you get that to me. If it's too hard, then obviously this . . ." pointing to the hologram, ". . . isn't as serious as you say it is. If it were, you'd find a way."

"If they're seriously advanced with their uplinks," said Lew, "couldn't you try and run some sims on third-level abstraction theory? I've got a functional-psych degree, just that could give us some possibilities to model. . . ."

"Lew," Sandy said firmly. "They've got two brains." No disagreement from the Captains. "Unless you know specifically otherwise, but that seems to be the consensus. Fleet have been watching them a hell of a lot longer, I was only introduced last year. I'll bet anything Fleet Intel's been watching navigation patterns for decades, figuring what's physics, what's tech, and what's just going on in Talee heads. Assuming they have heads. Get me that, and you're right, I'm probably better equipped than anyone else to set up those sims, and I might get you some parameters. Unless you want to ask Ragi?"

"Don't trust Ragi," said Reichardt.

"Fine. You want results, you get me real data." She went for the door.

"Commander," said Bursteimer, "you free for a date?"

"With you?" Sandy said over her shoulder. "No."

"She likes me," Bursteimer said, smiling as she left, still chewing. "She took my fruit."

Vanessa had turned Briefing One into a holoroom when Sandy arrived, one of the fancier room setups in HQ. Projectors turned the space into a 3D graphic, blocked by occasional shadow as Vanessa moved within it, other projectors detecting and boosting to compensate. Holographics was always weak compared to VR clarity, but the little bundle in Vanessa's arms was unable to join her in cyberspace.

"Bothering you?" Sandy observed, as Vanessa frowned and zoomed on a building top that enlarged and rotated where the room's central table had been before Vanessa had pushed it aside.

"Yeah," said Vanessa. "Trajectory's this way, you were here." The building raced away, a red line tracing sniper fire toward Subianto Stadium, alight with intricate detail as it moved into the middle of the room. "That shot is 1,240-odd meters. At your cruiser's velocity it was a .61 degree deflection, plus the stadium makes slight deviation in the crosswind at that angle. What would you guess a high-designation GI would miss by, at that range?"

"Me, maybe twenty centimeters," said Sandy, circling the room to get a better view. "Rhian, maybe three meters. League don't use many above a designation forty these days. . . . I'd think at least a two-meter average. It's a strange shot to take." And she was distracted, predictably, by the sleeping baby in Vanessa's arms.

"Right, so look at the cluster." A new projected image appeared above the stadium—Sandy's cruiser. It enlarged, red dots highlighted where sniper rounds had hit it. They were quite close together, forward of the rear gens, aft and down of the cabin. "That's very tight for a forty."

Sandy folded her arms, considering it. "So either it was a high-designation GI with a bad sight, which isn't likely with a high-des League operative. . . ."

"Or whoever it was, missed on purpose," Vanessa finished.

"A distraction?" Sandy wondered. "Speaking of distractions . . ." She lifted the baby clear of Vanessa's arms, careful of the head. Little Sylvan wriggled a little and slept on. People said he had Vanessa's nose, and Sandy knew she was supposed to nod and agree, but she couldn't. Babies were such odd little things; it was hard to think of them as the same species at all.

"Focus," Vanessa reprimanded. "A distraction from what? It was just before Subject A's death. We know League were there, the dead GI at the scene is a bit of a giveaway and the autopsy matches, but we don't know if they killed Subject A or not. Has Cai confirmed that was him that killed the GI?"

"Cai maintains mysterious noncompliance." Looking at the baby. "Save for, you know, telling us the Talee could spontaneously combust at any moment."

"So it didn't really distract you at all, did it?" Vanessa was *very* focused, Sandy noted. She hadn't really gotten that stir-crazy. Phillippe was taking twins duties even more than her, but it had still been a two-month layoff when the twins emerged from the tank. Now she focused and talked like a woman with something to prove, if only to herself. "Knowing your capabilities, as a high-des GI would, you just changed cruisers and continued. The only thing it *did* do was activate all our fire-support backups, bring them into the area . . . but still not fast enough to catch this sniper. Fast enough to catch the next one though."

Sandy frowned. "Next one?"

"If there'd been a next one."

"You think this sniper was trying to *save* me?"

"Save someone. Activate our defences so the next attack is sure to fail. Which would indicate knowledge of another high-des GI, someone who wouldn't miss." Sandy thought about it. "Well, it's my theory for now."

"No no, it's good," said Sandy. "You're right, nothing else makes sense."

The door opened, a quick flood of light in the darkened room. Ari entered, and it closed again. Sandy showed him Sylvan, sleeping peacefully, and smiled.

"I know, I know, don't tell me," said Ari with a forestalling hand, racking his brain. "I know this one, let's see . . . it has no discernible intelligence or ability, it's quite dysfunctional, it's constantly demanding attention, and it screams and poos itself when it doesn't get it. So I'm guessing it's either a baby or a politician."

"Or an Intel Agent," said Vanessa.

"So either you're allowed to bring babies to work," Ari continued, "or we're now recruiting analysts very early." He peered at Sylvan from by Sandy's shoulder.

"Rank has privileges," said Vanessa. "I'm only doing analysis, and Phillippe's got Rupa since she loves the violin. If I can triangulate counter-com strikes while under fire and manoeuvring, I can certainly look at some damn holograms with a baby on my arm." Sandy detected a little tension. "You here for something?"

"We've confirmed identities on the gunmen Sandy knocked out at the wedding," said Ari. "Mostly foreigners, some former spec ops, one former Fleet marine. Underground affiliated. Say they were paid to hit Mr Moily. No idea on their employers, they genuinely don't know."

"So you think FedInt," Sandy concluded.

Ari shrugged. "It fits. Hell of a desperate move if I'm right, hiring armed goons to do their dirty work . . . but it happens enough among gangs and big corporate disputes handled by other means. I mean, we've seen it."

"Would have worked too, if Sandy hadn't been there," Vanessa said flatly.

Ari looked displeased but didn't argue. "Could be any of that, we can't prove it's FedInt, which is the point. I'd guess with Cresta dead, they panicked and tried to eliminate everyone linked but couldn't use their own people to do it, knowing how we'd all be out in force."

"Linked to what?" Vanessa asked with dry scepticism.

"If I knew that, I'd get paid a lot more. Obviously FedInt are linked somehow to Cresta. And Moily's the key."

"Moily knows nothing," Sandy replied. "It's his Pyeongwha friends that are the key. Subject A was talking to them, my guess is about NCT."

"Great," said Vanessa. "They can swap notes on the most efficient methods of genocide in the modern age." Again the tension. Sandy thought she could guess.

"Of course," said Sandy, "the most *likely* explanation is that League killed Subject A, given that he's, you know, friends with people who just succeeded in killing a League moon with a quarter million people on it."

"Without first finding out what he's doing here?" Ari asked.

"Maybe they already know?"

"No no," Ari shook his head, quite adamant. "*We're* not sure what he's doing here. Was doing here. No way is League's Intel in Tanusha better than ours."

Sandy was unconvinced.

"Spec ops meeting in ten minutes," said Ari. "Ibrahim's office, if you can make it."

"Why couldn't I make it?" Vanessa asked suspiciously.

"I was talking to the baby," said Ari. "But you can come too if you want." Sandy slapped his arm.

The door opened again, and Rhian entered. "Oh, a baby!" She came over, hands outstretched. "Give me the baby."

Sandy smiled. "What if I want him a bit longer?"

"You *must* give me the baby," Rhian insisted. "It's compulsive. Baby baby baby baby baby."

"Rhi," Ari said seriously, and put a hand on her shoulder. "What have I told you about this? You only came to this room because you knew you'd find a baby here, didn't you? Your addiction can be cured, Rhi, but first you have to admit that you have a problem and learn to say no. Just walk on past that door, Rhian."

"Baby!" Rhian said plaintively.

Sandy and Vanessa walked a hallway on the third floor, as the top floors where the big meetings would otherwise be held were still out of action with all the construction.

"You okay?" Sandy asked her.

"Oh, you know." Vanessa ran fingers through her short curls, looking a little like she didn't know what to do with her hands, now that Rhian had commandeered Sylvan for the next half hour. "Hell of a time to be raising twins."

"It'll always be like this," Sandy reasoned. "There'll always be a reason for people like us not to have kids, and it's never a good time. But kids are tough, and no kid was ever raised in a perfect environment. That's just human."

"It's just . . . hell, you know me. I like to work, I like to focus, and this stuff is so important. And now I'm distracted, and I feel guilty for it. . . ."

"I know."

"And I feel guilty if I'm not distracted *enough*. . . ."

"I know."

"I mean, it's only the survival of the entire human race. . . ."

"I know."

Vanessa managed a wry smile. "How completely unsurprising that you also do motherhood better than me."

"Oh, my kids are easy," Sandy said dismissively. Vanessa raised an eyebrow. "Well, compared to newborn twins. Mine had been looking after themselves in a warzone for the last five years, all they need from me is love and time. I think you're doing great."

"I don't feel like I'm doing great."

"I don't care *what* you feel like you're doing. *I* think you're doing great."

Vanessa smiled at her affectionately.

CHAPTER FIVE

Poole walked from the rear of the grounded SWAT flyer to the road in Safdajung District. All around were flashing lights, police vehicles, and barriers to keep back the swarms of locals. Some of the cops had light armour and assault weapons, a new development for Tanusha. Most just kept the crowds back and cast concerned looks over their shoulders at the new SWAT arrivals, as the flyer's engines wound down from their previously ear-shattering howl.

Poole led his new contingent of armoured, helmeted agents to the police command vehicle parked a hundred meters down the road. From there to the river bend, hidden behind looming apartment towers, all had been cordoned off. A lot of these crowding civilians were not just annoying spectators; they were locals directed to leave their comfortable apartments an hour ago, now wondering when they could go home again. Poole spied some children amidst the crowd, holding parents' hands or being carried. Behind the glass front to an apartment lobby, he glimpsed a temporary crèche, bemused cops even now carrying in armloads of stuffed animals and toys for the toddlers playing on the carpet and amidst the expensive leather lounge chairs.

Near the barrier around the police command vehicle, journalists and cameras clustered. The cop by the vehicle side door indicated they could enter. Within was a command station, police sitting at posts, uplinked and watching displays. In the middle of the vehicle, a cleared space for a central table with holographic projection, around which clustered cops and a single CSA Agent—Commander Arvid Singh, head of CSA SWAT.

Cops moved aside as Poole stepped in, retreating up the side aisle to make space. Poole took off his helmet, as did his group, spreading around the table to Singh's left.

"Commander Naik," Singh said to the senior policeman, "these are Agents Poole, Kiet, Dahisu, and Trong. Agent Poole is mine, SWAT One, the others are from different SWAT teams." All GIs, of course. Commander Naik studied them warily—the very picture of a senior Tanushan policeman, brown, moustachioed, stocky.

"Agents," said Naik grimly. "Did they make a mistake by parking over the river?"

On the holodisplay was the maglev line over this bend of the Shoban River in Safdajung District. It ran alongside a road bridge, now empty of traffic, cordoned on both ends by lines of police. Directly in the middle of the river, an eight-car maglev train was parked, its ends nearly spanning from bank to bank. All its lights were off, big windows polarised. The terrorists within had gained command of the train's systems, and police and CSA concurred that it was safer to let them.

"No mistake," said Poole. "It gives us clear line of sight, but the biggest threat to them is immediate access. If we get in amongst them at close range we can take them apart. Their current position makes that difficult."

"Difficult or impossible?" asked Naik.

"That depends," said Poole, looking at Singh.

"We've confirmed they have deadman switches," said Singh. Naik had no command authority here, despite the police's overwhelming numbers. The use of force on this level, in aid of domestic security, was exclusively reserved for CSA. CSA needed police to clear the streets, get civilians out of harm's way, coordinate emergency services and media, all the things CSA were not equipped to manage. But the cops would only join the shooting if things went seriously wrong.

"Which means they've thought this out," said Kiet, contemplating the hologram. The view was wide enough to include the nearby towers and thus all the most obvious sniper spots. "We can't just shoot them."

"That would be hard anyway," said Singh. "They've shielded their uplinks, we can't reverse hack, so we've no way of figuring where they are in the train. With ten of them the odds of one or more surviving a simultaneous sniper strike are very high, and with all their explosive vests linked, it just takes one survivor to detonate all of them."

"Eyes inside?" asked Dahisu.

"They've control of the train's systems," said Singh, seated at the table in full armour. Slim with intelligent eyes and a love of practical jokes, Arvid Singh was not exactly the image of the macho Sikh-warrior beloved in the movies. But, Poole had learned, he was much more effective. "We could probably hack it, but they'd see. It's not wise to underestimate these guys, they're almost certainly former Pyeongwha internal security, their capabilities will be advanced, particularly given their uplinks."

Because most Pyeongwha citizens used Neural Cluster Technology, of a sort banned in the rest of the Federation.

"What's your plan then?" Poole asked.

"We can use SoundBlast to make that train ring like a bell," said Singh. "It'll disorient, probably damage eardrums, which in turn affects balance. It won't kill, so the deadman switches are out of play. It should stop anyone from hitting their vest triggers for a good ten seconds."

"Should?" asked Kiet. Kiet was former League Army. All his previous, extensive weapons experience was lethal. Nonlethals were new to him and regarded with scepticism.

"So we've a ten-second window," Poole summarised. "To be safe, we should drop that to six."

"That's up to you," Singh said pointedly.

"Six?" Poole asked, looking around at his small group. The others thought about it, looking at the hologram. And nodded slowly. "Six seconds."

"Wait a moment," said Commander Naik, "there are nearly a thousand civilians on that train, at least sixty children among them. You're going to blow their eardrums out?"

"And in the process save their lives," Poole replied. "Hearing can be repaired. High explosive leaves a more permanent mark."

Naik nodded slowly. "I'll alert the hospitals."

Arvid entered the apartment tower lobby a few minutes later, past a couple of cops keeping guard, and into the main elevator. He shoved tacnet visuals aside long enough to take a call. President Raza appeared on his visor display, looking worried.

"Commander, I've had your plan explained to me. Are there any other options?"

"There are always other options, Mr President, but we're all of the opinion here that none of them are as good."

Raza was Interim President of Callay, as everyone on Callay was "interim" right now. The previous President, Vikram Singh, was under house arrest as his trial for treason continued—the "Trial of the Century," Callayan media called it, a claim complicated by the even bigger one underway against the previous Grand Council leadership. Raza had been a constitutional scholar at Ramprakash University, plucked from his post by Callayan Governor Thomas for the interim role, the Governor himself having declined the position. All constitutionally feasible, and Raza had been a member of Callayan Parliament for ten years, at one point serving as Attorney General. Arvid remembered him vaguely from then, CSA was at least partially a law enforcement agency, and a lot of senior agents had dealt with Raza before in that capacity and considered him solid. But only vaguely, ten years ago seemed another universe.

"I'm inclined to try further negotiations," said Raza, looking very worried. *"They are talking, that seems a good sign there might be something to gain from further discussion."*

"Well, that's your prerogative, Mr President," said Arvid, as the elevator took him up to the penthouse. "But I'm sure your psych experts are telling you the same as ours—this is Compulsive Narrative Syndrome gone crazy, these guys are unredeemable fanatics, and negotiations for them are a tactic to buy time and a means to get their message out for propaganda purposes against the Federal occupation of Pyeongwha. They've no intention at all of actually listening to what we say, and their brains are by this stage structurally incapable of absorbing a pattern-anomalous argument anyway. All the Pyeongwha radicals we've dealt with so far have been unstable; the longer we wait to implement a solution on our terms, the greater the odds one of them will just decide to end it on theirs."

"What is your assessment of our chances of success? Doing it your way?"

For a moment, Arvid mulled which answer to give. The correct answer was that he didn't have enough data to make that judgement—if he'd missed some vital information and it was all a trap, then the chances of success were zero; he just wasn't aware of it. Ditto if these guys weren't as good as their assessment, the chances were more like 100 percent. Professionals didn't deal with odds, they dealt with available options, and when the best available option presented, they took it and hoped.

But politicians worked by a different calculus, and he had to give a number. Well, he told himself, when talking to a politician, pick a political number. Somewhere between zero and a hundred. "I'd think eighty percent, Mr President."

Raza still looked worried. And well he should, given the nine hundred–plus people on the train, whose fates all hung on what he decided next. *"Should we call Commander Kresnov?"*

"Mr President, you can do that if you want, but I've worked with Kresnov for as long as she's been on Callay, and I can tell you that she'll say this is a team job, and the inclusion of certain individuals, even individuals as capable as her, won't make any difference. It could even hurt. I have the team I need in place, they've all trained together; putting an outsider in the mix would complicate things unnecessarily."

The elevator opened on the penthouse, eye-wateringly expensive in Tanushan style, a wide living quarters opening onto wide windows and balcony with river views, many towers beyond, all ablaze with urban light. Arvid walked past several CSA Agents on surveillance, back from the edge, where small units on tripods peered over the railing to compile a complete scan for tacnet. Tacnet's command function showed another twenty such scanners now surrounding the stranded train, on either side of the river, at all heights and angles in case one saw something the others missed.

"Commander Singh," said the President of Callay. *"How long until you're ready to move?"*

"Seven minutes, Mr President." He crouched on the balcony, flipped up his visor to get a look at the scene with real eyes. Sometimes there was no beating the old Mark I eyeball . . . even if his were technically at least Mark III by now. A commander could become too dependent on simulations. Actually looking at the thing made the brain realise exactly just how hard the thing was they were trying. Hard for normal humans, anyhow. "We will delay if you request it, but as I've said, in the CSA's expert opinion, the longer we wait the greater the likelihood of failure."

"Commander, please hold for a moment."

Great, thought Arvid, measuring distances by eye below and trying to reconcile them with what tacnet showed him, with all its electronic certainty. Another thoughtful politician. "The problem with these guys," his previous commander and mentor Vanessa Rice had told him, "is that they spend their whole career arguing some perfect model of civilisation, and when they're dumped in a position of genuine power, they discover it's all a fucking mess and they can't make a decision because it doesn't look like anything they thought they knew."

No good and bad decisions, buddy, Arvid thought, just bad and worse. Now hurry up before you pick worse by default. Tacnet showed him units in position, everything centering on the train. You'd struggle to coordinate something like this, with regular humans. With GIs, new capabilities emerged, not just on the individual level, but on the tactical and systemic.

Green came two minutes after the all-clear. Poole leapt from his rooftop, jumpjets kicking in as the suit powered into the night sky above the river. The kick was nothing like the 10G boost from an assault hopper—these were little modular add-ons to regular armour—but thanks to hopper practise, everyone knew how to use them.

Halfway toward the train, the riverside sniper cannon fired, high explosive, shaped charge calculated to hit the curve of the train's tubular roof at a precise angle. Poole cut the jets and fell toward his projected opening . . . with a flash multiple explosions ripped the train, sideways force directing the metal to peel up and out, a spray of shrapnel across black river waters, and arcing skyward, away from the train interior. Visuals indicated high-intensity vibrations as SoundBlast hit, a double smash to eardrums in the train, nausea and vomiting to follow.

Poole's jets fired, his opening matching perfectly, and hit the hole at a tidy 90 kph. Caught the ragged edge of the roof with an armoured fist, rifle in right hand, a cluster of passengers across open floor and seats below . . . and here an armed and vested man on the floor, Poole put a bullet in each leg and one in an arm, twisting from the dangling arm to find another, but an entry farther up shot that target first, and the next target along was on top of civvies giving no clear shot.

Poole dropped, bounced, and scrambled amongst screaming, writhing bodies, switched ammo-feed and shot out a window with hollowpoints designed for the purpose, grabbed the terrorist and threw him out. The vests had been identified as limited range, if a wearer's heart stopped when he hit the water, the twenty-meter range would limit detonations to one.

He searched for more targets and found none—all down. Six were still on the train though. "Can't cover all six," he said tersely. "Two more overboard."

Dahisu and Kiet grabbed one each, both wounded, and tossed them out. Several seconds later, explosions from below. Human "rights" observers would be troubled by that, but fuck them, even wounded a human bomb could self-detonate, and hostage safety came first. The deadman switches precluded uplink triggers, luckily, though these guys had probably discounted the latter, given Tanusha's known ability to reverse hack uplinks.

"HQ, target green, move the train now." Immediately the train began to move, terrorist-imposed restraints wiped out, the carriages headed for the nearest station a kilometre away, where emergency services were clustered waiting. Poole grabbed a wounded terrorist, twisted his good arm so he had no chance at the two-handed trigger, and dragged him up the train, yelling at bewildered, deafened civilians amidst the smoke and wind to get down the other end of the train, gesturing with his free arm. They swirled past him as he went the other way, upstream against the flow, some carrying screaming children, others holding up frightened friends, family, and elderly and all commendably functional, considering how all his training emphasized the possible hysteria. Terrified and in pain, but functional, perhaps knowing instinctively what had just happened, and the reputation of Tanusha's new security assets, and having confidence that their chances of survival were now pretty good. The way they looked at him as they passed suggested as much— relief, astonishment, even worship, mixing with the fear.

As the train reached the station, they had all the targets piled at the train's far end, cuffed and twisted irrespective of injuries, guarded by Dahisu and Trong, ready to put more nonfatal holes in them if they more than twitched. Poole stood in the long space of open, tubular train between human bombs and clustered passengers down the far end, weapon away, and took off his helmet in hope of inducing a calmer reaction.

"Medical!" he yelled at the passengers, in the hope maybe half of them could still hear something. He pointed with both hands to the approaching platforms, then to both of his ears. "Go with the medics! All good, all safe!"

And gave them a double thumbs-up. And was absolutely astonished when a few of them, fearful, nauseous, and injured, gave him a thumbs-up in return, some with ferocious approval, others with tearful relief and gratitude. It gave

Poole a feeling he'd never had before at this intensity. He didn't know quite what it was. But suddenly, he felt unbelievably, addictively good.

There were cries of relief when the platform arrived, swarming with medical personnel, police, stretchers, and wheelchairs. The train stopped, and they poured off, into the organised confusion of helper and victim, then out toward the exits and broad stairways to where the streets below were filled with flyers, cruisers, and ground ambulances, a cacophony of flashing lights and motion.

Leaving four calm GIs, standing alone on a big empty maglev train, contemplating the four pathetic, bleeding wrecks piled up at the end in a growing pool of their own blood. One of them whimpered.

"Shut the fuck up," said Trong.

Intelligence Director Naidu strolled in off the platform, rumpled like an unmade bed, belly out, tie askew. He walked to the captives and regarded them with a quizzical, unsympathetic eye. "Only four?" he asked.

"You can go looking for the other six," Kiet suggested. "Might be a few bits floating downstream."

Naidu adjusted his belt. "Very well," he said. "It will do. Nice job, by the way."

"Thank you for noticing," said Poole. "How about a raise?"

"Oh dear boy," said Naidu with wry wisdom. "Among the many formidable opponents you will face, internal auditors and paymasters you will find among the very worst."

The briefing room was circular, an auditorium with a holoprojector in the middle, at the bottom of the bowl, surrounded by ascending rows of seats. Sandy sat on the bottom row, stretching as usual, relieving a myomer hip twinge. With her around the circle sat Steven Harren, Reggie Dala, and Abraham Yusef. Their three-person agency now had more than three people in it, Sandy understood, but no more details were forthcoming. Neither did the agency now possess a name. In that absence, those who knew they existed had given them one—SuperPsych. It was meant to be ironic, and amusing. Instead, Sandy found the whole setup rather creepy.

But only as an institution, because Steve, Reggie, and Abraham were actually very nice. "Sandy, are you sleeping with Rami Rahim?" Reggie asked her now, slyly. Reggie's professorial suit was cut a little more stylishly than Sandy remembered from just a year ago and looked very good with her long African braids. Reggie was a professor of some standing at a major Tanushan university, as was Abraham.

"No," Sandy said mildly, pulling her right elbow back behind her head, right leg stretched out hard for maximum effect. "We flirt so much in the interviews, we don't need sex."

"Yeah," said Reggie, "well, I was thinking, after your last interview with him . . ."

"It's a game," said Sandy. "Rami's a performer. And his ratings are down twenty percent since last year, so he needs every boost. It's the least I can do."

"Strange that a guy who helped save democracy should actually lose ratings," said Steve. Steven Harren was small, young, and blond. He dressed like a businessman but looked about half his thirty years. One of Tanusha's infamous tech whizzes, he was uplinked even now, dark glasses on despite the dark room, no doubt doing all kinds of fancy things on uplinks while he waited for the meeting to start.

"By helping to remove two democratically elected governments?" Reggie countered. She was comfortably old enough to be Steve's mother and sometimes took on the tone. "I'm surprised the backlash wasn't larger."

Sandy made a face. "It's not a political thing. Rami was Mr Partytown. Now he's a partisan, a part of the establishment. Not that he actually is, he's pretty vicious about us sometimes, but that's how he's perceived. It's uncool." She gave up on her right side and began stretching the left.

"So who *are* you sleeping with, Sandy?" asked Steven.

"My kids' imaginary friends," Sandy said drily. Reggie laughed, with the amusement of an older woman who knew. "Are you looking at porn, Steve?"

The young man grinned, reclining in his chair even farther than Sandy, hands folded on his middle. "Why? You know some good stuff?"

"I don't think you could run my sims."

"Never underestimate the capabilities of an ambitious man."

"Ambitious," said Reggie. "Is that what they call it?"

Abraham said nothing, gazing at the blank holoprojector. From her own feeds, Sandy could tell he wasn't even uplinked. He was just a quiet, thoughtful man who often had nothing to say. Instead, he wrote—ten books at last count, seven more than Reggie. His topic was sociology, theoretical systems and their applications in modern societies. He was not just a premier Callayan expert, he was a premier *Federation* expert. Sandy guessed that made him quite wealthy.

"Hey," said Vanessa, arriving from up the back and making her way down between chairs. "Sandy, you talking about sex again?"

"'Course, babe," said Sandy, arching her head back to look at her. "Where's the tyke?"

"I'm not bringing a three-month-old to a top-clearance briefing."

"Oh, come on," Sandy laughed. "Who's she going to tell?"

"You're bringing your kids to work?" Reggie asked. "The FSA let you do that?"

"It's just datawork," said Vanessa, settling into the chair across the aisle from Sandy. She looked a little tired, Sandy thought, but otherwise good. "I could do it at home, but I need to get out. I have entire offices of ready child minders outside."

"Who's got her now?" Sandy asked.

"Sarita."

"Of course." And to Reggie, "Personnel manager, grandma with twenty-three grandkids."

"Good lord, women breed in Tanusha," Reggie exclaimed mildly. "I had two, and even with all the tech, I've no idea how they find the time for more."

"Colonial society has a breeding imperative," said Abraham. "All these worlds to populate. It's why feminine social roles are more traditional away from Earth, completely contrary to what League thought would happen."

"Yeah," said Sandy, "and League overcompensated by building synthetic people instead." Abraham smiled a little. "She's been good?"

"Oh, she was screaming for about an hour this morning," said Vanessa, repressing a yawn. "And two hours last night. And Sylvan was screaming another hour. You'd think twin babies could synchronise screaming so we only lose two hours sleep, and not three?"

"You think they'd make a systems mod for it," Steven added unhelpfully. "Twenty-sixth century and there's still no fix for screaming babies."

"If they do," said Sandy, "that'll be the point I know to resign from the human race."

Steven peered at her past his dark glasses. "You know, Sandy, for such a high-tech specimen, you're quite a luddite sometimes."

"You're not the first Tanushan techie boy to accuse me of that." The doors atop the main aisle opened, and three men entered. "Speak of the devil . . ."

Ari was there, of course, walking with Ibrahim, the dark leather jacket and the cool plain suit. The other man was dark, slim, with a round face and unremarkable, almost androgynous features.

"Hello, Ragi," said Steven, quickly taking his glasses off and sitting up straight. Sandy repressed a smile—obviously some GIs required more full attention than others. "Haven't seen you for a while."

"Hello, Steven," said Ragi in that mild, pleasant tone of his. He walked the aisle steps down but took a seat one row back from the bottom. "Good to see you once more. Reggie. Abraham. Cassandra and Vanessa, of course."

Ari gave Vanessa a dark-browed look as he took a seat beside Steven, who looked pleased at the gesture. "What are you doing here?" he asked her.

"Oh, that's lovely," said Vanessa. "Maybe this little baby factory still has some other uses left in her?"

"It's not the propensity to make babies," said Ari. "It's the propensity to spread chaos and disorder wherever you go."

"Cassandra brought her," said Ibrahim, taking a random available seat. "Insisting she'd be useful."

"No pressure, babe," said Sandy. Vanessa snorted.

"Is this everyone?" Ibrahim asked, peering around.

"No," said Captain Reichardt from up the top of the stairs. He sealed the doors behind him with a code. "Now it's everyone."

"A man in uniform," Ibrahim observed, as Reichardt came down the stairs. And beneath his breath, "Wouldn't that be nice." There were grins. Ibrahim was no tyrant, but he did occasionally let slip mild concern at uniform standards in the building of late.

Vanessa shuffled along a seat so he could sit beside her and across the aisle from Sandy. "Hello, gorgeous," she offered. "It *is* a lovely uniform."

"Goddamn, girl," said the yellow-haired Texan. "Darn shame, you bein' married an' all."

"Abraham," said the FSA Director quite mildly, "I seem to recall some literature of yours on the detrimental effects on procedural outcomes of too much familiarity between coworkers? I think we could all become acquainted with that work again."

"And while you're at it," said Vanessa, "catch up with the *Daily Gossip*'s latest article on asshole bosses who won't allow their overstressed workers *any fun at all*. It's a doozy." Even Ibrahim struggled against a smile.

"Thank you, darling," said Sandy. "And now he knows why I brought you."

"It was a minor work," Abraham told Ibrahim with an impish smile.

"Good," said Ibrahim drily, organising a comp slate on his lap. "Work. Reggie."

"Yes," said Reggie, and Sandy sensed the uplink connect to the room's holodisplay. "Preliminaries on the maglev terrorists. Again, the usual disclaimer, we are aware that not everyone in the room is a neuroscientist. . . ."

"Including you," Steve added with a wry smile.

"Well, sure," said Reggie, a touch self-consciously. "Let me rephrase that. None of us in the room are neuroscientists, but some of us have to borrow from that field frequently."

"While others of us are far too busy to dabble in a new discipline," Ibrahim summarised. "Understood."

"We don't yet have the complete files on them," Reggie continued. "A lot of Pyeongwha security personnel are blank IDs, very hard to trace. But the very fact that they've accumulated these advanced skill sets without leaving any official record trace is indication enough.

"We've been retracing their movements, which has in turn given us leads to their uplink records . . . they've been scrubbing, but there's enough left for analysis. The conversations are all in code, so the words themselves remain meaningless, but there's a significant amount of code integration . . . Steven will get to that later.

"The end result is a PT graph like this." She linked up the holographic display in the middle of the circular floor. "PT is 'psychological topography,' for those of you who don't regularly attend these briefings."

With a glance at Reichardt and Vanessa. "I was gonna say 'physical training,'" Reichardt offered.

"Perfect tits," said Vanessa. Strangled smiles. "Do go on."

"You can't actually graph that," said Steven. "Though god knows some of us have tried."

A 3D graph appeared in midair between them, shimmering. The nonexperts in the room frowned, squinting slightly as it slowly rotated. "You can see the star pattern here," said Reggie, as figures on the graph aligned to make a five-pointed star, "this is the intersection of . . . well, I'll stay away from the technical terms—the intersection of short-term memory recall, interactive emotion, spatial perception . . . and a few other things. But when this star shows up on a Kitamura Graph, you know it's probably Neural Cluster Technology. NCT creates this intersection in maybe fifty percent of long-term users. It's statistically, just . . . wildly improbable that it should appear in anyone else, under natural conditions. Or under non-NCT conditions anyhow. With nearly everyone uplinked these days we're lately struggling, in this field, to recall what a 'natural' template looks like."

"We call that a Ruben Star," Steven added, with a glance at Ari alongside. "It only arose from your initial work on Pyeongwha four years ago."

"Well, now you're just engaging in Jewish stereotypes," said Ari.

"It's a pentagram, you dill," said Vanessa. "Not a Star of David. Unless you've become a Wiccan lately."

"My rabbi would not be surprised," said Ari. "Could just as easily be a Kresnov Star though, half of those ideas I got from her."

With a glance at Sandy. Sandy just watched, a leg stretched out, thumbs in pockets. Observing carefully.

"And that indicates a Compulsive Narrative Lock?" Ibrahim asked.

Reggie nodded. "It's not a precise match, everyone's different . . . but generally yes. Most of the Pyeongwha regime radicals, and maybe thirty percent of the general population, were showing this to varying degrees. Of course, the more extreme they were, the more likely they were to be in the Pyeongwha regime themselves. And if you have a critical mass of the population locked in to the dominant narrative, it pushes enough of the remainder into a non-compulsive orbit, what we call a submissive mass pattern. Abraham's term."

"On Pyeongwha it seemed to work on the rule of thirds," Abraham explained. He was the sociologist, Reggie the psych. Reggie studied individuals, Abraham studied groups. "One third compulsively locked into the regime ideology. Another third, not showing the Ruben Star, but following anyway—that's the submissive mass pattern, the people who follow not because their brains have left them no choice, but due to natural, unaugmented social pressure and Compulsive Narrative Syndrome. Which leaves a remaining third, largely too afraid to oppose, even if they feel opposed."

"And of course a lot of that last third have the Ruben Star as well," Reggie added. "They just haven't locked into the regime ideology, they've locked onto something else. A lot of anti-regime activity on Pyeongwha was organised by ideology and institution, there was a lot of religious opposition, so of course the regime shut down the religious activity."

"So in some ways," said Steven, "the regime was right to be paranoid. The opposition groups really were out to get them, and the regime knew just how fanatical they were, because the regime had the same fanaticism."

"That's an international relations problem," Reichardt said grimly. "Rational Escalation, the polarisation of opposing sides in a zero-sum environment. Fleet Captains deal with that every day."

"So okay," said Vanessa. "We have this natural mental condition, Compulsive Narrative Syndrome. Pyeongwha's uplink tech was making it far worse. People who have it become fanatics. So how does the regime make sure they become fanatical in favour of *it*? I mean, I get that that last third, where the opposition groups came from—they weren't. The religious groups and so forth. So why aren't there more of them? I mean, if the condition is as . . . as malignant as it seems, why aren't people just becoming fanatical about all sorts of things? I know you have a random spread of that on Pyeongwha, but you still have this mass support for the regime. Why not more opposition, more diffusion?"

"The most relevant question," Abraham acknowledged. Vanessa looked pleased. "It is the one aspect that my field cannot account for. And it's her fault." Pointing at Reggie.

Reggie sighed. "There are so many variables. I mean . . . well, we know the reasons, we just can't narrow it down to a main one. The first possibility is input dominance, meaning simply that people accept that information which they receive the most of. If ninety percent of the information you receive tells you one thing, and ten percent tells you another, the ninety percent is what you believe. You see this in any politics and religion, people who grow up and live in environments where they are only surrounded by the same kinds of people who believe the same things rarely question their beliefs. On Pyeongwha, the regime had input dominance, it was everywhere. Compulsive Narrative Syndrome is just looking for a juicy narrative to swallow, and the regime gave it one, all day every day."

"Which in some conditions will just set up counter-narrative dissonance," said Abraham.

"Yes, well . . ." Reggie swept some braids, "let's not complicate things unnecessarily. The second possibility is good old-fashioned emotional conformity. The oldest human psychology, it's hardwired into the least-evolved parts of the human brain, the parts that fish use to school, or birds use to flock. Protection and cooperation in numbers, it's the foundation of all society, animal or human. It's the reason very nice children will not oppose bullies and will sometimes even join in with bullies, even if they're not bullies themselves in other circumstances. Joining the dominant group is the most natural of human instincts, as deeply embedded as sexual desire. It takes an act of extraordinary willpower to oppose it and take another path when doing so leaves you all alone."

She looked at Sandy. They all did. Sandy inclined her head, silent appreciation of the gesture. She did not add that sometimes she thought that her own rebellion against the League was only that in a military society that valued force and power, she *was* the dominant group, no matter how outnumbered.

"And the third, of course," Reggie continued, "is narrative resonance—the opposite of the narrative dissonance that Abraham just mentioned. Which is just to compliment the Pyeongwha regime on a good marketing job. That's the same thing political parties everywhere run on, or ideologies, or religions—the appeal to things that trigger a positive emotional and psychological response. With extreme CNS, the resonance is so strong it instantly produces emotional conviction, an extreme emotional response. It's not new, you see it in pre-infotech societies too, look at footage from the Nuremberg Rallies in Germany in the 1930s, you'll see people sobbing, hysterically happy and committed over a man and a regime that started a war that killed a hundred million people . . . including a good percentage of those in the audience."

"And from where did we Jews learn irony?" Ari said drily. "I wonder."

"And 'the collective' remains an emotionally powerful concept," said Abraham. "However you define it. A state, a nation, a religion, a football team, an ideological concept of philosophy or politics. The triggers of personal identity and belonging are powerful, and too often they drive the so-called intellectual reasoning. Usually these are contributing factors to human conflicts. Certainly they were in the League-Federation War. What we fear we are beginning to see now, in the League, the destruction of Cresta and elsewhere, and in the Federation with Pyeongwha, is that the secondary sociological phenomenon becomes the driver. The cart pulling the horse, if you will.

"Usually these phenomena have a cause. Most historians draw a clear line between the rise of Hitler and the consequences of the Treaty of Versailles after the previous World War. Cause and effect. Similarly, the League-Federation War was fought over one primary issue, the question of synthetic humanity and the future direction of the human species. Now whether an individual accepts that the war was necessary or achieved anything worthwhile, from a technical, sociological point of view, we can confidently say that it had a real world cause.

"Pyeongwha did not. There was no reason for this regime to start murdering hundreds of thousands of its own citizens. They just chose to. The reasons why are largely inside the regime's heads and those of its supporters. There were no shortages. There were no notable social or religious divisions. There is nothing remarkable about Pyeongwha on any measureable scale that one might expect to cause a violent sociological response. Other than the fact that they had Neural Cluster Technology and used it with irresponsible abandon.

"So this is what we are now faced with in the League. What might otherwise be solved as petty disagreements between worlds and social groups, now erupting into violence because of the extreme and uncompromising collective narratives and mindsets of its people. Modern societies require compromise to function. Some historically did not, in pretechnological days they could shut out all who thought, looked, or acted differently, or burn them at the stake, or whatever their solution. These days, societies that do that can no longer function, because the natural diversity of human experience is impossible to avoid. If the automatic response of all narrative groups toward disagreement with their narrative is violence, in modern society, then human civilisation will destroy itself en masse."

A silence in the room.

"And am I correct," Ibrahim added carefully, "that you believe that something similar may be happening not just in the League but in the Federation too?"

"It's not that we believe it," Abraham replied. Pensively, leaning forward on his chair, elbows on knees. "The evidence assures us of it. If you refer to our latest report . . ."

"We all read it," Ibrahim interrupted. "I do not wish this meeting to waste time reviewing very well compiled figures and analysis. I want to review this basic point. If this is not a League-specific condition, and is also spreading in the Federation despite our relative lack of Neural Cluster Technology in uplinks, what do we do about it?"

"I don't think it's arguable," said Ragi, from several rows back. Calm and quiet, as usual. "I think I understand the technical ramifications of the technology better than anyone else here—with apologies, Steven and Ari." Steven shrugged. Ari just waited. "As an experimental GI, my brain is struc- tured to comprehend these things better than most. And when one applies the methods of this team—mass-psychological analysis by network interaction— to recent events . . . look no further than Operation Shield, the analysis data from those events were sobering.

"I think that monitoring for the condition should be expanded. You must know what you're dealing with, ignorance is deadly in these conditions. You have results showing particular individuals and institutions displaying symp- toms, and we've just seen what those conditions lead to, left unregulated. A coup and a shootout in the Federation's capital city. If we can prevent that, we should."

"We," Sandy thought. When did Ragi become "we"? He'd barely been seen the last year, off wandering or hiding god-knew-where. Trying to come to terms with the difficult circumstances of his own existence, no doubt.

Reggie and Abraham were nodding. Steven looked pleased to have Ragi's approval. Ibrahim looked at Ari.

"I think my position's well known," said Ari. "I don't hear anything here that would change it."

Steven frowned. "I think the science is pretty well established here, Ari."

"No!" Agitated, in that hand-waving Ari-manner. "What you're doing here isn't . . . it's not science! It's theory . . . fuck, it's not even theory, it's *new* theory. Theory's bad enough, I mean, it's useful, sure, but it's a simulation. All theory *simulates*, it makes assumptions and generalisations on purpose, it's the only way to make a useful analytical structure without getting bogged in detail, and that's fine. But good theorists know they're generalising and skipping over bits, and they allow for that, but it's clear that you lot *don't* know that. And worse, you're doing new theory, which means it's in its infancy, it's unevolved and almost certainly wrong about . . . well, nearly everything. . . ."

"Ari," said Reggie with exasperation, "we just saw an institutional coup in the Federation, and in the League an entire inhabited world was destroyed. And you want more evidence?"

"Results are not evidence," Ari retorted somewhat incredulously. "Process is evidence. That you're not aware of that is alarming in itself." Reggie hung her head and exhaled hard. "You show me the process that caused those results, I'll be convinced, otherwise I'll tell you that babies are made by pixies in the garden, and the proof is all the babies being born—if I'm not required to explain down to the finest detail *how* babies are made, it may as well be pixies, right?"

"I think we've explained our findings quite well," Abraham said calmly and a little condescendingly.

"Right! By concluding that there's a nasty phenomenon going on, which quite certainly is going on in the League, and then *assuming* that because some events in the Federation look somewhat like what you've seen from the League and from Pyeongwha, that it must be the same thing! And you know what that looks like? Narrative association, Compulsive Narrative Syndrome again, another version of the same thing you're studying . . . my cat has four legs, my dog also has four legs, therefore my dog is a cat."

"Ari," Ragi said calmly, "the tests devised to demonstrate causal effects from hyperactive Compulsive Narrative Syndrome are showing the same phenomenon increasing in the Federation. It's comparable against a timeline, it matches in critical institutions just before the coup. I think the association is quite obvious."

"And you don't know what you're measuring. Would you apply those graphs to Talee society if you could?" Frowns. "Of course you wouldn't, you don't know the first damn thing about Talee psychology, you'd have no idea what you're looking at, whatever 'firm results' the data showed. And all this stuff about the interactions between human psychology, neurology, sociology, and uplink technology—it's *new*. You think you know, but you don't. You think you're an expert, because that's what it reads on the blurbs of your books and how you get introduced at university lectures, but you're fucking *not* experts. You don't know what the fuck you're talking about, any of you, and unacknowledged ignorance is dangerous."

"And the consequences if we're right," Abraham replied, "and nothing is done, are too horrible to contemplate. Human science exists for a reason, and that reason is to control our environment to the greatest extent possible so that we can maximise the good things while minimising the bad ones. If this current circumstance does not qualify, I don't know what does."

Ari gave Ibrahim a "told you so" glare and slumped back in his seat. Indication that he'd said all he intended. Ibrahim's gaze turned to Sandy.

"Cassandra? Your thoughts?"

"I have a report to submit," said Sandy, quite relaxed. "You'll find it in your constructs in a few minutes, please read soon. I've been compiling it with my fellow Callayan GIs, now that there's enough of us to make a workable subject pool. The results suggest what I've long suspected—that GIs are far less susceptible to Compulsive Narrative Syndrome than straights. The psychological depth is lacking, we don't have the connections between memory, knowledge, and emotion, the hooks and triggers don't match up. We're entirely susceptible to input dominance, as Reggie explained it, but not too much else. Give us new inputs, we can change our minds, we don't form emotional attachments to abstract concepts to the degree that straights do. Which is why League are scared of their own creations and try to shield them as much as it can.

"So maybe this is our role in Federation society. The buffer between straights and the levers of self-destruction. Here in the FSA in particular. The objective observers who, with any luck, and a lot of encouragement, will not fall for the bullshit on either side."

Thoughtful looks around the room. A thinking frown from Abraham. A delighted smile from Steven.

"And how does that relate to our current discussion?" Ibrahim asked carefully. Knowing well that Sandy did not raise new issues at random.

"I'm increasingly certain that this is my own role in these discussions," said Sandy. "I understand the tech nearly as well as Ragi, but I know the functions and dysfunctions of human institutions better than nearly everyone here except you, Director." Ibrahim pursed his lips and did not disagree. "I have a balance. And I'm command senior of a large group of very capable combat GIs who are completely sick of political tyranny in any form.

"I see in this research the potential for a new political tyranny. Particularly given the new relationships I see being formed within the current provisional Grand Council. And while I don't agree with Ari on everything, I agree on this—that the imposition of a new political tyranny to deal with newly perceived threats is unacceptable. I don't care if you think the universe is ending. There's always an excuse. Every tyrant in the past has always had a sound logical reason that made perfect sense to him. Now we have *proof*. Today you promise me conclusively proven proof. I don't care. I'm for liberty. If that makes me an unreasonable obstacle, so be it.

"Just know this. I have great affection for you all personally. But any attempt to impose new authoritarian controls, even in the name of saving humanity, will first have to deal with me and every weapon at my disposal. I'm watching you. I'll only warn you once."

There was no smiling comradery now. Only consternation on some faces. And sadness on others. Steven looked upset. Ari, grimly satisfied. Ibrahim observed the new silence thoughtfully. His expression, as usual, gave nothing away.

CHAPTER SIX

C hief Shin walked in on Sandy's morning physical, black suit, slick hair, cool and calm as ever. Half-past six and God-knew what hours the Federal Intelligence Chief was working these days; Sandy had never seen him other than alert and immaculate.

She stood on a sense-pad in the middle of the medical room's floor, wearing tight gym clothes and sensor-bands around limbs and joints, reading every electrical impulse through her synthetic muscles. Instant analysis flashed across a wall screen, multiple scanners studying her every move, every shift of balance. She flicked the screen off, now with Shin here for company. They were otherwise alone, FSA medical staff not quite so dedicated to turn up at dawn, and Sandy not needing any help to set up this simple structural analysis.

"Commander," said Shin in that neatly accented English of his. It was an original Chinese accent, from Beijing, where Shin had been born. Homeland Chinese were often not well received by colonial Chinese, who thought them arrogant. Shin had that reputation, though Sandy did not know him well enough to know if it was warranted. And she'd not heard from local Chinese about him, because Callay had so few local Chinese—Chinese often avoiding settlement on worlds with too many Indians, and vice versa. Callay's settlement had been conceived and executed by predominantly South Asian business interests, and most Chinese settlers had gone elsewhere. "Is this a good time?"

"For what?" asked Sandy. She did basic Tai Chi. It gave the sensors good feedback on her muscles, coordination, and balance, the whole 3D structure flashing in multicoloured real time to her uplink vision, now that she'd turned the screen off. She'd not share that data with Shin, not even a glance.

"A personal matter," said Shin. Sandy frowned. Really? "My daughter Yu attends Canas School, as you know." She did. As a high-profile, security-sensitive individual in Tanusha, Shin and family lived in Canas, just a few hundred meters from Sandy. "She tells me that yesterday, your boy Danya and your girl Svetlana approached her. She said she felt threatened."

Sandy thought about that, continuing through a flowing motion. She didn't really know what all the movements were called, nor, tragically, any of the rich heritage behind it all—she just learned the forms and repeated them, as her synthetic brain did so well, to millimetre precision.

"Does she say my kids threatened her?" Quite calmly.

"No," Shin admitted. "But she said they asked questions about me, and about my attitude toward you."

"They do their research, Chief," said Sandy. "These are kids accustomed to looking out for themselves. Present them with a strategic situation, they'll look into it."

"They've not mentioned it to you?"

"We don't talk shop at home unless it's serious. And probably they'd know I'd disapprove. Why does Yu say she felt threatened?"

Shin put hands in pockets, watching her motions. He had the manner of a man accustomed to getting his own way and comfortable with power. A face like a shield, revealing only what he chose. "She said it was inappropriate," he said. "She says they should have known better."

"Oh, they do know better, all the time."

"So you will reprimand them?"

"No. My kids will look out for themselves on matters concerning their security or my security. If they threatened your daughter, I'd reprimand them. But I don't believe they would."

"Commander," Shin said firmly, coming about to see her face better. He was frowning, very serious. "Your eldest two children are no strangers to violence. The presence of two of them together, asking questions of a slimmer and less experienced girl, can surely be taken by my daughter as threatening."

"I suppose that depends what your kid has been told about my kids." She paused the Tai Chi and did a sudden lunge-punch. Shin may have jumped back, just a little. New data flashed across her inner vision, muscle groups, reaction densities, little flurries of feedback-and-response. "My kids don't bully. They know it upsets me. Your daughter will always be completely safe with them."

It was bullshit, and she knew it. "Always" was a long time, things between FSA HQ and FedInt were rocky, her kids knew it, and purely civilised morality was not always foremost in their minds when they, or she, were threatened. Dammit, she'd have to talk to them.

"I ask you very seriously, Commander, to warn your children away from my daughter. I do not wish to make an issue of this, but I will."

"Good," said Sandy. She did a fast combination, more data flashing back. Shin frowned, as Sandy glanced at him. "Good," she insisted. "My kids are reasonable, Chief. If I can tell them you're upset, and they can see the negatives in what they've done in making the FedInt Chief mad at them, they'll stop. If you're genuinely concerned, I'd invite you to talk to them yourself."

Shin blinked. She was inviting him to confront her kids in person? She saw fast recalculation. They're not scared of you, Chief. Not unless you try to hurt them. But who would dare, given their mother?

"I may do that," he said.

"Great," said Sandy, with a faint smile. "I'm sure they'll learn something." Whether it was what Shin wanted them to learn, she highly doubted.

"You've seen League Affairs' latest analysis of Cresta?"

"Yes." League Affairs were a separate department of the FSA, under Chief Boyle. They were now reporting that PRIDE, the collectivised term for the League resistance, were claiming responsibility for Cresta. Boyle was of the opinion that the only target worth PRIDE's killing on Cresta was League ex-President Edwin Balasingham. "What do you think?"

She did another fast combination, elbows, fists, and forearms flying. Something twinged above her hip, a short flash of pain across her middle. Graphics showed the right shoulder restricted at the rotator cuff. Old injuries that had never healed a hundred percent. Ninety-eight, maybe.

"In the absence of more information, it's impossible to be sure." Shin watched her carefully. She may have turned the wall monitor off, but he knew why she was here, why she had to watch all these old injuries. GIs were high maintenance, and she was no exception. Against a clever opponent, who played a long and indirect game, it could be a weakness. "It seems a stretch to suggest that PRIDE destroyed an entire moon, and a quarter of a million people, to kill one man."

"It would play to the nature of the disorder," said Sandy, resuming Tai Chi. "Emotive targeting, rather than strategic. Balasingham was a leader of the Centralists, the Worlders never liked him. Killing him is a statement, PRIDE are all about statements."

"You're suggesting this is not actually a military act, but the largest-ever act of terrorism?"

"Semantics." She blew hair from her eye, never losing posture. "All irregular warfare has elements of terrorism, whatever we think of the cause. But I wouldn't put it past PRIDE. League was founded on uncompromising idealism, stands to reason their breakaway splinters will employ the same in a different form."

"You had any direct experience?" Shin asked. "With PRIDE?"

Sandy gave up the exercises and went to get some water. She was hot and sweaty; maintaining muscular density for long periods could generate nasty temperatures.

"A bit." She sipped from her bottle and wiped her face with the towel on the bench. "A couple of marine commanders, a couple of army officers, back in the war. Now confirmed separatists. It's in my reports." All of which Shin had read, she was certain. He was fishing for something.

"Subject A was PRIDE. We can confirm it."

"Ah. Any ID?"

"No. But a visual match from League-side Intelligence." FedInt maintained that network still, spies all through the League. FSA HQ, based here on Callay, coordinated all the different arms and gave the instructions. But if FedInt didn't want to carry them out, FSA was a toothless tiger, with limited assets of its own. Those assets were blunt, like Special Group—Sandy and Vanessa's responsibility. And like Special Agency, the small group of Callay-based agents amongst whom Ari was now senior. FSA HQ ruled on Callay, and FedInt couldn't function without Callay. And the FSA's primary asset, its network of spies and agents elsewhere throughout the Federation and the League, were run by FedInt, and FSA HQ were just as helpless without them. Both sides were stuck, unable to work together, unable to work apart.

"So why was he talking to Pyeongwha terrorists?" Sandy asked.

Shin made a faint gesture of his head, perhaps a shrug. "Why was he talking to a Talee representative?" Pointedly. "I'm advised you have access."

Ah. Now they came to it: Shin's real reason for being here. "He's our guest," she said, taking another sip of water. "He doesn't want to talk to you."

"Why not?"

"Because you're supposed to do what we say." Her eyes flashed with barely controlled intensity. "And he talks to who's in charge."

Shin looked thoughtful. Careful, as always. And not rising to her bait. "If I cannot conduct my own interviews, I'll need access to yours. Transcripts."

"We'll consider it."

Raised eyebrows. "You'll *consider* it?"

Sandy nodded. The air between them might have crackled. Sandy fixed her eyes on his, knowing this was her advantage to exploit. She barely flinched at explosions—eye contact was nothing.

"Captain Reichardt says Cresta was not as undefended as early analysis suggested," Sandy added. "Our Fleet has sources on League Fleet no one else does."

"I'm aware." Drily.

"He says League reinforced Cresta's orbital defences a year ago. They were well guarded from random attack, despite the tricky lunar dynamics of those approaches. He says that a standard V-strike trajectory would typically have only a five percent chance of success against those defences."

Shin's brow furrowed again. "He thinks it was an inside job?"

"He thinks PRIDE did it," Sandy replied. "But he thinks someone on the inside gave them precise information on Cresta's defences."

Sandy's IR vision detected no real acceleration in Shin's pulse. He was very cool, she gave him that.

"Interesting," said Shin. "May I have access to *that* analysis?"

Sandy smiled, wryly calm. "You can talk to Captain Reichardt whenever you like."

"Good," said Shin. "I shall. I see Special Agency is now commissioning GIs. Another intake expansion, it seems."

"That's right."

"And Ms Togales is now FSA spokesperson."

"Uh-huh." With a hint of defiance.

"And for how long will this expansion of FSA HQ capabilities continue?"

"We're not sure yet," said Sandy. "We have quite a lot of capabilities now, with all these new GIs in town."

"Yes," Shin agreed. "Yes, you do. And the appearance of a power imbalance does not concern you?"

"Not yet," said Sandy. "But if you think too many GIs in the one institution makes for an imbalance, perhaps you could try recruiting some yourself?"

Shin did not look impressed at the suggestion.

"Try not to alarm him beyond a certain level," Ibrahim told her after the morning's combat drills, as she showered in the women's open stalls. *"I approve of the warnings, FedInt need to know where we stand, and strong disagreements are less dangerous than meek misunderstandings. But let's not overdo it."*

"Did I overdo it here?" Sandy asked, head under the water jets as she formulated silently, other women talking in neighbouring stalls.

"No," Ibrahim admitted. *"But I sense the potential, given that your children are involved. And his child."*

"I think he exaggerated that as an excuse to come at me hard before asking his real questions about Cai."

"Exactly," said Ibrahim. *"You moved automatically to a defensive position regarding your children, as every good parent does. Thus my concern."*

"I understand." Another GI paused at her stall but guessed she was uplinked and refrained from whatever she'd been going to ask. *"He thinks FSA HQ are loading ourselves up with new GIs to build up our military capabilities for whatever shape the Federation looks like after Ranaprasana's committee work is finished."*

"And he'd be right," said Ibrahim. Lucky there was no chance anyone was hacked into this call, Sandy thought.

"He thinks we're in danger of becoming the new autocratic power."

"It is a danger. If I were removed, or you were. But the situation has left us little choice, and that's Chief Shin's fault as much as ours."

It was still unclear just how much of a role FedInt had played in Operation Shield, but it was unthinkable they hadn't been heavily involved. Shin being Shin, he'd covered his tracks very neatly, and word was the ongoing investigations from FSA, CSA, or Ranaprasana himself weren't finding anything conclusive. Shin, and much of the Federation-wide intelligence network he ran, didn't want to be run by a central organisation on Callay dominated by former-League combat GIs, and run by a Director who didn't worship at the altar of established doctrine. And Shin believed, no doubt, that Ibrahim would pursue Sandy's own interest in GI-emancipation, perhaps simply to gain more manpower.

Federation had fought a war to protect the human race from unconstrained synthetic biology. Sandy had tried explaining to various people away from Callay, where attitudes changed more slowly, that GIs in the FSA did not signal that the League had actually won the war. On the contrary, no one was more concerned about how synthetic technology had been misused in the League, than GIs who had defected out of disgust at their personal experiences. And now, League was paying for its misuse of the technology in the most frightening way imaginable.

But what if GI production stopped completely? Certainly it remained illegal in the Federation and would remain so for indefinite years to come. A certain percentage of those GIs commissioned in the League would continue to trickle into the Federation, and that would keep the numbers here rising, though manageable. To date, Federation GIs were limited exclusively to Callay, though it was theoretically legal for them to move elsewhere — they simply chose not to for fear of less-adjusted attitudes elsewhere in the Federation. Amongst these Federation GIs, a sense of community was growing, a sense of "us." It was not at all chauvinistic, and Sandy was determined it would not become so, but certainly not all were happy at the prospect of an indefinite ban on making GIs.

Did any GI want to see the "species," such as they were, die out completely? They dodged the issue neatly in the Federation, condemning League for mistreating GIs but relying on them too for new members of the community. What if she and the others were growing old, many years from now, with all League production shut down, and no young GIs anywhere? Could she sit still and let her people fade into oblivion? Even if it was, by some metrics, the best outcome for the human race as a whole?

Captain Reichardt appeared and leaned on the tiled wall alongside her stall. Sandy raised an eyebrow at him and continued to rinse her hair. He wore full uniform as always—FOG, they called it, for Fleet-On-the-Ground. FOG protocol said that among high-ranking non-Fleet, he was required to identify himself at all times. In strategic terms, a warship overhead changed everything.

"Hi, Arron," said Sandy through the steam of many showers. "Wanna come in?"

"Hi," he said. "No thank you." And produced a memory stick in a plastic cover. Placed it on top of the soap dispenser; no doubt it was waterproof. He indicated to it, then used his hand to mime conversation. Indicated himself, then mimed his throat being cut. Sandy nodded. Not a word, then. And the showers were smart, especially the female showers, sensitivities being what they were toward visual monitors here. But audio was always possible. "Just came to say thanks for the Scarlotti. It was fantastic."

Sandy smiled, dunking her face in the water stream. "Sure. They're the best secret in the Goyal Valley. They don't have too many vines so they don't want to mass produce. But I haven't found a better red for that price on Callay."

"Ndaja and a few of the grunts are down that way touring," said Reichardt. "I'll tell them to check it out." Sandy couldn't quite imagine Lieutenant Ndaja of the *Mekong*'s marine complement touring wineries on her shore leave . . . but then, she of all people should know better than to prejudge. "And I'll wire them a procurement order from Fleet allowances to bring back an extra box or two."

"Ah, officer surplus wine supplies," Sandy reminisced. "I made good use of it, League-side. I was the black market's top customer." Whatever his innocent intentions, Reichardt's gaze was straying. She turned. "Do my back?"

He grinned. "No . . . no, I think I'll um . . ." He jerked a thumb back toward the exit. "I'll just go."

"If you must," she sighed and resumed washing herself. Reichardt turned and made way for Amirah, wearing that friendly grin as she passed and nothing else.

"Hi, Captain," she said, padding to her locker as she towelled her hair. Just because she was lately on an administrative track didn't mean she neglected her combat exercises.

"Dear Lord," said Reichardt as he walked to the exit, speaking loudly enough for most nearby to hear. "Thank you for female GIs."

A 42 series named Lata paused at Sandy's stall, observing Reichardt's departure with disapproval. "You let him go," she observed. "Why?"

"Steady girlfriend," Sandy explained.

"Straights!" Lata exclaimed, walking on with an exasperated shrug.

When she got home, the kids had already made and eaten dinner and were now doing homework together at the kitchen table—all under Danya's supervision. Other parents sometimes asked her what they could do to induce similar behaviour from their kids. Send them to Droze for five years to be terrified and starved, she'd replied. If they survive, they'll come back so mutually dependent and desperate for normalcy that even cooking and homework would seem a joy.

"Wow, guys," she said as she ate her fish with vegetables on the table amidst their homework. "This is delicious."

"Svetlana made it," said Danya, looking up from his physics problems. His hair was a mess after swimming at the Canas School pool, his arms bare and tanned. He'd grown ten centimeters since he'd come to Callay, and though he'd never be more than average sized, he would still be taller than her in another year or two. In four or five years, she'd probably barely make his shoulder. It still amazed her, teenagers and their growth spurts. Teenagers and everything, in fact. Her lack of familiarity made even the things most parents complained about seem interesting.

"Nice job, Svet."

"It was Danya's recipe," Svetlana said with a shrug, stylus paused between math sums. "He bought everything on his run this morning, I just followed the recipe."

"I made the sauce!" Kiril insisted. He was halfway through a page of meticulous handwriting, which Tanushan schools still insisted on. People like Ari thought it a stupid anachronism, of course. "The sauce is the best bit!"

"It is the best bit, Kiril," said Sandy. "You're right." His brother and sister smiled and did not protest. "I hear you guys talked to Shin Yu the other day."

"You mean Yu Shin," said Kiril.

"She's Chinese, Kiri," said Svetlana. "Surname comes first." Suddenly concentrating very hard on her tablet.

"Who told you?" asked Danya. Carefully.

"Her dad." She looked at him, waiting for the explanation she was not sure would come.

"Are you angry?"

"I don't know yet," said Sandy with mild amusement. "Should I be?"

Danya looked a little relieved that she was at least not *immediately* angry.

Not that her anger with them was ever real, just occasionally projected for effect. "Kids sometimes say more than adults," he explained. "I wanted to see if she let anything slip, about her dad and FedInt."

Sandy bit another mouthful. "And?"

"Not really. She doesn't talk much."

"She's a really good student," Svetlana piped up. "She's top of her classes in nearly everything. And she keeps to herself and has almost no friends."

"Thing is," said Sandy, "her dad says she felt threatened." Undeterred by Svetlana's attempts at distraction. "And tried to get me to reprimand you."

"She's lying!" Svetlana protested.

"We didn't threaten her," said Danya very seriously. "Not even close."

"I know," Sandy said mildly. "I told her dad I didn't believe you would. And I think he was probably exaggerating, just so he had some leverage on me."

"He's an asshole," Svetlana complained. "It's no wonder she looks unhappy all the time, with a father like that."

"I don't know that he is a bad father," Sandy replied. "I've heard other people say he's great with his daughter. But being the only child of a man like Shin is hard. They've travelled around a lot, and he has a lot of personal security concerns. She hasn't been able to make many friends, I think, because they keep moving, and she's been told not to talk to people about so many things. Like you."

"That's what Danya said," Svetlana admitted reluctantly.

"The difference between her and you is that she's all alone, while you have each other. And while I'm sure she's had the usual security training for the child of such a high-level man as her father, she hasn't actually lived it, like you guys have. She's been told there's threats everywhere, and she's probably been told I'm one of them, and therefore you guys are too. And probably that makes her scared. Especially when two of you talk to her together."

Danya made a wry face. "Yeah. It's just that when I talk to people, girls especially, they usually react better if Svetlana's there."

"Sure," Sandy agreed. A lot of people found their relationship very sweet, having rarely seen brothers and sisters so close at this age. "But there's two of you, and she was outnumbered."

"So you think I should have gone alone?"

"I think you probably shouldn't have gone at all." With a good-natured *look*. Danya smirked. Adult-sensible or not, he was still a teenage boy on some things. She may as well have told him not to surf on the really big waves. "But if you must, why not let Svetlana do it?"

"Alone?" Another smirk.

"Hey!" said Svetlana.

"Probably talk about shoes," said Danya. Svetlana slapped his arm.

"She might have done better talking about shoes," said Sandy. "Then, a few days later, she could talk about hairstyles. And a few days later, boy bands. Then, two weeks later, 'how's your father?' You see?"

Svetlana grinned triumphantly at Danya. Danya looked thoughtful. "You're such an ignoramus, Danya," said his sister. "You know so much about everything except people."

It was unfair, but not without some truth. Danya viewed everything as a technical problem to solve. With people less serious than himself, as children usually were, he didn't always relate.

"Sandy," said Kiril, "how many people live in China?" Sandy smiled. While Kiril, meanwhile, lived in Kiril-land, a bright and happy place filled with interesting facts that had nothing to do with the topic at hand.

After dinner, Sandy helped them with homework. Danya's grades were okay but predictably depended on whether his teacher engaged him or not. The technicalities of maths and languages did little to excite him, but applying them toward actual results, like in Applied Design, had gotten him good marks, and renewed enthusiasm for the skills that went into it. At history he was best of all, the more brutal and bloodthirsty, the better. People and politics made sense to him, and few of the horrors in history books surprised him.

Svetlana struggled, having missed most of those early years of education Danya had at least received. They'd used some basic education tape on Droze, but it was very limited, and often she got frustrated with how far she was behind. Sandy helped her now with some basic maths, sipping coffee while pointing her way through some algebra on Svetlana's slate, converting sums into simple diagrams with her uplinks that demonstrated the problem in some different way. Sometimes she substituted funny comic-art animals for numbers, eliminating them as subtraction demanded by an equally comic boot up the backside, making Svetlana giggle—she'd discovered the best way to curb the frustration was to break up the learning with laughter. It sobered her to recall how once, when she was very young in the League, she'd been dismissive of straights and their relative lack of maths and other basic mental skills. Less intelligent, less important, she'd thought. How wrong she'd been.

After homework she apologised and went to her room, with a promise to join them a bit later for a game they'd discovered they liked. In the room, she inserted the memory stick into her personal autistic drive, which established her local construct with no external connectivity whatsoever. It had no memory either, so no intruder or warranted search would find any trace of its use.

The memory stick loaded constructs in Fleet format, heavily encrypted, and Reichardt hadn't bothered to give her a decoder, knowing she could break it in a few seconds. She established the first construct . . . it was a nav map, from a ship's cruise recorder. The date had been not merely hidden but scrubbed, so she had no idea what ship it was, or when it had been recorded, or where. A bit of detective work could solve that, she supposed, sipping tea as she watched the recording play on her double desk screen, to save herself from the mental ache of too much uplink vision in one day. She could hear crew talking, and a voice-print match could find the personnel in question, the dates they'd served, and put the pieces together from there. Also, system features were clearly marked, planets, moons, stations, identifying names also scrubbed, but she knew quite a lot of that stuff from her time League-side in the war. Reichardt knew his career was over if anyone knew he'd shared this, names or no names.

This feed looked like a third-watch ship, twenty-four-hour cycles divided into three eight-hour slots. They were inertial, 31 AU from a star, twenty-three degrees nadir on an insystem heading. There was the usual system chatter, quite a lot of sensor data. Sandy guessed from the feeds it might be a Destroyer; the trajectory didn't suggest the jump engines of a Runner or the stealth of a Ghostie.

Suddenly an entry, a flare of jump energy . . . just 2.3 AU. Loud calls of alarm, scan and nav shouting figures in unison, helm sorting through incoming response trajectories, all-hands flashing red. The incoming vessel was far too close to the star for comfort, on a trajectory taking him across and also insystem . . . and now a second vessel jump-flared in behind, in the almost identical spot the first had arrived.

Only now they both turned, simultaneous flares of jump-energy to shift trajectory as only Talee could, and both disappeared in a flash of power. Leaving stunned Federation bridge crew to analyse the continuing scroll of incoming data, radiation levels, last trajectory, mass and power projections . . . all impossible, of course, for human ships. Listening to the crew gave her a cold chill up the spine, as seasoned Fleet professionals tried to keep the incredulity from their voices and do their jobs.

The ships had come in on different trajectories and arrived at nearly the same moment. So they couldn't have coordinated that manoeuvre beforehand. That had been spontaneous. And therefore impossible, because when you ran into someone else's light-wave you had no idea what they were actually doing at that moment, only what they *were* doing, several seconds or minutes ago, at the light-wave's source. But somehow they just knew, turned together in perfect synchronicity, and left on the same heading on the same trajectory. Unless it was a fluke, both ships turning instinctively to a familiar destination, a safety route. But this trajectory took them toward Federation frontier space, she heard nav telling the newly awoken Captain in terse, disbelieving tones. No Talee ships went that way, everyone was quite sure. Which meant they'd probably known a rock out there in the dark that Fleet did not, some point of mass they could arrive at, reorient, and jump out again some other way.

Unless they'd short-jumped it. In unison. With no preparation. That was impossible too, even preplanning short-jumps were fraught; with the star's fading mass behind them, getting out of hyperspace was hard, and making it stick, harder. Coordinating between two vessels and emerging within the same 100 AU, really hard, even if the Talee were using the tech everyone thought they were.

Sandy looked through two more cruise recordings. Both showed equally amazing things. The pattern, she was beginning to see, was that none of them could be completely explained by technology. All involved Talee ships, always two, appearing to guess each other's actions. Unless one believed in telepathy, and even that would surely be constrained by the laws of light and the fabric of the universe.

What was Reichardt suggesting with this selection of recordings? Some great mystery that Fleet had been puzzling at for . . . decades? Longer? Were Talee simply that predictable to each other? From everything she knew and had learned, Talee were never regarded as predictable, they were creative thinkers who often applied what seemed to humans risky or daring solutions. But then the magic act always seemed daring to clueless viewers in the audience who did not know how the trick was safely performed.

Talee were not a hive mind, and they had wrapped their minds around human psychology well enough to produce a synthetic copy like Cai. And Cai, squeezed between human wiring and Talee programming and (he confirmed) face-to-face friendships with actual Talee, had somehow turned out sane and reasonable. And was utterly loyal to them, and affectionate . . . although Talee knowing whatever they knew, perhaps they could program him that way. With human emotions. It seemed unlikely. But then, perhaps that was human bias showing, herself not wishing to believe her own mental processes were so easily manipulable by some alien species.

She sat and stared at a window, thinking as hard as she'd ever thought about anything. On an uplink she was barely aware she was accessing, she could see and hear the kids playing their strategy game in the living room, with shouts, accusations, and laughter. When she looked again, another hour had passed. If she was going to try to model this, she needed more data. She didn't see how she was going to get it though; Reichardt had gone to enough risk as it was.

Unexpectedly, she found herself looking at an image of a medieval castle. It was under assault, by swarms of armoured men, arrows pelting the walls, more arrows flying back . . . Sandy blinked and backed off her connections to view them more broadly. The kids! It was their strategy game, why was she suddenly seeing it on internal visual? Well, she was uplinked to the living room, and that . . . shouldn't have been giving her a close-up feed? Unless . . .

"Oh shit!" she said, and leaped from her chair.

She came quickly down the stairs, then slowed herself. No need to create unnecessary alarm. Best to see what was going on first.

They'd set it up on the coffee table, just a marker the house network could fix on. The rest was displayed on synchronised AR glasses, invisible to anyone else . . . but patched into the house network, Sandy could see the projection very clearly. A large old castle, under attack, the scene of ferocious battle. Svetlana was directing attacking forces, moving siege engines, directing archer fire, pushing covered battering rams into position with flicks of her finger. And Kiril was fighting back, with help from Danya, who suggested good ideas to him while Svetlana alternately protested or made evil threats.

"Sandy, Danya's helping him too much!" Svetlana exclaimed, as one of her ladders up a wall was pushed off by Kiril's forces. Armoured men leaped clear and fell to their deaths. If Sandy adjusted her volume, she could hear their screams, above the roar and clang of voices and steel. "It's two against one!"

"He's not helping me," Kiril retorted. "You're just losing!" Flaming oil ignited a siege engine.

"Hey!" said Svetlana. "Danya, how did he know to position his oil there?"

"Everyone knows that," said Kiril. Danya tried to look innocent and spoiled it by grinning. Svetlana fumed and schemed, circling the table to check her flanks, while Danya whispered in Kiril's ear once more. Sandy wondered if wishing they played a less violent game made her the universe's biggest hypocrite. To the consternation of some in the Education Department, growing up traumatised in a warzone had not turned her little darlings into trembling pacifist bunnies.

As Sandy had suspected, the image on her internal vision matched exactly Kiril's viewpoint. She quietly hacked his AR glasses feed . . . and yes, there it was, a precise match. But the glasses were not sending data; the kids always ran them silent, even at home, after being taught the dangers of broadcasting their locations on the net. The only one sending data was Kiril himself.

"Kiri," Sandy said innocently, "do you have any idea that your uplinks are sending data right now?"

Kiril blinked up at her. "No. They are?"

"Yes. In fact, they're accessing nearby networks."

"Not outside the house?" Danya asked in alarm.

"No no," Sandy said mildly. "Inside." She tapped by her ear.

Danya stared. "He's accessing *your* uplinks?"

"Yep. He does know me best, I guess it's natural enough." She kept the worry from her voice with effort. Scaring them would achieve nothing.

Svetlana took advantage of the distraction to send a hundred troops rushing to reoccupy a pair of abandoned siege engines from a previous, failed assault. Danya paused the game.

"Hey!"

"Shush, Svet," said Danya. Svetlana pouted. "That's not supposed to happen. His uplinks are supposed to be dormant."

"I think we'd better take him in. Kiri, you want to go visit Dr Kishore?"

Kiril enjoyed FSA medical far more than anyone else did. He sat on the bed with the little monitor band on his head, amidst small receptor paddles that captured whatever activity his uplink was generating. Dr Kishore watched his monitors, and talked with other doctors in quiet, intense conversations, while Sandy sat on Kiril's bed, Danya sitting on a chair alongside, AR glasses on and watching the little projection construct Sandy had set up using the hospital room's systems.

"Try to turn the lower part yellow, Kiri," said Sandy. "Can you do that?" Sure enough, the little 3D puzzle changed colour, several of the lower bars and junctions turning yellow. "Good, now you see that connection node on the right? Can you fold the pattern across, using that node as a hinge?"

A pause. "No," said Kiril. "It won't move."

"What does that mean?" asked Danya.

"That it's only receiving input from a small part of his brain," said Sandy. "But it's more than it was six months ago."

"But it wasn't supposed to be growing more at all."

"I know," said Sandy.

"I think it's cool," said Kiril. The lower part of the pattern now turned red. "Look! I can turn it red now, I could only do yellow and blue before!"

As with their castle game, Sandy didn't need glasses to see the projection, hovering in mid-space before them. She glanced at Svetlana, asleep on the neighbouring bed, tired from dance class and well accustomed to Kiril's hospital trips by now. Beyond her, Cai entered the room. Even the doctors stopped what they were doing when they saw who it was. So he'd been introduced to the FSA's top medical staff, then. These days there wasn't much more top-secret than neural-uplink expertise, given what was going on in the League.

"Hello, Cai!" Kiril said cheerfully.

"Hello, Kiril," said Cai with a smile, walking to the bed. "How are you feeling?"

"Everyone always asks me how I'm feeling!" Kiril said with exasperation. "I feel normal, it's just uplinks."

"You invited him?" Dr Kishore asked Sandy, no doubt wondering who had.

Sandy nodded. "If anyone knows what the hell's going on, he might." Dr Kishore offered no comment on that assessment of his expertise.

Cai sat on the end of the bed, as Sandy deactivated her little test construct. "Now, Kiril," he said. "I want you to think of nothing. Can you do that?"

"No," said Danya, with a faint smile.

Kiril frowned. "How do you think of nothing?"

"Well, try to not to think about anything specific."

"But if I'm thinking about not thinking, then I *am* thinking." Sandy smiled proudly. Not bad for a seven-year-old.

"All right," said Cai. "Try to think of an empty space."

"That's more Svetlana's talent," said Danya.

"Hey!" said his sister, rolling sleepily to whack him on the arm. "Not while I'm sleeping and defenceless, that's not fair."

"But you weren't asleep," Kiril pointed out.

"I was too!"

Cai looked at Sandy, with the beginnings of frayed patience. Sandy hadn't known that was possible. "Aren't they adorable?" she said.

"And other things as well," said Cai. It was the closest to thing to humour she'd yet heard from him.

"Kiri," said Danya. "Try holding your breath. Just concentrate on holding your breath for as long as you can." And to Cai, "He'll have to focus, might be the same thing."

Kiril took a deep breath and held it. Cai's face gave no indication, save a slight furrowing of one eyebrow. On the monitors, a flash of network activity. Kiril kept holding his breath, cheeks puffed out. He looked from one of them to the other, giving no sign of anything odd.

"That's fine, Kiril," Cai said calmly. "You can breathe now."

Kiril gasped. "I could have held it much longer," he insisted. "Do you want to see?"

"Kiril," his brother told him, "you're missing the point again."

"Am not." He held his breath defiantly.

Sandy didn't need to ask Cai anything. Her gaze asked all questions loud enough. "It's growing again," he admitted.

"It's not supposed to do that," said Sandy, all amusement vanished. She glanced sideways at Dr Kishore. "They stopped it."

"Well, it unstopped itself," said Cai. "Cassandra, it is Talee tech, but it's modified, so I can't be certain precisely what it's doing. But I don't know that it's harmful . . ."

"Putting uplinks in immature brains is nearly always harmful," she said coldly. She shouldn't have said that so bluntly in front of them. But sugar-coating with these kids didn't work.

"Standard uplinks have limited feedback responses," Cai said reasonably. "Kiril's uplinks are all feedback. I'd estimate from what I see here that more than ninety percent of the activity is measuring Kiril's brain growth and adjusting its own growth accordingly. It's measuring itself to fit him. I think the reason he keeps having these unexpected events is that the feedback mechanism needs to create activity in order to provoke a response. That's a part of the measuring mechanism."

Kiril gasped, letting out the breath he was holding.

"Is this a normal part of Talee uplink technology?" Sandy asked. "Does it usually work this way?"

"I can't answer that question."

"Goddamn it, Cai," Sandy said darkly. "Don't give me that."

"I'm sorry, Cassandra," he said, not sounding sorry at all. "I'm not at liberty to discuss that technology."

"And yet here you sit. Feeding us bullshit."

"Sandy," said Danya, and put a careful hand on her shoulder. Sure enough, her vision tinged red, motion-sense heightened, colours leaping at every twitch of Cai's eyelids, the rise and fall of his breathing. "Sandy, it's not worth it. You can't make him tell us."

"Don't count on it," said Sandy, unblinking.

"Cassandra," Cai tried again, "I can only guess at how Chancelry have modified these uplinks. The good news is that the work seems quite advanced. The bad news is that immature nascent-state uplink technology of this variety is mostly unresponsive to remote query. It can't tell us what it is. We can only observe what it does and make educated guesses. Chancelry were searching for a cure to the sociological effects of League uplinks operating on an invasive spectrum of too great a width, and . . ."

"That's if you diagnose the problem on the individual level," Sandy interrupted. "There are people here who believe the problem is more sociological than neurological, and that therefore the type of technology being used matters less, and that we're seeing the same phenomena manifesting in the Federation as well."

"Chancelry does not share this assessment," said Cai. "The League believes in technological solutions."

Sandy took a slow breath. It made sense. "So they'll be measuring degrees of invasiveness. Taking Talee tech that does things they don't fully understand."

"Cassandra, why put it in children?" Sandy considered him with deadly intent. Trying to discern clues from posture and mannerisms of what he wasn't telling her. "They have plenty of adults available. Unwilling ones, but that doesn't matter to Chancelry."

"You want me to believe it's safe?" Sandy asked. "Ask why they didn't use their *own* damn children."

Cai nodded, conceding. "Cassandra, this technology does what Neural Cluster Technology does, in that it wires all the portions of the brain into the uplink. So you get a broad spectrum of transferal—emotional, conceptual, everything."

"Great," Sandy muttered. "Just great." NCT had turned everyone on Pyeongwha into freaking zombies. Or so it sometimes seemed.

"But NCT is a blunt instrument. The technology in Kiril is subtle, reactive. On Pyeongwha, children were given NCT close to full neurological maturity . . . I know," he interrupted her interruption, "it's debatable, but close enough. What if adaptive uplinks at a young age are the *solution?*"

Sandy stared at him. Kiril looked back and forth, following with interest. Lacking any real concept of the dangers, Sandy knew. Technology was cool. *She* was technology, and she was cool. Uplinks would make him more like her. God help them both.

"You're saying full-spectrum invasiveness can be *controlled?*" she asked.

Cai nodded. "I think so. We cannot remove Kiril's uplinks without harming him. You've tried halting their development using your usual nanos and growth modulators, and that hasn't worked either. If I could suggest it,

I think your best chance is to work *with* the technology. Work with Kiril. Exercise with him. Teach him how to use it properly. That way, the technology learns what it needs to know of his brain function, and learns to grow in the way that does him the most good, and the least harm."

Sandy stared at him. She hadn't blinked for several minutes now. Still the red tinge, highlighting every breath Cai took, every slow beat of his heart. It was a hell of a thing he asked her, to take on faith. Was this Cai making a judgement call, deviating from the rules his superiors had laid down regarding how much information he was allowed to reveal? Dropping hints as to what he knew would actually work? Or was this just a part of some larger experiment?

"I think that sounds cool," said Kiril, unsurprisingly. Danya and Svetlana made no comment. Watching her, awaiting her decision. Trusting her to know the right thing to do. She'd previously held the fates of a hundred million Callayans in the palm of her hand. This felt worse.

"Will it work?" she asked Cai.

Cai considered for a moment. "I think it offers the best chance of a positive outcome," he said carefully.

Sandy looked at Kiril. His cheerful innocence made her heart ache. "I'm tired of threatening people I like," she said to Cai. "Do I need to?"

Cai smiled faintly. "I understand your feelings."

"Do you?" Sandy asked bleakly. "Do you really?"

For once, Cai had nothing to say.

CHAPTER SEVEN

Sandy took the short run-up that Ari had shown her and delivered the cricket ball with a flick of wrist and fingers. The ball fizzed down the pitch, looped and gripped beautifully off the turf, turning sharply sideways. But Poole got his foot to the bounce and smashed it out of the field, flying high up into the Santiello Stadium stands.

"It's a good delivery," Poole informed her, his bat on his shoulder as they watched the ball hit the seats twenty rows back. Up in the empty stands, some of the local club members' kids scampered to retrieve it. They'd been doing a lot of that, the past half hour. "I just don't think you're going to get a GI out by bowling spin. I could see it turning on the way down."

"Hmm." Sandy thought about it, playing through several scenarios in her head. "I think you could get a GI out with spin, but you'd get hammered doing it."

"But spin bowlers always get hammered," said Ari, flipping his own ball expertly in his hand. "The batsmen always *think* we're easy targets, and that's why we get them out."

Santiello was one of the three biggest stadiums in Tanusha. Ari wasn't the only FSA/CSA Agent with contacts here, lots of the augmented staff had friends in professional sports. But Ari was the cricket enthusiast and had been very curious to see what GIs could do on a cricket pitch. And so this semi-regular meet-up of Sandy's best synthetic friends took place in the middle of Santiello Stadium, with the practise lights on and lots of Tanusha's best professional cricketers watching on from the stands or the field perimeter—a front-row seat being their reward for allowing this access.

"I think you're wasting your time," said Rhian, preparing off her twelve-pace run-up. "Brute force usually beats cunning." She ran in and accelerated to a high-speed action, textbook, despite having only learned to do it this evening. The ball blurred down the pitch at over 200kph . . . and Poole belted it low and flat back over her head.

Yells of "watch out!" from the stands, warning to the ball-retrieving kids, but this ball was heading high into the upper tiers where none were present. Then laughter and sounds of awe as it hit the seats with an audible crack! Even augmented athletes hadn't seen hitting like this. Poole was pretty accurate, but the ball kids were all wearing helmets, just in case . . . even a hundred and twenty meters away.

"You're bowling too close to the stumps," Ari told Rhian.

"But that's what I'm supposed to hit, right?" said Rhian.

"Sure, but that's also the easiest thing for the batsman to hit. That's why you aim *past* him, try to get him to nick it, then it'll be caught behind by our imaginary wicket keeper." Rhian had been wicket keeper for the first five minutes but had gotten bored with nothing to do. In GI cricket, very little got past the batsman, at whatever speed. "Or the imaginary slips cordon. You just have to get him to edge it."

"Let me try," said Ragi. Sandy was thrilled that Ragi had turned up. She invited him to a lot, but he rarely came. She knew it was hard for him, being the smartest GI anyone had ever seen, in human space at least, and having no real idea of his origins. Lately he'd been keeping to himself and doing a lot of reading and thinking. But cricket, as Ari said, was the most civilised of games, and if one word described Ragi, it was civilised. But he was also a non-combat GI, without a combat model's more obvious advantages, and Sandy could see Poole practically licking his lips.

Ragi bowled spin, unable to generate Rhian's inhuman pace, and again the ball looped down the pitch, spinning madly. Poole leaped forward as it dropped short, and swung hard . . . and got a huge inside edge onto his shins . . . as Poole, of course, wore no pads. Ari threw up his hands and cried out at the closeness of it.

"Hmm," said Poole, picking up the ball and tossing it back. "That was different."

"Ragi!" said Ari with excitement. "The flipper!" That was a top spinner, Sandy had gathered.

"It's about the position of the seam," said Ragi, catching the ball. "There's a position that plays tricks on a GI's eyes. It looks like it's spinning sideways, but it goes straight on."

"Really?" asked Sandy. "How does that work?"

"Find your own special delivery," Ragi told her with a smile, walking back. Sandy grinned, suspecting he was playing mind games. A very high-des might do that successfully to a lower-des. And if anything was going to interrupt Poole's awesome hitting display, it would be the uncertainty that he could trust what he was seeing. Which was actually quite a fun thing to explore. Since she'd been introduced to GI-racquetball last year, she'd been slowly discovering that she wasn't as bored by sports as she'd thought. A few of them could actually teach her things, about herself and her kind, that nothing else could.

"Ami!" Poole called to the far fence, and they turned to see Amirah arriving, dressed in gym shorts and runners. "You made it!"

And others by the fence turned to look at her in astonishment, having no idea that the slim, bushy-haired girl in gym shorts could possibly be a GI . . . until she accelerated off the biggest run-up anyone had ever seen, a ball in hand she'd collected from the ball kids, and hurled it down at Poole at twice what a regular human could. She aimed straight at him, and Poole hooked it, and got a top edge that went rocketing into the night sky.

"It's high!" Ari shouted. "If it lands in play, it's caught and out!"

Sandy saw where it was heading. "Danya, Svet! Watch out!" Danya, Svetlana, and Kiril were over by the side fence, bowling tennis balls at Rhian's little Salman, who was a year older than Kiril.

"Danya, catch it!" Svetlana shrieked. But it was a mile in the air, and the lights made it hard to see against a black sky . . . and Danya, with no intention of trying to catch a hard ball falling from that height, pulled Kiril well clear and let it hit the turf. The ground erupted with ironic cheers, from perhaps a hundred people gathered. Danya grinned and threw the ball back.

"Have a bat, kid!" someone shouted to him.

"No thank you!" Danya said loudly. "It looks like a firing squad out there."

"Ami," said Poole, offering her the bat, which she took graciously. "You know how to play?"

"Of course I know," Amirah scolded, "I'm the only socialised one here."

And gave Poole's backside a playful whack as he passed to prove it. "I picked it up from TV. And the boss explained it a bit."

"Ibrahim watches cricket?" Sandy asked.

"Of course," Ari said, frowning. "You've known him eight years, how do you not know that?"

Sandy shrugged. "Never came up."

Then Kiet arrived, the last invite, with more greetings all around. Sandy could have invited more, but this seemed a comfortable number—all her closest synthetic friends, plus Ari. It had been Vanessa's idea, even as Vanessa had ruled herself out from coming. "You guys need to talk about your stuff," she'd said. "Because GIs in Tanusha, you've got *lots* of stuff to talk about." And Sandy had to agree.

They talked about new asylum seekers, who continued to arrive from different parts of the League, and the progress of other asylum seekers through the Callayan legal system and finally into their chosen professions. That was usually CSA or FSA for combat GIs, which the majority of them were. Not only did they have the abilities for it; it was where most of their new friends and support networks were—support networks like this one. This very night, Sandy knew there would be groups of GIs out at bars or nightclubs, or restaurants or concerts, or just staying at home, hanging out. Mostly they would mix with the Tanushan population quite well. If anyone disapproved of them, they were usually too smart to make an issue of it. And every week, Sandy heard gossip of hook-ups, Tanushan locals and new synthetic citizens meeting and getting along, carnally or otherwise. It was even becoming a tourist attraction—visit Tanusha and you might run into a real-life combat GI. For Federation citizens it remained a novelty.

Then, inevitably, conversation turned to the Synthetics Caucus Kiet wanted to set up.

"League's about to start churning out tens of thousands of new high-des GIs to try and stabilise their internal situation," Kiet insisted with his usual intensity, "and we're not going to try and make anything out of it? There's nearly six hundred of us now in Tanusha, we've got the ear of some very powerful people, some of us are pretty powerful in our own right. . . ."

"Kiet," said Sandy, "the best thing we can do to guarantee the rights of those new League GIs is to try and help stabilise the League's internal wars. And you don't stabilise the League by pushing the Federation—which is without a properly elected government right now, you might have noticed—to declare universal emancipation."

Ari bowled his legspin to Rhian, who blocked it neatly, elbow raised and bat straight with perfect form. Ari had given up asking them not to patronise him.

"League's taking an awful big risk making so many new GIs," said Rhian, taking guard once more. "I know the technology's supposed to be more like Jane's, they're not supposed to be thinking for themselves . . . but we haven't seen the long-term effects of that. I mean, who's heard anything about Jane lately?"

Sandy bowled—her new invention, the fast spinner, high speed but rotating like crazy. It turned so much that Rhian nearly missed, and a big edge went flying into the off-side stadium seats. The two kids out that way went racing to get it.

"Yeah," Sandy conceded. "It sounds like fifth column material to me too." She walked back to the bowler's end. "But problem is, if Jane *has* become a free-thinking individual, I bet it's taken her a damn long time to get there. Possibly we could turn these new GIs against the League, but at the rate the League's disintegrating, it'll be too late."

"You want to go around saying GIs are fifth-column material?" Amirah asked. Poole charged in, and Rhian belted him back over his head. "Because they say that about *us*. It was the fear used to justify Operation Shield, which then became the near-reality in the counter-coup."

"Look," said Sandy, flipping the ball as she waited her turn, "I'd love it if we started joining other institutions. But no one else will have us, and Callay's the only world granting citizenship."

"Wouldn't want to go anywhere else anyway," said Poole, walking back. "I mean why be the first GI on a new Federation world, get stared at and prodded, when you could stay here where people are getting used to us?"

"We are causing a power imbalance though," said Amirah, as Ragi bowled. This time Rhian took him on, and put him into the upper stands, but not in the direction she'd intended. Ragi smiled, taking it as a moral victory. "I mean FSA spec ops is now pretty ridiculous, even by League standards. Even Dark Star."

Sandy nodded. "Yep. Easily the highest combat capability anywhere, Federation or League. Nothing else comes close."

"And this is just the start," Amirah continued, "because the GIs who are defecting are the cream. League never concentrated them together much, because when concentrated together, high-des GIs get ideas. This little gathering would scare the shit out of League command."

"Worse if you start talking about God," Ari added. "Can you imagine, an army of religious GIs?"

Sandy jogged in and bowled with massive backspin. The ball kicked up and Rhian barely swayed aside in time, the ball striking her temple on a shallow angle. "Ouch," said Rhian, which was funny, from a GI. Sandy grinned, as the ball hit the rear fence with a loud crash, a hundred meters away.

"Well, FedInt's welcome to stop whining about power imbalances and recruit some of us," said Kiet. "Just cause we're combatants doesn't mean we wouldn't make good spies. Look at ISO's high-des spies."

"If you were FedInt," Amirah retorted, "would *you* trust a Federation GI? One of us? I mean, is there any doubt really where our loyalties lie?"

"Well, I don't think that's true," said Ragi. "Using myself as an example, I'm still unsure where my loyalties lie. I consider you all my friends, and I'll always endeavour to help my friends, but that's a different thing to a political loyalty."

"Not for me it's not," Kiet said firmly. "Friends *are* politics."

"Agree," said Sandy. "It's more complicated, as Ragi says. But for most of us, friendships and politics, with Callay and the current FSA leadership, are pretty much the same thing. Of course if anyone ever moved Ibrahim that could change."

"Well, this just proves my point," said Ragi. "We do have different ideas and loyalties, and we're all individuals. To suggest that there's only one side for GIs to support is to deny us free agency, which is . . . well, to borrow an old and imprecise term, racist."

"Synth-phobic," Ari offered. "Keep up with the lingo, Ragi."

"I try."

"Ahem!" Rhian called from down at the stumps. They'd all gotten so caught up talking, they'd forgotten to bowl. Amirah ran in, and Rhian cut her like a bullet into the off-side stands, with a bang that announced a damaged seat. More raucous laughter from onlookers, unable to believe what they'd seen. Sandy jogged to track down an incoming throw from the fence, as the ball kids finally retrieved her ball.

"Speaking of loyalties," Ragi continued, "I have a question for everyone. Who here follows a sports team? Not a sport, but an actual team?" He looked around, questioning. Shakes of the head, mild disinterest.

"I quite like football," said Amirah. "And cricket. But I like a good game, I don't mind which team."

"Rhian!" Sandy shouted down the far end. "You follow a sports team?"

"Subianto Shock!" Rhian called back, to cheers from the stands, who could overhear. It was the local team, of course.

"She's being polite," Sandy explained to Ragi. "She doesn't care."

"How about these damned dancing competitions?" Ragi persisted. "Tanushan Dance Star?"

"Oh, I love that!" said Amirah, quite predictably.

"Ever pick a favourite really early? Lots of people do."

"No, usually they're all really good." Amirah looked at him thoughtfully, guessing where he was going. "I suppose if I knew someone personally, I'd cheer for them. But from a distance . . . no. I guess GIs don't really do that much."

"No, we don't, do we?" said Ragi, flipping the ball. Ari bowled, and again Rhian blocked him. Boos from the stands. "Straight humans typically have an emotional compulsion to pick favourites. With politics it's understandable, because politics determine how people live. But football teams don't matter in real terms at all, yet some straights cheer their team as though it were life and death."

"I think it's dangerous to say too loudly that we're more objective than straights," said Sandy. "Someone might overhear and think we're getting a superiority complex."

"But we do," said Kiet. "Comes from real superiority."

Sandy gave him a wary look, unsure of just how much he was joking. "But on the whole I think it's pretty obvious. I think we'd make good judges or lawyers. We only take sides when we have to. It's not compulsive, like with most straights."

"Funny you should say," Amirah added, and paused, as Poole finally got Rhian to edge one, which counted as an automatic dismissal. And left Rhian looking at her bat, which was now missing a chunk of its edge, removed at 250 kph. "The new girl acting as Grand Council liaison is really unpopular with some of the HQ admin girls. You know, bitchy girl stuff."

"You know I never understood that," said Sandy. "But go on."

"Well, just my point," Amirah pressed. "I made sure I had a coffee with her for ten minutes, and I can see why they don't like her, she's pushy and doesn't listen well . . . but I'm sure I don't dislike her. I'm not about to become her best friend either, but once I thought I'd figured her out, I found I could manage her bullshit without getting that emotional response. I spoke to that new admin GI, Tanu, about her . . . and he didn't have a problem with her either. But the straight girls especially all hate her."

"Odd to think that we might be the peaceful ones, wouldn't it be?" Ragi suggested. "The ones preaching tolerance and understanding?" He gave Sandy a meaningful glance. They'd had similar discussions before, with regard to SuperPsych and its various findings. But they couldn't discuss that here. "But it would be nice to think that if we saw some conflict coming in Tanusha, at some point we might be able to head it off."

"Yes," said Amirah doubtfully. "But that's dangerous too, because it creates the impression we're more loyal to each other than we are to the institutions we work for. And if GIs become a separate power center in the Federation, we could become a real threat to lots of people who don't take threats well."

As Sandy pondered it, Rhian walked up, with a new bat from behind the stumps, and tossed it to her. "Your turn," she said. "You know it's what everyone wants to see."

Sandy walked down and took guard—an unorthodox stance, bat as horizontal as vertical, farther back from the stumps. Back and waiting, baseball style. She could see Ari wincing. "I hope you've got some clever theory," he called, "because that looks horrible."

"Well, the whole 'vertical bat' thing is to eliminate batsman error from variable bounce. I don't think I need it. And if I tempt you to bowl at my stumps, you'll just put it where I like it."

Ari bowled first. Sandy felt many things toward Ari, but chivalrous and patronising weren't among them, and she lofted him into the far stand. "G-22," she said. The ball hit a seat with a crack, but not hard, as Ari's pace was low.

"What's G-22?" Rhian asked.

"The seat number," said Ragi. "Incurable show-off. Here, let me try." He bowled, and Sandy saw how the seam scrambled as it spun toward her, but this one was spinning . . . off. She lofted it again, not especially hard.

"G-23," she said. Five seconds later, the ball hit the seat neighbouring G-22.

"Oh, no way!" said Ari.

"But can she do it against pace?" said Poole, and charged in. He bowled wide of the stumps, a blur that reached her in barely a split second . . . and she hit it dead flat, barely any arc on it at all.

"G-twenty . . ." she said, then "Dammit!" as the ball smashed a chair back and split it.

"H-24," Poole observed. "You missed!" From a hundred and thirty meters, aiming at chairs that look like little dots high in the far stand.

"Yeah, and here's why," said Sandy, showing him the bat. It had folded at the handle, more from the force of her swing than the impact with the ball. "If GIs are going to play this game seriously, we're going to need steel bats."

The kids found it fun to meet the Subianto Shock players as they watched some cricket on TV. But Sandy only hung around long enough for some brief conversation and to sign a few of Justice Rosa's books. She was more interested in sport than she had been, but the athletes themselves were never going to awe her, given that she played their sport far better than they ever could and with almost no experience.

"Sandy," said Kiril in the cruiser on the way home, "are we gonna be rich with the book?"

"No, Kiri," said Sandy from the driver's seat, "it's not our money. It's Justice's money because he wrote the book."

"That's not fair," said Svetlana. "It's your life he's making all this money from."

"Oh well, I'm used to that." Her seekers were returning only light "interesting" traffic tonight—some stuff on a controversial asylum case, a report on Chairman Li's upcoming trial, some speculation on new GI technologies employed by the League's illegal new production facility. All nonsense, of course. Nothing on tonight's little gathering yet, though that wouldn't last. "Besides Justice is donating most of it to war charities."

"Hey, the war orphan lady who visited last month!" said Svetlana. "So we *will* get some of it!"

"We're not eligible, Svet," said Danya, as Sandy repressed a smile. "We do pretty well with Sandy; the war orphan charities only go to kids that actually need it."

"So why was that lady talking to us?"

"I guess there aren't that many war orphans on Callay," reasoned Danya. "She just wanted to make sure we knew about it."

"Sandy, will the street kids on Droze get money?" Kiril asked. Quite seriously, Sandy saw with a glance back.

"No, Kiri. The Federation has no official contact with Droze or any of the New Torah systems. It's in the League, we're not allowed to touch the League."

"You went there."

"I went there for security reasons."

"But you helped us." He looked troubled, looking more out the window than at her, as light from passing towers slid across his face.

"Yes, I did," Sandy affirmed.

"So why don't the Federation help other Droze kids?"

Sandy glanced at Danya. Danya was craned all the way around in his chair to look at Kiril. Danya thought this significant then—Kiril's sudden recollection of all the other kids who *hadn't* made it out. "Because we're not allowed to, Kiri," she said. "League will say it's interference in their internal affairs."

"Helping street kids?" Kiril asked. With a faint incredulity that seemed too subtle for his age.

"Yes," Sandy said solemnly. "Helping street kids."

"That's stupid," said Kiril.

"It's very stupid," Sandy agreed sadly. "But a lot of things are stupid like that." In the backseat, Svetlana took Kiril's hand. And gazed at Danya silently. Danya turned back around in his chair, head back, knee up. With that thousand-yard stare thing he did sometimes, more typically seen on combat veterans.

Sandy was about to ask further, but something interrupted—a general alarm, this one CSA-coded but forwarded through FSA. The encryption-grade was Fleet.

". . . *we have an alert signal on inner perimeter*," came Reichardt's voice. She checked logs . . . Reichardt was still in Tanusha, wasn't due to return to

Mekong in orbit for another three days. "*New arrival, signature indicates hard jump, he came from a fair way off. Well off the main entry lanes, FOG recommends preliminary emergency status.*"

That would give everyone shivers, given what happened to Cresta. Svetlana started to say something else.

"Hang on, Svet," said Sandy, putting the feed to the cruiser's screens. "Something's happening."

"*FOG, this is Ibrahim. Who's up?*"

"*Bursteimer's in best position.*" Sandy checked the feed on Fleet positions and found it was true—*Caribbean* was on station out that way. As usual from Fleet, no explanation of why. "*Preliminary trajectory calc is coming through now. Looks like 182 by 23. League-wards. Could be a long jump.*"

"That's a new ship, right?" Svetlana asked, frowning. "Could it jump all the way from the League?"

"Way too far," said Danya, listening carefully. "But there are mass points through the Federation that are hard to guard, someone could three-or-four-jump it."

"That would take a long time though," said Svetlana, no doubt remembering their own trek from Pantala, weeks locked within narrow metal walls.

They landed at Canas and drove in, watching the situation unfold. The media were still not reporting it, plenty of amateur astronomers would have seen that entry pulse, but it took longer for amateurs to tell the difference between scheduled and unscheduled activity without access to Fleet feeds. No doubt a few of the more advanced amateurs would be guessing by now, but the credible ones didn't just blab everything to the media at first notice. But as Sandy and the kids settled for a late hot chocolate and snack before bed, still there had been no ID signal received from the ship. That was odd, because most ships newly arrived in a system automatically sent an ID package. In an important, populated system like the Callayan System, failure to do so would get you intercepted, or worse.

"Maybe they're damaged?" Svetlana wondered. Sandy's kitchen display showed the arrival's position, a holographic glow above the stove and fruit bowl. Coming in fast, less than two days from Callay at that velocity. Usually new ships took a week.

"Can we stay up and watch it?" Kiril asked.

"Sure," said Sandy, sipping her chocolate. Danya and Svetlana repressed smiles—Kiril always wanted to stay up late but always fell asleep anyway. Usually he got to sleep faster if he was allowed to stay up than if he was sent to bed complaining. Sandy was not above taking devious advantage. "But I warn you, watching ships arrive from the outer system is deadly boring."

"But the world might end!" Kiril insisted.

"The world's not going to end," Danya said calmly, checking some database on his AR glasses. Probably something about ships, trajectories, and physics—Danya always felt compelled to know. "That ship will be intercepted by a whole bunch of defensive systems before it gets anywhere near Callay."

"But League ships get to Callay all the time! That's how League agents end up in Tanusha all the time!"

"Those are stealth ships," Sandy told him. "They're small things that only hold thirty or forty people, they don't have FTL drives so they piggyback on bigger ships that arrive in the outer system. Then they coast in, usually from zenith or nadir, so we can't see them against black space. They're not fast or big enough to be a threat to the planet."

"Have you been on one?" Svetlana asked. Sandy nodded, sipping her drink. "In the League? Did you do insertion missions for the League?" Another nod. "Oh, come on, tell us! What did you do?"

And Svetlana glanced at Danya, as though by some telepathy, to find Danya giving a small shake of his head. No. Svetlana looked at the floor.

Sandy sighed. "Svet, it makes you more of a target if you know these things. League don't like lots of people knowing this stuff."

"That's not why, though," said Svetlana reproachfully. "You don't trust us."

Danya's faint roll of the eyes told Sandy what she already suspected—it was one of Svetlana's little manipulations. Sandy didn't fall for it as often as she'd used to.

"Sandy trusts us with all kinds of things," Danya said firmly. "Don't be unfair." Svetlana looked exasperated.

"Svet," said Sandy. "You want to know the truth?" Svetlana nodded earnestly and came to stand closer. "The truth is that I don't really like talking about it with you. I was a different person back then. I did a lot of things I'm not proud of. Back then, the only use I had to anyone was to the League, as a killer. A lethal weapon. I'm much more than that now. Or I like to think I am. And I don't like you to think of me that way, or have nightmares about what I've done."

"I wouldn't have nightmares," Kiril said earnestly.

"I do," Sandy said quietly.

"But that's not fair, is it?" Svetlana insisted. "You get to watch us grow up, and you get to see how we change as we get older. And probably when we're all adults you'll say all kinds of embarrassing things about what we did when we were kids. But you won't share your growing up stories with us?"

Sandy watched her sombrely. Svetlana gazed back, with those pretty blue eyes. Delicate, at first glance, within that pale, fine-boned face.

"Wow," Sandy finally deadpanned. "You're good."

Svetlana struggled against a treacherous smile. "I know."

"I especially like the big orphan-waif eyes. 'Please, Sandy. It'll mean ever so much to me.'"

Svetlana lost control of her grin. "She's always done that," Danya observed.

"Security stuff," Sandy told her, "and fighting, I'm excellent at. None better. This other stuff, I'm not so good at. Like you, like everyone. So I'll tell you eventually. But I'll do it when I'm ready. Deal?"

"Deal," said Svetlana. "Can I use my orphan-waif eyes to get you to break out the marshmallows?"

"Yeah!" said Kiril.

"Can't really have hot chocolate without marshmallows," Danya offered in support.

Nothing made Sandy more skeptical than when they started teaming up like that. "Is that some kind of law, is it?" she said drily.

"It is," Danya agreed. "It's an immutable law."

Vanessa was helping Phillippe feed the twins when the alert sounded. She dashed for the cruiser, with baby food and drool still on her shirt, and in eight minutes on emergency lane privilege was halfway across town to rendezvous on a rooftop pad at Surat. She jumped from the cruiser the moment it was down, and it flew away on auto to park itself somewhere secured.

The spec ops flyer was down on the pad, hulking black and heavily armed, engines keening but no running lights. Even as she ran up the rear ramp, her other team members were jumping from other cruisers and running to join her. Up the rear aisle between armour racks, and people quickly wriggling into armour, powering up, testing feedback.

"Where we at?" she yelled as she stripped outer clothes before her suit and stuffed them into the foot locker.

"Tacnet up!" Munde shouted back above the engine shrill, checking weapons and helmet interace alongside. "Target's in Bhubaneswar CBD, Lotus Tower!"

Dammit, Vanessa thought, ducking to slither into her upper-half armour. Anywhere in central Bhubaneswar was crowded; the market there was one of Tanusha's biggest. Central planners had added extra subway lines just to compensate for the numbers and had expanded the residential zones for more and taller towers around them. Operations in densely populated zones were a nightmare.

The last team member arrived three minutes later and the flyer lifted. By then Vanessa had the armour on, and completed the final adjustments automatically, full attention on tacnet as it showed her the scene.

Lotus Tower was two blocks from Bhubaneswar Market, above bustling streets lined with expensive shops and restaurants. Worse, it was Friday, just after 9 p.m., with rush hour faded and nightlife well begun. The market would be crammed with tens of thousands; there had once been entire roads of traffic there, but planners had blocked it all off for pedestrians about twenty years ago when it had emerged how popular the shopping had become. She called up traffic central, where monitors gave her rough estimates of people-density, and sonofabitch, even the lead-in streets were crammed, just below crush densities on the underground, and just as bad on the huge interdistrict maglevs. People came from the other side of Tanusha for a night out in Bhubaneswar. A high camera shot showed her crowds pouring down the steps of the maglev station from the latest train arrival. At 9 p.m. the maglevs arrived every four minutes, the underground every two. Add to that the rapidly filling parking lots. . . .

"*Hello, Vanessa, how's it looking?*" came Amirah's voice in her ear.

"Hello, Ami. Crowded as fuck. Where are they?"

"*We've units in position now, our intel says forty-ninth floor.*" Tacnet updated even as she spoke, showing the blue dots of friendly units on various floors of Lotus Tower and several floors shaded red. No eyes-on yet . . . which raised the question . . .

"Our Intel here is pretty weak, what's the rush?"

"Our tip says they're about to move. Could be a big one."

"Who's the tip from?"

"We don't know. But seems accurate so far."

Which could mean anything. Vanessa knew better than to start wondering about that now. It was the Pyeongwha terrorists, of course, and Lotus Tower would supposedly mean they'd been staying there, for a few days at least. Again, how they'd managed *that*, there was no way of telling.

"Okay, they'll be on this feed," one of their techies in HQ said, and Lotus Tower feed came through, all the data security services were usually not allowed to look at, people in rooms, security setups, elevator and stairwell activity.

"Yeah . . ." Vanessa fiddled with the inputs, not as good at juggling all these feeds simultaneously like Sandy, "damp that down a bit, the fucking targets will be on the building net, they'll see we're linked in. . . ."

"Vanessa, I've got it," came Sandy's voice, calm as ever, and Vanessa felt that particular tension flee her. Like a cool drink on a stinking hot day, everything felt right again. The incoming building feed modulated, just a trickle of incoming data, nothing they'd notice . . . only somehow multiplying here on tacnet, cross-referencing data adding up to more than was escaping. God knew how she did that, some trick of multiple sources adding up to more than the sum of their parts. . . . *"Can we get eyes-on, give us an ETA."*

"Snowcat, ETA is . . . can we get a . . . ?"

"Ten seconds," came someone else's voice, from inside the building. *"Keep your panties on."*

"Not wearing any," said Sandy. A few years back that would have broken tension amongst nervous troops in the back, gotten a few giggles. Now it provoked only lazy or minor smiles among cool, professional troops who'd seen this all before and were visualising exactly where they were and what was about to happen. GIs, nearly half of them, in separate squads but mixed teams.

SO1, Vanessa's flyer, now orbited Bhubaneswar a kilometre out, low amidst the teeming air traffic so as not to draw attention. Sandy was in transit too, SO4, now entering a similar orbit. SO2 had hoppers aboard, armoured troops with jumpjets, useful at altitude, but they wouldn't fit comfortably in those tower corridors. Standoff firepower only. On the ground, cops were gathering, Vanessa could hear multiple shouts and terse calls for direction in the background noise—someone had that under control, she couldn't worry about that now. A move too soon, and whoever was in Lotus Tower would see, and they'd be blown.

Then a new vision feed, fast and darting outside a window. Fly-cam, the troops called it, not easily spotted, but the feed was clean enough. Here a living room, tables and chairs, some odd-looking equipment . . . two people, in conversation with a third, unseen off-screen. Tacnet added those two to the schematic, its first hostile red dots. Then a third, as the camera bobbed and panned. The third person was working on something at a table, invisible at this angle.

"That's good," said Vanessa, looking at all the rear rooms in this apartment suite that tacnet still painted a blank, static grey. "We need more, backrooms if you can."

"*Looks like they're going somewhere,*" someone else remarked. It did, as one shouldered a bag. A fourth, a woman, entered from another room, pulling on a jacket. Tacnet added another red dot by the bathroom doorway, tracking across the carpet to the balcony window. Fly-cam gained altitude, and the red dots froze, blinking, indicating last-seen position. "*That's four. No weapons yet.*"

"*There's more,*" said Sandy. "*I'm seeing a loose communication matrix, like a low-grade version of tacnet. They're not all on this level, and they're not all in this room.*"

Fucking great, Vanessa thought, as her general level of optimism plunged several points. "Sandy, can you fool them? Pull the wool over their eyes? We gotta move these people. If we go in hot like this we're gonna have some motherfucking collateral."

"*I'm geographically limited on that capability,*" Sandy replied, slow and clear to be sure Vanessa would understand. "*I can only get the targets in the room.*"

"Great. Do it. I want . . ."

"*This is infiltration. We're reading explosive, mil-grade. Someone's got bombs in there.*"

New vision acquired from some nearby tower, blurred and looking through the windows . . . several people in the apartment were definitely preparing to go out, pulling on jackets, carrying bags. Once they got out of the apartment, into these crowds, the best chance of settling it relatively quietly disappeared. But one did not just walk out the door on the way to a terrorist operation; they'd be methodical. She still had some minutes.

"Sandy, if you can blind them, I'm going in hot. Everyone, spec ops is hot on my command. Let's get those cops on the ground and clear the streets on my signal."

She half expected to see the little light in the corner of her vision flash, indicating someone higher up wanted to talk to her. President Raza technically had a say on the maglev train, but that was because of the visibility. If she stopped this now, it would only be visible after the terrorists were all dead. Ibrahim, of course, would not call her at all. He trusted his people and would back her decisions whatever the outcome. And wear the blame if it all went wrong.

"Vanessa, they're transmitting on NCT bandwidths, so no guarantees. But I think I've got them. Go now."

"This is Jailbait, go go go." As Gs pressed them flat, the flyer turning hard and shrieking at full power. On the feed she could see police cars rushing the streets, sirens blaring, speakers yelling at everyone to move, run, get the hell away from Lotus Tower. Somewhere in that apartment on the forty-ninth floor, their targets were now locked into Sandy's VR matrix, the same trick Cai liked to pull on everyone, using uplink VR functions to activate in combination with actual surroundings, causing people to see whatever Sandy wanted them to see. Or not see. Like the view out the window, as the teeming streets around the tower suddenly cleared of traffic, and then of pedestrians, replaced instead by swarms of red-and-blue flashing lights and uniforms.

"Fifteen seconds," said the pilot. *"Stand by."*

"Squad One, fast rappel, main window," said Vanessa. "Squad Two, side window. Get the corridor, come through fast. Squad Three, reserve rappel." Illustrating with mental diagrams on tacnet as she did it, little dots and arrows as second nature as sentences. "Got it? Good."

Pointless question that was. They practised this, one aspect or another, every single day.

Heavy Gs as the flyer howled and flared, rear door cracking to let in the gale. Tacnet showed her their position, and then the towertop landing pad was coming beneath them. . . . "Move! Move! Move!" And she was unstrapping, coming last down the aisle as those before her leaped from the rear, twisting and rolling on the pad . . . then she was out, a quick fall then impact and roll, the suit made it easy, taking all the force.

Then running to the edge of the pad, rappel hook over one shoulder as the mechanism activated. She paused at the rim, a four-hundred-meter drop sheer off the edge of the world and no time to think about it, fed the hook through the belt loop, crouched and placed it on the steel rim of the landing pad. Pressed the seal, and it flashed, smoke and fire, welding hard and immovable in a second. A hiss of steam as coolant released, then it was firm.

A quick glance about the pad showed the rest of her team in position, silhouettes against the urban blaze of a Tanushan night. Tacnet showed all good, no vocals required.

"All good! Go!" She jumped, head-first down the building side, the suit feed automatically orienting her as she came down on the whizzing windows, a hand squealing against high-speed glass to steady as the other grasped her rifle, strapped on the shoulder in case she lost it. Far below, like ants, police vehicles and a chaos of sweeping lights.

"*Vanessa, I lost them,*" came Sandy's voice. "*They're out, they've seen us.*" A brief visual showed her a glimpse of someone staring out the window at the cars below.

"SO2," Vanessa called her fire support. "Fire." A mark appeared on tacnet, accelerating as it went. The viewer at the window saw, eyes wide, and ran like hell. Vanessa kept her head down, sliding fast, leg entwined with the steel cord at speeds that would have shredded an unprotected leg. Below her, a missile streaked into the forty-ninth floor window, and a massive fireball blew out.

She reached it four seconds later, pushing out with a hand then swinging in and head first. Hit the floor amidst smoke and flaming debris, fire retardant blasting from the ceiling, and cut the cord. And walked forward in formation, weapon ready, searching the impossible visibility. The walls seemed intact, the missile charge had been an airburst—the surrounding apartments occupied and as yet uncleared.

Gunfire erupted from a hole in the wall, return fire shredded it. Vanessa pumped in a grenade, in no mood for compromise, and debris blasted back across the room. More gunfire from a new angle, and everyone hit the ground, rolling for cover, returning fire . . . fanatics to be fighting hard in these circumstances, and Vanessa remembered the explosives here and rolled up to dash down the corridor.

Came face-to-face with someone in a doorway, blood streaked and wild eyed. Shoved them flying across the room and shot the next armed man through the head, a spray of brains across the wall, attention then to the woman on the bed. . . . Medical equipment, life support, bandaged sides. Half alive, it looked, but raising a gun at her with one hand. . . . Vanessa sidestepped and smacked it from her hand.

Another explosion outside, then a huge one, smashing through the walls and deafening her audio. Gunfire, as the second team came through the corridor outside, having gained access from the neighbouring apartment. And tacnet showed one down and vitals unsteady. . . .

"*Galley's down!*" Azim was yelling. "*Need a medic in here asap!*"

"*I'm okay,*" Galley replied dazedly. "*Just winded.*"

"*Clear! Clear, all clear! Level 49 is clear!*"

"Check those neighbouring apartments!" Vanessa yelled. "No blind spots! Clear it up!"

"*Vanessa,*" came Sandy's voice, "*that's a human bomb you've got there. Put her out.*"

Vanessa stared. The bandages were recent and bloody. On neighbouring tables were covered cases, perhaps for tools, perhaps medical. The life support was definitely medical, monitoring heart rate, blood pressure, just a small portable screen running a downloadable program.

"I can't put her out, I'm not equipped."

"*Then shoot her before she self detonates.*" The woman's eyes were staring madly, lips trying to form some words beneath hearing. Some incantation. A shot from behind Vanessa blew half her head off, and Vanessa swore, turning away.

"*Sorry,*" said Taga, not sounding a bit sorry. He stepped past her to check the rest of the room. "*Still got a live one here?*" Looking at the one Vanessa had pushed flying into the wall, head lolled, eyes closed.

"Might not be rigged," said Vanessa, walking away. Really wishing she hadn't seen that last bit, her head pounding, an awful taste in her mouth. "Be nice to question one of them."

"*The one that got Galley was rigged,*" said Taga, moving to check the unconscious man, tearing away clothes to check for scars or bandages. "*Just blew himself up.*"

"Sandy, if you're right we've still got some loose in the building." She walked into the hall, through showers of fire retardant and smoke, flashing lights and sirens from the building emergency systems. Someone killed the noise, mercifully. Here in the entry hall, all the door and wall were gone. Vanessa stepped past shattered remains into the corridor outside, and here lay Galley, on the point of entering when the human bomb had detonated. His helmet was still on because of the smoke, and Vanessa thought he was likely stunned rather than hurt—a GI, they got rattled by explosive concussion just like straights.

"*Got one,*" came a call from farther down. A stairwell, tacnet informed her. "*Heading downstairs, pulled a gun on me.*"

"Alive?" asked Vanessa.

"*Um . . . nearly.*"

"Dammit guys, Intel needs some more live ones if we're gonna find the source." As Azim and Wolder grabbed Galley under the arms and dragged him to the farside elevators, heading upstairs for some air. Vanessa headed into the neighbouring apartment door, smashed off its hinges by her second squad into an identical suite layout. The fire retardant poured down here too, a mother and father clustered in the kitchen hugging two terrified, screaming children . . . great. She strode to the smashed windows where the second squad had gained entry, disconnected rappel cables swinging in the breeze.

"We're gonna have them coming downstairs fast! Don't let them get into the streets or we'll . . ."

"*Too late!*" someone shouted, with a blurred, jolting visual from somewhere on street level, a man in a long coat sprinting, bag in hand, from tower doors onto the cleared sidewalk. Cleared, except for several cops, who were now in the line of fire of other cops, yelling and shouting at each other to get down.

Vanessa pulled her rifle up, sighting down the tower side as shots rang out, glass fracturing along the retail sidewalk, holographic displays imploding. . . . "Snipers!" she yelled. "Someone get me an angle!" Because she had none, she saw, sidewalk trees blocking the way, and banners for some upcoming parade strung across the road every thirty meters.

"*Got nothing!*" came the return call.

"*I'm blocked!*"

And the cops, terrified at nearly hitting each other, were now recovering to aim at the running man's back . . . only to find the street behind him still full of crowds clearing the area, and more cops doing crowd control with their backs turned.

"Shoot him!" Vanessa yelled on police frequency. "This is SO1, shoot him now, he's a bomb, he'll take a hundred with him!" Someone fired, hitting a tree. Another shot, a window collapsed. "Fuck!"

The running man plunged into crowds and cops. *"He's heading for the subway entrance!"* A bomb in there could be worst of all, entire train platforms massacred. . . .

"Hang on," came Sandy's voice. And tacnet showed her jumping, lightly armoured with no rappel line, off the top of the nearby three-hundred-meter-tall building. Spread-eagled as she fell, and aiming, rifle to shoulder.

Exclamations from her soldiers watching. *"No fucking way!"* Ming summarised. But in free fall, the gaps between those cursed banners opened up, and the angle past the obscuring trees. A GI's arm would brace steel-solid if need be, internal armscomp and weaponscomp aligning; she could see to millimetre precision exactly where the bullet would hit. Account in turn for a gathering 300-kph crosswind, downward velocity, deflection, five hundred meters range, on a single target amongst all those running, milling crowds. . . .

Sandy fired. The man's head snapped forward in a bloody spray. Sandy hit the road, hard enough that the crack! could be heard from Vanessa's forty-ninth floor. Arms out to save weapon and upper armour from damage, one knee down and probably a hole in the road. Got up, cricked her neck, and began walking back, limping slightly where her armour leg had gone dead, worn now like a heavy trouser leg. Her actual leg, no doubt, was fine.

"Gives me a hard-on," said Johnathon from Vanessa's side.

"Yeah, me too," said Vanessa.

CHAPTER EIGHT

"**S**o this is what it looks like," said Steven, lighting the holodisplay on the table. It showed another of his PT graphs—Psychological Topography—with the Ruben Star prominently displayed. The 3D lines that, when taken together, demonstrated a kind of technologically induced insanity. "Only I can do better than that. Look at this."

The graph was replaced by a 3D holograph of a human brain. Implants were in red, tendrils clawing, organic into the brain's crevices. "This is a brain activity average compilation," Steven explained. "Take all the terrorists' brains that we could recover and that were still working . . ." a hard glance at Sandy; he'd warned her he needed more live samples, ". . . and make an average of their activity profiles. What you're looking at here is an average of FSA Agents' brains, voluntarily given, of course. Similar combat augments, similar institutional life experiences, combat experience, tape teach, et cetera. And here is the average of the terrorists."

The image changed. "Son of a bitch," Ari intoned. You didn't need to be a neuroscientist to see the difference. A five-year-old could see it. The brain was different . . . well, the brain-average. Some sections were swollen to double normal size. Others were shrunken. One natural cavity seemed to have doubled in size.

"Now these Pyeongwha guys had Neural Cluster Tech implanted at, what, fourteen?" Steven said. Ari nodded. "And I mean these are the fanatics, worst-case scenario, they locked themselves into an institution that was committed to creating a super-race, using a particular kind of uplink tech that they knew damn well was changing their brains. But they liked it. They thought it was a good thing."

Does an extremist know he's extreme? Sandy wondered. Most extremists seemed to think they were normal and everyone else was nuts.

"Average age here is about forty-eight," Steven continued. "Often you find the younger ones are more extreme, life experience tends to be random, the longer you live, the more moderate most people become. Most," he emphasised, as Sandy opened her mouth to object. She held her tongue. "But here we're finding it gets worse. The technology doesn't stop. It's like water in the sand, once it's begun to carve a channel, the channel just gets deeper and deeper, until it's a canyon. More and more information passes along those brain pathways, and the others shrivel and die. You could put these guys in reeducation for ten years; I don't think you could reverse this. They're committed for life. The only thing that'll stop them is a bullet."

"Well, that would keep the prison expenses down," Ari offered. He glanced at Raylee, seated alongside in the dark, face lit by the holographic glow. She wasn't smiling and was biting her lip.

"Ari," Ragi said quietly. "You think this is what PRIDE were doing here? Talking to these terrorists about their condition?"

"Exchanging notes about the voices in their heads, sure," said Ari. "Looks pretty clear, we know they were talking; I've even got some chat-room notes. They didn't cover their tracks as well as they'd thought." Unsurprising, Sandy thought, considering Ari was the one tracking them down. "PRIDE are fighting the League. That takes commitment, given how League treats rebels. Extremism's a virtue for these guys, it looks like commitment, like giant brass balls. They're even aware of League's uplink tech problem, it's becoming hard to miss, there's outbreaks everywhere. But they don't see it as some medical condition, they see it as League's comeuppance. So they wanted to talk to other extremists with fun ideas about neural uplink tech, so naturally they talk to our Pyeongwha crazies . . . only they can't go to Pyeongwha to do that because it's kinda under Federation occupation, so they come here."

"Fun conversations those would be," Steven offered. "You murdered a few hundred thousand nonbelievers, I killed a whole moon, let's get together for breakfast."

Sometimes Sandy thought the small blond whiz kid was just a bit too excited about his field of work to think twice about what it actually meant.

"Pity our one solid lead on a PRIDE agent got his head splattered all over a room before we could examine it," said Ari. "Interesting to compare the brain scans."

"Oh, we've got data," Steven assured him.

"Reliable?"

"Sure. We have sources, in League. They come through FedInt, but they're reliable."

Ari's face darkened at the mention of FedInt. "And?"

Steven shrugged and put up a new image. Another brain scan. Nearly identical to the horror show it was replacing. "Averaged again," Steven explained. "That's why League's falling apart, right there. The technology's different to NCT, more advanced. But the effects are nearly identical. And League probably knew for decades and didn't tell anyone."

"Same thing as Pyeongwha," said Sandy. "They're crazy, but they *like* their crazy."

"And boom," Ari said flatly, "we're all dead."

Silence in the room. It was entirely possible that Ari wasn't wrong. For everyone. Mutually Assured Destruction didn't deter ideologues. Ideologues weren't frightened of dying, only of being proven wrong. And sometimes dying was the only way to avoid that. Sandy thought of her final years in the League's horrid war, all the officers and soldiers still clinging to the rationales that had killed so many millions, desperate to prove that it had all been worth something. Recalled a staff HQ in chaos because some staffer, who had never fired a weapon in combat, had pulled the pin on a grenade while sitting at her desk. Lieutenant "Last Ditch" Maloney, they'd called her, because of her endless lectures about the need to fight till the end. So much for that, then.

"So all the League's like this now?" Raylee asked, pointing at the hologram. Sandy thought to ask what she was doing here, but wasn't so rude as to ask.

"No, just the extremists," said Steven. "The degree of suggestibility implied in this model is . . . well, neighbours would be killing neighbours by now. You saw some of the Pyeongwha interviews. It got scary."

"Raylee found another terrorist," Ari told them. "A dead one. Was killed a month ago before this whole thing started, but no one knew he was one, just another cold case until Ray went back over the records looking for clues. This guy was in a VR chat room, trolling for underground contacts with security access. He got into an argument with a guy, then tracked that guy down in real life and picked a fight with him in a bar. Only the guy turned out to be an augment, part-time bouncer, so he killed him, got off on self-defence."

"What was the argument about?" Steven asked curiously. "The Pyeongwha occupation?"

Ari smiled and indicated for Raylee to speak. Raylee abandoned chewing her thumbnail. "Mitchi Wong. A popstar." Steven, Ragi, and Sandy looked at each other blankly. None had heard of her. "She's big in a few systems; she's not even from Pyeongwha, but she has Pyeongwha parents and is big in Anjula. This chat-room guy said she wasn't much of a singer. It escalated. That's it."

"Goddamn," Steven murmured. "Can I have your files for SuperPsych?"

Raylee nodded. "Only found it yesterday, you'll get it asap."

"Mitchi Wong Extremism," said Sandy. "We've found a new standard."

CHAPTER NINE

That morning, Poole came for breakfast. The kids were thrilled and chatted with him about all kinds of stuff, and were happy to have Sandy home in the morning for once. She'd been out all night, debriefing from the Bhubaneswar operation, and had only come home for food. Over cereal, fruit, and toast, she noted another priority FSA feed coming in.

She opened and saw FOG was monitoring *two* new incoming ships. These had entered considerably closer to Callay than the last one and were now right on that previous vessel's tail. She doubted the media would stay silent about it much longer and so opened the feed to the kitchen display so they could all see.

"They're chasing him," Danya observed, as they all stared at the real-time graphic of trajectories across Callay's spacelanes. "Can we hear audio?" Sandy looked at Poole. Poole gave a shrug. "They're your kids," that said. "Ship communications are always intercepted," Danya reasoned. He spent a lot of time reading about these kinds of security issues. "It's Tanusha, they'll decode it, we'll hear it eventually."

He was right, it was nearly impossible to narrowcast ship communications in heavily populated systems, someone would always intercept stray transmission, then feed it to others. Fleet encryption was heavy duty, but in Tanusha, that just gave them a few days' lag before someone decrypted it. Another reason Fleet usually didn't say much in populated systems, and in this system in particular.

"Okay," said Sandy. "If anyone tells that I let you hear this, I'll be in trouble." Usually that was enough. She activated audio.

"*Okay, I'm getting weapons active.*" The voice was Bursteimer's, on the Runner *Caribbean*. The feed showed him burning hard on intercept, but the audio graphic showed a five-minute unadjusted time lag. Meaning that while Bursteimer was fifteen minutes light away from Callay, this communication was five minutes later than that, and the feed was replaying the last recorded transmissions, in order. *"I'm getting pings. Comp profile says League, possibly EG-40 or 42."*

Everyone looked at Sandy. "Destroyers," she said, slowly chewing her toast, gazing at the projection above the kitchen bench. "Both of them."

"We are maxed out and running, projecting intercept in mid-zone-2, deflection mid 89 point three, probability slight. Fire grid linkup initiated, all protocols red, await my termination signal."

"League destroyers jumping into Callay's system this deep is technically an act of war," Sandy translated. "The whole system's about to go red."

"Whoa," said Danya, eyes wide. The kids had all stopped eating, staring and listening wide-eyed. Sandy kept chewing. She'd seen it a hundred times in the League, though usually from the other end, on board some incoming ship that scared the crap out of a system's residents with some hostile approach like this. But it hadn't happened to Callay through the entire thirty-year war, save for the usual false alarms. And the war was supposed to be nine years finished.

"Captain Bursteimer's the lead asset on the intercept," she added. "He's first responder on the time lag, so everyone coordinates off him. The armscomps will all talk to each other and start plotting fire tracks to cover as much of the League's approach vector as possible. Then it becomes about guesswork and statistics, but at the very least they'll make them dodge."

"What if they're not enemy?" Svetlana wondered. "I mean, League's enemy . . . but I mean what if they're not hostile?"

Sandy shrugged. "That's their problem. Everyone knows the rules, you don't make hostile approaches into defended systems if you don't want to get blasted, especially not this system at this time."

"But they're after that ship. That first ship." The first ship had begun broadcasting as "friend" in IFF mode. Not that anyone was prepared to believe it yet, but with these two latest arrivals bearing down on it, it wasn't implausible.

"And that ship is now within Callay's protected zone." Sandy sipped juice. "We're obligated by Federation law to protect it. Besides, it might be a trick, they might not really be after that ship at all."

"He said mid-zone-two," said Danya. "What's that?"

"There's five zones in a system's defence grid," said Sandy. "Five is outer, one is real close. Bursteimer's calculating intercept in the middle of zone-two."

"So that's really close?"

"Yep. Too damn close."

"What if they're Talee instead of League?" Kiril wondered.

Sandy smiled at him. "Then we'll all be completely screwed, Kiri."

"Gonna be an interesting day at work," Poole suggested.

Sandy rolled her eyes.

The media were crazy with it on the flight in. Every live broadcast had headlines with graphic titles of "crisis," or "attack," or Sandy's favourite, "Callay in Peril!" Most were running graphical simulations with commentary from experts, most of whom were civilian spacers, but a few ex-Fleet as well. There were enough civilian systems covering Callay's spacelanes that they could do quite a good job following the interception, though of course they had no audio yet—that would come later. Otherwise there was Amirah's network press conference, since no one wanted to leave their feeds to gather in a room and fire questions at her in person.

"We estimate intercept in seventeen minutes from now," Amirah was telling the several thousand direct-linked media units. *"We can confirm that ordnance is outgoing and incoming at this time. The FSA will not speculate on League intentions or implications for current relations with the League. Two League ships do not constitute League policy. We have no idea what they're doing here, and we don't intend to speculate. What is clear is that a jump entry this close to system homeworld, with warships, at hostile velocities, will be considered a threat in ANY system, League or Federation, and will result in all defensive measures being taken."*

"She doesn't say that in seventeen minutes the fight actually starts," said Sandy. In the passenger seat, Poole looked out the window, as though preoccupied. "Then we find out what they're doing here."

"That first ship's real quiet, aside from IFF," said Poole. "You'd think someone wanting us to save his ass would be shouting and screaming about now."

"Hmm." Who did League want to kill so badly they'd send warships into Callayan system space to destroy? "Could be PRIDE. Could be something else. Be nice to interrogate more than a cloud of dust."

"Bet it's nothing good," said Poole. Sandy glanced at him. "What is, these days? Coming from that direction?"

Sandy said nothing. For a moment, they flew through the late-morning rush in silence, a gentle weave between soaring towers. Panic or no panic, morning rush looked the same as ever, throbbing, alive. Below, express-ways streamed automated traffic, and maglevs whisked along elevated rails. Millions of people, all in motion.

"I don't think we're going to make it out of this," Poole added.

"Don't say that," Sandy murmured.

"I just don't see how it can last."

"How long what can last?"

"Me. Being happy." Poole had taken his time adjusting. He was only eleven years old, commissioned two years before the war's end and too young in early phase development to see any combat. He'd "grown up" in adminis-trative mess, at the war's end, unwanted and unneeded, as most high-desig-nation combat GIs had suddenly become. In that mess, trying to puzzle out what his life was for, made for a war that had recently ended, he'd encountered stories of Sandy Kresnov's big break for freedom in the Federation. It had seemed better than the mess he'd been in, so he left. Or so he told it.

"You're happy?" Sandy asked.

Poole shrugged. "Sure. I guess. Better than two years ago. But it doesn't seem the natural state of things, does it? I mean, it's such hard work."

"I find it's as hard as you make it."

Poole smiled. "Well, you're higher des than me. Things come easier."

"Happiness is not a designation.

"If you say so."

It took half an hour for the fight to start, Callay time, adjusted for lag. When it happened, there was very little for them all to hear, clustered into Reichardt's office on the fifth floor, where his bank of monitors made a miniature bridge for him. Even Ibrahim came down, leaning against a wall and stroking his goatee, helpless like the fifteen others in the room, as Reichardt watched the screens and doubtless wished he were up with *Mekong* . . . but *Mekong* was at full power away from Callay to effect a third-layer of interception defences if required, and God help any League cruiser that got within range of that firepower.

"Mark One is evasive," Reichardt observed, peering at events that happened a quarter of an hour ago, millions of kilometres from Callay. Mark One was the first unidentified entry. That meant the League ships were shooting at it. "Very evasive," Reichardt corrected, reading new data.

"Defensive weaponry?" Assistant Director Hando asked. Tall and bald, Hando was an Earth native. Upon the war's end, he'd been offered a senior political role in Mozambique, where he'd been born. Instead, he'd remained FedInt, and now FSA. "Anti-missiles?"

"No telling," said Reichardt. "The feed's not clear, probably League jamming. Maybe . . . oh wait. Jump pulse. Next manoeuver. Counter-pulse, I think Burstie saw that . . . detonation, armament scale. League's evasive, shooting back, they're serious."

Sandy leaned against the doorframe and said nothing. She didn't need to see the screens to read them, uplinked to internal vision, displayed across the room before her. Bursteimer's support made it four-on-two, about to be seven-on-two as the next Fleet ships came into range. Two station firepoints out that way had sent ordnance that would be arriving shortly—bundlers, Fleet called them, a package of missiles that scattered, shotgun-like, across whole sections of space, course-adjusting all the way. Two League ships had no chance, just hanging in long enough to hope for a lucky hit on their target.

Occasionally a captain would speak, a terse exchange, so laden with jargon and strained with heavy Gs it was unintelligible to any but the more experienced. Sandy translated it nearly as easily as Reichardt, having spent many hours locked in cramped ship holds, trying to follow data feeds just like this one, which would determine whether she lived or died. She'd hated it then, and hated it now. The memories brought tension, tightening her hands, dropping the redness onto her vision.

Then: "Big flash. That's a kill, he's gone." On the screen, one of the League ships disappeared. No one celebrated. It was all so unglamorously brutal, a play of numbers and chance, the mathematics of velocity, mass and energy. The League captain gambled against high odds, and lost.

"*Yeah, scratch that,*" came Bursteimer's voice, strained at G. "*Re-calc, Caribbean is boosting to fraction five on tangential! All grids, re-calc and re-load!*" As the attack pattern swung its full force onto the remaining League vessel.

"He's boosting up," Reichardt added, meaning the League vessel, as it pulsed its jump engines to gain velocity. "He's running, heading for jump."

"God knows where he'll go from here," someone muttered. "He can't do a U-turn, he's carrying too much V. He'll end up deeper in Fed space."

Another boost, then another, and the speed became tremendous, a measurable fraction of light, racing away down the gravity slope. Then a pulse of energy, and he was gone.

"Caribbean has hot pursuit. Nav comp to follow. See you on the other side."

Bursteimer would have some ideas where that League ship would arrive and would head for the most obvious, and hope to catch him there. Others were following. Well, that was the last they'd see of Bursteimer for a few weeks, at least. However annoying the man was in person, Sandy was in no doubt that Bursteimer possessed the mental stamina and discipline required to do that job, as his record indicated he did.

"Amirah," said Ibrahim. "Make the announcement, please." At her place beside Reichardt's desk, Amirah nodded and left.

"Hold it," said Reichardt, and Amirah paused. He highlighted a new feed coming through. "That's Mark One. Looks like a manifest."

There were crew names. A captain, officers . . . twenty of those, a big ship then. To get here through Federation space, hightailing it with League cruisers in pursuit, probably it was big with powerful engines. More names, regular crew . . . and passengers. Sandy's gaze froze on the first listed.

Renaldo Takewashi.

"Wow," someone murmured. "Didn't see that one coming."

Raylee first noticed something wrong as she walked from the bathroom to her bedroom, wrapped only in a towel. Some window blinds were open. She lived on the twenty-seventh floor of Denpasar District hub, with a partial view of a river bend, lots of nightlife, and good restaurants. But when the blinds were open, the five-star hotel guests across the road could see right in, so she usually kept them closed . . . and why hadn't the room minder polarised the windows?

Then she saw the man in the kitchen doorway, eating an apple.

"Bakav sa!" she yelped.

And froze, because her apartment was very secure, and anyone who wanted to get past that security must be a serious operative. Serious operatives didn't mess about, so if he was going to kill her, he'd likely have done it by now. Unless he wanted information and was going to torture her first.

The man looked her up and down, munching the apple. He was powerfully built, square-jawed and handsome. A GI, she could just about smell it on him. And high designation too, given his nonchalant style and the masculine way his eyes travelled over her. It was personality, for better or worse. Lower designations didn't have it.

"Nice," he opined. "For a straight."

"Nice for a GI too," she retorted, dry-mouthed and heart thumping. Maybe if he liked her, she'd be safer. GIs didn't rape, she remembered Ari saying once. Though high-des GIs were inventing new, atypical behaviours all the time. If this one wanted to, then there wasn't a damn thing she could do about it, new augmentations or not.

Augmentations! She tried her uplinks, and got . . . nothing. Not even a failed connection light, just nothing. No portal view on her vis-cue, where the graphic usually appeared to show her what connections she could make. Someone was jamming her. No prizes for guessing who. How it was possible, with Ari's various security measures built into the apartment, she wasn't qualified to guess.

The GI made a face. "GI girls aren't built like you," he said. "You're leggy, not built for balance or speed. But you're hot, considering you're useless."

Great, a synthetic chauvinist. And a lippy one. "What the hell are you doing in my apartment?"

"Want to talk." He bit the last part of the apple—so he'd been here a few minutes at least. "These are great, can I have another?"

"Sure." Drily. Maybe she'd live through this after all. "Help yourself. Meanwhile I'm putting some clothes on."

"Sure, spoil my day." She headed for the bedroom. "Leave the door open. So you don't go for a gun."

"Why would I go for a gun against a high-des GI?" she retorted, heading for the wardrobe. It was in clear line of sight through the bedroom door. She repressed the impulse for modesty, tossed the towel, and pulled on her nearest pants and top.

"Some straights panic," the GI explained, settling on the arm of her sofa, munching a new apple. His gaze never left her. Ari also said that GI men were not the slightest bit sexist, due to GI women being so formidable. Or did that fair-mindedness not extend to straights? "Ever have sex with a GI?"

"No." Her heart, slowly settling, now galloped again. "And I'm not starting now."

An offhanded shrug. "Just asking. I'm not here to hurt you."

"Why then?" She pulled on the top and strolled back out, barefoot on the floorboards. Forcing herself to calm, recalling that a GI would see her racing pulse, with IR vision that would show the blood pumping in her veins. She was a cop, and this was an information source. Act like it, silly girl. "You're League?"

He nodded. Slightly spikey, raffishly cut hair, a jawline and neck that suggested zero excess body mass, and a ripped physique beneath shirt and jacket. Hot, it occurred to her. If she'd seen him in a club, back in the days she still went to clubs, she'd have been interested.

"You here to defect?"

He smiled. "Like Kresnov? She's an idiot."

"Kresnov is many things," Raylee said firmly, "but she's no idiot."

"She wants to live famous in the bright lights," the GI replied. "She wants to be a big hero. She doesn't like what GIs are, she wants to be free to pick flowers and join the circus. It's bullshit. We're killers. And that's okay. It's the price we pay for being superhuman. We have great lives and less choice. But rather than dealing with it, she sulks and stamps her foot and comes out here where she works as a security professional. A professional killer, yet again. So much for choice."

He bit his apple again. Raylee padded past to the kitchen, the GI watching her all the way. "You're Internal Security Organisation," she observed. He shrugged. "Their GIs are League patriots."

"Plenty of military GIs too," the man countered. Raylee poured herself some makani juice to wet her dry mouth. "League military's pretty stupid, they haven't treated their GIs the best. I get that. But they're improving a lot now. Kresnov thinks all the League GIs are going to follow her, but she's wrong. League love GIs. Federation don't. Her vision of a synthetic-friendly Federation's a mirage."

"You came here to tell me *this*?" Raylee leaned in the doorway, sipping her juice. If this man liked her for her looks, and wasn't going to take without asking, she wasn't above exploiting it. She angled her hips, just a little.

"No. Federal Intelligence is not your friend. You know they killed the PRIDE Agent we've both been chasing? FSA called him Subject A."

"You didn't kill him?" Just like Ari said, then. "Even though PRIDE killed Cresta?"

"It's called intelligence," said the GI. "We gather information. It doesn't work when the source is dead. Which is likely why FedInt killed him, to stop us both from learning."

Raylee frowned. "Us both?"

"He was talking to another GI when he was killed." The GI's gaze held and fastened, intense for the first time. Half lidded. "What do you know about him?"

"Nothing I'm allowed to say."

"We're not allowed to talk about him either. It makes a logjam. I can't talk, you can't talk. I think we have the same problems and enemies. So I came here."

"Your superiors don't know?" No reply from the GI. "Ah. A free thinker."

"FedInt knows more about that GI than they're saying. And more about the Talee."

A silence. If there was one thing Raylee knew that she and her shiny new FSA clearance were *not* allowed to talk about, it was the Talee. Least of all with the enemy. Which she was pretty sure League still were, particularly with the way things were looking lately. Federation patriot that she was, she knew that this conversation now teetered on the verge of treason. And yet . . .

"He's our guest," she said. "We don't tell him what to do. You know his capabilities. He comes and goes as he pleases."

A solemn, sober stare. "I'm not sure that's wise."

Raylee rolled her eyes a little. "Well, *obviously* the League doesn't want us friendly with Talee. You think they should be best friends with *you*. So you can get all their technology, restart the war, and wipe us out."

The GI pressed his lips together, appearing to think about something. It was the kind of subconscious facial gesture only high-des GIs did. It suggested depth. "President Balasingham was killed on Cresta. Ex-President Balasingham. Now there was a guy with Talee connections. He was former ISO, you know."

"I know."

"Was President for eight years, two terms during the war. His ISO background made him a good choice for the war effort. ISO helped."

Raylee nodded. She'd heard some of this too. Hearing it from a top ISO operative, however, gave it a whole different kind of gravity.

"His whole power base was there," the GI continued. "Quite a few former ISO on Cresta. It was a bit of a hub for retired Intel. Not all of those guys like beaches and mountains, some prefer full enviro-habitats and low gravity. Go figure.

"No real reason for PRIDE to want him dead. And President Balasingham was the only high-value target on Cresta."

"Sure, but Cresta was a symbol of League government power," Raylee disagreed, trying to sound like she knew more about it than she did. "Lots of big former government retirees, some think tanks, research institutions. PRIDE are separatists, Cresta was an available target."

"Wasn't," the GI disagreed. "Very well defended. Someone tipped the attackers. We think it was FedInt."

Oh fuck. Raylee closed her eyes. She'd been used as a conduit for awful, world-shaking secrets before, and it had cost her her arm, parts of her face, and nearly her life. Now it was happening again. She wanted to order him from her apartment and find some way to have her memory erased.

"Great," she murmured instead. And looked down at her drink. "Just great. Why?"

"We're not sure. But FedInt is made up of old Federal Intelligence. They have a long history with President Balasingham and that crew, right across thirty years of war. We think they're hiding something, something President Balasingham was into. Something involving the Talee."

PRIDE never claimed responsibility, Raylee recalled. Never denied it either, but it wasn't typical behaviour for genocidal fanatics. "So FedInt are using League's problems as a *cover*? Kill Cresta and blame it on PRIDE?"

"Oh, PRIDE might have done it," said the GI. "But it wasn't possible without FedInt help. FedInt have sources in League security. We think they found out Cresta's defences and leaked it to PRIDE. Or did it themselves."

"So why are PRIDE here? Talking to Pyeongwha terrorists?"

"Hell," said the GI. "They don't pay me that much."

CHAPTER TEN

Ari blinked hard against the blurred vision of G-stress and tried to flex. It was hard to breathe, and he tried to remember the training—short breath, hold, short breath, hold, tense the diaphragm. Prolonged Gs were now causing vision flashes, something about the compression of the optic nerve about the augmentation nodes. Spacers got different kinds to guard against exactly that, but they weren't as effective . . . and how likely was he, a groundie who hated spaceflight, likely to be this frequently in space anyway?

He glanced sideways at Captain Reichardt, similarly reclined in his acceleration couch. Reichardt seemed to be sleeping, though more likely he was uplinked and processing. Vanessa, typically restless, was raising arm and leg against the Gs, considering how it felt. Director Boyle looked uncomfortable, but he had wisely had several shots from a strong-smelling flask before launch and looked to be managing. Farthest down the command hold, the two GIs, Poole and Tuli, were completely unbothered.

"That transfer shuttle just docked," Reichardt announced above the dull roar of thrusters. Despite the consistent 2.8 Gs, his voice barely sounded strained.

"Yeah, their manifest is a mess," Vanessa replied, uplinked and checking that. "No way it's legal."

"You can file against them if you want?"

Vanessa made a face. "Bit petty at this point."

The shuttle had come from Nehru Station, the main civvie station, to Hanuman Station, the main Fleet station. It was under FedInt jurisdiction, and thanks to the manifest screw-up, they had no idea who or how many were aboard. Renaldo Takewashi's ship was about to dock at Hanuman, and now FedInt were pouring faceless operatives onto station. Thus this rapid launch from Tanusha, at speeds that were only legal under emergency conditions, now requiring a full deceleration on approach to dock.

"Who has your confidence, on station?" Vanessa asked Reichardt.

"Next question," said Reichardt. Vanessa gave him a long look, an arm in the air, flexing her right hand against the Gs. *Pearl* was docked at the station, with its full complement of marines—a First Fleet carrier, so far noncommittal on most of Callay's recent politics. *Mekong*, Reichardt's ride, was accompanying Takewashi's vessel into station . . . but that meant its marine complement was off-station. "Got a final number on FedInt operatives on station?"

"Pick a number between ten and twenty," said Vanessa. "They've been Fleet infiltrating like crazy, it's not FSA HQ jurisdiction, nothing we could do."

"And Ibrahim says we can't bring Sandy," Ari muttered. The thrust suddenly cut, and he gasped with relief. Optics showed shuttle trajectory matching station, now less than two Ks out, *way* within safe zone for approaches. No shit someone would notice that. Almost immediately the side thrust hit, shuttle reorienting a final time for hub docking.

"It was a good call," said Vanessa. "It's too personal with her."

"Yeah, well, I'm tired of getting shot at," Ari retorted. "And Sandy has a deterrent effect."

"Hey," said Poole. "What am I, chopped liver?"

"We're here to get Takewashi before FedInt do," Reichardt replied. "I think we can do that without shooting anyone, or having to worry about Sandy shooting Takewashi."

That wasn't a real possibility, Ari knew. More that Sandy would set a tone and make Takewashi defensive, which could clam up whatever information they needed immediately. Or other, unforeseen possibilities. Vanessa was right, Sandy and Takewashi in the same place made complications. Takewashi was the self-pronounced father of the synthetic neurology that had created Sandy and all self-conscious GIs. Given what was now known about the true origins of GI sentience, Sandy had a real issue with Takewashi. Even more than she usually did.

"Boyle," said Ari. "What's your prediction on FedInt? We've got a betting pool, twenty gets you in."

"I think they're defending a special recipe for meatloaf," said Boyle.

"Yeah, me too." Ari glanced at Reichardt.

"This fucking war," Reichardt said calmly, watching the shuttle's docking approach on uplink, "was fought over a series of ideological positions that all proved untenable. The thing with hypocrites is they all have secrets. FedInt's built up thirty years of secrets in the war, and now nine more after it finished. Whatever it is, it's big, and it's probably got friends."

"If FedInt helped kill Cresta," Poole volunteered, "seems logical that whatever they killed ex-President Balasingham to hide, Takewashi might know something about. Which might explain why he's suddenly here."

And thus the mad rush to stop FedInt getting to him first.

They got off at Hanuman Station hub, a clash of locks and a blast of freezing air, ears popping, then down the tube to main hub, hauling at handles along the guideline in the zero-G with Reichardt in the lead, flipping salutes at spacers who saluted back harder. Vanessa set up tacnet for him as they moved, something she did far better than any spacer, and let it propagate on station networks Ari could vouch the security of.

"*LT I want you here asap*," Reichardt told Ndaja, his marine commander, as they went. "*Damn the procedures, just blast it to the rim lock and come in armed.*"

"*Aye, Cap*," said Ndaja.

"*Po, put the second shuttle at three-quarters off diameter, full weapons. I don't want anyone sneaking up on this sucker in dock. Hold Mekong at two point five and await further.*"

"*Aye, Cap.*" That was Po, Reichardt's second, currently acting-Captain with Reichardt off-ship. Po was new, an experienced Captain of a smaller vessel in the last few years of the war, but carriers were something else again, and no one commanded one without first holding second-chair. Ndaja had been with Reichardt for nearly twenty years, an extraordinary partnership by any measure.

They made the personnel elevator, grabbing rails without time for proper strapping as the car took them down—Ari missed his hold and would have hit the ceiling had not Reichardt snagged an arm and dragged him with the car's motion. They were all armed, Vanessa, Poole, and Tuli with short rifles; Ari, Reichardt, and Boyle with pistols . . . not that Boyle looked to have any idea what to do with it; it threatened to drift clear of his suit pocket now as his jacket floated up in the descent. No armour, that would have been a breach of protocol too far.

"Tell him to stay in his damn ship," Reichardt said aloud as the shaft whizzed by the car windows, airless and smooth. Talking to station, Ari saw with a glance at tacnet audio, fighting disorientation as the gravity increased. "Tell him he doesn't have clearance to leave."

"*He wants to get out,*" came station's reply. "*He's insistent.*"

"Well, his own people keep trying to blow up his ship," Vanessa reasoned, off-line. "Figures he's safer with us."

"*Tell him . . .*" deep breath, "*. . . tell him I can't guarantee his safety if he leaves his vessel.*" He glanced at Ari. Could a neuro-synth genius take a hint? Vanessa pulled on a cap from her thigh pocket, calculated the brim to keep the overhead lights out of her vision, then sighted the rifle against the wall, adjusting optics. All business, and preparing to shoot people, if necessary. She was as good at it these days as a lot of GIs. Ari felt his heart thump harder.

"We can't run, or we risk drawing fire," Reichardt told her. "At a brisk walk, how long?"

"Twelve minutes," said Vanessa, calculating on the station map. "Thirteen if Boyle finds a brisk walk too much." Boyle was too distracted by nervous tension to reply. He was a bureaucrat, not a soldier, but he was coping so far, sweaty brow and all.

"Okay, I've got people at strongpoints on the main junctions," Reichardt continued, making mental references on the tacnet map. An incoming audio began flashing. "It's mostly station security, didn't rate them more than a bucket of spit in the war, it's less than that now."

"I did a two-week exercise run with them a few months ago," Tuli volunteered, waiting patiently with weapon ready. "A bucket of spit is generous."

"S'not their fault," said Vanessa. "They're techs with guns. You gonna answer that?"

Reichardt answered the new audio. "Captain Reichardt."

"*Hello, Captain, please stand by for a connection with the Grand Committee Chairman.*"

"Yeah," said Reichardt, glancing as the elevator dial counted toward the rim, and gravity approached a full G, "could you tell the Chairman I'm a little busy . . ." Click, as the connection went through. "Great."

"The Chairman can't make his own calls?" Vanessa wondered.

"He's a busy man," said Reichardt, drily.

Click. *"Captain Reichardt,"* came Ranaprasana's voice, *"I'm somewhat concerned about what I see described to me as a . . . situation, aboard Hanuman Station. I have a complaint from Chief Shin of Federal Intelligence that you and FSA Command are seeking to deny him access to Mr Takewashi. Is that correct?"*

Reichardt looked at the wall as the car's motion slowed. Lips twisted as he considered. Tell Ranaprasana that they worried FedInt were going to have Takewashi killed? That FedInt were involved in an active cover-up, which, it appeared, had included assisting PRIDE to destroy an entire League moon and kill a quarter of a million people? That FSA HQ had just gone red on FedInt, effectively regarding them as an enemy entity?

"Mr Chairman, this is Special Agent Ari Ruben," Ari cut in. "I'm with Captain Reichardt at this moment. Sir, you might recall that the FSA's final report in the aftermath of Operation Shield concluded that there were unaccountable and dangerously autonomous elements within Federal Intelligence whose actions during that crisis remain largely unilluminated. Sir, we feel that those elements may now have negative intentions toward Mr Takewashi."

The car stopped, and the elevator doors opened. Everyone yawned to pop their ears as the pressure changed, Vanessa immediately in the doorway with rifle ready to be extended, checking quickly one way then the other.

"Agent Ruben, it is my task to investigate all agencies involved in the Operation Shield events, including FSA HQ and the CSA." Vanessa indicated that they move, Tuli joining her side, Reichardt behind, then Ari and Boyle, with Poole guarding the rear. The tight metal corridors were nothing as pleasant as the civilian stations, all exposed rivets and panels, with no sign of people. *"I'm alarmed by FSA HQ's tendency to accuse other agencies of improper conduct, and then to declare jurisdiction and run by decree. Federal institutions and agencies should work collegiately together on these matters. I would like to see FSA and FedInt working together on this Takewashi matter, with equal access to all. Failure to do so could see FSA receiving unfavourable mentions in my final report."*

"Understood, Chairman Ranaprasana," Reichardt said sweetly, striding on long legs after Tuli and Vanessa. "We will endeavour to cooperate with your wishes in entirety."

And disconnected before the Chairman could try again.

"Say, where'd you learn to speak fluent bullshit?" Vanessa wondered, quick-scanning up side corridors as they passed, small legs at nearly a jog to stay ahead of Reichardt.

"Academy," said Reichardt. "They run a special course, along with brown-nosing and ass-licking."

"Aren't those kind of the same thing?" Poole wondered from the back.

"Well, *you'd* have failed," said Reichardt. They turned left onto a junction corridor, past station security watching them warily. No one saluted—on duty they didn't have to, but Ari thought it was more than that. Fleet, so united during the war, remained riddled with factionalism. Reichardt was as loathed by many as he was loved by some.

"*Captain,*" came Ndaja's voice, "*we're docked. Two minutes to unseal, we'll be on scene in seven.*"

"Copy, LT."

At the next junction more security were blocking the way, several with face masks. A station officer stepped forward to Reichardt, a hand raised.

"Captain, we've a pressure drop in Section 14 A through D, pressure doors are down."

"Open them, we'll risk it."

"Sir, I must insist you detour to Level Three rearside, that will take you through . . ."

Reichardt pulled his pistol and levelled it at the officer's head. "Open the doors. You have five seconds."

The officer paled and hurried to comply. Station security stared wide-eyed. Vanessa and Tuli watched them intently. Any twitch toward their weapons would see them gunned down well short of firing, and they all seemed to know it. Ari recalled those constitutional arguments claiming that the mere presence of GIs in one security institution but not in others upset the fundamental power balance. Damn right it did.

The heavy doors opened to a wail of sirens. Reichardt holstered his pistol. "Thank you, Lieutenant. Carry on."

They walked fast, Poole walking half-backward to keep all in sight. Trying his reflexes would be just as much the death sentence as with Vanessa and Tuli.

"What if there really is a pressure drop?" Ari wondered.

"Then the whole station will absorb the pressure difference for a few minutes and there might be a slight breeze to ruffle your curly hair," said Reichardt. "Fucking amateurs."

Ari didn't ask if Reichardt would have pulled the trigger.

They exited onto station docks opposite Takewashi's berth, a wide, cold expanse of curved steel decking. A glance each way up the sloping horizon showed no pressure doors down, no sign of emergency or depressurisation issues. Gathered around the main access tube to the newly docked ship were station personnel and several dark suits. They turned now to see Reichardt approaching with his small group.

"*Marks left,*" Vanessa formulated on tacnet audio. Tacnet highlighted several watching suits along the inner left wall, another behind a dock transport two berths down, scattered personnel in between. Tuli and Poole could put bullets on those marks in a split second if required; Vanessa, only a fraction longer than that. Still Ari wished Sandy were here—she could do it in several directions at once, almost doubling her killing arc over even high-designation GIs.

"*Marks right,*" Poole added, highlighting targets that way. They formed out, three killers, open on the dock with guns still pointed at the plating but ready to come up at the slightest provocation. Ari and Boyle continued behind Reichardt, up to the berth.

"Agent Raman," said the lead FedInt, empty-handed and palms out. That was smart. "FedInt wasn't provided with any explanation of your purpose here, Captain?"

"FOG claiming jurisdiction on Fleet authority, on behalf of FSA HQ."

"Ah." Raman scratched his nose. "Would have been simpler if you'd said that from the start."

"But so much less fun." From up the sloping docks, a vehicle came humming, dodging working runners and pedestrians. On its back, Lieutenant Ndaja and four more armoured *Mekong* marines.

"Director Boyle," Boyle identified himself, though the FedInts doubtless knew that. "Chief, League Affairs. We get first dibs."

A dry smile from the spook. "Ranaprasana doesn't think so."

Sandy sat in the command chair of SO1 and watched the operation unfold. The shuttle carrying Takewashi was arcing about on final approach, through multiple looming thunderclouds. SO1 circled Balaji Spaceport, an hour's flight from Tanusha. Two other FSA flyers flew support patterns, and drones made low passes over jungle and farms between here and the city outskirts.

FedInt agents were accompanying Takewashi also, by Ranaprasana's order. It made everyone nervous. Word was that Takewashi had shut up completely upon seeing those tensions for himself and was now not talking to anyone. The four GIs who had accompanied him were coming down on another shuttle. All noncombat designation, all female. Voluptuous, the word was. Subservient. It made Sandy want to smack Takewashi around even more. A few of her male non-GI colleagues were more amused at her reaction than at Takewashi's companions. "Feminism" had never been her thing—it presumed a degree of identification with mainstream Federation gender roles that she simply didn't possess. But this, she understood. And had some satisfaction that Vanessa might smack him around for her on the way down.

In the meantime, she had to keep Takewashi alive. The weather was poor, flight control showed the shuttle bounding in the thermals on the approach. Ari would hate that, being as disenchanted with flying as with space travel. Vanessa would probably be asleep. Or pretending to be, while keeping an eye on the FedInt agents on the shuttle with them. Rain swept across green forest in sweeping grey veils, hiding the nearby mountains. Such pretty country, across the northern continent. So little of it she'd gotten to see, even now. Her life was the city, and her rural recreation was the beach.

The shuttle landed, a cloud of white smoke from the tires. Another ten minutes until transfer to a flyer. Then a secure transmission from Ari.

"We have confirmation of new FedInt agents on standby at shuttle docking. Request clearance for removing Takewashi clean, if we have to."

"You have clearance," came Ibrahim's reply. *"Just try to make sure it doesn't come to that."*

Because Takewashi might provide the first clue what the hell was going on in the League, and who killed Cresta, and why. Well, PRIDE killed Cresta, that much seemed certain . . . but the GI who broke into Raylee's apartment said FedInt leaked them the information they needed to do it. Which jibed with Captain Reichardt's assessment of Cresta's considerable defences, and that it had to have been an inside job. FedInt could have done that. But then, it seemed to Sandy, so could ISO, or League Fleet, or any other combination of League forces. So why the suspicion on FedInt?

Because FedInt had been around a long time, came the obvious reply. All through the war. FedInt had even used GIs, granted them by Takewashi for one, experimentals he simply wanted to see granted life when his own authorities refused to allow it. FedInt had done deals and dirty tricks, including with people in the League. Former League President Balasingham had been involved in a lot of these old games, and certainly FedInt had dealings with him and his agents. Some said that over a thirty-year war, the stalemate had begun to drag on both sides, leading to a lot of backdoor conversations about who might concede what, if some theoretical deal could be reached. Many had agreed, for a long time, that a military solution was impossible. And then League had begun to lose, changing everyone's minds. But not before a lot of secret exchanges, carried out by Intel organisations of both sides, that could conceivably have gotten various leaders executed for treason.

Secrets big enough to kill an entire moon to cover up? League had been keeping one damn big secret—that synthetic humanity, the signature achievement of League independence and free thought, had actually come from the Talee. It undermined all League pride and credibility on issues they'd gone to war over and lost millions of lives . . . enough that they'd tried to nuke Droze rather than let the secret get out. That, and the other secret, of how all League was now going nuts, thanks to the widespread use of that technology in uplinks that they didn't truly understand.

It all seemed to fit. And now the League GI told them it was FedInt behind Cresta's destruction. Or told Raylee, anyway. Who just happened to be Ari's girlfriend, and Ari was a somewhat conspiracy-prone guy who hated FedInt with a passion . . .

She connected to Amirah as the flyer bumped through heavy turbulence, grasping a handle above the command chair. "Ami, what's the weather forecast telling you?"

"*Lots of activity,*" said Amirah. "*Doesn't look good at all. I think Shin might try something.*"

"Against *us*?"

"*We're making him look bad. We got Takewashi before he could, and if we have* sole access to that intel, FedInt's at a real disadvantage. FedInt has its own politics, Shin's position won't be secure if that happens. He has to be under pressure."

Dammit, thought Sandy. The gnawing discomfort got worse. "Ami, does this seem odd to you? This FedInt killed Cresta theory?"

"*Well, it doesn't really matter if it seems odd, what matters is that it's credible, and in the absence of more information we have to act on all credible intel.*"

"But that's just the problem, the absence of more information is because the only people who could give us that information are FedInt."

A short pause from Amirah. "*The old man seems pretty sure.*"

"Ibrahim's been burned by FedInt before, he has to defend himself. But that's the problem, we're locked into institutional opposition, and after a while we stop thinking. It's just reflex. And I've done that before, Amirah. I did that when I was a soldier in the League. It was just the way things were— League were good, Federation were bad, that was my reality. I don't want to do that again."

A longer pause from Amirah. Sandy tightened the seat buckles harder as the turbulence got worse. From the back, one of her troops complained to the pilot.

"*It is a bit strange,*" Amirah admitted. "*I didn't want to say anything, but it's a lot of faith to be putting in the word of a League GI, our enemy, who has every reason to lead us astray and make us fight each other.*"

"Thanks, Ami," said Sandy, and reconnected to Rhian on the shuttle. "Hi, Rhi. How's things?"

"*Rolling to berth now,*" said Rhian. "*Watching FedInt agents pretty close. Sandy, are we sure these are the bad guys?*"

"Go on." Her heart was thumping a little harder now. This had been a theory of hers for a while—GIs not thinking so much like straights. Could this be the moment when it proved not only true, but useful?

"*Look, I don't like FedInt either. But killing Cresta? It's convenient that we can't prove it, don't you think? And we can't just ask them if they did. We know someone helped PRIDE kill Cresta . . . but maybe PRIDE had inside sources of their own. They're a League insurgency, insurgents have spies, right? What if they've tricked us into suspecting FedInt, and right now we're falling for it?*"

"Are Ari and Vanessa convinced?"

"*I think so, yeah. That's kinda why I didn't say anything.*"

"Yeah," Sandy said grimly. "That's becoming a recurring thing."

She called Poole, on SO5. *"Sandy, I don't like this,"* he told her as soon as she raised it. *"We're doing this on the say-so of an ISO agent? You remember what happened the last time you trusted an ISO agent?"*

Sandy ran her eye over the listed assets grounded at the spaceport . . . five flyers, all unarmed transport. Three previous shuttles, currently at various stages of refuelling. She was in charge of this part of the operation, but she wasn't in *control*—the setup was largely out of her hands, and that made her uneasy.

"Ari," she tried again, "update please." No reply. Her link was good. She just wasn't getting a response. Spaceport control was showing a flyer's engines running at a nearby hangar. Taxiing, the visual showed. More ground vehicles moving near the shuttle. What the . . . "Tacnet propagation," she announced as the network went tactical, shutting out all external sources. "We have a situation, I'm not getting a response from inside the shuttle, all units . . ."

"Nothing," came Arvid Singh from SO2. *"I get no response either, something's going on."*

"SO1 is on fast approach," said Sandy, sending that uplink signal to her pilot. A sudden crush of Gs as the flyer powered up and turned hard, directly toward the runways. Full weapons came up, an active scan across the entire spaceport . . . Sandy kept a close eye on spaceport defences, remembering an incident seven years ago at Tanusha's main public spaceport, but FSA had full control of spaceport defences and the networks that controlled access, network superiority being the one thing they were guaranteed of against FedInt. "Amirah, get me Chief Shin, right now."

They were several kilometres away, and on this angle the shuttle, nosing up to berthing gantries, was blocking their angle on the taxiing flyer. But if she took personal fire control of a missile, she had enough visual sources to loop it in by eye.

"Sandy," came Arvid, *"if they're making a getaway, they're using that flyer to do it."*

"I know," said Sandy, as turbulence tossed them again, harder this time, at speed. "I'm not shooting unless we're under fire."

"They incapacitated our agents inside . . ."

"We don't know that." Her combat reflex was up but calm. Shin knew he couldn't win a shooting match here. It was a hostage play, take Takewashi on the flyer, and FSA wouldn't dare shoot it down. Maybe they'd even take someone else along for safety.

"*Cassandra,*" Ibrahim cut in, "*you are authorised to take all measures to prevent Takewashi falling into sole FedInt custody.*"

"Understood." It was the first time in her life she'd found Ibrahim's advice unhelpful. The runways were rushing past now, the flyer's weapons tracking on multiple possibilities. An alternative-access vehicle was pressing its walkway to the shuttle's opposing side door. They'd take Takewashi off that way, down stairs to the flyer on the tarmac, then back to FedInt HQ in Tanusha. "Amirah, how's it coming on Chief Shin?"

"*No response, Cassandra, I'm trying everything.*"

"*I could take out that access vehicle?*" the pilot suggested.

"Okay, I want everyone to stop making suggestions and do what they're told," said Sandy. "Orbit at five hundred, please."

The flyer went into a low orbit around the shuttle, five hundred meters out. Sandy diverted enough of her attention to the network to get a full picture of FedInt HQ construct, a huge multilayered thing, as all security net constructs were. All barriers were up, gleaming trails of data now dead and blocked. Parts of that system had to respond to external signals, that was why hackers existed, and there were few more effective hackers of A-grade code than herself, when she had to. But unlike more subtle hackers, if she broke in, she'd truly break it. Plus it would take her long minutes that she didn't have.

"This is SO1," she said, blinking her vision back on the scene before her. "We are deactivating weapons. Pilot, increase orbital diameter to a thousand, thank you." The pilot was slow responding. She overrode and deactivated the flyer's weapons for herself, just to make the point.

Baffled silence on the coms. The pilot levelled out to find his new circling perimeter. Ibrahim came back. "*Cassandra, please explain your . . .*"

A signal from FedInt HQ, via some very fancy relays. "Just shut up for a second," Sandy told her boss, and connected. "Chief Shin."

"*Cassandra.*" Nothing more. No explanation. It was possible she was wrong, it occurred to her. But she didn't think Shin was suicidal, and if he'd hurt Ari or Vanessa . . .

"Our weapons are off, and you appear to have won this round. Congratulations. I'd like to discuss round two."

"I'm not sure there will be a round two, Cassandra. FSA's recent actions suggest them incapable of acting in the Federation's best interests. I'm sorry to have to do this, but under the circumstances I've had little choice. Your agents on the shuttle are fine, they have not been harmed. Please do not pursue Mr Takewashi further. Mr Ranaprasana is expecting your full cooperation on this matter."

Great. Ranaprasana was backing FedInt. Shin would not use that as a bluff. If Ranaprasana got angry at Shin, Shin was history—FedInt answered to Earth factions above all others.

"Fine," said Sandy. "We'll have a little talk with Ranaprasana, about how we'd all be better off if he took his sides *before* we get to drawing weapons, instead of after."

"Cassandra, please tell your boss that threatening Ranaprasana would be the worst and last mistake of his career."

"We're all well aware of that," Sandy said calmly. "You have your assets, Chief, and we won't mess with them. Neither should you forget ours."

Already the flyer was backing away, engines powering. It climbed rapidly, then tilted and began its flight. SO1 turned and moved into formation alongside, three hundred meters off the flank. Fast, Sandy thought with suitable respect. FedInt had quality people who executed well. She wondered how they'd pulled it off.

"We shall not forget, Cassandra. And FSA are welcome to speak to Mr Takewashi once we have finished questioning him ourselves."

"Oh, he won't tell you anything," said Sandy dismissively. "You forget that I'm his baby. He'll only talk to me."

CHAPTER ELEVEN

Federal Intelligence Tanushan Headquarters (FITH-Q in security parlance) was located in one of Tanusha's stranger buildings. In the style of a French eighteenth-century chateau, it was originally built with private money as a place of entertainment by business interests and as a six-star hotel for VIPs. But most VIPs, it turned out, liked to stay in Tanusha's multitude of thriving commercial hubs, not here amidst the leafy, quiet suburbia beside a lovely walking park. The chateau had been used variously since as an art gallery, a museum, and a performing arts school until someone in the Callayan government had offered it to FedInt as a new base following the relocation of Federation government to Callay. They'd been joking, the story went, but FedInt had snapped it up, and occupied it thoroughly the past five years.

Walking from the cruiser, boots crunching on driveway gravel, Sandy had to admit that FedInt had done a very nice job of maintaining the place. The stonework looked old and heavy, though modern laser cutters and robotic construction would have taken a fraction of the time of its predecessors in France. Lights gleamed from old wrought iron lanterns, about which darted a flicker of moths. She trotted up the stone steps, and someone inside opened the heavy wooden door.

The entrance hall sported a black and white checkered floor, old furnishings, and chandeliers. Sandy handed over her pistols to the FedInt agents on duty, then followed one's lead from the anteroom to the main ballroom. Here was a double-arched staircase to die for and some distractingly high-tech desk displays across an open floor, processing a lot of interesting data. Nothing sensitive, Sandy was sure, as she walked down the center aisle. Not with her visiting.

FedInt agents watched her pass. Most here were data processors, like Intel operatives anywhere. Analysts, selected for their attention to detail, ability to work in groups, and tendency to keep their mouths shut when required. At least half, Sandy knew from FSA reports, were from Earth.

Her guide led her up one of the staircases, then down another hall, where open doors showed smaller offices for higher-ranking operatives. Interesting that the doors were all open, Sandy thought—considering FedInt was in the business of secrecy. But then, truly secret meetings could be done uplinked or on VR. Face-to-face time was best for conversation and sharing ideas. The FSA under Ibrahim worked in a similar way.

At the end of the hall was a closed door. The agent knocked and entered. Within was a beautiful room, high-ceilinged with extravagant wall panels, all in eighteenth-century style. Wooden floors, old furnishings, only some framed paintings gave lie to the ancient feel—watercolours of sunrise on a moon mining base, and another of some alien reptilian bird in flight. Sandy thought it must have been quite nice to be noble, and French, in the eighteenth century. Right up until the people who unwillingly gave the nobility all this wealth started chopping their heads off, anyway . . .

Renaldo Takewashi rose from his grand embroidered armchair with difficulty and the help of a cane. He looked no more gaunt and skeletal than when she'd last seen him six years ago, but much weaker all the same. Though maybe that was just the recent travel.

"Cassandra!" he exclaimed in that thin, reedy voice. Narrow-eyed, his scalp close-shaven and pepper-grey, looking every one of his hundred-plus years. "Dear girl, you came. How good of you."

The other chair was occupied by Chief Shin, immaculate in his dark suit, sipping a drink. Another man in a tuxedo appeared from the adjoining door, through which Sandy could see a bed and possibly a kitchen. VIP accommodation, then. The butler (Sandy thought, never having seen an actual butler before) stood by the door, as Shin also stood.

Sandy went to Takewashi and took his frail hand, wrist draped in purple kimono sleeves. Takewashi smiled at her—at this range like the grin of a corpse. But that was unfair, she told herself. She must try to be fair. Much depended on her being so. Even now, the smile flickered, then abruptly vanished, like the dropping of a mask.

"Cassandra," he rasped. "You must help. They're trying to kill me!"

Sandy glanced at Shin. The FedInt Chief was impassive as ever. "I'm sure Chief Shin will do his best to protect you from the League, Mr Takewashi," she said. "Though his resources are limited, against League GIs." Drily. "That you helped to build," she could have added. Doubtless the irony was not appreciated. "I'm quite sure you would be safer with the FSA."

"Not the League!" the old man hissed. "Well . . . yes, the League, but you can guard me well enough against them."

"Who then?"

"The Talee!" Sandy blinked. And looked at Shin. Again, there was no response. "The Talee are coming! They may even be here, now! You must have me moved to a more secure location, somewhere without net access, somewhere so hidden not even your top operatives know where it is! Net access is death against them! Death!"

He gasped and regained his balance with a weight on his cane. Sandy grasped his arm to steady him. And regretted it, as Takewashi managed a shaky smile and patted her hand. Sandy felt the slow spread of pins and needles, a flush of cold, creeping dread. She did not like Takewashi. But he was no fool and would not get this worked up over ghosts and demons.

"I will say no more," he said, and sank back into his chair. "I cannot talk here. It is too dangerous. Everything net connected, far too dangerous."

"He told you this?" Sandy asked Shin, her heart thumping in slow acceleration. Combat reflex red-tinged her outer vision, uncertain of just how far to spread. Combat reflex was for immediate threats. What Takewashi was suggesting was . . . existential.

Shin nodded. "And no more. I asked for you."

Smart move. Sandy nodded, more respect than appreciation. A shift to IR showed Shin's pulse, hot and thumping somewhat faster than normal. Her vision detected a faint tremble of the hands. Fear.

She took a knee beside Takewashi. It put her eyes on a lower plane, but she did not care. "Renaldo. Why are the Talee trying to kill you?"

He shook his head. "I cannot. This is not the place."

"Renaldo, I was on Pantala. I saw. I know where we come from."

Takewashi smiled sadly and reached a gnarled, brown hand to her cheek. "Yes. Sweet child. That is the origin."

A thousand accusations boiled up. A thousand hatreds. All were irrelevant now.

"So why are the Talee trying to kill you?" she persisted. "Did you steal something? Do something to them? You used their technology to make us, to make GIs. Are they angry?" But how could they be angry, they'd known about it for as long as humans had made GIs, and done nothing, indicating no displeasure.

"Mr Takewashi," said Shin. Again, Sandy's hearing registered the faint tremor in his voice. "We have a suitable location for you. Will you discuss it when we get there?"

"Yes. Yes, with Cassandra. She will understand."

"Renaldo," Sandy tried again, but Shin was shaking his head. He indicated the door. Evidently he'd tried pleading, and other things. Sandy got up and followed Shin's direction to the door.

Shin shut the door, crossed the hall to the next door, and opened it. Within was a much smaller room, tasteful but not extravagant, with a modern desk and holographics. The night view, past garden trees, was the park and path lights on green grass.

"We're preparing a location now," said Shin, walking to his desk. Sandy closed the curtains. Shin lit a cigarette. That old habit still thrived on Earth; it was barely seen on Callay. Shin's lighter was silver and stylish, like his watch. He took a puff and sat against the desk. "If he's right, it will have to be total information blackout. Given what Cai can do."

His gaze asked questions. "I can't call HQ about Cai," she answered. "If Takewashi's right, we can't stop Cai from hearing." Cai. Dear God. How did you fight someone who hacked eyes in real time? Who put entire collective networks into involuntary VR? "Shin, we're going to have to work together on this."

"Can you?" Regarding her, serious and skeptical. "Can Ibrahim?"

"Ibrahim is the most fair-minded man I've ever met."

Shin smirked and took another puff. "Yes. Well, you should meet more men."

"You're plotting to remove us," said Sandy. Shin said nothing, smoking warily. "I get it. FedInt is the long-term structure, FSA HQ is short-term, the head of the snake. We're more replaceable than you. Your problem is that this is the relocation all over again. Earth interests dominating Federal interests.

That's why the Grand Council is now here and not there. Your institutional base is far broader than ours, but we have more popular support off-Earth, where it matters."

"You really think this is the time for such discussion?" Shin suggested with some disbelief.

Sandy walked to him, face-to-face. His wariness increased. He did not believe she would hurt him, or he'd never have allowed himself to be alone with her. But a man sensitive to mortal threats could not help but recall what she was, at this range.

"It's okay," she said. "We're plotting to remove you too. Eventually. And to reshape FedInt into something less Earth-centric and more FSA friendly."

Shin tapped ash into his desktop ashtray. "This I already knew. I'm a spy."

"No, you're *the* spy." A faint smile from Shin. She couldn't say she thought much of his nasty habit's smell. "My theory is Compulsive Narrative Syndrome. FSA and FedInt. GIs are less susceptible to it. The non-GIs in FSA were becoming convinced you were the enemy; you were becoming convinced we were the enemy."

"And apparently, since each was plotting to have the other removed, we both were correct in that assessment."

"No." Sandy shook her head. "Incorrect. I think all uplinks accentuate the process of CNS, the selective interpretation of data. SuperPsych have been picking up on that. Institutionalisation makes it worse. You were plotting because we were plotting. We were plotting because you were plotting. Chicken and egg, at some point, we have to stop. I think this is a good place to stop. What do you think?"

Shin thought about it. Tapped more ash into the tray. "Your presumption is that our differences are not grounded in functioning realities. I can't say I agree. FSA and FedInt stand for different things. Naive fools in the media cry that all squabbling political factions should just get along and put those differences aside. Until they realise that one of those differences is important to them, whereupon they become partisan players like the rest of us. Only the ignorant and the uninvolved crave bipartisanship. We're neither."

"We can talk about it," Sandy insisted. Her gaze inviting agreement.

"And we can talk about it *later*. If every fundamental disagreement spirals into out-of-control narrative ideology and institutional confrontation, then we'll end up like the League, tearing itself to bits."

Shin nodded slowly. "Yes. I have confidence that this intelligence takes priority for both of us. If Takewashi is not delusional."

"We can't presume that." She took a deep breath. "Shit."

Shin nodded again. "Shit indeed." Took a long drag and stubbed out his cigarette. "Let's begin."

Everyone was waiting for her in HQ's briefing room, the most secure room in the building. She hadn't even sent an emergency signal, just a low, meaningless pulse, with a few random beats thrown in. It meant nothing. Which in turn meant everything.

"Talee," Sandy told the gathered faces around the long table. It was past midnight, and the absence of so many top FSA figures from their usual routines, in the absence of an announced emergency, might be noticed. "Takewashi says the Talee are trying to kill him. The League too, but mostly he's scared of Talee. Says they're coming for him. He wants to be taken somewhere with no net access. That's why I couldn't say anything on the way back. Considering Cai."

Ashen-faced silence around the room. Barely a breath was heard. Ari was there, cold pads on his skull under a cap, head still throbbing after the sonic pulse that FedInt had hit the shuttle with. It had been inside the cabin, new tech that no one had known to look for, probably on the walls. Designed especially for use against GIs in enclosed spaces, it had concussed even Poole, Tuli, and Rhian. They were no worse for wear than Ari, save for their good humour. It had been cunningly done, all were aware. FedInt were players, and being spies rather than soldiers, perhaps somewhat better at playing the cunning angle.

"We need to go red," Reichardt said quietly. "The whole system."

"But they're only after Takewashi, right?" Hando asked.

"Yes," Sandy answered Reichardt, ignoring Hando. "Quietly." And glanced at Ibrahim. Ibrahim looked as grim as Sandy had seen him. Partly that was unhappiness with her, she knew. He'd given her orders on FedInt, she'd ignored them. Now, FedInt had Takewashi and were calling the shots. She'd explained her reasons, and he wasn't buying it. Sandy wasn't sure she'd be any different in his position. FedInt had a gun pointed at their heads. Unconditional trust, in that circumstance, was not feasible. Even if she was right, from Ibrahim's point of view she still might end up being wrong.

He nodded. "Give the signal. The system goes red. We must alert President Raza and Mr Ranaprasana."

"Sir," said Hando, "the more people who know, the more inevitable that Cai will find out. We simply can't keep him out of our systems."

"Then we'll have to keep the systems quiet," said Ibrahim. "Verbal communication only on this matter. And we'll have to implore those we tell to do the same."

"Safer not to tell them anything," someone volunteered.

"Given the Federation is still nominally a democracy, we don't have that luxury. Cassandra, Cai. Suggestions?"

"I could kill him," she said. And took a deep breath. "Or I could try. I'm not sure even autistic can stop him . . . and if he gets into my head, there's the killswitch . . . which can't be activated by any technology known to humans, but . . . well." A grim silence. "I think I'm a better soldier than him, to judge from Vanessa and Rhian's assessments from Pantala, but we've never seen him at full stretch, so that's uncertain also. All up, I'd give that a less-than-equal chance of success."

Ibrahim pursed his lips. "Yes. And Takewashi may be delusional. Best to let him explain himself fully first."

"He's being taken to a more secure location," Sandy continued. "Obviously they'll need to limit access, the location will be blind to most of us."

"Better and better," Hando muttered.

"Shin is frightened." Sandy looked firmly around at them all to make sure the gravity of that sank in. "I saw it, elevated pulse, trembling hands, nothing out of the ordinary, but real nonetheless. And he's sure as hell not scared of me, he's too smart for that. He agrees we have to work together, FedInt and FSA. On this, we can trust him."

"No, we can't," said Ari. Sandy stared at him. He was sitting farther up on the table, feet on a chair, face drawn in a permanent grimace. "This is an initial shock, but we've seen Talee get interventionist before. If they're just after Takewashi, then he'll readjust and we'll be back in the firing line . . ."

"What if they're not?" Sandy interrupted. "Just after Takewashi?"

"Then we'll need a secure foundation we can depend upon, and Federal Intelligence isn't it! Shin is pathologically incapable of accepting FSA leadership on this issue, and the higher the stakes get, the more he's going to grab at the steering wheel . . ."

"Ari!" Sandy snapped. "No more! This is Compulsive Narrative Syndrome, and it nearly got us all blown to hell out at the spaceport! We have to work with FedInt, because if there's anything to Takewashi's fears, we're going to need them!"

"Sir, this is a mistake," Ari said to Ibrahim. "They'll knife us first chance they get."

Ibrahim's craggy face looked deadly grim in the low light. "I agree with both of you," he said finally. "They will knife us, and we can't trust them. But for now we have no choice. We'll walk the tightrope because we have to." With a dangerous stare at Sandy. He wasn't happy about it. That being the case, Sandy knew that eight years of friendship wouldn't count for much, if Ibrahim felt she was becoming more liability than asset. If she pushed too hard, Ibrahim would sit her out.

She nodded. "Good enough."

"Cassandra," said Amirah, more composed and calm than most. "Any thoughts on Talee motivations?"

"To kill Takewashi? Hell, any number of reasons. *I've* wanted to kill Takewashi, and we know the Talee aren't pacifists." She ran a hand through her hair, thinking. That mannerism was new. She'd never made random, subconscious mannerisms in the past. "But targeting an individual, if they are, is a new step. We know they can do it, that's possibly what Cai and others like him were intended for in the first place. As to why . . ." she shrugged. "It's dangerous to guess too much. Let's wait to see what he says."

"Why not just give Takewashi to them?" Hando asked. "I mean, he's not that important to us that we're going to stand between him and the Talee?"

"No, you don't get it," said Reichardt. "Fleet have code for degrees of Talee contact. Talee have been minimally interventionist before. Pantala was a huge escalation, them destroying a League warship, but that was defensive, not aggressive. Takewashi's one of the best-defended people in the League. Was. And didn't think League could protect him, and now suggests we can't either. That means he expects Talee to come through us, to come through anyone, to get him. That's the nightmare scenario. We know Talee can be unstable and incredibly destructive. If that starts coming here . . ."

Deathly silence. Sandy had never seen outright fear in an FSA briefing before. But it was a time for firsts.

"Danya?" Danya started awake and remembered immediately that he had to keep still and quiet, or the drug pushers on the floor of the warehouse below would hear and send someone up with a gun to investigate the loft. But the air on his cheek was warm, not chill, and . . . no, that was the wrong memory, and the wrong reflex. He was on Callay, in Tanusha. In Sandy's house, in his own room, in a comfortable bed, with a surfboard against the wall and AR glasses on the bedside bench so as to check on Svetlana and Kiril any time he wanted . . . "Danya!"

He blinked and lifted his head to peer at the doorway. Kiril was there, in his Moondog pyjamas—his favourite cartoon character. Scruffy-haired and lightly freckled, and now a little confused . . . but that was Kiril, much of the time. "What's wrong, Kiri?"

"I just got a message from Cai."

"From Cai?" He blinked wider awake. "On your uplinks?" He picked up his glasses and peered at the timestamp . . . it was quarter past one in the morning. Cai had been helping periodically with Kiril's uplinks, giving advice to Sandy on how to help them grow in non-dangerous ways. But why would he be sending a message after one in the morning? "What did he say?"

"He said he just wanted to see how I was." Kiril wandered into the room to stand at Danya's bedside. "I was already awake, I was trying out some things."

"On your uplinks?" He wasn't wearing his headband, the one with the repressors that would talk to his uplinks and tell them to stay quiet, for a time at least. To help him sleep, as these days they were waking him. "Kiri, you have to leave the headband on. Sandy says you're giving them enough exercise during the day, you shouldn't do it at night as well."

"But I wanted to try something." With no real fear about the trouble it might cause. Kiril was brave. Danya tried to remember what it was like to be that brave.

"So what did Cai say?"

"He just said hello and that he couldn't sleep either. I think he's nice." Danya sighed. Kiril thought everyone he talked to was nice.

"I think he's nice too. But he's a very unusual GI, so we have to be careful with him. We're not sure if he's actually nice, or if he just seems nice. Understand?"

Kiril nodded. Danya didn't believe it. He'd had this conversation with Kiril a thousand times on Droze, be careful of this person, don't trust that person, but as soon as he turned his back, there would be Kiril, chatting away with some new friend.

"Now go and put your headband on, do you know where it is?"

Kiril nodded. "It's just by my bed." Danya ruffled his hair and kissed him.

Svetlana came in. "What's going on?"

Danya rolled his eyes. "Kiril's just going back to bed, with his headband on this time. Aren't you, Kiril?"

"I was just talking to Cai on my uplinks!" Kiril sat up on Danya's bed, all eager to start this new conversation, as though the previous one had never occurred. Danya groaned. "We were both awake, I think he could see me on the net. Sandy says that can happen when I'm awake, or with Cai it can happen anyway."

"Sandy's not here," said Svetlana, bouncing on the end of Danya's bed. "She hasn't been back all night."

"Sandy sent me a message an hour ago saying she had to work tonight," Danya explained. "She doesn't know when she'll be back."

Svetlana pouted. "That's not fair, why does she only message you?"

"Because I asked her to, and she doesn't want to wake you up." Danya was a light sleeper at the best of times, and Sandy had quickly learned that he would sleep less, and worry more, if he woke to find her gone with no explanation, than if she woke him herself with a quick message.

"I bet I could talk to her on my uplinks," Kiril suggested.

"No, Kiri," Danya said sternly. "She'll be very angry if you do, you know she doesn't like you using them at night at all." And far less than that, in fact. "Why don't you both go back to sleep?"

"I don't like how she's never here," Svetlana complained, lying on the bed by Danya's feet. "Doesn't she get tired?"

"She doesn't need as much sleep as we do," said Danya pointedly. "And we see her a lot more than some kids see their parents. I was talking to Raul Esparza, he was saying he only sees his dad for an hour each day, just before he goes to bed. We see Sandy much more than that."

"She's never here at night lately."

"But you're asleep, it's not like you're missing her at night."

"I just feel safer," said Svetlana. She stretched out tiredly, head on the covers.

"Svet," said Danya, "go back to bed."

"U-hmm," Svetlana agreed, dozing.

"I had a dream I was back in Droze," said Kiril. Svetlana's eyes opened to look at him. "That's why I couldn't sleep. I dreamed I was running away from a big lizard, and I was trying to find you, and you were looking for me, but you couldn't see me and you just kept walking past. And I tried to talk to you, but you couldn't hear me, and . . . and then a storm came up, and . . . and the lizard . . . I can't remember the next bit." He bit his lip, looking downcast and upset. "And Cali Wiley was there, and she kept trying to steal my apple." He frowned. "I can't remember how I got the apple. But she kept trying to steal it."

Svetlana's eyes flicked to Danya. Concern. "Cali Wiley died, Kiril," said Danya. "You remember that, don't you?"

"Yes, but she was trying to steal my apple. In my dream." His eyes were far away, concentrating. Evidently it had not been a nice dream. "I should have given her the apple. Cali Wiley was nice."

Cali Wiley had been a loudmouth fool, Danya recalled very well. But she'd been only twelve, and she hadn't deserved to end up dead in a ditch by an old warehouse in Rimtown. No one knew how. In Droze, they rarely did, and few people asked.

"Danya," said Kiril with sudden conviction, "we should go back to Droze with Sandy and get all the other street kids, and bring them back here. It's not fair that they're still in Droze, and we're here."

"We've talked about this, Kiril," Danya said quietly. "She's not allowed. I know she'd like to. But she wasn't really allowed to help *us*. She broke the rules for us."

"She could kill all the gangsters," Kiril said stubbornly. "She could stop them hurting street kids." Not all of them were gangsters, but to Kiril, every bad guy in Droze was a gangster. He hadn't been old enough for a more detailed understanding.

"Don't you think it's unfair of us to ask Sandy to go around killing people for us?" Danya asked him. "She's very good at it, but she doesn't really like to do it." Again he looked at Svetlana. Svetlana gazed back sombrely.

"I think she would," said Kiril, his brown eyes wide and earnest. "I think she'd kill anyone for us."

"Yeah," Svetlana murmured, in a more quietly adult tone than Danya had ever heard her use. "I think she would too, Kiri. But that's all the more reason why we shouldn't ask."

Danya woke at 7 to go running as he usually did, slipping out quietly so he didn't wake Svetlana, still asleep in her pyjamas on her side of the bed. Kiril had adjusted to sleeping alone, but Svetlana still came in sometimes, when something bothered her. Lifetime habits that your lives had once depended on were hard to break, and the kids at school who'd found out and teased them and made dirty jokes could go to hell; it just increased the number of kids he had no interest spending time with. Give *them* five years in Droze, scared to sleep in case someone killed them in the night, and see how fast *they* started sleeping in groups.

He came downstairs carrying his shoes, to find Sandy already in the kitchen, with a small arsenal laid out on the benches. The understairs secure safe was open, a steel compartment behind the panelling, unlockable only with secure uplink codes. Within, now laid on the benches, were a pair of snub-nosed assault rifles, three pistols, various magazines, an underside grenade launcher (currently detached) and a brace of multipurpose grenades, to be fired or thrown.

"Morning," she said breezily, cleaning the stripped-down barrel of one rifle. She had synthetic oil out and cleaning implements. Every weapon gleamed, and the air smelled of lubricant. She wore neat-fitting cargo pants and a sleeveless shirt, bare arms lean with muscle.

Danya submitted to the morning kiss so that he could take a closer look at the weapons. "You keep grenades here?"

"Sure. They're actually safer than guns. You can't set them off without uplink or biometric triggers." Meaning that the molecular sensors would have to recognise her finger contact, or her breath, before priming. Unactivated, the charge was as chemically inert as granite; you could play cricket with them.

Danya fetched a banana and some juice, watching her fast hands reassemble the weapon, automatic, like tying shoelaces.

"You mind waiting until Poole gets here?" Sandy asked him.

Danya blinked, stretching his quads, mouth full of banana. "Poole's coming?"

"Yep. He's on security detail for you guys today."

"He's coming to school?" Sandy nodded, disassembling one of the pistols at similar speed. "Cool." Cautiously. It had happened a few times before, and the school didn't mind, Canas being the neighbourhood it was. "Something going on?"

"Nothing I can talk about." Threading the barrel with the cleaning tool. "And I'll be taking Kiril today. He gets the day off school."

"Okay." He did his calf stretches against the bench with the just-cleaned rifle, getting a better look. "When are you going to teach me to use one of these?"

"Hopefully never. But I can't stop you from learning when you're old enough."

"Yeah. Cause whoever might want to hurt us will be nice enough to wait until I'm older."

Sandy looked at him, eyes lidded as she cleaned. Weighing options, but for now, unconvinced. "You gonna carry to school?" she asked drily.

"Seems a pity to have them at home and not be able to use them if I needed to," he reasoned.

"And Svetlana will want lessons if you get them, and we all know how that turned out, last time she had a gun."

"Yeah. She saved my life." Sandy's gaze remained unreadable. That was odd, usually her guard was down at home. Reminders of Svetlana's most recent and profound trauma usually got a reaction. Today, nothing.

Sandy polarised the cruiser's windows on the way in, so that Kiril could not see where they were going. In reality, it was Kingly, a beachside suburb beyond the main Tanushan grid and not far from her favourite surfing spots. All network traffic blanked and Kiril wearing his repressor headband, she landed on a sandy vacant lot that was used as a temporary transition zone, then drove to a nondescript suburban house using forward cameras and into the carport. She depolarised the windows as the carport sealed behind them, and interior lights revealed bare concrete.

"Sandy, where are we?" asked Kiril, looking up from his compslate.

Sandy fought back a smile, shutting down the cruiser systems individually to make sure none of the automatics would relay something they shouldn't. "Why did I polarise the windows, Kiril?"

"So I couldn't see."

"So why would I tell you where we are?"

Kiril thought about it. "Oh. Sorry."

"Don't be sorry. Stow that slate and let's go. Out this side, please." Gesturing him to climb across and come out through her driver's door. He did, as she pulled her pistol. "Here." She picked him up with her right arm— he was getting too big for that really, but weight was hardly an issue for her.

"But I wanna walk!" he insisted as she went to the only obvious door in the carport's concrete walls.

"Tough," she said. "Open the door, would you?" He did that, as her hands were full. Sandy stood side profile for a moment in the doorway, pistol not raised but ready. Ahead, another stretch of corridor, all dark.

"Why do you have your gun out?" Kiril asked, noticing that for the first time. He'd seen her handle weapons before, but never like this, entering some strange Tanushan place.

"I'm being very careful this morning," said Sandy, walking down the corridor, adjusting her gait for Kiril's weight. "We're going to see an old friend of mine."

"Who?"

"You'll see in a minute."

"I can't see anything."

"That's okay, I can see fine."

At the downward stairs Sandy saw defensive emplacements in the walls, probably gas, possibly those sonic blast weapons they'd used in the shuttle. Anti-GI defences, for sure. But FedInt would never risk hurting Kiril. Assuming they knew all of what Kiril was. Given they had Takewashi to talk to, she didn't doubt it.

The corridor ended on a new door, which opened as she approached, flooding the darkness with light. Here was another bare room but for a pair of lean, doglike creatures who stood and studied her with unreadably curious demeanours.

"Oh look," said Sandy, to blunt any misgivings Kiril might have. "Nice doggies."

"They're not dogs," said Kiril. "They're asura. They come from Emerald, they're really smart." The asura circled aside from their bed baskets on the floor, lean-faced and sinewy. Bodies more catlike in their agility, but the faces were all dog, thrusting snout and pricked ears. "They're kind of dangerous," Kiril added as he recalled what he'd read.

"Well, luckily for us, so am I." Sandy walked slowly past them to the next door. The asura weren't there for fighting, she knew. Their smell was exceptional and when combined with intelligence made them suitable for anti-GI work. She wasn't especially worried—if FedInt hadn't trained these two to behave, they'd be searching for two new ones very quickly. She usually liked animals, but not these ones, with Kiril on one arm. And not some humans either.

Beyond the next door was an open-plan house, pale-blue floor tiles and white walls, overlooking a beach. As Sandy had suspected, the tunnel had led beneath dunes to another house. It appeared to be built into the dune face here, with sand above. It meant there was only one point of assault for any attacker—the windows onto the beach, about which there were doubtless many other defences.

In the living room before the windows, Shin got to his feet. With him were three other agents, two men and a woman, similarly rising. And Ragi, wearing a nice suit, but semi-casual without a tie. Like a young man dressing up for the first time for a formal function, Sandy thought . . . which was not far from the truth.

Amongst them all sat Takewashi in his usual kimono, this one was white with silver trim, in a comfortable white chair before the brilliant sunlight of a Tanushan beach. Sandy glimpsed a surfer, out beyond the break, awaiting a wave. The swell did not look promising today, but surfers were optimists.

All stood for her arrival, Takewashi shakily, on his cane. Seated alongside, Ragi hovered, ready to offer assistance. Sandy refrained from rolling her eyes.

"Cassandra!" said Takewashi, his face creasing into a smile that hid his eyes completely. "Oh, and you have brought me a visitor! This young man must be Kiril Kresnov." Sandy let Kiril down, to stand by her side. But he took her right hand, unasked. "Kiril, my name is Renaldo Takewashi. I'm an old friend of your mother's."

It made Sandy edgy, this man pressing these concepts into Kiril's head.

None of the kids were entirely clear on the whole "mother" thing—Danya and Svetlana had known their real mother, and Kiril had heard stories about her. Sandy did not want them to forget and had even helped them to find information on Lidya Seravitch, with photographs and life history, as much as Federation investigation into League archives could reveal from this distance. They'd not yet taken to calling Sandy "mum," and Sandy wasn't sure she wanted them to. She was their legal guardian, and best adult friend, and lethal protector. The head of their family, such as it was. That was plenty, but now Takewashi, for his own purposes, came thrusting that word at Kiril. Imposing judgements on him.

"Hello," said Kiril. "I've heard about you. Sandy told me."

"Kiril," Sandy reminded, "call him Mr Takewashi. That's the proper thing to say with an older man."

Kiril nodded. "How did you get to Tanusha?" he asked, completely forgetting what she'd just told him. Sandy nearly sighed. "Were you on that ship that the League were trying to blow up?"

Takewashi straightened, with a look of amazement that was part real and part exaggeration for the boy. "Well! Cassandra, you have a smart one! Yes, I was on that ship, Kiril. And do you know? You were one of the reasons I wanted to come back to Callay so badly."

Kiril looked unsure, a half-frown half-smile. Uncertain if he was being made fun of. "Me?"

"Yes. Please, won't everyone sit?" Takewashi gestured around. All the agents looked to Shin first and sat only at his indication. A two-person sofa was beside Takewashi's chair, at ninety degrees and angled to the windows. Sandy took it and patted the cushions for Kiril to get up alongside.

Shin and a few of the agents were looking with some concern at Kiril. "Cassandra," said Shin, "why did you bring him?"

Probably it upset their psych profiles. They knew she was protective, dangerously so if threatened. They wouldn't think she'd bring him to work, especially not *this* work. Which told her that they *didn't* know the full details of what he was. Or not what she suspected. And any time she did something that violated FedInt's psych profile, they got nervous.

"He knows," said Sandy, looking at Takewashi. "All these little seeds he's sowed across the galaxy. Ragi was one. Weren't you, Ragi?"

"It would appear that way," said Ragi. Looking at Takewashi with something approaching . . . not worship, no. Ragi had an IQ off the charts and was far too rational for that. But there was longing in his eyes, and the hope of answers. "From the beginning, there were few other explanations of why I could exist. Different as I am."

"The uplinks in Kiril's head are another," said Sandy. "Renaldo was hooked into the corporate research programs on Droze from the beginning. After all, he's old enough to have been in on the original discovery. Weren't you?"

With a steady gaze at Takewashi. Takewashi's gaze dropped briefly to consider the pistol, still in her hand. No one had demanded that she put it away or give it up. All knew that she was nearly as lethal without it, and one did not invite Cassandra Kresnov into a room unless you were confident she would not hurt you. Thus their disquiet at unpredicted behaviour.

"Its immediate aftermath, yes," Takewashi conceded. "Understand, Cassandra, Chancelry Corporation was only small then. A few scientists and businessmen, making a joint exploratory venture. They discovered Talee outposts on Pantala and wanted to monetise their discovery. Before League Gov stepped in and took it from them."

"Which they did."

"Oh, but with a large slice for Chancelry," said Takewashi. "But they did not know how to make sense of what they'd found. Thus they called for my expertise, and I was able to understand the technology. It was *so* advanced, Cassandra. So advanced. I used every simulation then available to me, every processor, every AI matrix, and still I felt that my brain would bleed from the effort." He spread his hands widely within flowing sleeves. "And yet here we are." Indicating both her and Ragi.

"Mr Takewashi," Ragi asked earnestly. "How did you make the leap between the second- and third-generation neural models? The technological concepts involved had nearly nothing in common with where human research—League research—had reached at the time, and . . ."

"He didn't," Sandy interrupted. Watching the old man with half-lidded eyes. "Renaldo's initial training wasn't neuroscience, or biotech. It was linguistics."

"The neurology of linguistics, Cassandra," Takewashi corrected with a benign smile.

"You're a translator," said Sandy. "You translated what you found in Talee symbols and language into things humans could understand, you borrowed and copied, you didn't create anything."

Takewashi shook his head. "Now, now, Cassandra, that's not quite right . . ."

"And then you claimed all the credit for yourself, because how lucky for you, your government decided it would keep these discoveries a secret and let the Federation think that League science alone had made this astounding breakthrough. Or did you play some role in persuading them of that decision also?"

A flash of frustration crossed Takewashi's face. Perhaps anger, quickly suppressed. The too-wide smile replaced it, like a slash. "Cassandra, I have come this far to help you. Perhaps you should think of that before hurling these grotesque accusations. . . ."

"He's not your creator, Ragi," Sandy told the bewildered young GI by Takewashi's side. "He's a fraud. Always has been. He's been playing with things he's never truly understood, and now he's reached the last page of the Talee instruction manual, and he's scared and out of ideas."

Takewashi glared at her, jaw set hard. FedInt agents looked urgently to Shin for guidance, for hints of how they might intervene. Shin merely watched, always cautious.

Sandy leaned forward and put her arms on her knees, pistol loose in hand. "If you've set them on my boy," she said coolly, "if you've made some trouble with the Talee that brings them here and puts Kiril in danger, then you and I will have a real problem. Do you understand?"

It had scared her since she'd known where Kiril's uplinks came from. Takewashi's insider at Chancelry Corporation—Margaritte Karavitis, a mole of his, who Sandy suspected but had never been able to prove had played a key role in Kiril's operation.

"Did you give her the tech?" she persisted. "Karavitis? You had all these pages of Talee manuals you hadn't gotten to yet, or hadn't found a way to make work—that's why there's so many different kinds of synthetic neurology, isn't it? Why I'm a rare and unusual kind, and Ragi's another kind again. And Jane was. More pages in the Talee manual—let's try this one, this one looks like fun. And so another one of us is born and spends an entire life wrestling with the bloody consequences of your curiosity."

"Cassandra, you don't understand," Takewashi said sternly. Nearly composed, with effort. "League's use of Talee technology uplinks is causing a neurological and sociological condition, as you know . . . or rather, a neurological condition whose manifestation is only observable in sociological outcomes. A group condition, of transmitting thoughts, of forming collective identities.

"We were working on cures. But we were not working fast enough, so League Gov went to the Torah Systems, to Pantala, where the regulations are . . . less onerous. They were desperate, and still are. You saw the results there, the GIs used for terrible experiments. Synthetic brains are similar enough to human brains that they make a good template to study the technological effects of uplink activity and data-process distribution. I would not allow it!"

His voice shook with anger, his gnarled knuckles tightening upon the cane.

"I would not allow it in my labs, and so they left and took it to Pantala, where the Corporations were beyond my reach. But I had a mole there. Karavitis, a talented researcher. They knew she was mine, but they did not fear me, and valued what information she possessed. My research was advanced, and the Corporations of the Torah Systems have no real knowledge of the information they possess—it is all residual data, their only advantage comes from their utter lack of morals in pursuit of results. Karavitis suggested to them a technique. It is the best thing I have yet developed. My brightest hope. I did not ask that they implant it in a child, but in children it achieves the best results."

"What is it?" Sandy asked. Takewashi knew better than most what her unwavering stare meant.

"It is . . ." Takewashi exhaled hard and stared down at the floor. "It is something I have not dared to use before now." He looked up. "Cassandra. You are aware that the Talee are a dual-ELE species?"

Sandy nodded. No surprised looks or frowns from the others. Of course not, they were spies. If the FSA knew, FedInt would know. "Self-inflicted, I know."

"Twenty years ago," Takewashi continued, "I had a visit. From a synthetic woman who was not of human construction. You are aware of these individuals." Again, Sandy nodded. "Fleet and ISO had known of them for some time before, but this was my first encounter. She warned me that there was one branch of research that I could not explore. That the Talee would make certain would never succeed, should we try. She was quite explicit.

"And so for fifteen years I did as she asked, and avoided the field entirely. Until League's problems began to manifest, and I returned to it. The synthetic neurology involved led me to new uplink technology, which grew by self-analysis and learning. I could not have attempted it twenty years ago even had I tried. But now, the technology has moved along, and whatever its Talee origins, Cassandra, we *do* now understand considerably the fundamentals."

"So test it on your own damn kids, why don't you?" Sandy replied dangerously.

"I was not able to develop the technology sufficiently to create a working model," Takewashi said quietly. "But Chancelry succeeded, with Karavitis's help."

"Were there others? Or was Kiril the only one?"

"There are others," Takewashi confirmed. "Still in Chancelry custody. All in good health."

Sandy looked at Kiril. He was quiet in that way he got when adults were having interesting conversations, listening intently. A smart boy, but not so genius-smart that he could join in. Just a regular smart kid, who didn't deserve this. Sandy took a deep breath.

"Why are the Talee trying to kill you?" she asked.

"The technology that I was warned against is feared by the Talee," Takewashi said sombrely. "They think it responsible for their dual catastrophes. They do not allow anyone to possess it. Amongst their own kind, the punishment for possession or development is death. I was warned that that exclusion would extend to humans too."

"Oh dear fucking god," said Shin, and got to his feet to stare out the window, hands on his head. And muttered something else, in Chinese. Otherwise, stunned silence from the spies, if only to see their implacable boss so upset.

"Sandy?" said Kiril, gazing up at her with dawning concern. "Sandy, what does that mean?" Sandy couldn't move. Her heart was thumping, her vision dropped into full multi-spectrum. Ready to fight and move, but with no one to kill.

"But our real problem," Takewashi continued sombrely, "is that the technology may be the only way of stopping the League's condition. If it works, we can adapt and upgrade the population. But at present, even if we were sure it does work, which we are not, such a policy would bring us into a full-scale war against the Talee, which we would surely lose."

Shin stood, hands on hips, and looked at Kiril. Kiril now looked a little scared. And not before time either, Sandy thought. She grasped his hand.

"Sir," said one of the FedInt agents, "if this one boy brings down Talee assassins on our heads . . ." And left the sentence incomplete. Considering the gun in Sandy's hand.

"This one boy," Ragi said coolly, "could be the best hope of preventing humanity from destroying itself. Why such fear of aliens, when the real monster is ourselves?"

"Yes, Ragi," Takewashi agreed. "And so I came here, to warn you. League got wind of my departure and wanted it stopped at any cost, given my knowledge, and the blow to League prestige. But what I share with you here is paramount. The Federation must assist the survival of this technology, even should it mean resisting Talee agents. The League insists it does not need Federation help, and fears that Federation help would mean the end of League as a political, independent entity. They may be right. But that has always been secondary to me, against the advancement, and survival, of the human race."

"There's not another way?" Shin asked. "We have advanced labs, in Tanusha. And funding beyond anything the League could offer, should we offer it. With your help, you could achieve in months what in the League would take years."

"The advantage of this technology is that its success is already established, amongst the Talee themselves," said Takewashi. "It is known to work on them but to have deleterious side effects. To develop entire new technologies from scratch is an operation of guesswork and trial that takes unavoidably enormous periods of time. Time that we do not have."

"What side effects?" Shin pressed. "On the Talee?"

A keening wail filled the room, rising up, then falling down, with full, alien vibrato. The FedInt agents looked at each other. One went to the other room, but the asura were already coming into the main room, loping and circling on sinewy legs. Another let out a wail, like the first, body taut, muzzle searching the ceiling. The agents looked alarmed. Sandy stood, gesturing for Kiril to stay on the sofa.

Shin pulled out a small handheld radio, the simplest of old-tech, and unhackable. "The asura's upset," he said shortly. "Anything?"

Another wail from an asura, its diaphragm throbbing. "Everyone's autistic?" Sandy asked in a low voice. Combat mode seemed strange without uplinks, no cross-referencing of data on her sub-visual.

"All uplinks are off," one of the agents confirmed, weapon out, backing slowly toward a wall. He plucked at the elastic band around his wrist and winced as it snapped his skin. Clever, Sandy thought—Talee-GIs fought by VR, but most straight-human VR failed to accurately replicate pain.

"Kiril's uplinks aren't full emersion-capable," she said, crouching by the boy. "Kiril, if you see anything, you tell me, yes? Anything that shouldn't be here."

Kiril nodded fast, looking frightened.

"They can't be here so fast!" Takewashi muttered, still in his chair, having nowhere safer to be. "I had more time!"

"Sandy?" Kiril volunteered nervously. "Cai called me last night."

Sandy, Shin, and the FedInt agents all stared. "What did he say?" Sandy asked.

Another wail from the asura, circling now by the windows but with eyes still directed to the ceiling. "Just hi," said Kiril. "I couldn't sleep, and he couldn't sleep either, and he said that maybe I should have a glass of warm milk. But I don't like warm milk very much."

"Cai?" said Takewashi, frowning. Then with dawning comprehension, "You have Talee agents here *already*?"

Sandy thought furiously. A Talee attack would establish a VR framework around the target, simultaneously fooling it and every system in it that nothing was wrong. Everyone here was autistic, systems allowing no external communication. So the Talee *should* find nothing they could hack into. . . .

Shin's radio crackled. "*We have a cruiser breaking lanes. Hold on . . .*" A whine from beyond the front windows. Sandy looked and saw a flat angle of concrete arising from the front garden wall amidst the sand . . . a defensive mount, on this FedInt property, searching the incoming cruiser. Beneath was a mag-launcher, targeting on an articulated mount.

"Is the defence grid autistic too?" she snapped.

"Yes," said Shin, "but it's . . ." and looked to the rotating mount out the front windows. "MOVE!"

Sandy grabbed Kiril and threw herself toward the rear wall. All hell exploded about her, high-velocity rounds shredding walls, furniture, people, eardrums. She rolled behind the supporting wall at the rear of the living room, covering Kiril as best she could, then grasping him beneath her as she scrambled on hands and knees for the hall as rounds smashed fist-sized holes in the walls above her.

She glimpsed fast around the corner, saw devastation, white walls sprayed red, Ragi low against one wall with his hand gone, Takewashi still in his chair but missing head and arm. She ducked back as rounds from the emplacement tore across the near wall, just missing Ragi, then swivelled back to some new motion. . . . She leaped up the hall, rolling to collide and slide back-first with a wall, cradling Kiril from the impact, then scrambling again on hand and knees. Grabbed a doorframe one-handed and shoved hard, shooting herself in a power slide up the hall, figuring that if the design of this place was like she suspected, the other hidden entry tunnel would be up this end by the second bathroom. . . .

And here before the bathroom doorway she found a FedInt man crouched, waving frantically to her . . . and just as abruptly his eyes glazed, and his pistol raised straight at her. But he was too close, and Sandy smacked the pistol from his hand with force enough that he gasped and clutched his hand.

"Autistic!" she yelled at him. "Autistic or they'll hack you!"

"I wasn't . . . I mean I didn't . . ."

And she dove into the bathroom, aware that someone else was following— a wall in the shower stall was false, and she ducked through and down stairs three then five at a time, then a corner at the bottom and running in the dark. A sprint, clutching Kiril, reminding herself not to do that too hard, usually even her subconscious combat-mode brain could still recall to do that.

Then up stairs and into a basement garage, empty of vehicles, just utility pipes and the ongoing echo of hammering gunfire nearby. And a FedInt agent atop the stairs, who gestured frantically for her to come, and then as she got close, abruptly swung a gun to her head. Sandy slammed the woman back against the doorframe with a forearm.

"Fight it!" she yelled. "Stay autistic, dammit! Don't let them in!" The woman's stare was confused, no telling what mental state she was in, half in and out of VR . . . but if she could see her . . .

The shriek informed her of an incoming round and she hit the floor, covering Kiril once more as the explosion tore through a far wall and peppered the halls with debris. These were beachfront houses, lightly built holiday homes . . . her fine-tuned hearing caught the howl of the cruiser. . . . She smacked the woman's head back against the wall, and she slumped unconscious, but at least the Talee would no longer be targeting through her eyes. Then the hacked air defence emplacement next door began to blast through the walls, and she ran at a big window and jumped, turning her back to take out the glass and sailing to hit a dune on the far, downward slope. She slid, shielding Kiril all the while, as staccato shots shredded the house behind them like paper.

A glance at Kiril showed him in shock, clutching her frantically, all sandy but not obviously hurt, but she couldn't ask if he was okay, as the cruiser circled in, one gull door lifted in flight, a weapon scanning ominously out the window. She'd barely scratch it with a pistol, she knew, before that door gunner took her out. He'd be a GI, perhaps as unlikely to miss as she was. She had to jump, from an angle the gunner couldn't hit, and take them hand-to-hand . . . but the pilot was being smart and careful, not getting too close. If he kept circling, he'd see her, and with this soft sand beneath her she wouldn't have the leverage to jump that far. . . .

A shot hit the cruiser. She could barely see it, but from somewhere behind came fast, accurate rifle fire. Five shots a second, slower than weapon-auto, but faster than unaugmented human fire—a GI then. The cruiser veered, wobbling as its rear gens took all the damage, and fleeing before it took more.

"Come on, Kiri, just a bit farther." She struggled along the dune, horrified by how slow the burden of a child could make her, now she couldn't just leap and crash through and over things. She did leap the next house's low wall, an easy enough thing to calculate without a great impact, then up the side of the property to the rear, then paused at the carport exit to peer out. Running up the road was Ragi, clutching his damaged forearm. A little inland, and up the hill overlooking the beach, came a crackle of fully automatic rifle fire—her guardian angel again. Was one of the FSA's GIs out here, looking out for her on Ibrahim's orders? She couldn't use uplinks to find out.

She pointed uphill for Ragi's benefit, then ran that way, along the road, then the first left, heading sharply upslope. Return fire was coming in from the cruiser now, but only rifle fire, hitting a house near the crest. Again the sniper fired, from a different window, changing positions before new fire came back. Aside from a few dogs barking, there were no people to be seen or heard—the beachside suburbs were sparsely populated on weekdays, thank all the Hindu gods.

And here, parked by the side of the uphill road, was a groundcar. Sandy put Kiril down beside it, fished in her pocket for the cord that was always there, and plugged it direct into the insert socket at the back of her head. Connected the other end to her belt unit, unhooking it to press it on the door lock . . . flash, it felt as though her head had been grasped in a giant vice, with pressure about to split her skull.

She tore the unit away from the door, gasping . . . the short wireless distance between unit and door lock had been all it took for Talee GIs to access and reverse-hack the most sophisticated combat GI yet commissioned by humans. Dear god.

"Sandy," Kiril protested, "we need an aircar, not a groundcar." If she'd had time to feel anything, such lucid thinking from her little boy under pressure would have made her the proudest ever.

But, "Cruisers use air traffic command," she said, and smashed the window with her fist. "It'll get hacked and flown into something. Groundcars don't." She got in, plugged herself directly into the console, and got an override two seconds later. "Get in."

She dragged him over her lap and into the passenger seat, as downslope Ragi came running, with one of the asura loping panicked circles about his heels. Kiril scrambled to try and open the rear door for him but couldn't reach. Ragi did it himself, tumbling in as the asura followed, and Sandy gunned the car into fast reverse and a skidding one-eighty. If the sniper was as smart as he seemed, he'd have seen this and would know exactly what was going on.

Sandy roared uphill and screeched to a halt by the house. And the front gate *opened*, thank you very much, and a middle-sized female figure with a baseball cap and a large rifle exited and closed it neatly behind her. Kiril scrambled between the seats into the rear with Ragi and the asura, as the sniper got in, and looked at her . . .

Sandy's pistol snapped up and levelled at the woman's face. Unremarkable features, though strong, and calm. Shortish brown hair beneath the cap. A combat GI, unseen by Sandy for the past six years. At the time, the very worst of enemies.

"Hi there, sis," said Jane. "We gonna go, or you want to sit here until they find a new cruiser and kill us all?"

CHAPTER TWELVE

It wasn't much of a signal that Poole received. Just a blip, a heavily encrypted and rerouted nothing, an accidental static transmission from some random function of the network. But it was enough. He clipped the little autistic plug to the back of his head, linked it to his earpiece, and stood up. Walked six paces to Svetlana's desk in the classroom, where she sat with other kids considering the best way to solve a maths problem.

"We have to go," he told her.

Svetlana stared up at him. "Now?" Poole nodded. "I'll get my bag."

"Leave it here, the school can look after it."

Svetlana excused herself from the group, the other kids now also staring. The entire class turned to watch them go, and the teacher came uncertainly to intercept them by the door.

"Can't talk," Poole explained, not halting. "Have to go." The teacher, being from Canas high-security school, nodded and asked no questions.

They walked into the empty school corridor. "What's happened?" Svetlana asked.

"Prearranged signal," said Poole. "I'd rather not say here." Between these echoing walls, sound travelled. "Let's get Danya."

He'd memorised their schedules, as there was no way to check Danya's location by uplinks. Danya was in chemistry class, also performing some exercise in a small group, with beakers, white coats, and protective eyewear. Poole got his attention from the doorway, a fast military signal of "leave now, this way." Danya nodded, took off coat and glasses, and left. The class barely noticed.

"Trouble?" he asked, as they descended stairs to the ground floor.

"Precaution," said Poole. Danya nodded and walked fast.

The day outside was warm and sunny, barely a cloud in the sky. It seemed impossible that something, somewhere was less than perfect. The school playing field gleamed green and humid from recent watering as they walked across it.

"We're not going home?" Danya guessed.

"No. Rendezvous with Sandy. Prearranged spot."

"She never told me."

"Only came up with it this morning," Poole explained. "We think it might be Talee." Through the gate surrounding the playing field and onto the sidewalk beneath leafy trees.

"Talee?" Both kids stared at him. "You mean Cai?"

"Possibly Cai himself."

"That's why we're not driving?" Danya guessed.

"Not for now. Sandy doesn't trust Canas systems if Cai's involved. The higher the network intensity, the more control Talee-GIs get over it."

He half expected Svetlana to take his hand for comfort. He'd seen other girls her age do that, when upset. But Svetlana left his hands free, in case he needed a weapon in a hurry. Thank god he was looking after *these* kids. The prospect of Talee-GIs as enemies was scary. *He* was a bit frightened, if he thought about it. Luckily, he didn't make a habit of thinking.

Sandy drove fast along winding suburban roads, tires skidding on sand patches and slopes. The landscape remained wild out here, Tanushan central planners kept wanting to landscape like the main city, but locals resisted, preferring the rustic beach-side feel. She dodged light traffic and a couple of cyclists, heading back toward a trunk road that would in turn get them to the freeway.

"We should slow down," said Ragi, pale and wincing with his bloody stump squeezed under his armpit. "Traffic central will register us as speeding, and a stolen vehicle. Talee will hack traffic central in no time."

"Yes, but so will FedInt," said Sandy. Driving with a direct cord from her head to the dash, she had full access to car systems without risking a wireless hack. But mostly she monitored the cabin rear-view camera, to watch Kiril in the backseat. He was crying, the great, gasping sobs of a child badly terrified. "FedInt know what just happened, they'll be looking for an escaping vehicle. We might get help."

"Do we want their help?" said Jane, patient in the passenger seat, rifle propped to the ceiling. "Given what we just saw?"

"Maybe." She rounded a fast bend and guessed the best turn ahead. No net access meant no maps, so she didn't even know the way. And no one in an infotech dreamworld ever thought to put up road signs. "They could at least run interference."

The road looked less promising, turning into a house-lined cul-de-sac. She screeched the car sideways, then roared back the way they'd come, seeking the other turnoff.

"Look," said Jane, "you can either watch the road or the kid." Sandy shot her an evil look and screeched into the next turn. "We could use your shooting if they come at us again, you're still a better shot than me." Though with Jane, they both knew, the margins were so close it would be very hard to measure. But if Jane took the rear seat in another attack, would she use her body to shield Kiril with rounds incoming?

"Take over," said Sandy, unplugging herself and moving to the rear seat, taking Jane's rifle with her. At speed on winding roads, regular humans would have found it difficult, but she and Jane made it work in barely two seconds. Only now she displaced the asura, who instinctively knew to get out of her way, and squeezed into the just-vacated front passenger seat.

"Hello doggy," said Jane, scratching the animal's muzzle while steering them into a sharp deceleration and corner through a stop sign.

Sandy hugged Kiril. "It's okay, Kiri," she said. "You had a bad shock. You'll feel better in a minute." Thank god he hadn't seen very much, pressed to her chest. But he was well old enough to know they'd both nearly been killed, and others had been, and that was bad enough. "It's okay, Kiri. You'll be okay."

"I'm fine too," Ragi said drily. "Save for my hand. Thanks for asking."

"You're a GI," Jane told him. "Suck it up, princess."

"Yes, but I'm not a combat GI."

"And it shows." She found a larger road with a bump and Gs pressing them to one side, then a roar of acceleration, and passing several other vehicles.

Ragi looked disbelievingly at Sandy, with a jerk of his head to the front seat. "This is your . . . sister?"

"Same designation," Jane said calmly. "Different styling. Different tape teach. Different attitude. She tried to kill me."

"I let you live," Sandy corrected coldly.

"Don't worry, sis, I learned my lesson. I've changed."

"That was you before, the day Cresta was killed? The sniper who hit my car?"

"Warning shots," said Jane. "There was a PRIDE team about to drop the hammer on you guys. I thought I'd break you up."

"And the informant who gave us the tip on the Pyeongwha terrorists?"

"One and the same."

"Whose orders?" Sandy demanded. "Takewashi's?"

"Yep."

"Takewashi's dead."

"Figured as much," Jane said sombrely. "I think he knew they'd get him, whether he stayed or came here. He sent me ahead to look out for you."

"Why?"

"He never said. But I figured it was the Talee, since you wouldn't need protection from anyone else. Only the Talee aren't after you, are they? Or Chief Shin, or anyone else, now that Renaldo's gone. They're after the kid."

Sandy gave her another evil look, thankful Kiril was still sobbing too much to hear. "Thanks a lot, that's a real help."

"What are you going to do, keep it from him?" Sarcastically. No kidding she'd changed. There was expression now in Jane's tone, inflection and personality. But Sandy was far from certain she liked the personality she saw. "When those damn alien GIs keep shooting at him, he'll figure something's up. That reminds me, where are we going?"

"We're getting my other kids."

Jane frowned. "Wait, they've got alien uplink implants too?"

"No. But I've got an evolving psych profile of the Talee running, and they're methodical as hell. When they intervene, they go all in. Anyone with direct personal knowledge of Kiril's uplinks is at risk. Plus they might just want to stretch me defensively by going after multiple targets."

"Thereby luring you into predictable locations so they can kill you," said Jane. "Which you're doing, strategic genius that you are."

"You know, I heard having a sister can be a pain in the neck," said Sandy. "I'm beginning to see it."

Danya, Svetlana, and Poole took light rail from outside the Canas gate six to nearby Ludhiana. Ludhiana was walking distance; they'd all done it after school to visit the markets or the adventure playground in Ambedkar Park, but the rail was much faster. It let them off at the maglev station at Ambedkar Park, and Danya caught Svetlana's glances at the playground's mazes and games as they ascended the escalator. Wondering about normalcy, he knew, and when she'd get to play there again.

Station traffic was light at midmorning, and the board showed five minutes until the next train. They'd have known that already if they'd been using AR glasses, giving kids a similar but much simpler capability than adults had with uplinks. But now, they were all dumb and blind. Normally in any emergency, Sandy would have called immediately and given word about Kiril. They'd had no communication on Droze either, but their little patch of Droze had been Rimtown and its immediate neighbourhood, and they'd known where everything was and had arranged many rendezvous points in case something went wrong. Without coms, Tanusha seemed impossibly vast, a jungle of people and randomness.

Poole, Danya noticed as they waited against the wall farthest from the platform edge, was calmly scanning one way then the other. Mostly working people on the platform, a more predictable crowd than the exuberant Tanushan evenings. A number of young mothers with strollers going about their baby-centred day. Some older folks. A train arrived on the other platform, a gentle whoosh that defied its gleaming size.

"Can you see them?" Danya murmured to Poole. "Their body temperature?" Human-made GIs had lower body temperature that could give them away. But not always, beneath clothes.

"Maybe," said Poole. What was Cai's body temperature, Danya wondered? Had anyone thought to check?

"Danya, I don't like this," Svetlana said quietly at his side. "We should hide."

"We have to get to Sandy," Danya replied. "That's the only way to be safe."

"We're too exposed."

"Well, we can't take a cruiser, Cai could track anything on the grid."

"And you don't think he could track trains?" Svetlana retorted.

"Maybe. But he can't track people walking to the station. Just keep an eye out."

"Gee, *duhh!*" said Svetlana. Her eyes hadn't stopped tracking even as they talked.

The opposing train left, and their own arrived. It was barely a quarter full, most passengers finding seats against the curving tube sides. With so few interior partitions, the whole length of the maglev was visible from within, and everyone in it. Danya realised Svetlana was probably right.

"Svet," he said as they took seats, "why don't you . . ." But she was already gone, wandering up the train as the doors closed and platform fell away almost soundlessly, building to a steady rush of speed. She swung on the support poles, like any eleven-year-old girl on a day off. Most passengers barely noticed her. A little boy on his mother's lap stared, and Svetlana waved, continuing on.

By the next station she was back, plonking herself nonchalantly down beside Danya, with an attitude that said "nothing up that way." She was good at spotting odd things in crowds, and being a kid, she could do things that would be suspicious in an adult. She blew a bubble on some gum and put some sunglasses on her face. Not *her* sunglasses, Danya noted.

"Fucking hell Svet," he muttered.

"Oh blow it out your ear," she said calmly, looking the other way down the train through her new shades. It was something Sandy said from time to time.

"Poole?" said Danya. "That woman by the door two carriages down? She's in the sunlight, but she's got no shades on. And she's not squinting."

The train accelerated once more, now holding another seventy or so people. Poole said nothing until the train began to slow again, several minutes later. "Let's go," he said.

It wasn't their stop. Danya's heart beat faster as they walked to the door, waiting behind several others. The maglev was so smooth they barely needed a handhold, and just leaned. Poole put his own AR glasses on and clipped the connector cord to the insert at the back of his head. It looked like a blocker, Danya thought—the kind of thing that prevented any direct transmission to or from uplinks.

The train stopped, and they got off with the rest. Svetlana "dropped" a candy wrapper from her pocket, turned back to pick it up, then scampered to rejoin Danya and Poole. "That woman's following us," she said in a low voice. Frightened, and ready to run.

"Not yet," said Danya, still walking, eyeing roof columns on the plat-form and chairs and information boards, anything that might make temporary cover. His heart was pounding fit to burst. If these were GIs of any descrip-tion, let alone Talee-made GIs, he had no idea how they could get away. Though surely, with all these people about . . .

"Fuck," said Poole, and staggered. Went down on his haunches, a fist down for balance, as though trying to focus. Danya and Svetlana stared. Poole's jaw was tight, teeth clenched, as though in pain. "Run," he said. "Use the crowd."

He went for his pistol and stopped abruptly, his whole body in seizure, contorting. Danya stared back up the platform. The woman he'd spotted was coming, dark, nondescript, normal. She wore jeans and carried a handbag and was coming straight toward them.

Danya grabbed Svetlana's arm and turned to run. Blocking their way was a man, middle-sized, Caucasian, wearing a suit. Normal. But staring straight at them.

"Help us!" Svetlana screamed at the passing passengers. "Help us, they're going to kill us!" No one even looked. It wasn't cowardly indifference. They just kept walking, not seeing, not hearing. Danya realised that it was over, these GIs could do anything to them, in full view of everyone, and no one would notice a thing. Not even the security cameras. Nor the people watching them.

A third person walked up, passing outgoing passengers to join the man in the suit. Chinese features, round-faced, handsome. Cai. He, and the man in the suit, and the woman with the handbag were the only people on the platform who seemed to see them. Danya stood behind Svetlana and put his arms around her. She trembled. Cai pulled a pistol. His companion in the suit glanced at him, as though wondering why he'd done that.

Cai shot him in the head.

Danya flung Svetlana to the platform and fell on her, as more shots erupted, rapid like firecrackers. Then nothing. Danya raised his head, gasping for air against the adrenaline overload. The woman with the handbag was down too, pistol in her own hand. Cai checked her, picked up the pistol, and pulled several extra mags from her bag. Then back to the man in the suit, who'd only been shot once and was still moving. Shot him repeatedly in the skull, point-blank, then recovered weapon and mags as well.

And finally stood before Danya and Svetlana, both half-crouched and watching, wary like frightened cats. About them on the platform, people continued to talk, laugh, wander, and wait. But several babies were crying. They'd heard the noise, Danya realised. Their uplinked mothers were puzzled, wondering what had triggered the sudden screams. There were no other kids on the platform; they were all at school. Just adults, trapped even now in the Talee net.

"So," said Cai quite calmly. "I think you'd better come with me."

"I'm sorry, Chief," Raylee insisted, as ahead her cruiser's nav comp plotted her toward a high-security "event" she'd normally not be allowed into. "They won't say when I'm released."

"*Ray*," her precinct chief replied with frustration, "*I can't run a precinct if my officers keep running off for days on end. You're going to have to decide whether you're a cop or not.*"

"Well, sir, it's not entirely up to me, FSA have the authority to put police on secondment at any time, and . . ."

"*That's bullshit, Ray, and you know it. If you're gonna spend all your damn time with them, take the offer they've had on your table for months, and at least get paid like a damn spook.*"

He disconnected. "He has a point," Rhian offered from the passenger seat. "It is more money, for basically the same job."

"You're okay with this?" Raylee changed the subject.

"If it gets me on site, I'm okay with it," said Rhian. Raylee found her difficult to read. Found most GIs difficult to read, in fact. Lean and pretty, Rhian deadpanned much of the time, but not like some clichéd automaton. More like . . . well, Ari, she supposed. It was personality, of the mild, quirk-less variety that high-designation GIs did.

Nav comp brought the cruiser down, field gens whining, over haphazard rows of beachfront houses, through the ocean haze of an onshore wind. The scene below drove the frustrations of work from Raylee's mind—the streets were swarmed with vehicles, mostly aerial, lights flashing, forensics lugging gear, suits talking and gesticulating amidst the roadside sand and scrub. The beach was cordoned, uniformed cops getting the grunt work again, manning a line to keep gathered onlookers from encroaching, and interviewing anyone who claimed to be a witness.

All were centred by a beachfront house atop a short, sandy cliff. Several small anti-aircraft mounts were visible, hidden defences used by an alarming number of Tanushan high-security zones these days. The one at the rear appeared to have been fired directly into the house. Raylee didn't see that the terrible damage could have happened any other way—much of the rear wall was gone, the roof caving in with little to support it. The opposite walls, at the front of the house, were studded with high-velocity holes from rounds that had gone straight through. The neighbouring house, across a patch of unoccupied scrub, had also been hit, from an angle that seemed to line up with that rear gun mount.

She selected a landing zone and was rejected by the onsite net construct. She selected another, closest to the barrier now placed across the road, and it rejected that one too. Maybe Chief was right, she thought drily—time to get a promotion. She selected a new LZ on the beach instead.

"Don't do that," Rhian advised her, and suddenly her LZ had changed back to the street.

Raylee frowned. "You hacked the system?"

"No, I used my FSA clearance," said Rhian. "I'm not walking from the beach."

"Aren't GIs supposed to be without ego?" Raylee suggested.

"Ego doesn't have anything to do with it," Rhian said mildly. "But I'm not walking from the beach."

"Right," said Raylee, field gens throbbing as she followed the landing path down to the crowded, sandy street. "Let's just hope they don't ask to see my FSA ID."

"You worry too much about rules," said Rhian.

"You do understand what police officers do, in Tanusha?"

"Patronise thirty-nine-series GIs, apparently." Raylee blinked. She'd probably deserved that—Rhian was technically a lower designation than Kresnov, or Togales, or any of the other GIs she'd met at the top of the FSA chain, but she was a long way from stupid.

Raylee always felt nervous flashing her police badge at a scene that was clearly beyond what police usually handled. But the badge ID, followed on uplink, led to FSA encryption that various suited spies and agents let pass without so much as a raised eyebrow, and Rhian followed after her.

The main room was a mess, floors covered in glass, fractured plaster, and blood. Everywhere were high-velocity holes from the rear emplacement, drilling through walls, and sprayed with red like wine on Swiss cheese. Agents had set up various scanners and forensics posts, the show run by CSA Investigations, Raylee guessed. FSA didn't really have any crime-solvers of its own, were truly just an administrative body with a special-forces wing, on this planet. Thus this resort to outsourcing, CSA most of the time, and TPD when they were truly desperate.

Ari was here, and Commander Rice, standing to one side where they couldn't contaminate the scene and looking concerned. Rice was in full armour; no doubt the rest of her team were around somewhere, providing security. They seemed to be in uplinked conversation, no doubt something to do with the FedInt spies on the other side of the room. Raylee could tell they were spies because their suits were old Earth style, two buttons, rich weave. And the haircuts of the men, again traditional, none of the shaved undercuts and little trims of Tanushan men. Sometimes police work was hard, but other times the little, ridiculous things people and institutions did made it easy.

"Hey, Rhi," said Rice as they came over. "Raylee. What brings you here?" We didn't ask for you, that meant.

"She's with me," Raylee explained, not taking her eyes off the scene. "I attached her."

"And who attached you?" Rice asked cautiously. Vanessa Rice was not yet her "friend," as such. She was Kresnov's friend. Who was Ari's friend. Who was staying suspiciously quiet.

"I attached me."

"You can do that?"

"Apparently. FSA gave me clearance on homicides connected to terrorist operations in Tanusha. I'd guess this qualifies."

"We're not actually sure it does," said Rice. And no more, with a glance at silent Rhian, wondering how much a homicide cop on secondment was supposed to know.

"It's Talee," Raylee told her. "Or Talee-created GIs."

"How'd you learn that?" Rice wondered, with a glance first at Ari, then at Rhian. Raylee knew that Ari had seen some strange stuff on his last trip to Pantala. The one he wasn't supposed to tell her about, but had, because she knew too much elsewhere for lying to be credible. But he hadn't told her about the alien-origin synthetics.

"I have sources," Raylee said blandly. "That's Takewashi over there, right? So it was a debrief. Which means Shin was here, and Kresnov. But Kresnov's alive, of course. . . . How about Shin?"

"We don't know," Ari said cautiously. As the spec-ops commander gave him a questioning look. "Ray, this isn't exactly a homicide investigation, we kinda know who did it."

"That's what you think." She strolled to the scene, stepping carefully around debris on the floor, boots only where her trained eye told her was safe.

"Rhi?" the Commander asked her for an explanation.

"Rhian, with me, please," said Raylee. And Rhian came, similarly careful, and still silent. To the astonishment of her friends. Raylee attempted to make a connection. . . . It was always hard, the sudden disorientation of netspace, the graphical balance shift, the little icons she was meant to indicate. . . . Rhian came to her rescue and made the connection with a profound click in her inner ear.

"*So Sandy got away,*" said Rhian. Relief didn't always translate through uplink formulation, but it was clear enough here. "*And Poole was guarding her kids this morning, so I guess they're safe too.*"

"*Can you check?*" Raylee asked.

"*Can't check anything. Talee can hack anyone—if we know where Sandy is, they'll know. We have to stay ignorant on purpose.*"

Made sense, Raylee supposed, stopping by the headless body in the kimono, still upright in the chair. And to think that higher-grade uplinks had recently seemed like a good idea. The FedInt spies were watching her now, from over by their wall. God save them from these childish little games.

"*Asura,*" said Rhian. Raylee looked, and saw the hindquarters of what had once been an animal of some kind. Perhaps a dog.

"*Asura?*"

"*Fed Fleet used them against GIs in the war. Hearing and smell combined means they can tell if a GI's near. They still don't understand how it works. And they can detect transmissions.*"

"*They're uplinked?*"

"*No, it's natural. Their brains just detect some kinds of wireless transmissions, it's like natural radio reception. Again, no one understands it, it's pretty spooky.*" Rhian,

Raylee recalled, had an advanced degree in child psychology, of all things. A lot of which overlapped with basic psych, so surely she'd take an interest in brains of all kinds.

A FedInt agent arrived, Asian, dark glasses. "FSA's so short they send for homicide cops?"

They knew who she was. If FedInt were as involved in Operation Shield as FSA thought they were, damn right they knew. "Tell me this," said Raylee. "Your boss was nearly killed here. A couple of your best people were killed here. FSA nearly lost Commander Kresnov. Yet all you guys are standing over there . . ." indicating the far wall, "and all the FSA are standing over here?"

"Ask your own people," the spy said stubbornly. Japanese accent, Raylee thought. She'd seen enough old samurai movies to know.

"I already know what they say."

"And somehow," the spy added darkly, "it's never their people who get killed. Only ours."

Raylee glanced at Rhian. Rhian looked sombre. "You think this is some kind of FSA setup?"

"If it were," the spy replied, "do you think you'd be the first to know?"

Commander Rice heard. "Hey, asshole. She brought her own kid here. You think she'd set this on her own kid?"

"For all we know about Kresnov," the spy replied, "she's using those kids as a cover to get everyone to trust her. She's a machine. He's a bag of meat to her, we all are."

Rice took a step forward. Rhian pulled two pistols, Kresnov style, and gave each side a nasty look, tensed for threats in both directions. Everyone froze. Rhian was the only GI in the room. With weapons drawn, it made her the automatic center of attention. Rice and Ari stared, in disbelief.

"I'm in the odd position here of being an outsider from both sides," Raylee told the room. "FSA gives me independence to form judgements as I see fit, given the value of an outside opinion. What I see here is dysfunction, two groups of people fighting over a pile of bullshit. And I think our enemies are using it against us, like that League GI used me, to get you lot to hate each other more than you already do. This is exactly what's killing the League. You want a good look at Compulsive Narrative Syndrome, you've got it right here, all of you."

Rice was unimpressed. "And you took it upon yourself to march in here," she said coolly, "and inform us all of your lofty judgement?"

"Not hers," said Rhian. "Ours too."

"*Ours?*"

"GIs. All of us think you're nuts on this FedInt thing. All of us. No exceptions, Sandy, Amirah, Poole, Kiet, everyone. Me too. Vanessa, Ari, you're my friends, and I love you both. But pull your fucking heads in before you get us all killed."

She glanced at Raylee. Raylee nodded, and they headed for the door.

"*They're very quiet, aren't they?*" Rhian formulated as they left. It was definitely irony, Raylee decided. A calm, understated variety, rather than Ari's sandpaper-dry brand. They emerged into sunlight, cordons, guards, and clustered vehicles.

"*Haven't seen a room so stunned since I was a beauty queen contestant in junior college,*" Raylee offered. Rhian raised a curious eyebrow at her. "*A bit of cunning sabotage in the swimsuit contest caused my main rival to um . . . disrobe, right onstage.*"

"*I'd thought that means she wins.*"

Raylee grinned. "*It's not that kind of contest.*"

"*Maybe it should be.*" Still with just that faintly bemused eyebrow raised. Okay, Raylee admitted to herself—for all her misgivings about GIs in Tanusha, she was coming to like Rhian a lot. "*Did you do it?*"

"*The sabotage? Of course not. I've always been a good girl.*"

"*You're not built like a good girl.*"

"*Neither are you.*"

Rhian's amusement faded. "*Why would Sandy bring Kiril here?*"

They reached the cruiser and got in. Raylee waited until they were sealed in before replying, for the relief of not having to formulate. "She would have been trying to protect him, I guess. Keep him with her. Which means she thinks the Talee are after him."

"That stuff in his head," Rhian murmured. "Shit. Even Sandy can't fight the Talee. I saw what Cai did at Pantala, it's crazy."

"Cai?" As the engines fired up once more.

"I'll fill you in." With a cautious glance. "You believe that stuff the spy said back there? Sandy not caring?"

"No. Of course not."

"But you're no fan."

Raylee frowned. "She's very powerful, Rhi. All GIs are, and now you're all in the one place, which is making FedInt nervous."

"And you."

Raylee pointed to her right arm. "Last time we had a civil war here? I lost this arm."

"But we're not the ones making trouble with FedInt. GIs, I mean. You regular humans are the ones falling for this stupid narrative syndrome. GIs are seeing through it. So why are you scared of *us*?"

Raylee powered the cruiser into the air as the field gens reached full charge. "Don't confuse me with your logic," she muttered, plotting a course and allowing the com to find her next call.

It connected. *"Hello, ladies,"* came Steven Harren's voice on the cruiser com. *"Nice work, we already have some good data running."*

He and SuperPsych had been listening the whole time. With herself and Rhian on the inside, they'd been able to run a large enough infiltration program, using FSA constructs against themselves, to let them monitor the entire confrontation in the house. That, Steven had insisted, would be enough to run the voice stress analysis, along with visual data, required to establish the last data point against which all other data points could be measured. A face-to-face confrontation, FSA against FedInt.

It was also very illegal and could land both her and Rhian in jail, not to mention unemployed. But they'd all agreed that the stakes made it worth the risk.

"What's the deal?" Rhian asked.

"Swing by and we'll show you."

CHAPTER THIRTEEN

Sandy strolled the Harihan tech market with cap and shades on, as rain poured on the transparent awnings and plunged down pipes between stalls into drains underfoot. Lights strobed the interior stalls and crowds, kaleidoscopic on wet plastic, making electric puddles gleam on the tarmac floor. People moved between shelves and displays, teeming hundreds, examining the latest gear, uplinks and AR glasses bombarding them with specs and advertising.

The kids loved it here, and it was a good place to hide—a natural rendezvous. Svetlana could no doubt steal her way into a serious juvie record in a place like this. Sandy scanned the commotion, her own AR glasses just a disguise, as usual for her in public. She didn't dare uplink here, or anywhere, internal or external. Her uplinks were firmly on autistic, completely disconnected, and impossible to access remotely. Her head felt empty without the cacophony pressing on her awareness. That swarm of electronic context, giving shape to every fact.

There was a tree amidst the market stalls where food stalls continued brisk sales despite the downpour, awnings redirecting runoff toward the tree in a curtain of silver water. Normally to find the kids, she'd have bet on food. But now the food courtyard seemed too obvious a central gathering spot, and a quick scan did not reveal them. Every body shape was heat and colour, her combat mode augured up to reflex maximum. She was finding it easier to stay here, one sudden motion away from instant violence, than to confront what lay outside of it.

She walked past rows of robot helpers, one of them juggling to entertain an audience. Another mimicked passersby, like a street performer begging for coins in his hat. Sandy detoured and glimpsed a girl up the far end. Beret, short hair. About Svetlana's size, but disappeared about a stall corner and lost amidst the press of bodies. Sandy walked briskly. Audio thundered and boomed from a nearby VR game display, people lying on flat recliners, eyes covered, lost in their dreamworld while their actions were watched by others on displays.

She walked parallel to the girl's last direction . . . and glimpsed her again, up ahead, one stall over. Again no clear view of her face. It didn't seem right, and suspicion tingled. She pressed on, hand itching for the pistol within her jacket. Some unnamed sense made her turn, to see a woman amidst others standing before a display . . . but only that woman . . . posture . . . body temp . . .

Her uplinks hit her like a hammer blow, her knees folding. Gunfire, screams, and she overrode it in a millisecond, bypassing to the auto-cutoff, rolling up and moving fast through the pandemonium, gun in hand. More gunfire from the left, firing elsewhere, and she aimed straight through displays, expensive screens erupting in sparks and liquid crystal, and dove to a roll and dead-stop by an aisle, braced three-points to the ground and waiting.

Movement down a neighbouring aisle, a figure hurdling bystanders, just the right approach axis to cut her off from flanking her previous target. . . . Sandy exploded that way, through a stall, saw the pistol training on her from the airborne hurdler and shot it, and the arm, then crashed through displays in a flying tackle. The GI was already adjusting as she hit him, twisting to an arm lock even as they hit the plastic wall and rebounded . . . but Sandy counter-pivoted, came down on a leg to brace into full rotation. Locked out the arm as they crashed down, predicted and ducked into the counter-strike, wrenching the arm from its socket as her balance shifted. The GI rolled, trying even now to escape that grasp, but she went with it, coming to a crouch as her grip shifted, and tore the GI's head half off.

Dropped the lifeless bundle of synthetic parts and leaped on a new flanking run. That had been high designation, a Talee-GI, no question. Not invincible then. But damn, if she'd been off by just a millisecond . . .

Shots tore through displays as she ran, aiming at sound and motion more than plain sight, and she slid behind a heavy power unit. Screaming, panicked shoppers ran past. Again the buzzing in her head, activated uplinks trying to swamp her . . . how the hell? They weren't even connected.

More shots, this time from the right, aiming *at* her opponent. Who made the mistake of returning fire, and Sandy was off before the first cartridge hit the ground. And came into line-of-sight as the female GI was still firing, then tried to change direction. . . . Sandy's trigger finger blurred, even as the target flung and twisted aside, tracking to put most of a clip into her head. Still the GI somehow managed to bounce up, face torn and ear hanging . . . to receive Sandy's flying fist through skull, brain and display wall behind. The whole lot collapsed on her and set off chain-reaction sparks and small fires, gantries supporting the plastic walls tumbling down. But Sandy was off again, figuring whoever had fired on that target would now take advantage to make sure she was down. And sure enough, when he came fast down the neighbouring aisle, he froze at a stall entrance as his peripheral vision showed him what he dared not turn and face directly—Sandy already there, pistol aimed at his head. Eyes wide, face speckled with blood, fist stained with synthetic gore.

"Me or them?" she said. "Think fast."

"You," said Cai. And amidst the ongoing confusion, Sandy's hearing zoned on a familiar running stride, short steps and light weight. And another behind.

"Sandy!" Svetlana shrieked and ran to her. It would have been the easiest thing to collapse and sob with utter relief. But combat reflex wouldn't allow it, and Svetlana wisely pulled up short in the stall, tears on her cheeks and wanting a hug but not daring. Danya arrived behind and grabbed her to be sure, looking at Sandy's red-stained fist. Behind them, Sandy saw Poole, looking grimly about for new threats.

"Sandy, he saved us," Danya said breathlessly. "There were others, and Cai killed them."

"Why?" asked Sandy, staring unblinking at Cai.

"Not here," said Cai. "Where is Kiril?"

They stole another car from a parking unit and drove in the spitting rain along streets strangely empty of law enforcement. People stood in clusters in the light rain, talking wildly, hands waving, looking about for support and authority. Several police cars were surrounded by crowds, everyone wanting to talk, the cops holding them back and making no effort to advance toward the market. Evidently they'd been told. Exactly *what* they'd been told, Sandy couldn't guess, but it involved leaving the market space clear for a while and not bothering with roadblocks or other traffic inspections, even when a simple check-and-match of passengers with vehicle registration would have revealed a stolen car. Someone higher up still had her back and left her space to get away the only way she could.

Sandy sat in the rear seat with Danya and Poole, pistol out, as Cai drove. Svetlana sat in the passenger seat, upset and trembling. Sandy watched all ways at once, or tried to. Here in busy northern Tanusha, she felt naked without her uplinks.

"How many are there?" she asked Cai.

"No way of telling," said Cai, steering by pure visual and no connection to traffic central. Normally that was illegal and would have cops on their tail in no time. Now, nothing. "Numbers are not their style. They would not have believed you could survive their initial attacks, in this network environment. Their tactics will now change."

"Why?" Danya asked, voice low and hard. "Is it Kiril?"

"Yes," said Cai.

"So why attack us?" Svetlana demanded.

"To split Cassandra's attention and draw her out. Remove Cassandra, and Kiril's primary protection is gone. It nearly worked."

"Not so nearly," Sandy growled. "They're dead. I'm not." Still the combat reflex remained. She could not read the kids' expressions clearly, though their upset was clear enough from their voices, posture, and racing pulses. The faint muscle tremors, all the little things that fear did to straight humans, but rarely to GIs. She had no desire to drop out of combat reflex and face that.

"I helped," Cai pointed out.

"Yeah," said Sandy. "Thanks" didn't quite pass her lips. She didn't yet know if it was warranted. But if he hadn't started shooting when the first net attack had hit her . . . "They got past my barriers when I was completely autistic. How the fuck?"

"Have you been hit by assault barriers in the past day?" Cai asked.

The stolen car, Sandy recalled. At the beach, she'd tried to access wirelessly and had been reverse-hacked for the briefest moment. . . . "Yes," she said.

"They plant traces, activated remotely."

In another mode, Sandy would have sworn. "Can you get them out?"

"Yes," said Cai. It still shouldn't have been possible. Damn alien tech. The car reached a freeway onramp, and accelerated into the traffic stream. Great flashes of white light lit thunderclouds behind nearby towers.

"Why can she beat them?" Danya asked. "I mean, aren't they more advanced? Aren't *you* more advanced?"

Cai shrugged. "If your most advanced soldiers today were to go back in time to fight ancient Roman gladiators with swords and spears, even with all their training and augmentations, they'd probably lose. We become dependent on technology. Talee fight by network, by wireless assault and computer assist. Cassandra remains the latest word in guns and fists."

"Who are they?" Sandy asked. "Exactly?"

Cai said nothing for a long moment. Hell of a thing, Sandy realised. To find yourself at violent odds with the people who made you. She knew exactly what that felt like, and even in extreme combat mode, she retained some sympathy.

"Something that shouldn't exist," he said finally. "Talee can control their own technology, but not that of humans. For that, they had to create others."

"Combat units," Sandy said flatly. "Assassins."

"Yes. And me."

"And who do you answer to? Who do they?"

"We should wait," said Cai. "Even cars have microphones. In any networked space, my people's technology can find a way to listen to anyone."

Sandy glanced at Poole, seated between her and Danya. He looked grim, unspeaking. "You okay?" she asked him.

"I can't fight that," he said. "I'd be dead if Cai hadn't shown up. Don't know what use I'll be."

"I hope to live long enough to see GIs no longer defining themselves by how useful they'll be," Sandy replied. "Thank you for guarding them."

"If Cai hadn't shown up, we'd have been killed," Poole said blandly.

Combat vision intensified. Sounds deepened, broke into individual throbbing vibrations. Sandy fought back the hyperfocus with difficulty. "You did what you could."

"I'm okay too," Svetlana muttered, wiping tears. "Thanks for asking."

Sandy tried to say something but couldn't. This was why she'd originally never wanted kids. How did a combat GI mix these two sides of her life and stay sane?

Cai wiped the car's memory with a direct cord and sent it driving on auto back to the city. There it would reconnect with traffic central, finally find a park, and alert its owners where it was. In a city of sixty-two million people, rogue cars and glitches happened frequently enough that checking each one would be time-consuming. If found, the car could not tell where it had been, and its location would be central Tanusha.

A hundred kilometres north of Tanusha, Sandy led the group along a path by the riverside. Thick tropical foliage overhung the dark waters, insects flittered, and fish broke the slow-moving surface. Here and there, a few house lights shone through the trees. This was Greenwood, a light residential zone more than a town. Most folks out here commuted but preferred life away from the urban crowds. Aircars had hollowed out many Earth cities, leading to urban collapse as citizens chased cheap land to commute from by air. Around Tanusha, environmental protections made this land even more expensive than the central city, and the houses that peered through the lush forest were large.

The path passed several riverfront homes, their gates lit by small lamps, swarming with flying bugs. All had cruiser ports—no roads here; they were air access only. Four houses up, beside a leaning swarm of riverside bamboo, Sandy pushed through the gate of a house on stilts, front porch well over the river.

The asura bounded on the porch to greet them, ears pricked attentively. Danya and Svetlana were not surprised, having been warned. But they ran as Kiril emerged from a doorway and grabbed him in a three-sided embrace. A lump fought its way into Sandy's throat, but here in the house there were approaches to guard and security possibilities to consider, and all without the usual assurance of uplinks. Combat reflex reasserted, and she walked the perimeter to check, noting Ragi on the sofa with heavy bandaging where his hand had been. Jane was around the back, lying flat on a mattress in the rear bedroom, rifle by her side. Eyes watching impassively upstream, even as Sandy passed before her. She'd be changing positions every five minutes, Sandy knew—endless pacing just drew attention. Anyone scouting this house would watch for a long time, so there was no need to keep moving. Just watch each approach, intently, for any sign of movement or observation.

Jane volunteered nothing, and Sandy went back to the living room, a wide space surrounded by windows with river views. Not the most defensible, perhaps, but with window tints it was easier to see out of than into . . . and when defended by high-des GIs, line of sight was nothing to mess with.

"Whose is it?" Poole asked, cracking a beer in the kitchen. When he'd acquired that taste, Sandy didn't know. CSA training, perhaps.

"It's on the market," she said. "No personal connections to trace, it's just empty. We won't be here long." Poole offered her a beer, forgetting that she'd rather drink the brown river water. Offered it to Ragi instead when she refused, cracking it for him first so he could drink one-handed. Sandy looked at the tight bandaging on his wrist stump.

"Kiril helped," said Ragi, looking worn and pale. Worn and pale for a GI, anyway.

"This is really good, Kiri," said Sandy, as Cai put a kettle on for himself and Sandy. Searched the cupboard for coffee or, failing that, tea. "Did you help wrap this?"

Danya and Svetlana were still standing with Kiril. Kiril was crying again, softly, as his siblings comforted him. Which had set Svetlana off too. She looked at Sandy now, accusingly. Do something, that meant. Sandy felt offended. Keeping them alive was going to be hard enough . . . now she had to keep them emotionally stable as well? She barely knew how to do that for herself half the time.

"Kids?" Cai asked quietly from the kitchen. "Would you like some tea?"

"No!" snapped Svetlana. "I don't want anything!" Danya looked at Sandy helplessly. Looking back at him, Sandy felt the combat reflex dropping, for the first time since the beach.

"Guys," she said. "Guys, look . . ."

Suddenly her heart was pounding, and her face was hot. For a moment she thought perhaps she'd been hacked again, those damn Talee trace codes still lurking in her system to ambush her . . . but this felt nothing like that. Her gut tightened, and suddenly she was short of breath. She gasped, a hand on the sofa for balance.

"Cassandra?" asked Ragi. "Cassandra, are you . . . ?"

Cai came over. Sandy's head was pounding, and she felt nauseous. Still her heart accelerated further, galloping fit to explode. She went down on one knee, trying to breathe, trying to stay focused and get enough air as Cai knelt before her and tilted her head back to gaze in her eyes. Slapped her cheek, quite hard, to gauge instant response. . . . Sandy felt the combat reflex kick back in briefly, an abrupt calming of the heart . . . but it was only Cai, and her conscious brain didn't believe what the automated hindbrain was telling it.

"Sandy?" Danya came over, all concern. "Cai, what's wrong?"

"I think she's having a panic attack," said Cai.

"Oh fuck," Sandy muttered, and put her head down, focusing just on breathing. "First time for everything." She'd never seen it before, in any GIs. Had never heard of it happening. But if anything could get her this paralytically scared . . .

"Just breathe," said Cai, a hand on her back. "It will pass soon, just breathe."

"Sandy," said Danya, kneeling and putting an arm around her. "It's okay, we're all safe. You saved us, Sandy."

She looked up at him, and her eyes filled with tears. "I've never been so scared," she managed. "It's one thing when it's just me or my friends, but they're trying to kill my babies and I've never been so scared. . . ."

And then Svetlana was hugging her too, and apologising, and she clung to them both tearfully until her heart began to calm and her breathing returned to something approaching normal.

"Svet," said Danya against her shoulder, "Sandy has to focus. She can't comfort us and fight them at the same time."

"I'm sorry," Svetlana repeated. "I'm sorry, I'm sorry."

Sandy wiped and blinked her eyes clear. Took a deep breath. "Okay. Svet and Kiri, you do what Danya says. He's in charge. And he'll do what I say. We have to be a team. Can we do that?" Earnest nods. "And I'll try to be nice, Svet, but when I'm in combat mode it's just really hard. You just have to trust that I love you and not keep asking for reassurance, okay? I know it's hard when you're scared."

Svetlana nodded. Sandy smiled and kissed her. "I want a hug too!" Kiril complained.

Sandy laughed and went to him. "Oh, you poor neglected boy, come here." She scooped him up and smothered him in kisses until he laughed.

"Good lord," Jane said drily, watching from the bedroom doorway. "I used to just accept that you could kick my ass. Now I'm embarrassed." Sandy showed her a middle finger with her free arm.

"Talee have words for it," said Cai a little later, as they sat in the living room with the auto shades drawn. With both Cai and the asura, the potential for ambush was slight. Kiril sat by the animal on the floor rug, having decided it was his friend. Sandy didn't like that either, but the asura seemed to know who it shouldn't make angry. "But the words won't mean anything to you. Talee language is difficult."

Sandy watched him carefully, sipping coffee, pistol on the coffee table. Poole alongside, with Danya and Svetlana beside that, eating sandwiches they'd bought from a store on the way here.

"Talee are double-brained," Cai continued. "So are humans, technically, with left and right hemispheres, but in Talee the separation is even more pronounced. In humans, conscious thought can be traced to specific locations, in the left or right sides. In Talee, the conscious thought arises from somewhere between two hemispheres. Like binocular vision, if you close one eye, you see only what that eye sees. But open both together, and the brain combines them to make a composite image, overlaying one image atop the other."

"But that's an illusion," Ragi said cautiously. He was reclined on another sofa, bandaged arm across his middle. The shock of losing a hand was mostly psychological, Sandy knew. Though not a combat GI, physically he could take far worse damage and still function. For a while at least. "There is no single image, it's the brain creating an entirely new one. A third image, an internal construction."

"Exactly," said Cai. "Talee consciousness is a construct of a third image, if you will—neither entirely left nor right brain, but something in the middle. It makes them very clever, perhaps cleverer than humans, if one can measure such things. Talee have vast imaginations. Arts and science, for Talee, are much the same thing."

"You know," said Jane, "this would be absolutely fascinating, if they weren't trying to kill us." For once, Sandy found Jane's derision agreeable.

"It sounds like they would be less susceptible to compulsive narrative syndrome than humans," Ragi offered.

"Yes," Cai agreed. "Normally that would be true. But Talee psychology has a drawback. Mostly in the form of drugs. Talee have used them to alter chemical neurology for as long as they've known how to brew, just as humans with alcohol. But the effect on Talee is different, and targets different parts of the brain. This shuts down the cross-referencing process, or parts of it. Which turns a Talee from a thoughtful, cautious, farsighted individual into a far more focused and straightforward one."

"A drone?" asked Ragi.

"No. A believer." A quiet pause. The asura yawned, a flash of long, sharp teeth. Kiril scratched its head. Sandy wondered if the animal enjoyed the sensation as much as Kiril thought it did. "Most Talee are thoughtful. Though flexible, they can be conservative in their own way and not rush to judgement. But an 'impaired' Talee will think in straight lines. The uncertainty of cross-referencing between hemispheres disappears, to be replaced by something far more predictable.

"When humans are drunk, all judgement is impaired. When Talee are impaired, mental faculties actually improve, in some directions. Linear thought process improves. Mathematics, certainly. Many of the great geniuses who have driven Talee scientific progress have been 'users.' Today, many still use, despite death penalties for usage and possession. This is the attraction, the ability to focus mental process. Talee in this state are significantly more intelligent than the most intelligent humans. It's not a boast, believe me."

"I believe you," said Ragi. Ragi, of course, was the most intrigued of them all. The smartest of them all, perhaps, though with Cai that was uncertain. The one with the most questions to answer about what it was that Takewashi had used to create him, and why. "And the Talee blame this . . . 'impaired' state for their two near-extinction events?"

Cai nodded. "Current research indicates a spiral of competing interests forced into usage by the need to keep up with each other, and that usage descending into mindless animosity."

"And how do they stop people from using?" Sandy asked. "A police state?"

"There is less diversity in Talee society than human," Cai explained. "They do not fragment so easily. Consensus on large matters does not require a police state. But enforcement is strict, yes . . . though largely consensual."

"Largely?"

Cai shrugged. "Every society has its criminals."

"And its revolutionaries."

"And there are types of uplink technology that create a similar effect to other forms of drug usage?" Ragi pressed.

"Yes," said Cai. "The worst." He looked at Kiril, sitting by his new animal friend.

"What does it do?" Sandy asked quietly.

"Like the uplink effect in humans, it's not noticeable in individuals or small groups. Only when you monitor the overall direction of large group thinking does it begin to appear. Individually, our narratives are small. Favourite foods, favourite activities. Favourite people. Our preferences do not shake the world. But all uplink activity establishes commonalities over time. Uniformities.

"Neural Cluster Technology is humanity's version—it's very crude, very simple technology compared to anything Talee use. It does not differentiate between different kinds of mental signals to be shared. It shares too much, and absorbs too much, without filters. The consequence is somewhat akin to brainwashing, as you've seen with your Pyeongwha terrorists here.

"The condition is called *aiwallawai.*"

Dead silence in the room. Cai's lips twisted to pronounce it in an accent unlike the approximate Federation-neutral with which he usually spoke. Alien technology, alien words, never before spoken on this world . . . that anyone knew of. And now here they sat, five synthetic humans, plus the organic kids. Listening to the words and sounds of this strange species whose thoughts had made the technology that created them.

Sandy thought of Takewashi, now dead in his beachview chair. She'd hated him, once. Perhaps she still did. But that was a personal luxury, born of what it now dawned on her was misplaced spite. It was not easy to confront the things that made you, especially when you were dissatisfied with the result. And now she wondered if she should have accepted Takewashi's offer of fatherhood and been comforted. As Jane had. She glanced at Jane and saw sullen disapproval. Was that normal for her now? Or was it because she felt she'd just lost her father? It wasn't like they'd had any time to talk about it.

"Aiwallawai," Ragi murmured. "It's a phonetic palindrome."

"Double-brained," Sandy echoed. Perhaps that was connected.

"It is like chemical impairment, only more subtle," Cai continued. "The uplinks are designed to focus traffic into specific portions of the brain. The user experiences aiwallawai but also becomes a link in a conduit of like-minded neural interface. This interface can induce other brains into a similar state. Like an infection. The user does not realise the condition, and this adds to its lethality.

"Unwitting sufferers are rehabilitated in isolation. Implementers are executed. Most Talee have no difficulty with this policy."

"Do you?" Sandy pressed. It might explain his current situation.

Cai smiled faintly. "I'm not Talee."

"Semantics."

"No, it's not. I'm human. Being here has taught me about myself, and how I'm different. And made me wonder at the uses to which my creators put me."

"You're not an assassin," said Sandy. "You're a spy. These others trying to kill us are something else again."

"They have a name I will not share. They are from what you might call an internal security force. The one that implements the executions among Talee."

"Yeah, well, buddy," Poole growled, "we're not in Talee space anymore. You're trespassing."

"They have a foreign operations wing," Cai continued, ignoring Poole. "For humans. This is the first time they've used it." Something about that didn't sound right to Sandy. Was Cai's answer a lie? Or was it just incomplete? The difference between the cautious, sensible policy of Talee toward humans to date and now this all-out aggression and insanity was stark. Far too stark to be the result of disagreement between security agencies, surely? Was Cai merely feeding her that because it sounded like something she'd be familiar with? Cai still served his people, in his own way, she had no doubt. And serving his people, in the past, had meant only telling humans as much about Talee as suited Talee interests at the time.

"How long have they been scared humans would move on aiwallawai technologies?" asked Ragi.

"The information Takewashi and Chancelry Corporation recovered from Pantala over a century ago made it inevitable eventually," said Cai. "It's the primary reason my kind were created, though other intelligence activities have proved useful. To see if the technology would be reached here. Takewashi was warned. But League's circumstance caused him to ignore that warning.

"The war drove synthetic neural technology faster than Talee had hoped humans could progress. Cassandra was of concern to Talee higher-ups. Then Jane. And Ragi, of course." Looking at each of them in turn. "The final straw."

"Gee, thanks," said Poole. "Nothing about me, huh?"

"You three showed the proficiency that humans were gaining with the technology." Pointing to all but Poole. "But such are matters for Talee security. Ordinary Talee do not think much on security matters, for all their imagination. The twin catastrophes make such thoughts a taboo subject. Everyone is nervous to have strategic thoughts. It makes the authorities uncomfortable.

"It's not so dissimilar to the Federation, where most civilians leave trouble with the League to Fleet, especially after thirty years of war. They don't want to think about it. And they don't ask too many questions, so long as the job gets done."

"So Talee security created synthetic humans to assassinate us covertly, if necessary," Sandy completed. "And these guys answer to different people than you do." Raising her eyebrows at Cai, inviting him to jump in.

Cai smiled. "I share as much as I need to. But not that."

"That's okay, I can guess. More moderate forces." Cai shrugged. "And you dislike their methods?"

"I dislike the fact that they were created in the first place," Cai said flatly. "I find it an insult to my kind. To our kind." Looking about at them all. "We are free individuals, and most Talee treat their creations well. There are synthetic Talee too, you know. Most are subjected to nothing like this." Another bombshell, but a predictable one. Of course Talee made synthetic copies of their own kind before applying it to aliens. How could they not? "I and others like me have protested, and our Talee friends as well. Our protests have been noted, but ignored, on the grounds of security necessity."

The human-made GIs looked at each other. It all sounded depressingly familiar.

"That's great," Jane said sourly, from over by her bedroom doorframe. "How do we beat them?"

"I'm not sure you can," said Cai. "Not here. They have been surprised, and my defection has helped you. But they will recover, and they are more the combat experts than I."

"They're not so tough," said Sandy, eyes half-lidded as the combat reflex began to spread across her vision once more. She forced it back, with difficulty. "They'll need a lot more than what they've brought so far to get past me."

"And that's what they'll bring," Cai said quietly. And sipped his half-forgotten coffee.

"Well, then we've all got a problem," said Jane. Effortlessly hefting the rifle in her left hand. "Takewashi sent me here to look after you, sis." With a cool stare at Sandy. "And your brat. He knew what he was doing would bring them down on you. And him. But he said it was the only way."

"To do what?" Ragi asked.

Jane made a face. "Save humanity," she said vaguely. "Or something like that. I only did it because he made me promise. He sacrificed himself for you lot. I hope you realise that."

Or what? Sandy nearly asked her. Or you'll get upset at us? Since when had Jane ever been upset at the demise of anyone? Takewashi had created her but sold her off to the highest bidder when it proved the only excuse to allow her technology to see the light of day. Rapid-gestation high-des. Sandy had taken five-years-plus to become functional. Jane had taken months, perhaps a year. It meant shortcuts in mental development. Lots of tape teach. Drone-like behaviour. Murderous indifference . . . and indifferent murder. Now she claimed sentiment?

"Takewashi thinks the technology in Kiril's head is the only way to save humanity from killing itself," Jane finished. "I don't know how or why, it's not my field."

"Then we have a real problem with the Talee," said Ragi, gazing at Cai. "Because if we can't live without it, and they can't live with it . . ." He let it hang, unfinished.

"Cai, you said there were others?" said Sandy. "On Pantala? That Chancelry put the same technology into, like Kiril?"

Cai nodded. "Whether they're still on Pantala, or whether League has figured out what's going on and moved them, I don't know."

Sandy's eyes slowly widened. "Then the Talee will be going after them too?"

"Quite likely," said Cai.

"Then we need to find League representatives here and warn them," she said.

Ragi frowned. "Cassandra, if Talee are acting in unison to eliminate all those test subjects, it's likely they've already moved. And given Callay is farther away, it's quite possible the others are dead already and Kiril is the last test subject left."

Svetlana sat beside Kiril and hugged him. Kiril just scratched the asura's head, sombrely. The animal flicked its big ears.

"All the more reason to get the League onside," Sandy said firmly. "Because in that case, Kiril's *their* last hope too."

CHAPTER FOURTEEN

Ibrahim threw his coffee cup at the wall. It smashed, splashing coffee to the carpet. Everyone stared. No one had ever seen Ibrahim do such a thing.

"So you're telling me," he said, "that we are under attack by an alien race that everyone thought benign, and that there is absolutely nothing we can do to fight back."

They sat about the central table in the secure briefing room. All was dark, save flashlights and independently powered monitor screens. Room lights ran off the HQ grid, and if they powered the HQ grid, it was conceivable that power could be siphoned to activate the currently deactivated network. The only option was to power down completely and turn off the backup generator. If the network was operating, it could be used against them. The only way to fight the Talee was to give up electricity entirely. But most of the city couldn't do that.

"The attack appears limited," Reichardt offered. "Just the beach house, and our reports are that Cassandra was there, and her youngest boy . . ."

"And which of those reports do we trust?" Ibrahim asked the Captain bleakly. "Which of those people reporting to us are reporting things that actually happened, or merely experiences that the Talee placed in their heads by remote?"

Reichardt looked at the wall, the splatter of dark liquid running to the floor. Then he snapped the elastic band about his wrist for the sensation of pain that would tell him if this was a simulation or not. About the table, Hando, Amirah, and Ibrahim did the same.

"VR simulation in everyone's heads," Ibrahim muttered. "All for games. We could so easily do without it, but it's too entertaining. And now we don't even know if we're awake or not." He'd never felt so helpless. He wondered if there was really any point in him being here at all. Maybe he should go home to his wife and his bed.

"Sir," tried Amirah, "high-designation GIs will be least affected. We're not easily forced into VR without a direct link; Cassandra herself made that assessment after her encounters with Cai at Pantala last year."

"Well, if they can help," said Hando, "they're on their own. If the Talee are after Cassandra's kid like we think, we don't know where he is and finding out could kill him."

"We'd be better off with an army of children," said Ibrahim. "Completely without uplinks, they'd be more use than us."

"Sir," Hando said carefully, "in all seriousness, I know of some high school cadets who would likely volunteer for messenger duty. Scouts, possibly football teams. Community-minded kids. They couldn't be hacked."

"No, just killed physically," said Amirah with obvious disapproval. "We've already got one much younger child being targeted, they wouldn't stop at more."

"I was in Fleet Academy from fifteen," said Reichardt grimly.

Ibrahim stared at the wall for a moment. "Do it," he said finally. "Talk to their parents, get them out of bed if you have to. Courier by motorcycle or public transport; cars and cruisers are too vulnerable."

"Sir," Amirah began.

"We have to be able to *talk* to each other," Ibrahim cut her off. "I mean, what is a human being without the ability to communicate?" Amirah said nothing, unaccustomed to her boss's temper. Ibrahim had been through bad situations before, but this was too much. Before, there had been options. Now, their only option was to lie still and take it. He looked at Reichardt. "If Fleet have any more Talee stories you haven't shared with us yet, now might be the time."

"I was hoping you had something," said Reichardt. "No, we've got . . . biological clues, ideas about physiology based on what we know of their homeworld's atmosphere, ship performance . . . nothing helpful here."

"They have to know," Ibrahim muttered. "I mean they can't just let this happen."

Hando frowned. "I'm sorry, sir, who?"

"The Talee. This can't be the mainstream society attacking us, this has to be some fringe. They've been so meticulous not to aggravate us, and now this?"

"Sir . . . guessing games with Talee social and political structure is dangerous, we just don't . . ."

"I'm sick of being careful, Mr Hando. Careful got us here. The Talee are evidently sick of being careful too, since careful got them Cresta's destruction and the fears of species-wide extermination. That must be it, mustn't it?" Looking around at them all, faces underlit in the dark room. "Whatever uplink tech is in Kiril Kresnov's head, they must be terrified of it. And with whole moons being destroyed in human space, they've leaped from too-cautious to too-aggressive in one leap. Well, two can play at that.

"Captain, I'm putting Fleet on full alert. A war footing. The official announcement shall be 'pending invasion.'"

A very predictable silence about the table, though their faces did not show as much shock as one might have expected. Federation Fleet hadn't been in full alert since the war. "The whole Fleet?" Reichardt asked. "Even if we could get the word out, I'm not sure the whole Fleet would listen or respond, things as they are at present."

"The whole Fleet," Ibrahim agreed. "I'm overruling anything Ranaprasana may say, I'm invoking FSA's rule. The Federation has been attacked by an external entity. This means war."

"Sir?" Amirah ventured carefully. "You're going to take the entire Federation to war against the Talee?"

"They've left us no choice. We can't negotiate, they won't let us even talk to each other, let alone to them. Their technological advantage is so extreme that it demonstrates to us a clear existential threat. We either submit to their intervention whenever they feel like it, or we retaliate. The only retaliation they will notice, given the scale of their advantage, is total war.

"I cannot believe this is the entire Talee people in action. Surely this is only one small part, acting without consent from the majority. To have feared interaction with us for so long, only to intervene now so brazenly, makes no sense in any other context."

"Hell of a gamble," Reichardt observed.

"As was theirs," Ibrahim replied. "Thus my move."

"And if the Talee majority doesn't take the hint and drag this smaller group back into line?" Hando asked. "Or if the smaller group launches an all-out attack before they can do so? What then?"

"Then," said Ibrahim, "I doubt there will be very many of us around to debate the point. But there won't be many Talee either. We have to hope they won't make it *three* times extinct."

"Sir," Hando persisted, "consensus with the Talee has always been to tell the public as little as possible, to avoid the considerable public alarm that everyone expects if there were any incident. But your strategy is to provoke public alarm on purpose?"

"Yes," Ibrahim nodded firmly. "The more the better. They can only have calculated that we'll go along with them in keeping it quiet. They've miscalculated us, because now our only defence is to let them know that there is *no such thing* as safe intervention against humans. Every human being alive will learn of this and be alarmed. Let the Talee deal with *that*, next time they consider doing it again."

He snapped the elastic band against his wrist again and felt the sting. And thought, on an impulse, to pull up his left elbow to crack his shoulder—an old injury from many decades ago, as a young agent in the field. The shoulder joint enhancement cracked slightly off, and a twinge of pain followed. But this pain usually tingled. Today, it merely stabbed. He tried it again. Same result. He hadn't done that for a long time; the doctors insisted he shouldn't, and his wife scolded. The sensation wouldn't be stored in his short-term memory implant. Talee VR couldn't replicate it. They'd be guessing.

"Fuck," he said. Again the stares. He never swore either. Was that VR, messing up his head, or was that really him? He pulled his gun and strode from the room.

"Sir?" called Amirah. "Sir!" Out into the hallway, headed Allah-knew-where. "Director Ibrahim!"

He spun on her and put the gun to his head. "My shoulder has an old injury. The pain when I manipulate it is different. This is VR."

"Sir, no!" Real fear on Amirah's face, coming closer, her hand outstretched. "Give me the gun, the Talee could be manipulating that pain to make you think it's VR, and shoot yourself for real."

"Why not just kill me outright?"

"To not make a bigger incident, to not kill the FSA Director themselves, make it a suicide." Behind her, Hando and Reichardt were in the dark hallway. "Sir, let me take . . ."

Ibrahim levelled the gun at her head. "Are you really Amirah? Can they put us all in a VR together, or are you just a simulation?"

"If that's your question, then nothing I could tell you could convince you," Amirah said carefully, slowly creeping in that braced, dangerous way GIs did when threatened.

"The real Amirah could have disarmed me by now. . . ."

And in a flash his pistol was gone, his hand stinging from her speed. She pocketed the pistol and put her back to the wall. "Hit me here," she commanded, pointing to her left ribs. "There's a raw nerve in one that never entirely healed from the last shooting. Hasn't twinged for months. If it's VR from short-term memory they won't be able to replicate it, same as your shoulder. Hard as you can."

It still gave him pause. She was a slender girl compared to most GIs. Pretty, young and . . . yes, he had to admit, something like a daughter to him, in these last months, in what they'd been through together.

She saw his hesitation. "Seriously?" she asked him, half exasperation, half teasing. He recalled the speed with which she'd removed his gun and drove his fist as hard as he could into her left ribs. And immediately grabbed his hand and wrist, because it was only a bit more forgiving than hitting the wall. She blinked at him, bounced hard off the wall but unbothered. "Nothing," she said.

She pulled her own pistol, a heavier calibre than his. "I'll do it," she said, and put the muzzle in her mouth.

"No!" He grabbed her hand and would have made little progress with the steel of her grip, but she let him pull it back. "No. We don't even know if that works."

"Look," Hando intervened, "they must have cut in at some point. Seamless, so we wouldn't notice. Think back. What was the last time we can definitely agree was real?"

"Dammit, we can't afford this," Ibrahim muttered. "We have to find a fast way out and put the Fleet on alert, simulation death usually works. Give me back the gun."

"You think I'll let you do it but not me?" Amirah said incredulously.

"Right, first thing," said Reichardt in that Texan drawl that got more pronounced the worse a situation became. "Let's all take a wander, meet some other folks, see if they're stuck in this thing too, assuming we are stuck. More data, more possible outcomes. Then we'll see how far this simulation spreads. 'Cause if it *is* a simulation, we may as well call a press conference and tell the world we've just been invaded by aliens, 'cause then we'll overload those sons of bitches trying to simulate a realistic response. . . ."

"This man," Ibrahim snapped with a finger at Reichardt's nose, "is a genius." He strode off. "Let's go!"

The kids slept in the riverbank-side bedroom, away from the riverfront windows. Sandy dozed in the hallway, back to one wall, pistol in her lap. And opened one eye to see Jane approach and lean on the opposite wall, rifle in hand. She had more weapons in a Tanushan safehouse, as did Sandy. They couldn't get to them, as anything in uplinked, networked Tanusha could now be traced. And if the Talee had guessed who Jane was, then likely they'd found some network trace left by her old com traffic and had found her safehouse by now.

"You their mother?" Jane asked, with a glance at the bedroom door. Sophistry and explanation was tiresome, with Jane.

"Yes." She closed her eye.

"You do that because you felt it? Or because you thought you ought to?" Sandy said nothing. "It's an honest question."

"It's a boring, stupid, predictable question, from you. If you'd had any emotional growth since I saw you last, you'd already know the answer."

A silence. She thought Jane would leave. Instead, she slid down the wall to sit. Out beyond the windows, the black night, broken by a few lights on the far riverbank. The windows were polarised one way, central minder deactivated, unhackable. They thought.

The silence stretched for ten minutes, but Jane remained. Sandy opened her eye again and saw her just gazing at the windows. Similar face, but leaner. Not as pretty, but not unattractive either. The kind of face that would blend in with a crowd. Probably smarter to design a GI that way, these days, given the infiltration work they could do. But Sandy's kind were hunter/killers, with brutal skills and short life spans, with no need of built-in camouflage. She'd been expected to die in pitched battle, not end up running security for billions of ungrateful civvies. Physically, she and Jane were nearly identical. Middle-height, shapely, powerful. Based on the same design, she'd been told. To look at them, side by side, they could be mistaken for siblings.

"Takewashi sent you to protect me?" Sandy asked. Jane nodded, eyes not leaving the windows. "Why'd you accept?"

"'Cause he asked. 'Cause I had nothing better to do." A pause. A heartfelt rendition of true feelings from Jane was too much to expect. "'Cause he was the first person to care."

"Crap," said Sandy. "When we met, you killed everyone and everything with pleasure. You liked it. Don't give me this 'nobody cared for me' bullshit. You were homicidal, and you deserved to be killed. Painfully."

"Why didn't you?" Turning her head against the wall to look at her. Sandy thought it was a question Jane had been meaning to ask for the last six years. At the time, Sandy hadn't been sure she knew the answer. But now, if she was honest with herself, she did.

"Because I had to know what you'd become. Finding out that another version of me could be a homicidal drone was scary. Everything I do, I do by choice. Or so I thought." With a faint motion of her head, back to the bedroom. "The variable you were lacking was time. I gave you time. I had to see how you'd use it."

"That's right," said Jane with an unpleasant smile. "'Cause you're the humanitarian, aren't you, sis? Assuming GIs are really human. You want us to be the good guys."

"And you don't?"

"We're hiding in your hometown from the most advanced GIs ever made, and they're trying to kill your cute little seven-year-old. Why don't you go and explain your synthetic sisterhood concept to them?" There wasn't much Sandy could say to that. She didn't try. "You want to see the future of us? It's out there, making plans for our extermination. There's nothing inherently good about synthetic intelligence, never has been, never will be. Don't place your faith with false prophets."

"That why you came when Takewashi sent you? Is he the 'real prophet'?"

A flicker of resentment in the brown eyes. "Takewashi wasn't my master. It's not that we can't make our own choices. It's that even when free, our choices are stuck in a narrow multiple-choice between 'kill' and 'kill.' That's how we're made. And the kind of freedom *you're* after doesn't exist for us."

"That how you rationalise all those people you killed when you were last here?" Sandy asked. Jane said nothing. No reaction. "How about those two in the company you were using as a cover? The ones you smashed to a pulp? Sandeep Mishra, he was thirty-two, had two kids and a wife. She still hasn't remarried. Had to take full psych-tape restructure to get over the loss, still depressed to this day, has trouble getting steady work. And the other one . . .

". . . Timothy Larchey," said Jane. "Sixty-two, four kids, I imagine some grandkids by now. Coached the school cricket team, worked as an insulation specialist on construction projects. The wife's now remarried."

Sandy didn't know what to think. There was no evident emotion on Jane's face, or in her voice. Anyone could do the research and recite this stuff. Knowing what it meant was something else.

"How about all those Federation soldiers you killed in the war?" Jane asked. "You memorised all those? A few of them were probably from here."

"One of them was," Sandy whispered. "I tracked her back. A few neighbourhoods over from where I used to live, in Santiello." It hurt, even now. It would hurt all her life. Jane saw, watching sombrely. "That was before choice, for me. Choice set me free."

"Free to kill again. Free to kill . . . how many was it on Pyeongwha?"

"Lots."

"You gonna memorise all those too?"

"No. Because if you serve something that bad, I couldn't care less."

"Ah," said Jane with a dry smile. "Some deaths good, other deaths bad. Got it."

"We do the best we can," Sandy said coldly. "At least some of us make an effort."

"I make an effort."

"At what, exactly?"

Jane sighed and got to her feet. "You want to know why I came?" she said. "I made a promise to someone. And I couldn't let him down."

"Yeah, well, your master's now dead," said Sandy. "Time to find a new one."

"I told you," said Jane, "I don't serve him." Sandy frowned at her. "Lā 'ilāha 'illā-llāh, muḥammadun rasūlu-llāh," Jane explained.

There is no God but God, and Muhammad is his prophet. Sandy stared, mouth dropping slowly open. Jane nodded and walked away.

Danya awoke. He felt like he'd never really been asleep, waking fitfully, listening to noises in the night. Time and again he rolled to check the bags between the two beds—they were backpacks they'd bought with Cai and Poole yesterday, on Danya's insistence. He'd filled them with things too, water bottles, cutters, some rope. It wasn't nearly enough. Twice he got up to wander the house in search of extra things to bag, only to be intercepted by Sandy and sent sternly back to bed.

He didn't like this bedroom with no windows. Of course, windows were even worse, given what was hunting them. But he worried about line of sight, and escape routes, and warning times . . . silly to worry about, given they were guarded by a house full of high-des GIs, all of whom would know when it was time to go better than he would. But the old habits were back, a bit faded but never forgotten. Svetlana and Kiril slept together on the other bed, the exhausted sleep of younger children who had always had an older brother to look after them. He worried what would happen to them if he wasn't there.

Now he woke and rolled to find Poole sitting between the beds, back propped to the wall. Eyes closed, chin rough with stubble. The eyes opened a little, and looked at him.

"Can they hack you here?" Danya murmured.

"Don't see how," said Poole. "But that's the point of advanced tech, I guess. The less advanced can't see how."

"It works off the local network, doesn't it?"

Poole nodded. "Cai says they don't have transmitters in their heads. They just lock into the local network and take it over. So if we go somewhere where there's no network, we should be safe from it."

"We should go," Danya muttered. "Into the jungle. There's no network reception there. No high bandwidth, anyway."

"Nothing to eat either."

"Plenty to eat," said Danya. "You've just gotta kill it."

"You have jungle survival training?" Danya shook his head reluctantly. "It's not a dustbowl like Droze. There might be food and water, but there's a lot poisonous."

"Better than here." Uplinks had seemed like more of a liability to him for a long time. Now that they were definitely a liability, he wondered if he, Svet, and Kiril wouldn't be safer without any GIs at all. They were protection, yes, but they also attracted attention. And they kept insisting they could keep the Talee out of their heads, but the Talee always got in anyway.

"Danya?" said Svetlana. She was looking at him. "Should we go?"

"I think so." He gnawed his lip. "Anywhere with uplinks and networks is dangerous. But Sandy . . ."

"Sandy thinks we should rest first," said Svetlana, troubled. "Danya, I think she tries to protect us too much. We're tougher than she thinks."

Danya nodded and got up. Svetlana came too, careful not to wake Kiril. Poole stayed behind. In the living room, Ragi dozed on the sofa, while Sandy and Cai spoke in the adjoining kitchen. Sandy gave them a displeased look.

"Guys, you need to sleep."

"We need to leave!" Svetlana retorted. "There are too many networks, the Talee will find us!" Sandy and Cai exchanged glances. It looked to Danya as though they'd been planning something.

"What are you planning?" Danya asked cautiously.

"Best not discuss it further," said Cai. "Just in case." And frowned as the asura, which had been resting on a rug by the windows, trotted past him and headed for the kids' bedroom. Kiril, Danya thought, and followed. The animal turned into the bedroom and paused, staring at Kiril.

Poole considered it with a deadly stare. No one entirely trusted the animal, whatever good it had done at the beach house. It was FedInt trained, for one thing. And now, its muzzle pointed unerringly at Kiril's sleeping face. It moved forward, slowly, as though sniffing.

"Poole!" Svetlana hissed. But Poole barely glanced at her, one hand ready in case the asura had something else in mind. One-handed, Poole could take its head off without effort. Yet he watched, ready but curious. Cai and Sandy pressed in behind Danya and Svetlana to watch. The asura's radar-like ears pricked, and from deep in its chest came a low, thrumming whine.

"His uplinks," Sandy murmured. "What's it sensing?"

"I can't access myself without giving us away," Cai replied. "I'd guess Kiril's uplinks are active, but there's no telling whether it's passive or active."

"You mean he might be giving away our location?" Danya asked.

"Or he might be responding to an active incoming scan," said Cai. "Either way . . ." But Danya was already moving, grabbing his and Svetlana's backpacks, as Sandy told Ragi and Jane to move. Danya ran to the kitchen and stuffed some last cans of soft drink from the refrigerator into his pack and some eggs left by a previous occupant that he'd taken the time to boil so they wouldn't break in his bag.

"Cai," Sandy snapped as they collected final things and made ready, "as we said, you take Ragi and Poole, and . . ."

"Multiple incoming!" Jane yelled. "Move now!" Pulling a pistol and blasting out a riverfront window. Crash, as someone went through a neighbouring window, and suddenly Danya heard it, a whistle-and-whoosh from somewhere above, then a boom! that he felt in his ribs. . . .

"Go!" Sandy shouted, running from the hall with the bewildered Kiril in her arms, and Svetlana was already flinging herself shoulder-first through what remained of the windows. Danya ran to follow, was grabbed halfway out by Sandy and thrown farther. A brief moment of flying, then crash as the water hit him and obliterated sound . . . and a shockwave like a giant fist. Then upside down underwater, flailing as though he'd forgotten how to swim, until he broke the surface and gasped, the water bright with flames and pelted with falling debris. Something hit him on the head, hard, and he dove back underwater, watching heavy objects splashing down above, against a backdrop of flames. Bits of house, he realised.

Svetlana! She'd gone first, Sandy hadn't given her the extra push, she'd have been closest when it blew. He splashed in that direction . . . and heard his name shouted, from off to the left. And there by the neighbouring cruiser port, on a paved section of riverbank, were figures crawling on the riverbank, silhouettes against flames . . . two adults, two children. One of them must have grabbed Svetlana, and damn they were fast to swim over there already.

He struck out that way, swimming around floating, burning debris . . . and noticed that the upstream house was gone too, two walls still upright, but all aflame and shedding pieces into the river. When he reached the bank, Svetlana was there to help him ashore, and Sandy was crouched by a tree across the riverside path, pistol ready, Kiril already well hidden behind.

He joined them, and Kiril protested being picked up again, but Sandy ignored him and then they were running through trees, soaking wet. And immediately up against a perimeter fence, plastic wire and three-meter-high wall, but Sandy kicked one of the posts out of the ground, and the whole thing went down sideways like some bouncy obstacle in a kids playground for them to climb across. Then clambering up a short hill, and finally they paused, Danya and Svetlana gasping, Sandy and Kiril not. Again Sandy took a covering position, which they instinctively copied, and looked back down the hill.

Danya saw through the trees that every house along the riverbank had been hit, at least seven, each now a bonfire on the water. "Fuck," he said succinctly.

"Sandy, how many people are living here?" Svetlana asked.

"It's mostly empty," said Sandy. "Tanusha doesn't like people living outside city limits and commuting, the city would hollow out and the forest would be clear-felled for suburbs. These are mostly holiday homes. Danya, you're bleeding. Svet, check him."

It was brusque and unmotherly, but Svetlana remembered her earlier warning about combat reflex and emotions, and checked Danya's head without complaint.

"There had to be someone home in there," Danya muttered.

"Probably," Sandy agreed. "Could have come from anywhere. FSA and CSA have enough weapons systems that could be commandeered. They didn't have a direct fix on us, so they took out every house on the stretch."

"Sloppy," said Danya. "They gave us time to get out."

"Maybe they're flushing us out," Sandy replied. "Jane's scouting ahead. We stay here until she's back."

"She dragged me out," Svetlana said breathlessly. Her hands trembled as she searched in Danya's hair for the source of the blood. "Jane dragged me underwater, I thought she was trying to drown me, but then the house blew up, she was keeping me out of the explosion. Then she just shot through the water and the next thing I was on the bank, and she was gone into the trees."

"I'm thirsty," said Kiril. Danya glanced at Svetlana and saw her struggling not to laugh. He bit his lip.

"Yes, what time is it on Planet Kiril?" she asked.

"I'm not a planet," came Kiril's well-rehearsed retort. "I'm a star. Danya, can I have my water bottle?"

"You'll drop it," said Danya, rummaging in his bag. "Have a drink and give it back."

"Doesn't look bad," said Svetlana, giving up on Danya's cut. "It's just a scalp wound, they bleed a lot." Danya handed Kiril his bottle and realised the wetness on the left side of his jaw wasn't water but blood. Damn, that was going to get sticky when it dried.

"Where's Dodger?" Kiril asked.

"Dodger?" said Sandy.

"The asura. You know, because he keeps dodging every attack."

"I don't know if he dodged this one," said Svetlana, looking back down on the river. "Maybe he went with Cai. . . . Sandy, did Cai, Poole, and Ragi get out? I saw someone else jump, but I didn't see who."

"I saw them out," said Sandy. She was turning her head slowly, Danya saw. Taking in the dark forest, the undergrowth.

"Where are they going?" asked Danya.

"We've got a plan. Talee can dominate the city network, anyone trying to help us will be hacked, probably put into VR. Cai says he can stop it. He's going to set up a trap for them, Ragi and Poole will help."

"But how do . . . ?"

"Get down," Sandy told them, and they flattened to the dirt and dead leaves. For a moment they heard nothing. Then Sandy let out a small, low whistle. "Kiril, I think your animal's looking for you."

It came bounding through the undergrowth. "Dodger!" said Kiril, and patted the wet asura as it sniffed at him with whatever passed as "joy" in an asura's mind. Danya thought it looked happy, just restrained about it. Like GIs, maybe.

"Did save our lives twice," Danya offered.

"Yes," Sandy said shortly. "Useful." In a tone that suggested that however much Kiril liked his new pet, she wasn't about to risk any human lives to keep it alive. Danya agreed completely. She glanced back. "Here's Jane. Let's go."

They moved, and Danya didn't see Jane at all, just followed Sandy's lead, second behind Sandy as Kiril followed and Svetlana watched their backs. But it was comforting to know that Sandy's senses were so good that she could hear/see Jane well beyond anyone else's range. Now the two GIs used it to pass signals that unaugmented kids would miss entirely.

Downslope to the right were houses, lights blocked by foliage, appearing and disappearing as they moved. "Sandy!" Danya hissed as something occurred to him, heart suddenly thumping with fear. She stopped and crouched, not even looking at him. "What about aerial surveillance? If they can target those missiles, they'll be watching us from orbit or altitude! We'll be on IR right now, and . . ."

"Cai said he can block it," Sandy assured him. "Sorry, should have said. He said he knows what they're using to control the city networks, but they don't know he's against them yet, so they don't suspect."

"He'll feed them a false image?" Sandy nodded. Danya's heart restarted, realising they weren't just about to get blown to bits by incoming artillery. "Good. Then we'll need some more food, if we have to stay in the forest while Cai does his trap. Like that house there."

Sandy considered for a moment, then nodded. "Let's go." She gave a faint signal to Jane, who must have been wondering why they'd stopped, and moved downslope. A fast scout of the house wall showed a secure perimeter, and evidently no one home, given the explosions nearby yet no sign of activity within. Sandy wanted to jump the wall, but Svetlana stopped her.

"Can you get past security systems without your uplinks?" she pressed.

"No, but I can break something."

"And raise an alarm," said Svetlana. "This house is all uplinked. You raise an alarm, they'll drop a missile on it." She rummaged around in her dripping backpack.

"And you can get past it?"

"Sure." She pulled out a little black unit with wires and a couple of small pins, activated and touched the pins together. "Yep, still works. Danya, I need another conductor, you got a pen or something?"

Danya searched and produced one. "Front gate," he advised, as Svetlana stripped the pen for an inner spring coil. "Lock's good, but the paving's loose, you can squeeze under. And if you trigger something, just smash a window and run like hell."

"Yep," said Svetlana. "Rendezvous back up the hill if I fuck it up." And she scampered along the wall, Sandy close behind. Sandy had been about to say something about that entire conversation, Danya knew, but hadn't. Clearly she wasn't happy.

They waited for Svetlana by the wall edge looking onto the rough trail leading to the carport. "She's been practising breaking into our house," Danya explained, as they peered through the leaves of an obscuring bush.

"Yes, I know," said Sandy a little drily. So some of the combat reflex had worn off. "She bypasses primary settings but not secondary, I see those on replay."

"Canas is special security, a place like this won't have anything that advanced." He glanced back to where Kiril remained hidden in bushes farther back up the hill, with Dodger. He grimaced. Well, that was what happened when you let seven-year-old boys name pets. In Droze, he'd once kept a beetle named Flash. When he trod on Flash by accident, Svetlana had renamed him Splat. It remained a sore point between them to this day. "Sandy, what if Kiril's uplinks are giving away our location?"

"I think Cai would see it," said Sandy. "If Cai can access the net as much as he says he can without getting himself killed. And if he can cover us from aerial surveillance, which he evidently can or we'd be dead right now, he can cover us from Kiril's uplinks too."

"Something's not right about Cai," Danya muttered.

Sandy looked at him. "What do you mean?"

"I think he's on our side. I just don't buy his explanation."

"People have crises of conscience about their own side's goals," Sandy replied. "I did."

"He just did it so smooth, you know? I saw guys get antsy all the time in Droze, you know, you want the money but you don't want to do *that*. Kill someone, rob someone, whatever the job is. Droze was one big fucking crisis of conscience. But Cai just . . ." He shrugged, not knowing how to put it.

"Yeah," Sandy agreed. "I know."

"I mean he's alien, I get it. Or aliens built him, whatever. But what do we know of Talee politics? I mean, how many different groups of humans are trying to kill each other? Here, in the League, in the Federation? And how weird would it be if the Talee didn't have the same? I mean, the only guy we've ever heard a real explanation from about how Talee work is Cai, right? You think he's told us *everything*? How much more likely would it be that he was with some other group that disagrees with the main group all along?"

Sandy exhaled softly and kissed him absently on the head. "Who you think?"

Danya shrugged. "Who knows the Talee? But Cai's synthetic. And synth-tech caused the Talee to self-destruct, twice. That stuff's gotta be controversial with them like it is with us. I mean, look how we split on it, Federation and League, had a big war and everything. So now we've got the Talee, one moment the most peaceful neighbours ever, then suddenly trying to kill us, only Cai's trying to protect us and killing his own people. You think maybe Cai's faction was running their human-policy all along? And now the other faction has taken over, only Cai's not going quietly?"

"That would imply there's others like him who might help," Sandy said quietly. "Takewashi said he got a visit from another one like Cai, who warned him not to pursue Kiril's technology."

Danya nodded. "Only maybe that wasn't a threat? Maybe it was a warning, not 'I'm going to kill you,' but 'watch out 'cause these other guys will try and kill you'?"

"Dangerous to assume all Talee-made human synthetics are on the same side," Sandy cautioned. "The ones trying to kill us now certainly aren't, they're human-looking just like Cai."

"And Cai said he was offended by them even existing. What if his faction never *would* have made GIs like that, and that's why he was offended? What if Talee are all split on this synthetics thing, like I said? They certainly like to outlaw some kinds of tech, to the point they'll kill anyone who has it. If that's a thing in their society, a *trend* . . . maybe that's their politics. Or part of it. The synths or synth-users against the rest. And maybe it's dangerous too, 'cause Cai might not just be trying to help us, he might be using us to fight his enemies back home."

Sandy thought hard for a moment. Distant through the trees, rising smoke from the river. No emergency vehicles yet though, that was odd . . . but maybe not that odd, given how the Talee screwed up the whole network.

"That's it," Sandy said finally, "I'm deputising you to FSA Agent. That's as good an analysis on the spot as I've heard from anyone."

Danya managed a smile. "Doing that *and* school will be a bitch."

"You'll manage."

Svetlana reemerged at their side, quiet as a ghost and lugging a full back-pack. "Jesus, Svet," said Danya, "you steal a whole banquet?"

Svetlana beckoned urgently for them to follow, and they did, along the wall and up the hill to where Kiril and Dodger were. Jane, wherever she was, stayed put.

"Sandy, I saw the weirdest thing," Svetlana said urgently. "There were people in the house."

"Did they see you?" asked Sandy.

"No, that's the weird bit. They weren't in bed, they were watching TV. Explosions next door and everything, just watching TV. Only it looked . . . *strange*." Svetlana's eyes were wide, face pale. "I was going to run, but they just . . . I made a noise on purpose, just to see, and nothing. No response. So I figured the Talee were hacking them, and I just got into the kitchen, took stuff and left, and *nothing* from them. It was so creepy."

"Wow," Danya murmured. "Even out here. How much of the city can they cover at once?"

"Lots and lots," said Kiril quite matter-of-factly, seated on a tree root with one arm around Dodger. "I can see flashes of it on my uplinks. It looks really complex when it gets close, like when the missiles were incoming. I think they could put the entire city into VR if they wanted."

CHAPTER FIFTEEN

It was 4:30 in the morning, and Poole drove along streets as deserted as Tanushan streets ever got. He was dripping wet, as they all were, and newly a thief (or Cai was) in the stolen groundcar that was now the safest way to traverse the city. Or so Cai insisted.

"So how can you VR hack an entire city?" Poole asked, letting traffic central steer the car onto the winding outback road, lest some Talee monitor register his precise GI-driving style and get suspicious. Auto-drive wasn't compulsory out here beyond the Tanushan perimeter, but you needed to register as licenced to do it—the usual Tanushan regulatory straitjacket the free-everythingers complained about.

"It's a self-adapting matrix," said Cai in the passenger seat. "It takes a lot of work to keep it running. I think there's at least fifty infiltrators here."

"Some running the matrix, some hunting down Kiril and Sandy?" Poole glanced in the rear vision display to see Ragi in the rear seat. His damaged arm was stuffed under an armpit, and advanced GI or not, he didn't look well. "What percentage?"

"Hard to say," said Cai. "Depends on circumstance."

"The inherent contradictions within the matrix will cause an implosion in time," said Ragi, head back on his seat rest, eyes half-closed. "People not directly hacked will notice those that are hacked aren't responding. I assume they've hacked the FSA and CSA . . . both institutions talk to thousands of people every day, they'll notice if they're not replying."

"But they are replying," Cai said grimly. "False conversations, false interactions, or hacking the interlocutor's brain to change their mind about interaction in the first place."

"That gets obscenely complicated," said Ragi.

"VR *is* obscenely complicated."

"But this tries to seamlessly mesh together VR and real-world, one controlled and the other random. To track every permutation, every interaction, to infiltrate that many minds to prevent suspicion leading to realisation and a crash . . ."

"Yes," Cai agreed. "It has a twenty-four hour shelf life. Much longer, and the internal contradictions will cause implosion, as you say."

"So we need to keep Cassandra and the kids alive for twenty-four hours," said Poole.

Cai shook his head. "They won't last that long. I'm running interference on the infiltration matrix. I use the same technology so they haven't registered it's me. I'm fooling them the same way they fool everyone else, they're looking on aerial surveillance and seeing nothing, not realising I'm hacking them. But that won't last more than a few hours, if that. We need a distraction."

"We need more than a distraction," Poole muttered, noting a street sign, ten kilometres to the perimeter. Out here it was mostly trees, dark with no street lights, just the occasional glow of a small, passing settlement. "We need to take out the whole fucking matrix."

"That's just the distraction I mean," Cai agreed. "We need a place with a big, internally secure network. Independent processors. FSA and CSA are out, they're too compromised by now. Some place unsuspected."

"Sadar Institute of Technology," said Ragi. "Not the largest intranet, but largely autistic since they do so many classified things there. I'm friends with some researchers there, they'll help."

"Not in this they won't," said Cai. "Uplinked minds are too easily controlled. Human minds, straights. I can help, but I'll be most proficient helping GIs. Humans are too difficult. We need as many GIs as we can get, and we need to get them to Sadar Institute of Technology. There I can make us a little bubble of resistance, from where we might be able to mount a counter-attack."

"And how do we do that?" Ragi asked. "Even if we have numbers, you're the only one with a chance of unravelling the infiltration matrix. And if there's fifty of them, and one of you. . . ."

"I can disrupt it. We can, using the Institute systems, which I can reinforce from their net assaults. They'll have to attack it in person."

"Which they're sure to do," Poole observed.

"Which is where our GIs come in," said Cai. "If we can assemble a strong enough fighting force, we might be able to kill enough of the attackers to get their numbers down to somewhere manageable."

"So that's your grand high-technology plan?" Ragi wondered, staring at the car ceiling. "Kill enough of the operators that they can't run their matrix?"

"Yes," said Cai decisively. "And bullets and bombs remain the most effective ways to deal with high-des combat GIs as well. Or a well-timed punch in the head, as Cassandra just proved. The most effective solution to high-tech offence is low-tech defence, always will be."

Sandy crouched in cold water at the inner bend of a shallow stream. Undergrowth overhung, drooping green fronds into the flow. From above came the keening of a flyer's engines. Perhaps half a kilometre away and passing. They'd be back soon, sweeping on a search pattern. Behind her, Danya and Svetlana were sharing food with Kiril. Svetlana was shivering, skinny and worst affected by the cold.

About the stream bend Jane appeared, keeping her rifle above the water. "They'll figure we're in the water," she murmured. "They'll put boots on the ground to flush us."

"Good," said Sandy. "I want a better gun. Better yet, I'd like that flyer." They kept voices low, in case someone already was on the ground. It was an hour after dawn, and already their pursuers seemed to have figured out their aerial surveillance wasn't trustworthy.

"They won't fly that low," said Jane. "But you're right, we have to hit them. We're better than them in a fight, individually. Especially away from the city."

"Sandy," Danya said urgently, repressing his shaking jaw in the cold water. "You should go, both of you. If you stay and try to protect us, you'll get tied down. And by attacking and killing them, you not only do what you're best at—you take their attention away from us."

Sandy stared at him for a moment. Then out of their little overhang hiding spot, across the stream. "Kid's got a point," said Jane.

"Where's Dodger?" Kiril wondered. Looking at him up to his chin in river water, eating and shivering, was nearly more than Sandy's combat reflex could take. She steeled herself and forced down her thumping heart. Her kids hunted by anything but GIs, she could handle. But against the likes of these, she knew the odds. And it took a full-on effort to stay locked so hard into combat reflex that she didn't break down completely.

"I think he's scouting," Svetlana volunteered. "Lots of animals in the jungle, the Talee will think he's just another one. He won't give us away."

"Asura aren't native to Callay," Danya corrected. "If they bothered to check, he might."

He offered Jane some cold meat from Svetlana's food stash. "Kid's uplinks aren't transmitting," Jane observed around the mouthful, peering upstream. "If they were, we'd be dead. He's receiving, but he's passive."

Sandy looked at her. Jane returned a sombre gaze. "Kiri," Sandy murmured. "Over here."

Kiril waded past Danya, and Sandy helped him onto a low rock. The water up to his waist, he looked up at her, wet and scruffy and trusting. Again the desperate fight to keep combat reflex in place.

"Kiri, can you see anything else on your uplinks?"

Kiril shook his head. "No, I think we're out of range of any networks here. But when they scan it's like . . . I don't know. I just feel it, more than see it. It's like a dream."

"Kids' brains are wired differently," said Jane. "He might have a better intuitive sense of it than straights do. But that thing in his head is Talee, and no question it recognises what these guys are using against us. If he can do it passively, it might be our only chance to see what's coming before they see us."

Jane was right, of course. Sandy had been terrified of making serious use of Kiril's uplinks because of the dangers it posed to his young brain. But the worst that could happen was injury, and now they were facing near-certain death . . . unless they could find some kind of advantage.

"Kiri," she said, pulling the booster cord from her pocket and plugging it in to the back of her head. "I'm going to make a connection with you. A proper connection, you understand?"

"Wait, won't *they* see it?" Svetlana asked. Danya looked scared for an entirely different reason.

"I don't think so, the booster creates its own network." Sandy patted her pocket, where the cord connected to the booster unit. "It's all self-contained."

"But you have to make wireless contact with me," said Kiril, glancing up at the rock overhang above them. "But I guess it won't penetrate this."

"But keep an eye on it," said Jane, "because from what we've seen of Talee, they can hack into any network, wireless or otherwise, whether it was meant to be hacked or not. Autistic-external won't help you."

"Sure, but they have to see it first," said Sandy. The hum in her head indicated a network presence, the booster creating a cyberspace construct of its own. It felt like a line, an artificial horizon, running through her head. One flip, and all reality would reverse itself. "Danya, just hold onto him and make sure he doesn't fall over."

"You don't need that?" Danya asked, doing that.

Sandy shook her head. "Are you ready?

"Yeah," said Kiril a little nervously. "Is it going to feel weird, or . . ."

She flipped it . . .

. . . and was in a blank space. There were no walls or floor, which was always disorienting at first, so she tuned in the detail just a little more . . . and a floor appeared. Walls, corners. A square room.

"Sandy?" It was Kiril's voice, and she turned. He sounded tinny, bereft of detail. A light hovered, head height, above the floor. "Sandy, is that you?"

"Hi, Kiri. What can you see?"

"Um . . . I think I see a room. And a shape, it looks . . . yeah, it definitely looks like you."

"Okay . . . we're still not sharing very much data, that's why all the detail is low. How do you feel?"

"Um . . . okay. It's a bit strange."

"Do you feel the water? Anything from the river?"

"No, but . . . hey, I can see more now."

Sandy did a subconscious dart into the data stream and saw that, sure enough, the data feed was increasing. "Well, I'm not doing that," she said. It scared her, the sudden rate of increase. Almost as though . . . "I think your uplinks are doing that on their own."

"Cool!" said Kiril. Back in the VR room, the light representing Kiril was slowly materialising. Kiril-sized and Kiril-shaped . . . and god knew how it knew those dimensions so exactly. Most non-GIs doing VR for the first time had to have that data fed in externally. It even had Kiril's clothes. Detail continued to resolve, far beyond what it should at this level of integration.

Finally it was Kiril. He gawked at himself, looking at his hands and arms, then turning to stare at the unnaturally bare room. Then he turned to Sandy, grinned, and ran to hug her. Sandy hugged him back. Even that felt real, almost to natural standard.

"We shouldn't be able to make VR this real on a wireless connection off a booster, should we?" he suggested.

"No." She frowned and stepped back to look at him. "You still feel okay?"

"This is amazing!" He stepped back to look around. "I guess it knows what you think I look like, huh?"

Damn, of course it did. It amazed her that Kiril just seemed to grasp what the technology was doing. But then, as Jane said, he was intuiting as much as thinking.

"Can we go someplace?" he asked, all excitement. "Can we load some VR place?"

"No, we need a network to do that," said Sandy. "Something to connect us to a big computer. Right now we're just inside my little booster." Kiril jumped up and down. Then danced on one leg. Sandy repressed a grin. "What are you doing?"

"It feels a bit funny. Like . . . I don't know."

"It's a simulation," Sandy explained. "All the signal receptors in your brain that work when you're walking or jumping have to be stimulated exactly the same as when you're doing it for real. Since you're so new to it, your brain isn't reading quite the same signals, that's why it feels strange. But after a while, your brain will fill in the gaps on its own, without needing to be told." Because the human brain, worryingly enough, liked to be fooled and would compliantly play along when directed. Except for high-des GI brains, which broke information down into pieces and refused to accept the overall narrative quite so easily.

"I can't believe we're not actually here," said Kiril, looking around. "This is so cool." Most people in VR for the first time had some kind of nausea or cognitive difficulty before their brains adjusted. Sandy couldn't help but feel proud that Kiril showed nothing like it.

"Now, Kiri," she said, "come here, take my hand." He took it. "We're going to go into data mode."

"You mean cyberspace?" It remained the colloquial term. "I've been there lots, I can see that fine on my AR glasses."

"You ready?" She flipped again, and the blank walls disappeared. About them was infinite space . . . and yet finite, close range, and lit with light. Here was a huge, massively complex golden half-sphere, layered and gleaming with complexity.

"Woaw!" She could still see him, physical representations were not necessary in cyber, but for Kiril on his first adventure, it was probably easier. His figure was transparent, postureless with nothing to react against in this space. "What's that? Is that you?"

"Yeah, that's me. Or that's every bit of my brain and systems that's connected to a network."

"It's *huge*!" Again she had to smile. A seven-year-old's enthusiasm was infectious. "That's 'cause you're a GI, right?"

"Yeah, there's much more in my brain that connects to something. And all of that is able to connect to a network. See that over there? Look to your left." He looked. Not far off was a much smaller globe with a similar radiant layer, like atmosphere over a planet. "That's you. See these little fuzzy links between us? They're kind of whizzing around all over the place?"

"Is that the wireless? I mean, that's cyberspace showing a wireless connection?"

"Yep. Now let's go over and have a look at you. . . ." She did it slowly, because sudden movement in here could really create nausea, which the disembodied brain struggled to process, leading to a VR breakdown. Kiril's network construct came closer, intricate details emerging, like a tightly wound ball of microfilament wires. "Each of those little wires is an information pathway. And this outer shield is your barriers. So right here your barriers are hardly active at all, you're admitting me no trouble at all. That's why we can share a VR space together so easily without a proper network."

And that scared her again, because if his barriers were that easy to penetrate, he'd be completely defenceless to the Talee . . . but on the other hand, his net connections didn't link to anything very vital. Attacking them could sever connection between his brain and the uplinks but couldn't actually attack his brain at all. Yet. With the level of invasiveness of this uplink tech, that would come later, she was sure of it.

It looked good though. Solid. The detail in his construct was organised in ways that looked to her trained eye as though they shouldn't work with normal tech . . . clearly something else was going on with Kiril's tech, down on the molecular level. The tests the FSA doctors had done had suggested as much.

"How much does it connect?" Kiril asked, gazing at it. "I mean, these are the receptors here and here. . . ." he pointed to where the wireless tendrils seemed to be interacting with the construct, causing reciprocal flashes of activity. "So these are activating my VR capability? And I should be sharing all kinds of stuff with you, into that VR stuff?"

"Well . . ." It wasn't an easy thing to explain to someone without the technical lingo. "Sure. But see, this is the problem with Neural Cluster Tech, NCT—the stuff they were using on Pyeongwha. It shared *everything*. There was no filter, and then every other brain responded the same way, so you had this crazy echo effect, where people's brains were all trying to copy each other, and it changed the way their brains worked."

"See if you can feel this," said Kiril. And Sandy felt . . . wow. It was odd, a completely unwarranted change in her emotional state. Only it wasn't *her* emotional state, it was . . . Kiril? She felt excited, but not in the more complex way an adult might . . . it was just enthusiasm, without roots. But more than enthusiasm. Awe? "That's how I felt the first time I saw Tanusha from the air," Kiril explained.

"I can feel that, yes," Sandy said quietly. She didn't know what to think. All her years of uplinked and networked experience, she'd never felt anything like it. With anyone.

"How about this?" This one she recognised immediately . . . and she had to flip them out of cyberspace into the VR room once more, because she'd started to cry, and in cyberspace an unrequited physiological reaction could cause VR collapse. He stood before her now, in the blank white room, scruffy-haired and incurably curious, gazing up at her. Looking at him, Sandy felt love, so pure and intense . . . yet not *hers*. "This is when I think of all of us together," said Kiril. "You, me, Danya, and Svetlana. I mean, not all the time, but when I think of what it would be like if one of us wasn't here? And then I think of how much I like all of us together."

"I feel like that too," Sandy managed to say, her hands on his shoulders.

"I know," he said, smiling. "I can feel it."

This degree of interactivity was dangerous. The future implications . . . but screw the future implications; she was trying to keep them alive. And this degree of interactivity might just support . . .

"Kiri, I'm going to drop us out. Are you ready?" He nodded. She flipped again, and . . .

. . . they were back in the cold water, Kiril blinking on his rock, supported by Danya's arm around his shoulders. Cyberspace was still before her eyes, and she made a few frequency adjustments, adjusted booster power, and activated her own local tacnet. It fired up quickly, with just the booster to run on . . . and immediately she could see Kiril's construct grab it, interact and process it . . . and suddenly icons were spreading across her view, red and ominous.

It took her several moments to figure out what she was looking at. Hostile icons. Enemy, as tacnet processed things, friends and enemies . . . and then it hit her, as she registered ranges, trajectories, even numbers. The Talee synths were broadcasting some kind of search signal, filtered by their own uplinks, and Kiril's uplinks, being of a similar type, were picking that up and processing it while bouncing nothing back. Now tacnet gave it a framework within which to express what it saw, and these red hostile dots on her screen . . . they were the Talee synthetics hunting them. These were the enemy. And Kiril's uplinks meant she could see them, for as long as they kept active scanning.

"Jane!" she said, meeting Jane's eyes. "Tacnet, now!"

Jane connected her own booster, and suddenly Jane was there too, her icon reading green as tacnet failed to recognise her as friend or foe, and Sandy switched it to friendly-blue. Now Jane's eyes widened to see that display.

"Well, that's a start," she said. "But if you generate that wireless connection with Kiril in the open, they'll spot it like a giant fucking beacon. And if they've acquired armed flyers by now, which they surely have, they'll put a rocket on you before you can blink."

Amirah blinked her eyes open. She was in the backseat of a groundcar. Poole was leaning over her, removing an insert cord from the back of her head. A moment ago she'd been in FSA HQ. Arguing with the Director. It seemed indistinct now, like a dream. But it had certainly been VR. Hadn't it? VR recollections were always precise, never dreamlike.

"Where am I?" Poole was attending to someone unconscious beside her—there were four of them, she realised, crammed into the backseat of the car, Poole sitting across their laps. The car was moving erratically, unlike most car rides in Tanusha. Manual control, she realised, looking out the window. It was a regular Tanushan road, not a highway, but there were vehicles parked randomly across the verges, people standing about, talking in groups, pointing. What the hell was going on?

"Talee tried their mass-VR assault on all Tanusha," Rhian said from the driver's seat. She wore light combat armour, and various weapons were jammed into the gaps between seats and passengers everywhere. "Put all the FSA out, much of the CSA. Now the whole thing's collapsing."

She indicated out the windows, steering between stopped cars. Traffic net must be down completely, Amirah thought with incredulity. That never happened. A few of the stopped cars had been in accidents, mostly minor ones . . . but if it was like this all over Tanusha, there'd surely be worse elsewhere. Here in the front yard of a suburban house a cruiser was lying on its roof, attended by a small crowd of civilians.

"Cruiser crash," said the GI in the front passenger seat—Leon, she remembered his name. FSA spec ops, low-40s designation. "You ever seen a cruiser crash?"

"There's been about fifty," said Amirah, remembering something she'd read when researching her new home. "Most of them self-inflicted by idiots messing with traffic central. About five actual accidents, in seventy years."

They had the radio on the car's dash, one of those antiquated functions all vehicles were required to have in case of network emergency. It came through all garbled, auto-tune flicking from one to the next on some automated function—keywords and sender addresses, Amirah guessed. But the gist of it was clear. . . .

". . . *full-scale network assault! I repeat, Tanusha has experienced a full-scale network assault, no telling yet if this is work of the League, or some other entity. . . ." ". . . recommend to everyone to put their uplinks into full autistic, or better yet disable them entirely. . . ." ". . . got net expert Shanti Singh here, says it looks like an automated VR matrix that is putting people into VR involuntarily. . . ." ". . . equivalent to a network weapon of mass destruction, make no mistake if this was some foreign entity, this thing is an act of war. . . ."*

"It went nuts about an hour ago," said Rhian, steering them carefully through some malfunctioning traffic lights, a few concerned locals waving at traffic to warn them—Rhian waved back, acknowledging. "If the Talee are doing the same shit we saw Cai do on Antibe Station out at Pantala, there's just too many contradictions to pull that off here. We think the independents' pirate nets started picking it first, the VR matrix went after them and started putting them and their operators under . . . and of course those guys are all so paranoid they've a million counter-systems to fight that shit, and so . . ."

She indicated to the mess around them. Here ahead were a couple of police cars, lights flashing, attending to some commotion along a shopping walk. The Tanushan underground were legendary Federation-wide for being paranoid, at times criminal, ideologically libertarian-to-anarchist, and often more high-tech than the authorities charged with keeping them in line. Even Talee tech, surely, trying to suppress that many fragmented and ferociously autonomous systems, must have had a nervous breakdown trying to track all the spiralling trillions of permutations as each system fought back on its own accord.

"Well, you see this is the problem with fucking around with aliens," said Amirah, bundling her hair back, as Poole woke the GI beside her. "They're unpredictable. Looks like they underestimated how complicated we are." Poole moved to the last GI on the rear seat, as the near one rubbed his eyes and looked around. "How are you doing that?"

"Something Cai gave us," said Poole. "You've just been upgraded to Talee tech. Or something that interacts with it. Blocks them out, he says—makes you invisible on their matrix."

"Cai's with us?"

"Yep. Killed a couple of his own to do it."

"Really."

Poole glanced at her. "What?"

"Talee," said Amirah, making a face. "Speaking of unpredictable aliens. Wonder what's actually going on with them. Just because they wiped themselves out several times, doesn't mean they're all peaceful with each other now."

"Sandy always said this 'First Contact' romanticism was shit," said Rhian from the front seat. "'Cause you don't know what strategic balance the aliens have amongst themselves. Like if the Talee had first talked to the League during the war, they'd have made enemies of the Federation, and vice versa. We make friends with Cai, who's to say we haven't immediately pissed off all *his* enemies back home?"

"Cai made friends with us," said Poole. "That's different."

"Not to his enemies it isn't."

"So where are we going?" Amirah asked. They passed a turnoff to a major business hub. Down the road Amirah could see blocked streets, crowds of people milling, talking, gesticulating. As though the entire city had stopped work and come out onto the streets. Network "weapon of mass destruction" indeed. People were wondering if they were awake or not.

"Somewhere to fight back. Cai says he can upgrade GIs enough that we can't get hacked again, or not easily. Then we use big, powerful servers to attack their matrix with Cai's matrix, force them to come after us at the source. Where we kill them."

Amirah nodded. "Sounds like a plan. So it's just GIs?"

"That's right," said Poole. "Saving the Federation's ass again. But still they won't support emancipation."

"Now you sound like Kiet," said Rhian.

"Maybe it's time we all did," Poole retorted. "'Cause you might have noticed—the more crises we get into, the more we end up running the place anyway."

CHAPTER SIXTEEN

Raylee roared her car up the access road to Sadar Institute of Technology, dodging through malfunctioning road signals, then crashed the feeble access barrier, wincing at the damage it did to the bodywork. The car was a gift from Ari, the only truly expensive thing he'd ever bought her. He knew she didn't like being "his girl" in that way, the pretty thing the wealthy former-underground player kept happy by buying nice things for. But she loved to drive, and loved it still even after last year's crash that cost her an arm. Her driving up to that point was now legend in some circles, amongst FSA and CSA guys who knew what she'd been trying to do, and Ari had thought it fitting she had a car to match her ability. With traffic central down, it had certainly gotten them here faster.

She glanced again at Ari as she raced into the complex. He lay slumped in the passenger seat, eyelids twitching, mouth open. She wanted to check his vitals again, but the network wouldn't allow it. Last time she'd uplinked to anything, she'd awoken twenty minutes later face-down on the floor of Ari's apartment. Even as she thought it, another burst of nausea hit her, and her vision flickered like a display screen on the blink. She slowed past the sides of gleaming, high-glass building atriums and a green-grass campus with gardens and walking paths—she'd never been here before, but SIT was one of numerous Tanushan legends, one of the institutes that had helped make Tanusha the technology powerhouse it was today. All empty today; the crisis seemed to be keeping everyone at home.

She took a turnoff into the underground carpark beneath the major central building, headlights coming on to illuminate the space before her . . . and screeched to a halt, confronted by a man and a woman in combat armour, rifles levelled at her head with precision that just screamed "GI."

She popped the door and climbed out, hands raised. "Hey! I'm Detective Raylee Sinta, that's Agent Ari Ruben in the car, he's having a bad reaction to this fucking net virus or whatever it is. . . ."

But the GIs were already moving, one rushing to the passenger door to pull Ari out and dumping him over her shoulder. The woman led them on, talking on what Raylee guessed was a radio link, "Rhian? Yeah, Sinta and Ruben just turned up, he's having a bad reaction to the invader matrix. . . ."

"*Ray?*" Raylee could hear Rhian's voice on the GI's headphones . . . and now suddenly louder as the GI flipped them onto her speakers as they strode to the carpark elevator. "*Ray, I don't think this is the safest place to bring him. . . .*"

"Rhian, his heart's nearly stopped twice." She couldn't keep the quaver of panic from her voice, as they reached the elevator, and the other GI propped Ari against a wall to examine him, taking his pulse. "Ari said you'd be coming here, he woke up briefly, said he could help you, but you had to get him here. . . ."

"*Yeah . . . I don't know if we can stabilise straights against this matrix, Ray, you might notice we're all GIs here . . . wait, how are you still awake? You're close to Ari, they should have knocked you out first.*"

"I think it's because I got high-level uplinks late. It's . . . it had me for a while, but when I came to it's left me pretty much alone since. . . ."

The elevator opened, but Ari was beginning to convulse once more. "Rhian!" Raylee yelled, trying to grab him, as the GI tried to lift him once more. "No! No, you can't move him like this, he's going to need CPR again!"

And immediately footsteps were running, as Ari was laid on the floor before the elevator doors, Raylee turning him onto his side in case of an airways blockage. A Chinese-featured man skidded on the polished hallway floor on his knees and put an insert cord into the back of Ari's head. . . .

"Are you Cai?" Raylee demanded. "Cai, right?"

Cai paid her no attention, eyes momentarily closed. Ari stopped convulsing. Cai looked up. "Now you."

"Me? Oh no . . . what are you . . . hey!" As one of the GIs grabbed and twisted her arm, forcing her forward, where her hair was pulled aside to reveal the little insert that she still hated to use. . . . "No!"

And she awoke in a teacher's chair in an institute classroom, with a view across the wide sweep of river. No disorientation, no dizziness and looking around to wonder where she was. Somehow she just knew this was classroom H15 in E Block. She even knew the SIT layout now, an arc of buildings along the inner bank of a loop in the river, each one facing onto a central, inner building, connected with walkways and separated by gardens. This building was at the very tip of the arc, the center of the five riverside structures.

And here in the middle of the room, using the holographics, was Ari. He stood with Rhian, hands flying across the hovering icons, pointing things out to her.

"Hi, Ray," he said without looking at her. How did he know she was awake? "How do you feel?"

"I'm . . ." She got slowly to her feet, careful of moving too suddenly. But she felt fine. Except that . . . "Wow." She could see cyberspace overlaid on her vision. That was usually hard for her and would bring on a bout of nausea. Now, nothing. Her head seemed to be buzzing with awareness. "I can see stuff. Lots of stuff . . . is this the institute schematics?"

"Schematics, networks, mainframes, everything." He turned, looking at icons, and she could seem him grinning. "We've been upgraded. Talee tech. Fucking amazing."

They left the stream with five hundred meters to go to the river branch that Sandy's internal-memory map told her was up ahead. The stream joined with the river farther along, but only after a wide bend that took it very close to where tacnet was now telling them a ground party of four was approaching. The flyer had come down that way fifteen minutes ago and hovered above the trees, while tacnet showed single figures jumping from the back. Farther upriver, more Talee-GIs were down, another four with tacnet uncertain of two more behind. The tactic was obvious—squash them up against the riverbank and force them to cross.

Sandy pushed low through the undergrowth now at the bank, ankle-deep in mud. The river here was only fifty meters wide, and bendy, over-grown by thick forest on all sides. Infrared showed her little coloured dots of animals and birds in places, but a concealed GI would give a similar signature. There was movement everywhere, wind brushing the leaves, insects buzzing, small animals leaping from branch to branch. She had to consciously dial down her visual sensitivity—GIs were urban combat specialists, and out here, data became cluttered. But the GIs hunting them would have similar trouble.

Danya pushed up behind, more like knee-deep, holding a mangrove branch aside so it wouldn't snap back in his face. He was sweaty, tired, and muddy, but seemed to be holding up. Behind him, Svetlana helped Kiril, both exhausted.

"We have to cross," Danya whispered. Without uplinks, he couldn't see the threat that now moved to surround them, but Sandy had described it to him, and Danya could visualise a tactical situation as well as most grunts. "They'll trap us."

"If you get caught halfway across, you're dead," Sandy replied. Flyers had been passing near, on a search pattern. Her personal tacnet didn't have the range to see them unless they came close, so she had no idea how many. Perhaps no more than two, she thought. But if one passed overhead when the kids were halfway across the river . . . "GIs don't miss, Danya. It's not like exposing yourself to fire against straights. That's a risk. This is just dead, automatic."

Jane pushed up past Svetlana and Kiril, as Svetlana helped Kiril drink from their dwindling supply of water. "Cross or fight," Jane murmured, without preamble.

"Fifty meters, it takes too long," said Sandy. "If they've any suspicion we're tracking them, they could have someone transmission-blanked on the far side, they could have ambush spots along the far bank, waiting for someone to cross. It's what I'd do."

"They may not have that many people," Jane replied, her lean face deadly calm beneath the brim of her cap. "If Cai's plan's working by now, he'll be causing trouble elsewhere, that will divert some of them. . . ."

"They might just hack some heavy weapons and level Sadar Institute," Sandy retorted.

"Won't kill the mainframes," Jane disagreed, "they're underground, and I don't think Talee want to cause *that* big an issue, flattening an entire facility."

"You don't think a mass VR attack is big? Jane, this thing's the network equivalent of WMD, we can't count on them holding back for anything, which means we have to assume Cai's intervention won't work. . . ."

"Sandy!" Danya hissed impatiently. "You're being too defensive! You're thinking only about defending us!" With a jerk of his head back to Kiril and

Svetlana. "You're a Hunter/Killer! You're built for attack! If you just defend, against these guys, it isn't going to work!"

Sandy gritted her teeth. It nearly hurt to hear him speak of her like that, but combat reflex blocked most of it. Besides, she was becoming accustomed to hearing tactical common sense from Danya, and in situations like this he was more an asset than a liability. Except of course that he couldn't fight against these opponents, and she wasn't prepared to countenance any risk to him whatsoever. And now he was telling her that she had to countenance exactly that, or they were all dead. The worst part was that she knew he was right but still didn't want to accept it.

"Kid's right," Jane said firmly. "I figure they'll pick up our network within a hundred meters, and then they'll target us just like we're targeting them. They've got built-in output, but they rely on the city network for passive reception—otherwise they'd have found us by now. So if we're going to hit them, we can't be too far away from Kiril, or we lose tacnet."

Because whatever active signal the Talee-GIs were putting out, Kiril's uplinks were converting it harmlessly and processing it for Sandy's much-lower-strength tacnet. In Tanusha, the city network would have registered that tacnet and boosted the signal, allowing Talee to find it easily, and hack them. The Talee's active signal, Sandy reckoned, would be something that found autistic networks or network systems, and turned them on against their will. That would explain how they continually broke into systems that were supposed to be disconnected. But Cai had given her and Jane enough new barrier defence to limit the range of that, and now Kiril . . .

Sandy stared at him. He was muddy, tired, and panting, but uncomplaining. What else did Cai put in there, without telling them? Was what Kiril doing now a new function or not?

"If we're going to do this," said Jane, "it'll need to be from range. If we're too close they'll sense tacnet and hack us."

"No," said Sandy. "I'm better in close, and you're the only one with a rifle." She looked at the kids. "And you guys had better . . ."

". . . stick together," said Danya. "You need Kiril close, but Kiril can't move fast by himself if he has to. It's all of us or none."

Raylee left the elevator into the lower-level carpark, where several more cars were pulled up, and GIs scrambling to hand out weapons. They'd only been able to wake GIs from CSA and FSA, mostly, and didn't appear to think "straights," as they called non-GIs, were worth the effort anyway. Raylee spotted Rhian in light armour and ran to her.

"Rhi, you got anything spare?" Looking at the boot full of weapons, and various light armour being quickly strapped on. "I can help."

"I'm pretty sure Ari wants you to leave," Rhian said dubiously, checking grenades in the rapid-magazine on her front armour webbing. "Deb, is that A5 spare?" A GI tossed her a heavy sidearm and magazines, which she tucked into a belt holster.

"Yeah, well, Ari's not my boss." Her heart was thumping unpleasantly, and she couldn't quite believe what she was suggesting. But she was here now and apparently immune to the infiltration matrix for now, and she couldn't run away.

"What's your combat rating?"

"Standard police course, high marks." Someone snorted, amidst other conversation. Raylee gave him a dark look. "I know I can't fight high-des GIs directly, I'm not dumb. But you'll need someone running around doing odd jobs, carrying ammo, retrieving wounded. I can do that."

"You get wounded," said one of the preparing GIs, "we can't spare another body to help you. Combat assets are worth retrieving, and wounded GIs can still fight, even missing limbs. You can't."

"I know," said Raylee. "I get it, I'll stay in the rear and keep out of your way."

"*Ray?*" It was Ari, cracking in on their channel. "*Ray, don't you . . . Rhian! Rhian, don't be stupid, she's a cop, not a soldier, tell her to get the hell out of there!*"

Rhian turned him off. How Raylee could tell it was Rhian who did it, she wasn't sure. She could just see multiple sensory overlays across her vision. Audio made a small window on the bottom left, somehow synthesising itself across both eyes, not disappearing if she closed either one. Augmented reality just opened if she squinted hard enough, allowing network-uplink of surrounding rooms, and now the GIs' tacnet filled those rooms with friend-or-foe. Everything the network knew, she knew or could find out with a little effort. It was enough to make her head spin. This was what GIs saw, without trying.

"I don't like it either," said Rhian. Ari tried to break back in. "Ari, either leave her alone or get a different girlfriend." And cut him off again. And to

Raylee's grateful look, said, "The reason I don't like it is the same reason *he* doesn't like it—I actually like you, and I probably will risk my neck to help if you get hurt."

"I won't be a burden," Raylee said firmly. "I'm good under pressure." She was. The few times she'd been in dangerous situations with criminals, where guns were drawn, she'd made good choices and everything had seemed to make sense. Her augments now were way beyond what they had been then, and problem-solving was always her thing. Surely a whole bunch of combat GIs could benefit from an organic perspective here and there?

"Okay," Rhian sighed. "We're all big on free choice here, or so Sandy tells me." She pulled a remaining weapon from a car boot—it was an assault rifle, standard SWAT issue. "Used one of these?"

"A few times on the firing range." She took it, and it was heavy, but with her more recent augments, heavy didn't bother her.

"First thing, forget about the rifle. Use the grenade launcher if you have to—you know how to ricochet against GIs?"

"I've read about it."

Another dubious look from Rhian. "Okay, you don't want to get line-of-sight against high-des GIs, because they'll hit you first every time. So rely on tacnet, don't look at them directly, and fire short into walls and bounce the grenade onto them, a half-second impact delay should do it."

Raylee nodded, mouth dry, and as she activated the rifle's CPU . . . "Whoa." Suddenly the rifle itself felt like a 3D space opening within her head. And she could see ammo status, barrel temperature, targeting. She put the rifle to her shoulder and got a visual close-up of the carpark's far wall. Exactly the spot where the bullet would hit. "My uplinks are integrating with the rifle. That's incredible!"

"Don't trust it," Rhian said firmly. "You'll get tech-fixated, that's what we called it in Dark Star when we got some snazzy upgrade we were so impressed with it made us feel invincible. Always remember your opponent's just as high tech, and in this case far more high tech. This won't impress him at all, and it won't stop bullets.

"And remember the mission, mainframe computers are in central building basement. When we fire up Cai's counter-matrix, the Talee will be on it like flies on shit. We keep them out of the basement, simple. Got it?"

"Yeah, we keep them out of the basement." Raylee glanced toward the open carpark entrance. "Shouldn't we shut that door then?"

"We've got another carload coming from some guys who've rounded up some CSA GIs from their homes. . . ." Rhian glanced at the open door as she spoke . . . and yelled, "Get down!"

Grabbed Raylee painfully and hurled her at the concrete floor as shots erupted, bodies fell, and return fire roared in the confined space. Raylee rolled and scrambled behind the car's front wheels, the combination of wheel and engine assembly the only part of the car that might stop bullets, as Rhian angled her rifle at the ceiling above the carpark doorway, not exposing it, and pumped three grenades. Explosions followed quickly, and Rhian braced above Raylee's head and fired a burst. On tacnet a red dot briefly appeared and died just as fast.

"Got him!" Rhian announced. "High-grade opti-cam, like Cai said!" Raylee rolled to peer past the wheel and saw the oddest sight—a body lying on the ground, flickering like a damaged display screen. One leg twitching amidst the debris from Rhian's grenade explosions on the ceiling above him. More shots from someone else, and the twitching stopped.

The efficiency of it was mind-blowing. Rhian had made the attacker dive for cover with the grenades, so he couldn't shoot, freeing Rhian to pop up and shoot—and in that split-second had probably hit all skull. Suddenly it really hit Raylee why Ari didn't want her here. That any straight human could survive combat at this level, for any period, seemed incredible.

"Four down!" came a yell from one of the other GIs, and Raylee looked the other way under the car . . . four? Sure enough, there were bodies on the ground, GIs who'd just been talking and preparing. Someone else was checking on them. There had been seven plus Raylee . . . and she realised she had to get up, and did that, legs wobbling, overlaid tacnet graphics unnaturally bright upon her vision.

"Good news is they don't seem to be much better combatants than we are," said Rhian. "Probably a low-to-mid-forties average. Bad news is I could barely see that opti-cam, it's much better than we've got."

"I've augmented building sensors to compensate, based on this new encounter," Cai added. "But building-network tacnet isn't reliable, only tacnet from fellow soldiers can be trusted."

"Fellow soldiers are going to be dead before they can give tacnet anything," said Rhian.

Raylee rounded the car's end and found bodies sprawled, two clearly dead with penetrating headshots, one with a glancing headshot and unconscious, a fourth with a chest wound near the throat and struggling to breathe. One GI attended them, while Rhian and the other kept motionless under cover of the carpark entrance.

Another flicker on tacnet, and audio buzzing, voices distant until Raylee focused on the audio, which brought it forward, loud gunfire, explosions, and shouting. A friendly icon disappeared from tacnet, then another.

Raylee put pressure on the chest-shot GI's wound, as the carpark security door rolled down and latched with a thud. Then Rhian raced over.

"I've got it!" Raylee told them all. "You guys go and fight, I'll get these guys patched up!"

And they were gone, no arguing, just racing footsteps to the stairwell. Raylee's hand pressed hard on the wounded GI's chest; it felt like steel. How the hell did you put pressure on a GI's gunshot wound? Blood seeped between her fingers, but not nearly as much as she'd expect with a regular human. And it occurred to her that while she knew first aid like any cop did, she had no idea how much of it would translate to GIs.

"Open your mouth for me!" she told the wounded GI. He looked scared, fighting for breath. That shocked her. This wasn't some synthetic fighting machine, just a young guy in a lot of pain who didn't want to die. "Open!" He did, and there was no blood, and he wasn't coughing it up. "Okay, I don't think it's penetrated to the lungs. You're going to be okay!"

"Can't breathe," he muttered, still scared. As on tacnet there was yelling and shooting, and terse remarks from Cai and Ragi—they hadn't even turned the counter-matrix on yet, so the Talee must have figured out what was about to happen and hit them preemptively. So now they were turning it on. There were casualties in the outer buildings, as defensive GIs struggled to spot advancing opti-cam. And here she was, like so many grunts in battle, preoccupied with something else entirely while the war raged around her.

She checked the holes—it was a tight grouping of three, one above the collarbone, two below. The one above would have severed the jugular on a straight, and the two below would have punctured the lung. An attempted neck or head shot, as chest shots would disable but not kill.

"Where is it hard to breathe?" she asked. "Is your chest constricted? Or your throat?" She got no response, his eyes were zoned out with fear and pain, his breaths shallow and gasping. She racked her brain to remember some stuff she'd read about GI physiology . . . assault rifles could penetrate major muscle groupings but would fragment in the process and do no more damage. Internal bleeding wasn't an issue, GI blood was a different consistency and coagulated much faster when the victim was injured. But those muscles contracted to armour density against gunshots, then surely released some of that density . . . but this guy's upper chest continued to feel hard as a rock. . . .

"Shit," she said as she realised and pulled out her pocketknife—one of those things a cop learned to carry for those unpredictable moments. "Hang on, I'm going to get that bullet out." It wasn't hard to find, though it had fragmented to several pieces against something hard in the man's neck . . . and when she levered the biggest piece out, he gasped a deep, sudden breath, and she could see the tension relaxing around his throat. "That better? Good, I'm going to get you to cover, you're too exposed out here. . . ."

But the man stopped her and pointed to the unconscious head-shot victim, a woman. Raylee nodded, got an arm over her shoulder, and did a deadlift she'd never have managed before the augments, jogging with the woman's body over her shoulders. She made the stairwell by the elevators, shouldered the door, and deposited the woman inside with a brief check—she looked okay, a gash of white skull visible through the torn skin, and a lot of blood but already coagulating, and if the bullet hadn't penetrated skull she'd be okay.

Back outside the stairwell door, Raylee found the other man had recovered enough to stagger over himself, and he now lay on the stairs beside the woman, tearing off some cloth to attend to her head, with weapons on the steps alongside.

"We'll block the stairwell here," he whispered hoarsely. "Go."

She realised she'd left the assault rifle back by the car, ran back to retrieve it, a part of her brain firmly expecting to be shot at any moment despite the carpark security door firmly closed. So much empty space felt lethal, and she wondered if soldiers ever became agoraphobic, so great did their desire for protecting walls and cover become.

Back past the wounded GIs and up the stairs, fumbling with the rifle and surprised that her hands weren't trembling more. Perhaps that was the augments, damping down the worst of adrenaline overreaction—the doctors had given her all kinds of lectures about effects and capabilities, but she hadn't had the opportunity to test half of them and hadn't been game to try many others. The stairwell turned, once and again, and she stopped on the second floor, confronted by that most horrid of urban combat obstacles—a door, opening onto a length of space that could end in an enemy who could put a round through her eye faster than she could blink.

She put her back against the stairwell wall and stared at that door, heart pounding. Tacnet showed her that the fighting was in buildings two, four, and five about the perimeter, presumably Talee-GIs had come in by air, she didn't know. The computer mainframes were here, in the central building, down on the carpark level, but there was no access from there, they had to come up to these levels to cross and go back down again. Those approaches were guarded and booby trapped, tacnet showed her the locations . . . and she hoped again the Talee really couldn't access tacnet, but with Cai now running the network here, it seemed unlikely.

Inexperienced soldier that she was, Raylee could see the effect it was having—the defensive positions were spreading to the perimeter, more and more of the defenders engaging, attention being pulled outward. So with high-grade opti-cam, Talee-GIs could sneak in here, while attention was elsewhere, and get into the computers and shut down Cai's counter-matrix. She wasn't a soldier like these others, she couldn't engage on the perimeter anyway. So she wouldn't be distracted. She should just stay here, and watch, and hope that whatever modifications Cai made to the building sensors would detect a sneak-in opti-cam.

But first she had to get out of this stairwell. She reached, hand trembling, and eased the door open. And with one of the greatest efforts of her life, pushed all the way through it and into the kill zone.

Sandy saw all the red dots vanish from tacnet and knew that Jane wouldn't miss the distraction. And two rapid shots, from nearly a hundred meters off amongst the trees. Return fire came back, and even without tacnet Sandy could calculate their position from the sound. Two previous marks, who she'd have expected to shoot back, were not shooting. Jane was accurate.

Sandy came around the tree she'd been using for cover, targeting those gunfire locations. Two more GIs fell to precise headshots, and she skidded into the undergrowth to collect a fallen rifle from one of Jane's victims—the woman had an eye missing, blown straight back into her skull from precision rifle fire. The rifle was an FSA model, and Sandy rolled again, low in the undergrowth, and put a higher-velocity bullet through the head of her first victim, to be sure. She searched him, as tacnet reignited with red dots, scampering and changing position but none yet advancing. There had been only four in this flanking section, and all were down in several seconds. Surely it would give them pause.

Her network barriers registered assaults, a brief disorientation-flash into net vision . . . but back again as she realised she could handle it. Cai had given her a couple of crazy-intricate barriers that integrated with her own, and now the Talee net attacks seemed feeble compared to before. Probably that was Cai's counter-matrix now working—the Talee-GIs' active scan only established a connection to autistic units; it was the infiltration matrix that would exploit that connection and hack the target's brain. Without the infiltration matrix to back them up, these Talee-GIs could net attack her all they liked—without their nasty matrix, they couldn't disable her. Unless Cai's position was overrun and the counter-matrix destroyed at the source.

But now this pause. She'd wiped out the approaching southern flank, four GIs, but she couldn't escape this way because it was too obvious, and the kids were hidden by the riverbank and couldn't outrun GIs. But those Talee-GIs knew where she was now, and Jane, and so could figure roughly where the kids might be between them. Why not rush in and get them, if Kiril was the target?

Then she realised. "DANYA RUN!"

Danya grabbed Kiril, crashed through riverbank undergrowth, and fell into the shallows. He heard the missiles coming, a shriek through the trees, and grabbed Kiril for one last leap and dive into the muddy water. The explosions felt like a blow to the head, then the air was full of tearing bits of wood and shrapnel, and he dove full underwater, dragging Kiril with him. Things hit the water around him, then a submerged tree trunk was blocking the way, and he hauled Kiril over it, kicking and splashing to slide onto the other side . . .

. . . and looked frantically for Svetlana and couldn't see her. Two more explosions ripped big trees to pieces before him and blew him back off the trunk and into the water. He swallowed river water and grabbed the trunk, surfacing to find Kiril still clinging alongside. He couldn't leave Kiril, the water here was deep, swirling and full of underwater snags. He was the weakest swimmer of the three, and if he was hurt here, he'd drown. But he had to find Svetlana . . . and calling out to her would get them all shot.

Another rocket hit the riverbank twenty meters away, and he felt the shockwave through the water, like someone using his chest for a drum. Water sprayed down, and chunks of wood, and a rain of leaves. He held onto the trunk above Kiril, covering him with his body. If the rockets began hitting up and down the riverbank, they were dead.

Sandy ran through the barrage. They were airbursts, blasts and shrapnel scything trees like a lawnmower cutting grass, trunks crashing and falling all around. She figured she was fifty-fifty to get through it alive. But this deep in combat reflex, those odds flashed out at her like a beacon of hope, the best and only chance she had.

Shrapnel tore her, ripped her clothes, but she could hear the rockets coming and could tell from a lifetime's experience of modern combat where they were going to hit, and which way to run, to dodge, and when to fall flat and roll. The shrapnel caused no pain, though from the force of several strikes, she knew they could be debilitating, perhaps disfiguring, even to her. Smoke, fire, and thick clouds of dust hung airborne from the explosions and reduced visibility to a few meters. When she reached the first Talee-GIs, she was on them before they saw her.

She put rounds through faces, point-blank, kicked sideways off a tree to change direction as she rolled, shots kicking off splinters as she returned fire even as she hit the ground, tearing out the woman's throat. A shot hit her shoulder from cover, even as she spun to target while diving . . . and that man's head snapped back as another rifle shot cracked. Jane, she realised. Jane had followed her through that hell, guessing what she'd do. Now they had a chance.

They ran, moving fast, the remaining enemy deactivating tacnet to try and hide. But it did them no good—with numerical advantage fast dwindling, and network advantages neutralised, all that was left was raw killing skill. She and Jane moved as though with one mind, almost as though each knew the other's purpose in advance. Jane drew attention while she flanked and killed, and then vice versa, never stopping, never allowing the scene to settle. And when finally there was only one left, Sandy peppered her cover with fire, ducking low to avoid return fire, which Jane then used to target in a running leap and put a burst through the woman's chest before she could reacquire.

Sandy was at her as she tried to stagger back up, shooting the gun from her hand, then smashing her back against a tree. An average-looking woman, nondescript, infiltration-model. Looking dazed, with no particular fear or emotion. Sandy put bullets through her knees and caught her by the jaw before she could fall, holding her up.

"Nothing?" she asked, as cold and hard as death. No response in those eyes. She smashed the GI's arm, saw the shoulder dislocate, and smashed it again for good measure. Grabbed the broken body from the ground and threw it back against the tree again, still breathing, and gasping. "Nothing at all?"

Jane walked close and watched, saying nothing.

"You still uplinked?" Sandy asked the wrecked GI before her, staring her in the eyes. "This going back to your masters? Good. You picked the wrong fight. We adapt fast. Your tech advantage has just been neutralised. You haven't crippled us. You've improved us. These drones are the start. You're next. You're not the most dangerous species in this corner of space. We are. And we're coming for you."

And she smashed the GI's skull like a melon.

"*Cassandra?*" It sounded like Ragi, though the connection route was unclear. "*Cassandra, the infiltration matrix suddenly collapsed. I'm reading a massive reduction in the enemy presence keeping it stable.*"

"*That's me and Jane,*" she replied. "*We just killed a dozen plus out here . . . and we've been under fire from foreign artillery, they must have commandeered some combat flyers. Can you lock that down for us?*"

"*Of course, Sandy, I'll have it down in a few moments. With the matrix down FSA and CSA will be back on line shortly.*"

"Where's Cai?"

"Cai's dead. It got very nasty here, but we think it's nearly over." The shock of that registered past combat reflex, though just barely. "How are the kids?"

At which she took off sprinting, as *that* got past her combat reflex. "Danya!" she yelled as she ran. "Danya, stay in cover! We got all the GIs, but they've still got flyers! Danya, where are you?" Because where there was Danya, there would surely be all of them, safe and well, hidden with all the cunning of a veteran at hiding.

"Sandy!" came the return yell, from over by the river. "I've got Kiril, but I can't see Svetlana!" Relief and terror, all at once.

"Stay where you are, I'll find her!" If he was in the river shallows, he and Kiril would be relatively safe if indirect fire started once more. "Svetlana! Svetlana!" There was no reply. She ran through a carnage of shattered trees, leaping piles of wood and leaves, ripped clothes flapping.

"Can you see her?" She ran to Danya's voice, vision on full infrared, searching for telltale heat signatures. There was heat everywhere from recent explosions, but shrapnel made small dots, and hot dirt was just a haze of colour, not the dark red and yellow of a body. Jane arrived at her side and took the bank to the right, while Sandy went left. Then a yelping howl, from Jane's direction, that sounded like an asura.

"Here!" yelled Jane, and Sandy reversed at full speed. And crashed through undergrowth to find the asura, anxious by the riverbank, looking at Jane in the shallows, who was cradling a small, limp figure in waist-deep water and looking alarmed, perhaps even scared. The water around her was red with blood.

Sandy screamed.

CHAPTER SEVENTEEN

Sandy sat in the FSA hospital ward at Svetlana's bedside and stared at the sleeping girl. She had a tube in her nose and mouth and various things patched to her arm. There were little gel seals on small cuts across her face, and her hair had been shaved up the sides to allow access to several more. Her left eardrum had been ruptured and was now covered by a big white bandage. And her left thigh had been sliced wide open by shrapnel, now wrapped in a nano-solution bandage beneath the covers and monitored moment by moment. Thankfully the blast had knocked her senseless, so she wouldn't remember a thing when she woke. Thank god. But if that shrapnel had been a little across, it would have removed her leg. A little higher, it would have cut her in half.

The doctors who had been in to check on her cast Sandy nervous looks. Three hours since arriving here, she hadn't allowed anyone to treat her. Her clothes hung in shreds, sliced as though she'd been used for sword practise. Skin beneath was torn and red, blood-caked and nearly black, in great streaks beneath her clothes. She'd pulled out the shrapnel herself, it was mostly larger, none of the fiddly stuff from smaller munitions, save the squashed round in her shoulder. Five main injuries, but nothing as bad as she'd thought, just muscle strikes of the kind she was specifically designed to withstand and keep on fighting. It was trivial, compared to what Svetlana had suffered. Less than trivial. And so she sat with her little girl, unmoving in the neighbouring chair, and waited until she woke. Another day, another week, she didn't care. She wasn't going anywhere.

Danya entered. He was showered and clean and wearing some borrowed clothes. He squatted by Dodger, who lay on the floor alongside, somewhat clean after Danya and Kiril had washed and dried the reluctant animal in a bathroom, so he no longer smelled like wet dog. Animals in the ward were against all regulation, but this particular animal had been more useful in warning of impending Talee attacks than all available technology, and Sandy was adamant that he stayed. Under an artillery barrage that would have scared most animals so much they'd still be running, Dodger had gone straight for Svetlana, found her injured, and gotten Jane's attention. That was good enough for her. Danya ruffled the asura's oversized ears, then walked to Sandy's side, and she put an arm around him. But her eyes never left Svetlana.

"Sandy," he said gently, with concern. "Sandy, she's going to be fine. The micros will fix her ear in barely a week, and her leg will be less than a month. She'll need crutches for a bit, that's all. She'll be more upset about her hair, that's going to take a while to grow back."

Sandy nodded, and said nothing. Thinking only of how fragile Svetlana looked, lying there with those tubes in her. And unable to shake that image, of Jane, cradling Svetlana, in waist-deep red water. Her lip trembled.

"Sandy," Danya tried again. "You're scaring the hospital staff. They have to come in here, and . . . well, you look kind of terrifying right now." Sandy couldn't see how that mattered. "Kiril doesn't want to come in here until you're cleaned up. He's upset to see you like this."

That registered. She gazed at him. "He's upset?"

Danya gripped her shoulder. "You're not functioning right now, Sandy," he said firmly. "Kiril needs you to function. We all do. This is you freaking out. That's okay for a bit, I know you love us, and this scared the shit out of everyone. But it needs to stop now. Okay?"

She blinked at him. And realised, with utter helplessness, that he was right. As always. "Okay," she said in a small voice. And hugged him tightly.

"Now go find one of *your* doctors, and get some treatment on those wounds, and get cleaned up so Svetlana doesn't freak out when she wakes up and sees you looking like a corpse."

Sandy nearly smiled against his shoulder. She drew a long, shaky breath. "Okay. I'm going."

"Love you," he said, and kissed her. It was the first time Danya had ever volunteered that first, without her starting it. Sandy kissed him back, not trusting herself to speak without crying. Then she leaned and kissed Svetlana, very gently. And finally dragged herself away and out the door of the ward.

FSA medical was now a GI repair yard, wounded GIs in various rooms, getting patched up. In intensive care, there were eight, at least half of whom might not make it. In the morgue, thirteen more, including Cai. Nearly all of them were wounded to varying degrees, and regular medicos who rarely worked on GIs were helping out with the biotech specialists, doing basic triage and applying micro-solutions where possible, and stabilising injuries for later treatment where it wasn't.

Sandy's injuries were more a matter of electro-stimulation for the beat-up muscles, micro-environment bandages for the wounds themselves, and a small plasma transfusion for blood loss. Finally allowed off the table, she went to Rhian's ward where she was having her head wrapped to protect the damaged ear and eye where a grenade had gone off near her head. The ear would heal, but the doctors weren't sure about the eye. Replacement parts in the League would be done and largely healed in five days, but in the Federation, laws prevented the creation of GI parts, even as they no longer prohibited the citizenship of GIs themselves. Everything was available on the black market for a price, but the FSA wasn't allowed to go that way, and these days League channels were tenuous. It looked like Rhian might be one-eyed for a while yet.

Sandy sat in clean underwear as a young doctor prepared the bandage micro-solutions and wrapped them around her worst scars. Rhian talked with a senior doctor about her eye and ear, head turned to help her hear. Sandy remained uplinked to Svetlana's ward, where Danya sat with her, and the room where Kiril sat with Ragi, who pulled the dual duty of scanning Kiril's uplinks for possible damage while having his arm treated and fitted for a robotic hand in the immediate absence of a proper replacement. Kiril seemed okay but subdued and upset. It made Sandy want to rush to him, but she remembered what Danya had said, and how all her hovering and worrying wasn't always helping. Being upset only made them more upset. She had to be strong for them, to show them everything was okay. If only she felt it.

Rhian's doctor left. Sandy's doctor had only some wrapping to do on the legs, which Sandy insisted on doing herself. When they were alone, Rhian smiled crookedly. "You know," she said, "there was a celeb magazine offering a lot of money for photos of us two without clothes. We should take a photo and make some cash."

Rhian wore only a hospital gown. They both looked like wrecks. It was almost funny, but only because it was Rhian saying it. Sandy found that she still had nothing to say. Rhian patted the bed beside her. Sandy came over and continued to wrap the bandage around her calf. In her life, she'd had plenty of practise.

"Sandy, you saved them," she said gently. "They're safe now."

"No," said Sandy. "Talee still want them dead. And now with Cai dead, we can only guess what's actually going on."

"Well, then, we'll just have to deal with them first," said Rhian, ever practical. "We've proven we can beat them now. Or you did."

"They're not much better than you or most high-des combat GIs in a straight fight. With Cai's assistance they no longer had the tech edge."

"Proving that you really *are* the most dangerous soldier in the known galaxy," Rhian added. "Given that our known galaxy just expanded a lot."

"Yeah," Sandy murmured. "Though Jane's nearly at my level now." She cut and stuck the calf bandage. "I'd have been screwed without her. Two high-des GIs don't increase capability by addition, it's multiplication—combat effectiveness squared. And we coordinate like . . ." She searched for the word.

"Like siblings," Rhian suggested. Yeah, Sandy thought. That was the word she'd been avoiding. "We'd have been screwed too, without our cavalry. They'd breached the final defences right when Cai got killed trying to stop them."

Rhian's "cavalry" had been Tanusha's usual complement of League GIs. Uninvited, covert, and hostile insofar as they were implementing League policy at the Federation's expense, they'd been untouched by the Talee-GIs' infiltration matrix and had maintained enough network insight to see what was going on. A quick debate had brought them to realise that the success of Talee assassination squads was in no one's interests, and perhaps the League's interests least of all. And upon deducing that a final defence was being mounted at the Sadar Institute of Technology, they'd acted as reserve, held back until the enemy was fully committed and hit them from an unexpected flank. Without it, the whole thing would have failed, and Rhian, Ragi, Ari, Raylee, and most other defenders would be dead.

"Damn," Sandy muttered, thinking about it. "We're all going to have to have a talk. All us GIs, before the Grand Council and FSA take over once more."

"They're not in charge now?"

"That's what we're going to have to have a talk about."

Rhian thought about it, nodding slowly. "You know it doesn't make sense? Talee attacking us? I mean, Cai says they're terrified of the tech in Kiril's head, and that makes sense—I mean, Takewashi confirmed it, and the Talee chased Takewashi here because he's the guy who gave it life in human form. But it was a desperate, stupid thing to do."

"I know," said Sandy, tightening the wrapping about a forearm.

"I mean, if it didn't work, and they took casualties, we'd basically have their tech. And we can reverse engineer, and suddenly humans are catching up with Talee, and they've lost their edge on us . . . just after having pretty much declared war on us."

"There's only one way that it makes sense," said Sandy. Rhian looked questioning. "If they thought Cai was already giving us all that tech anyway. Whether they attacked us or not. Then they'd have nothing to lose."

"But . . ." Rhian frowned, puzzled. "But that would mean Cai was their enemy from the start. Not their representative like we thought."

"Yeah," Sandy agreed. "But he's not one of ours, he's clearly Talee-made. Makes you wonder what actually happened in their second catastrophe. How they actually wiped themselves out, and who actually survived it."

"You think . . ." Rhian's one good eye registered shock as it came to her. Damn, she'd gotten so much smarter in the past five years, Sandy thought. It made her happy for all synthetic-kind that it was possible, given a long enough, and full enough, life. "Oh shit! What if the Talee *didn't* survive their extinction event? What if only their synthetics did?"

Sandy nodded. "Like if organic humanity wiped themselves out, and GIs were the only ones left." Rhian stared at a wall, trying to take that in. "In which case, think about it. Would we bring them back? If we had enough tech and enough DNA to do it?"

"You think . . . you think organic Talee are the creation of synthetics? That synthetic Talee brought back their organic creators from extinction?"

"And are now wondering if it was such a good idea," Sandy said grimly. "We can't be sure, but it's worth considering. Certainly there's a big division between synthetic and non-synthetic Talee, and the synths seem to have been running a lot of their foreign policy until now. This would sure explain how that ended up happening. I bet you anything that was what Cai was—the representative of synthetic Talee, not the organics. Only in this case, the synths aren't the copies, they're the original. And what if they laid down some laws to the straights when they brought them back, like 'you guys will always be more numerous than us because you reproduce so much more quickly, but synthetic rights will always be determined by synthetics alone.'"

"Damn right," Rhian murmured. "That's what I'd do."

"Which is why Cai was so offended by these fucking drones sent after us. Organic Talee wouldn't have been *allowed* to make synthetics, synths would have reproduced themselves. Like we were doing briefly on Pantala, at Chancelry."

"And now they're having a falling-out," Rhian finished, "synths against organics. And the organics thought Cai was trying to get humanity onto *his* side, the synth side, and panicked."

Sandy skimmed the net briefly on her way to FSA HQ's interrogation rooms. Tanusha was in chaos, and everyone had been told to take the day off. There was too much speculation flying around to follow without a concerted search, but some of it seemed alarmingly accurate. "Talee net attack" would have been laughed at not long ago, but now it seemed quite prominent, discussed with seriousness by leading experts on various media. The Tanushan tech sector knew what was possible and impossible with today's technology, Federation and League, and what they'd just seen was the latter. Impossible for humans, anyway. It didn't leave many options.

Then came the observations that FSA and CSA had been targeted hard, that there were riverfront homes on a wilderness stretch of northern river ablaze where the infiltration matrix had acquired FSA military assets, presumably chasing someone to kill them. Others were connecting Takewashi's ship's arrival in-system, and rumours it might have been carrying someone the Talee were chasing. The breadcrumbs were everywhere, and Tanusha's techs aboveground and below were too smart not to follow them. This genie was well and truly out of the bottle, and humanity would never be the same.

She ID'd past heavy security doors, then into a corridor where fully armoured FSA troopers stood guard. Beyond a window, several armed agents were interviewing a man shackled to his chair, tubes in his arm. Sandy entered without asking if it was okay, pulled up a chair and sat on it backward, arms crossed on the backrest. The interviewing agents stared at the breach of protocol. The interview subject gazed back at her, unsurprised. Brown-skinned, handsome, broad. A combat GI, currently drugged and restrained to safe levels. And matching exactly the description that Raylee had given, of the GI who had shown up in her apartment, and fed her tall tales about FedInt.

"Name?" she asked him.

"Hafeez."

"Designation?"

"Forty-four and change."

"Commander," said the interviewing agent, "if you don't mind, we're in the middle of . . ."

"This is more important," said Sandy.

"I don't think it's that . . ."

"Get out," Sandy told him and his companion. Flicked her eyes to the door and back, a stare that would take no argument. "Now."

They got up and left. This was not technically her field, nor was this her accustomed part of headquarters to be giving orders in, but still she outranked them.

"You being treated okay?" Sandy asked.

Hafeez looked down at his cuffs and the tubes in his arm. Sedative, that kept a GI's synth-alloy muscles from contracting to critical mass. He shrugged. "Sure. Nothing unexpected."

"I've been right where you are now," she said. "I always ask."

"You've never been right where I am now," Hafeez corrected. "A prisoner of the Federation, while still loyal to the League."

Sandy nodded, conceding. Smart, this one. It wasn't surprising. "You're ISO?" No reply. "Of course you are. Why not run when you had the chance? Before FSA arrived and took you and your people prisoner?"

"We're not all prisoners," Hafeez corrected. They had five of them. *Which* five, and how many more were still loose in Tanusha, they didn't know.

"You're the leader?" Sandy asked. No reply. "Okay. I think you got caught because someone needs to see how the FSA reacts from the inside. And in case someone like me wants to talk about things League would like to talk about. Like Pantala. Takewashi said there were others on Pantala like my boy Kiril.

With that same new-gen tech in his head that the Talee are so scared of. That they warned Takewashi years ago they'd kill him and everyone around him if he started playing with. Know anything about that, Hafeez?"

His stare told her he did. "Go on."

"His uplinks work," said Sandy. "My boy's. He's seven years old, and they were automatically decoding Talee active transmissions and nullifying them." His stare widened, just a little. This was why GIs should always interrogate other GIs—a straight might miss it. "They're not supposed to work this well in kids. I haven't noticed any bad side effects yet; they might happen, but so far nothing. Takewashi thought they could overwrite League's uplink problem. New tech, replacing all the existing tech that's causing League straights to go crazy and kill each other."

A hammering on the window. Sandy looked and saw Hando on the other side, in the observation room, lights switched on so she could see him. He beckoned to her; the interview was over. They didn't want her discussing this stuff with a League GI. Sandy ignored him.

"I have the key," she said as calmly as she could. "The key to saving the League's ass. Possibly the Federation's too, if we end up in a V-strike war with the League. Unfortunately this key is lethal to the Talee, or they think it is. They'll do anything to eliminate it. Only *they* is a little bit more complicated than we knew, isn't it, Hafeez? What do you know about it?"

Hando burst through the door. "Commander!" he said angrily. "This interview is over!"

Sandy barely looked at him. "Either you go outside," she told the FSA's second-in-command, "or I will put you outside."

There were advantages to being known not to bluff. Hando stepped back out, a hand to one ear, no doubt formulating wildly. There was only one higher-ranked person he could go to.

"Speak fast," she told Hafeez. "We may not have much time." Hafeez's jaw tightened. Sandy guessed at the difficulty. "Let me start, so you don't have to worry about revealing this particular secret. Talee ships are all piloted by synthetics, aren't they?" There was as little reaction as she'd expected. But it was there, if you knew where to look. "I've seen some tape, of the coordination in those manoeuvers. A Federation Fleet tape. I'm sure League Fleet has far more experience. However the organic Talee psychology works, I can't see how any organics can pull those manoeuvers, with that coordination. But for synthetics it might be possible, sharing off a common calculation matrix.

"Which means synthetic Talee pretty much run Talee foreign policy, because foreign policy is run by the people in the ships. We know about their dual catastrophes, Cai told us, and I'm sure League's known for a lot longer. But Cai didn't tell us why synthetic Talee seem to run everything, where policy toward humans is concerned. My running theory is that the synths were the only survivors of the last catastrophe and haven't trusted organics since. Given what the organics have gone and done here in Tanusha, it looks like they might be right about that. It also explains why Talee policy toward us has been so sensible and cautious until now, before turning abruptly insane. Organic Talee are deadly unstable. We've just never dealt with them before, only the synths."

Hafeez leaned forward as far as his manacled hands would allow. "What are you offering?" he asked.

"If Takewashi's right," said Sandy, "Pantala will be under attack right now, news just hasn't reached us yet. Kiril's tech originated in Droze, in Chancelry Corporation, after Takewashi loaned it to them. That's a far bigger target than Kiril, he's almost an afterthought by comparison. Whatever their ships, I don't think the synths have the balls to fight their own people over humanity. Clearly the organics have ships too, probably a lot more ships—they just haven't been allowed to use them near us.

"I'm offering cooperation. Federation and League, together, to save Pantala and to give the Talee organics a butt whipping they won't soon forget. And to share this new tech, if we succeed, with all of the League and keep everyone sane."

Hafeez sat back in his chair, considering her. More than slightly amazed. "You have Talee tech. Cai gave you a whole bunch, you've got a bunch of their GI-infiltrators' bodies, and Tanushan tech can reverse-engineer anything. If you help us, you'll have to share that with us too. We won't survive long against Talee warships without it."

Sandy nodded. "That's what I'm saying. I doubt we can replicate their uplinks for a long time, the hardware will be technological generations ahead. But Cai knew enough pure software patches to . . . well. It'll completely change everything everyone thinks they know. And while it doesn't put us on their level, it puts us close enough that they can't just wipe us out by 'magic.'"

Because every sufficiently advanced technology will look indistinguishable from magic to those less advanced, a wise writer long ago had said. Everyone who knew infotech knew that quote. Prior to Cai's intervention, Talee tech had been magic to humans. No longer.

Sandy entered Ibrahim's office at Hando's heels and saw Amirah for the first time since the fight. The girl was uplinked, racing through data on newly safe networks, hair falling roughly about her face. She disconnected as Sandy entered and gazed at her tiredly—the thousand-yard stare of a veteran who had seen one too many horrible things. Amirah never used to have that look. Sandy hugged her.

"I'm so glad your kids are okay, Sandy," Amirah said with feeling. "I was really scared for them."

Sandy believed her and kissed her with feeling. She felt so proud of her fellow GIs. Many of them had died, for nothing more than a sense of civic duty. They weren't so long in Tanusha that they felt connected to it like she did, but they volunteered anyway, out of concern for others, and the unquenchable optimism of the newly arrived.

Amirah left on other business, and Sandy stood before Ibrahim, choosing not to sit, as he was only leaning against the edge of his desk, while Hando glared from the side.

"You don't make the Federation's foreign policy," Hando told her.

"Neither does the FSA," said Sandy. Her uplinks showed her Svetlana, unwaking in her ward, with Danya seated alongside, holding her hand. And Kiril, still with Ragi, now impatient and tired with something. "The Grand Council does, and the Grand Council is out of action. Someone has to make foreign policy, and I'm putting my flag in the ground."

"You can't just . . ." Hando began, and broke off as Ibrahim held up his hand. Ibrahim looked tired. Being in forced VR for all that time could be wearisome, like sleep deprivation, Sandy understood.

"You're right about the Talee," he said. "We have to hit back, or this will become a habit for them. Cai's death is unfortunate, we can't be sure exactly how far the Talee synthetics will be prepared to go to oppose their own kind, and to restore their preeminence in Talee foreign policy."

"We can't even be sure that's actually the situation!" Hando protested.

"But I can't sanction this attempt of yours to co-opt League GIs to get the entire League onboard," Ibrahim continued. "Asking League to invite and collaborate full-scale Federation military intervention in League territory seems foolhardy. The last time we intervened at Pantala it nearly restarted the war."

"I'm not asking League Gov to sanction it," Sandy said flatly. "I'm asking League GIs to sanction it."

"League GIs follow orders," said Ibrahim, eyes lidded with that familiar, wary intelligence.

"Right," said Sandy. "Who else is there from the League chain of command on Callay? This guy Hafeez in our holding cell might be the highest-ranking League operative on the planet."

"'Might be' is not a lot to go on."

"ISO have put high-designation GIs in charge before. He says he's a forty-four series, but he's probably lying. He said 'forty-four and change.'" Ibrahim's always-arched eyebrows arched a little more. "That's a very old expression, from the days of a cash economy. 'Change' is what was left after you'd paid for something with a larger denomination. Most GIs just aren't interested enough in abstract sociologisms to go searching for vocabulary there. I picked some up because I watched old movies and read old books. League makes that hard because League doesn't like old stuff. It's available, but it's not fashionable."

"You're going to trust an enemy GI with Federation foreign policy because he watches old movies?" Hando seemed quite agitated. It only convinced Sandy more of her present course.

"I think he's probably another fifty or fifty-one, like Mustafa," she continued. "I just get that sense, I was running speech-rec as we were talking, and it spiked in all the right places. ISO trust their high-des operatives, and if they've got more like Mustafa, and we know they do, Callay's exactly where they'd use them. Which means Hafeez is effectively the rank of a League carrier captain. Maybe a bit higher."

"Cassandra," Ibrahim said carefully. "I understand what you're saying, and it's a nice idea. I'd like nothing more than to put differences with the

League behind us for a common cause. But consider the Federation's present political situation. . . ."

As Ibrahim spoke, Sandy's uplinks showed her Kiril, abruptly upset and shouting something at Ragi. On the verge of tears. Sandy uplinked, something she wouldn't have dared do before yesterday.

"*Kiri. Kiri, it's me.*"

"*Sandy?*" He was speaking aloud at his end, Ragi looking a little surprised. But only a little, because Ragi would have known anyway. "*Sandy, where are you?*"

"*I'm in a meeting with Director Ibrahim. I'll be with you in a minute. I love you.*" The linkup was broad width, transmitting far more than just words, and she thought hard on that feeling, with no real faith that it would work. But a faint glow came back, and her heart beat a little faster.

"*I love you too. I'm okay, I'm not upset.*"

"*I know. Just be good with Ragi for a few minutes, okay?*" Some mothers she'd heard sweet-talked their kids a lot more, with "brave boy" and "good boy" and "sweet boy." She didn't know how to do that; her brain didn't process platitudes, and, like his siblings, Kiril wouldn't appreciate being patronised. She'd always thought she was lacking something before, as a parent, that she couldn't do such things. Only now was she coming to realise that she truly didn't need to, and that her kids didn't want some mythical, perfect parent—they wanted her.

Ibrahim's explanation finished, she'd been listening with the other side of her brain—the expected thing about the Federation being ill-prepared to take collective military action anywhere, with the mess the Grand Council was in. And the firm expectation that FedInt would block it anyway, especially if it was being led by FSA.

"I understand," she said. A silence followed.

"Cassandra," Ibrahim said carefully, "I must warn you of the dangers of any unilateral action on your part. I know you think the current conflict between FSA and FedInt to be trivial—I must assure you it is not. You don't know everything that I know. Promise me you'll keep your head down for a change."

"I promise," said Sandy.

"*But he told you to keep your head down,*" Ragi formulated as she strode down the hall in medical. "*Are you going to keep your head down?*"

"*Fuck no,*" said Sandy. "*Physical assembly's going to be too difficult, but I want everyone together, and soon. We need to talk about this properly, all us synthetics.*"

"*Sandy . . . you're not planning an insurrection of artificial people against organics are you?*"

"*No, but we've a bunch of things we need to get done, and I absolutely refuse to put them through the process, because the process right now is broken. We don't need process, we need results, and GIs are the only ones who can deliver it. Once we have results, we can present it as a fait accompli.*"

"*Hmm.*"

Sandy entered the med ward and found Kiril sitting on a bed between monitor paddles, more patches stuck to a baseball cap on his head, and looking uncharacteristically disagreeable. "Hey, kid," said Sandy, and sat alongside him with a kiss. "What's up?"

"Ragi's doing all kinds of uplink stuff," Kiril complained. "And it's making me feel sick. I'm tired and I want to go home!"

"Good lord," Sandy said mildly, "what happened to 'oh my god I love uplinks so much! I want to use my uplinks all the time and never stop using them!'?"

"S'not funny!" Kiril retorted. "My head hurts."

"Just the usual full-spectrum checks," Ragi answered Sandy's questioning look. "Cai did some things on the barriers that will take weeks to decipher. Otherwise it all looks remarkably stable."

"He's going to get tape," said Sandy, looking at Kiril but trying to keep the most obvious concern from her face. "They all are."

"I don't want trauma tape!" Again the lip was quivering. "Danya says it turns your brain to mush, I don't want it!"

"Tough," said Sandy. "You're all getting it, because I'm boss and I say so." Kiril started crying. "He's tired," Sandy explained to Ragi, who looked concerned. "And he's been through something that would have given most adults a breakdown, and he's completely pissed off." She put an arm around him. "But you're still getting tape. I'm an adult combat vet, and I've had lots of trauma tape. You don't fuck with post-traumatic stress disorder, Kiri, it's no fun. Even GIs get it."

This was a new phase in her parenting, then. A few months ago she'd have been guilty and anxious at making him cry. But now, she knew she was right, and the insecurity that he'd stop loving her if she got tough with him had disappeared. Kids cried sometimes; she just thanked her lucky stars Kiril cried so rarely. He was the only one who might, at less important things. If either of his siblings cried, something was badly wrong.

"*Tonight, half-past-ten,*" came Ragi's voice in her ear. "*I'll have the VR set up.*"

When they got back to Svetlana's ward, she was awake, and Danya was lying on the bed beside her as they talked. Kiril forgot his bad mood and scrambled up onto Danya, who held him there as he assaulted the sleepy girl with a recital of all the weird things that had happened to him lately. It was Kiril's way of saying hello, and Svetlana seemed happy to receive it.

Sandy just looked at them for a moment, all together on the big hospital bed. Such great friends, with a bond like she knew existed between combat vets. She could almost feel like an outsider, watching them talk . . . or rather, watching Kiril talk while Svetlana and Danya listened. But Svetlana looked over at her, wantingly, and she came, and sat alongside, and grasped her hand and tried very hard not to cry. Without much success.

"I don't actually feel very much," said Svetlana a little dreamily. "It doesn't hurt, they said something about micro-implants, I didn't understand it."

"It's micro-machines!" Kiril said enthusiastically. "They inject them into your blood, and then . . . and then they go woosh! and they multiply, and they get right onto your pain nerves and make them go quiet."

"I told her she's going to be here another five days," said Danya. "We'll bring you lots of things from home."

"Chocolate," said Svetlana. "I really feel like some chocolate." Sandy had to resist the urge to uplink and track down the biggest, richest chocolate gift basket for urgent delivery. And found Danya grinning at her, knowingly.

"You're such a manipulator," he told his sister, "even with a hole in your leg you're still working an angle."

"And a pony," Svetlana suggested. "I'd really like a pony."

"It'll live in your room and crap on your bed," said Sandy.

"Maybe a small one," Svetlana reconsidered. "It can live in my closet."

"You spoken to Jane?" Danya asked Sandy.

"No."

"You spoken to Ibrahim *about* Jane?"

Jane was in lockup, somewhere secure. Sandy was pretty sure she knew where. Jane had broken laws and killed innocent people the last time she was in Tanusha. But she'd stayed with Sandy and the kids all the way back to FSA HQ, despite knowing what they'd do with her when she got there. They couldn't be sure all the Talee-GIs were accounted for, and Jane was serious about finishing the job.

"No," Sandy admitted.

Danya looked curiously concerned. "Don't you think you should? She did save our lives."

"I know. Talking to Ibrahim doesn't help, it's out of his hands. FSA procedure means she gets locked up, she's guilty of some terrible crimes, and since she doesn't technically serve the League she's not a diplomatic prisoner either."

"But she helped us," said Svetlana, also concerned.

Sandy smoothed back the girl's hair. "Don't worry about it, Svet. I haven't given up on Jane. I'll help her. I just can't do it now."

"Sandy," said Kiril, "can Jane come and live with us? I mean, if she doesn't have to go to jail? She is kinda your sister."

"Truth?" said Sandy. They nodded. "I don't trust her. I know what her mission is this time, or what she thinks it is. But she was brainwashed once, maybe she can be again. Who knows what she'll think in another few months or years. And, to be honest, I'm not sure I'll ever enjoy her company so much that I want her around permanently. She's not a bundle of laughs."

"No," Danya agreed. "She's a mess. Like us."

Sandy was surprised. Her kids didn't form attachments to people lightly, or quickly. Except, it seemed, in this case. The main reason she wanted to limit contact with Jane, of course, was her kids. But if *they* thought she should help . . .

Ari peered in the door. Saw them looking and came over. Sandy hadn't seen him yet and grabbed him in a hard hug. Danya and Kiril followed, to Ari's surprise. "Hey, guys," he said. "Sorry I couldn't get down sooner, kinda caught up. Vanessa too, says she didn't want to get in your way."

"Oh, I'll get to Vanessa," said Sandy with a smile. "Gonna need her soon."

Ari gave her a wary look and leaned onto the bed to kiss Svetlana. "Hey, there, Svetochka. Cats finally tagged the little mouse, huh?"

Svetlana smiled. "Yeah, but you should see the cats."

Ari grinned, taking a seat on the neighbouring bed. "Yeah. I guess Sandy skinned 'em."

"*Slaughtered* them," Svetlana corrected, with a cold edge that gave Sandy a shiver. "I wish I was a GI."

"I think you're perfect just how you are," said Sandy. Which was a parental cliché if ever there was one, but she didn't know what else to say. And it was true. "Where's Ray?"

"Oh, somewhere about," said Ari, unconcerned. He looked tired and unshaven but had showered somewhere along the way. And his eyes darted a little more than usual, distracted. Focusing on a far wall as he talked. "Keeping her new buddies company. They all adopted her, all the GIs here. She saved about five wounded guys, took charge of some of the booby traps they'd set when a few of them were shot and couldn't get to them. And flooded a couple of floors with the fire systems so the damn Talee would make splashes when they moved, gave away their opti-cam. She's amazing."

Sandy smiled. "She is. I'm glad she's okay."

"You heard Kiet didn't make it?"

The smile vanished. "Yeah. And some real good kids I had big plans for. I'm getting sick of us GIs getting killed saving the Federation's ass, and no one giving a fuck about our opinions afterward."

"That sounds just like Kiet," Ari said sombrely.

"Exactly. You heard our latest Talee theory?"

"That Cai's GIs are the ones that survived the catastrophe and brought organics back from extinction?" A faint smile, incredulous. "That's . . . that's pretty screwball, even for you. No way of knowing if it's more than a guess."

"You don't like it?"

"You kidding? I love it. It explains everything . . . that's why I don't trust it, it sounds too much like the kind of science fiction stuff I read when we were . . ." A glance at the kids.

Sandy smiled. "Yeah."

"And that you hated."

"I didn't hate it. I just think that kind of thing's pointless."

"You know how warped that would've sounded to people a hundred years ago? Humanity's most advanced synthetic human hates science fiction?"

"Advancing technology's a fact of my life, Ari, and not often a nice one. I've got more exciting fantasies." She grasped Svetlana's hand. Ari looked at the entwined hands and smiled. "But the point of it is, synthetic Talee have a special place in their society. And if I'm right, and if it explains Cai's distrust of his fellow Talee, it means he thinks they're prone to going off the rails, psychologically."

"And you think organic humanity's doing the same thing," Ari completed. She had his full attention now, intense but cautious, like he wasn't prepared to say everything he thought. "Speaking of warped SF plots, you know how much like one this line of reasoning could get?"

Sandy nodded. "I know. But Ari, look around you. Humanity opened a can of worms when the League borrowed Talee tech they knew nothing about and started using it—it got them artificial people it didn't know how to raise responsibly, and uplink tech that started driving League society crazy. And that's caused so many repercussions, and so far it's been up to GIs to save the Federation's ass from those repercussions—twice now, if you count Operation Shield."

"Three times," Danya added. "It was you that uncovered the whole thing in Droze. Federation wouldn't know about it if it weren't for you, and Kiet and Rishi, and Gunter." All of whom were now dead, fighting the Federation's war, with little thanks from the Federation.

Sandy nodded firmly. "And right now, the organic Talee are after Pantala, if Takewashi's right, and we need to stop them. But with the current political mess here, it's not going to happen if we leave it up to business-as-usual."

"You've got a plan," Ari observed, with something between anxiety and excitement.

"I might."

CHAPTER EIGHTEEN

"*Kiri, are you ready?*"

"*I think so. Does it hurt?*"

"*No. I can see all of your construct readings, I think it should work. Here we go.*"

The empty dark of cyberspace faded to light and then resolved into colours and shapes. Yellow sand. Vast stone walls. They were standing in an arena. It stood huge and high about them, a great oval of seats and columns. All empty of people, save for several swarthy men in old robes, sweeping the sand flat.

Sandy looked and found Kiril beside her. He gawped up at the huge stadium around him, much like the great sporting stadiums of Tanusha, only two and a half millennia older. "Woah! Where are we?"

"This is the Colosseum," Sandy explained. "It's in a city on old Earth called Rome. It's still standing today, but it's all ruins. This is how it looked twenty-five hundred years ago." Watching Kiril carefully for any dizziness or disruptive link but seeing none.

"Did they play football here?" He spun about in slow circles at rows of empty stone benches. A few cleaners swept the aisles with whisk brooms.

"Football hadn't been invented then. They had gladiators instead. They fought each other for sport, with all kinds of weapons."

"For *sport?* No *way!* Did they kill each other?"

"Yes. About one in ten of the times they fought, someone died. Or that's what I read." It was an oversight not to have introduced Kiril to this history yet. But then Danya's concept of history was one war after another, and she'd hoped to expose them to more cheerful things first. "It was like religion to the Romans, they believed that fighting was like praying to the gods. Rome was the most powerful empire ever, for about five hundred years. Much of what we understand about modern civilisation started with them."

A distortion in the air nearby, resolving into human form. An outline, then texture, and finally colour, as Ragi appeared. He wore a white toga with embroidered hems, and both of his hands were functional.

"Ragi!" said Kiril, very excited, and ran to him. "Ragi, this place is huge! How did they build it so big two thousand years ago! Ragi, what are you wearing?"

"Well," said Ragi, with an offhanded shrug, "I figured 'when in Rome.'" Sandy smiled, considering his outfit. "A history lesson for small boys. This is called a toga, Kiril. Romans wore them on formal occasions, like we wear suits."

"Can you make me wear a toga?" Kiril looked back and forth between the adults. "Please! You can make me a smaller one, right?"

Ragi looked at Sandy. Sandy shrugged. "His connection's amazingly stable. Go ahead."

Kiril's form blurred for a moment, then flowed out to make a toga. Kiril stared at it, arms spread wide. Then laughed and jumped around in it. Sandy repressed a grin, hand to her mouth. He'd been traumatised a moment ago. Kids were amazing. He was amazing.

Kiril stopped jumping, alarmed at that sensation. "But I'm not wearing anything underneath!" he accused Ragi.

Ragi smiled. "You wanted a proper toga, kid." And he bared his chest beneath his own toga, to show he wore the same. Kiril laughed. "Want a toga, Sandy?"

"After second century BC only prostitutes wore togas," Sandy told him archly. "Women wore stolas; I'm not big on stolas."

"What's a prostitute?" asked Kiril.

"Whores."

"Oh," said Kiril, then laughed. He knew what *that* was, as any Droze street kid would. "Yeah, don't call her a whore, Ragi, she'll pull your arms off. Hey, where does this go?" He ran to the great entrance to the arena, sandals flapping.

"Incredible," said Ragi, watching him. "Seamless integration of upper- and lower-level functions. Extraordinary technology. It works better *because* he's so young, it's adapting as his brain adapts."

"If we put that in the brains of all the new kids in the League," Sandy said sombrely, "we'll change human evolution more in one move than anything since the invention of farming."

"Maybe," said Ragi. "But humans have been self-evolving for so long, it seems a logical next step. And who better to supervise it than us synthetics?"

Another blurring, and Poole appeared, in jeans and T-shirt. Clothes were a personal choice in a VR space like this, chosen at the entry portal. He looked around and squinted up at the far stands. "Great. Sandy and her Roman fetish again."

"Hey, Poole!" yelled Kiril from under the great entry arch. "Where do you think this goes?"

"No idea, Kiril. How do you like VR?"

"I love it! But it feels funny, the colour's not quite right and everything's a bit . . . I dunno."

Amirah appeared, then Jane. Amirah blinked around, then at Jane. And looked at Sandy, pointing at Jane, eyebrows raised. "You can get a stable VR matrix to reach her in isolation?"

"Such is my kung fu," Sandy confirmed. "Or Ragi's, rather. HQ might spot it, but I doubt it. I don't especially care at this point."

Jane looked around, hands on hips. "Nice spot. Needs some decoration though. Ragi, didn't they have training weapons or something?"

Dummy posts appeared in the sand, person-sized and scored with slice-marks. Alongside them, wooden racks with swords, tridents, and shields. Kiril came running back over, eyes wide.

Poole took up a trident and hefted it. "Much better," he said, and hurled it at a post. It stuck with a thud and quivered. Jane took up a short sword and twirled it. Amirah looked over the new setup distastefully and walked to Sandy, bundling her untidy hair with both hands.

"Ragi, I need a hairpin," she remarked. "Something period?" It appeared in the air before her and immediately fell. Amirah snatched it with lightning reflexes and pinned it to form a hair bun. "Thank you. Hello, Kiril! How are you?"

She knelt to give the boy a hug and kiss. "Hi, Ami. Did the gladiators fight with these weapons?"

"Oh, I don't know, Kiril. I'm just a poor twenty-sixth-century synthetic person, and not an especially high-designation one either. Ask Sandy, she knows everything."

"They did," Sandy confirmed. "That one Jane's holding is called a gladius. They'd use that with a shield, otherwise it's too short to defend with."

"Yeah," said Jane, putting the sword back and looking at other weapons. "I don't think this was my period. I think I'm more an eighteenth-century claymore girl." Sandy and Poole looked at each other. So Jane knew a little history too. If only about weapons. "I think one of us could have taken out an entire legion with a claymore."

"Don't be so sure," said Ragi, eyeing the weapons but not touching. "They lived a long time ago, but they weren't backward. If we ever have an apocalypse here and have to rebuild with stone and wood, I'd much rather have a bunch of Romans than Tanushans. We're quite helpless without our technology."

"Like the Talee," Sandy added. Ragi looked at her with nodding comprehension, perhaps considering one reason why she'd brought them here.

Rhian appeared, blinking with her suddenly-good eye as she readjusted to binocular vision. "Auntie Rhian!" Kiril shouted, and ran to her for a hug.

Rhian picked him up. "Wow," she said, "Sandy really outdid herself this time, didn't she? I think you might be a reincarnated Roman, Sandy."

"So it's just us?" Amirah asked. "Just GIs and Kiril?" With a questioning eyebrow at the latter choice.

"I brought Kiril because he's a part of this conversation," Sandy explained. "I know he's too young to understand a lot of it, but this is about him, now. I always hated other people making my life's decisions behind my back, I won't do it to my kid."

"Ari would be a useful contributor," Ragi added. "He can't help me too much at the far end of the Talee technology we're deciphering, but he knows far more about adapting it to regular humans than I do."

"And Vanessa's going to be essential once we need an actual plan," Sandy agreed. "Sure, we can't do this entirely alone. But this part is about us. Synthetic humanity. There are things we understand, and things we can do, that organic humanity can't share. We're in a position here to make decisions that could shape not only humanity's future, but our own."

Rhian put Kiril down. "It's sad Kiet's not here to hear you say that," she said.

"Sad, sure," Poole said flatly. "But probably better this way. The guy would go full speed ahead at any available cliff, he didn't help."

Amirah rolled her eyes. "Jason! A bit of tact, please. The man just died."

"And I'm finding the bright side," said Poole. "And don't call me Jason."

Another figure appeared between the training posts and materialised into a brown-skinned man, handsome, clearly a combat GI. He looked around in mild interest, with a frown of curiosity at the huge stadium surrounding. Amirah, Rhian, and Ragi stared.

"Hafeez," Sandy introduced the League man. "Internal Security Organisation, but you already know that."

"Hello again," Hafeez greeted them. "Under much nicer circumstances than before. And surroundings." He glanced at the racked weapons. "I think."

"So you're running a VR matrix that simultaneously incorporates Jane, who is in an FSA secure cell in some farther part of the city, and Hafeez, who is in an even more secure cell in the basement," Amirah observed. "Ragi?"

"Sure," said Ragi. "And I think Jane knows why."

They all looked at Jane. Jane pulled the trident Poole had thrown from the post and twirled it. Even here in VR, she preferred a baseball cap, down over her eyes. Was she hiding, Sandy wondered? Or was anonymity a reflex beyond conscious thought?

"Hi, Hafeez," said Jane, giving the trident a twirl.

"Hello, Jane," said Hafeez in measured tones. "I'm sorry about Takewashi."

"Yeah, him too."

Amirah looked from one to the other. "You two know each other?"

"Renaldo Takewashi was in regular contact with the ISO," Hafeez explained. He looked like he might want to take a weapon and fidget, as GIs often might. But uncertain in this company, he shoved hands into his pockets. "I saw Jane a few times. Other ISO agents reported her presence there at others."

"What'd you *do* there?" Poole asked. "Learn to pot plants? Read philosophy?"

"Actually, kinda, yeah." Jane took up a shield as well, testing its grip. "I did lots of reading. And I was Takewashi's busybody. General purpose bodyguard. Odd jobs."

"Occasional assassin," Hafeez added.

Sandy frowned and stared at her. Jane rolled her eyes a little. "Hey," she said to Sandy, "what'd you expect? Monk's robes? Some bad folks were never friendly with Takewashi, and his work was important. I kept him safe."

"How?" Sandy asked Hafeez.

"It's classified," the ISO agent replied.

"I don't kill civvies any more, sis," said Jane. She thrust with the trident, with effortless balance. "That was stupid, you were right to be mad. I didn't understand it then, and every bad thing you said about me at the time was right. I'm making amends."

"Yeah," Poole said drily. "You seem real cut-up about it."

Jane's eyes met his, a hard stare. "Allah gives me the strength to change what I can, the patience to tolerate what I can't, and the wisdom to know the difference."

"Dear lord," said Amirah unhappily. "So it's Allah now."

Jane pulled the trident to attention, then down once more, testing. "Call it what you like. A substitute for universal morality by any other name, I don't care. I read the damn book and I liked it."

"Why?" Amirah challenged. "Like having someone tell you what to do?"

"No," said Jane. "I like being reminded that I'm not the center of the universe. Psychopaths and atheists forget."

"Ami," said Sandy, cutting her off. Amirah rolled her eyes. What a strange bunch of synthetics they were, Sandy thought. Atheist GIs were as rare as believers, both required watertight belief systems and a personal investment in narratives. GIs rarely did that to the same extent as straights, leaving most as curious agnostics. Save for Jane and Amirah, at opposite ends of the spectrum. "Given where Jane's come from, that actually makes sense to me."

"You mean she was a psychopath before," Poole said unhelpfully.

"Well, yeah," said Sandy. "And now she's not. And it's important, given where we are right now. Ragi, what did you mean when you said Jane knows why this VR matrix is so advanced?"

"Because I think Takewashi was planning on spilling a lot more of his secrets in coming here," said Ragi, watching calmly and quietly as usual. Ragi had even less visible ego than most GIs. Easily the smartest person present, he could have dominated the conversation with brilliance and conjecture, but he listened instead. "But beneath that gruff exterior, it seems logical that Jane is really quite intelligent."

"I'm not," Jane deadpanned. "I'm as dumb as a box of hammers."

"She is basically your designation, after all," Ragi continued, looking at Sandy. "And any basic psych profile of Takewashi suggests that his fifty-series GIs were always his favourites. You in particular, Cassandra. He had closure issues with you, and given that he only had a few months to live regardless, I speculate that a part of his motivation for coming here was to tell you some things. He indicated as much to me, in our brief time talking."

Sandy glanced aside at Kiril. He had a gladiator shield before him, held up by Poole, who seemed as interested in Kiril's attempts to get his arm in the grip as in the ongoing conversation. Kiril wasn't understanding much, but he was listening, as was his habit when interesting adults were talking.

"Jane?" she said. "What else did Takewashi tell you?"

Jane hung up the shield and leaned on the trident. She was right—no GI would ever use the shield. Defence was not a GI strongpoint. "Not much," she said. "Only that we're all wrong in thinking the Talee are so advanced. Sure, their uplinks, that's freaky advanced hardware, but it's only hardware, we can catch that up pretty quick."

"What do you mean, not so advanced?" asked Amirah, frowning. "After what they just did?"

Jane smiled and sighed. "You're too close to it, you don't see it. The original mystery that none of you ever figured out, but you got so used to not knowing that you stopped asking the question."

"Sandy?" said Rhian. "I don't like it when she talks in riddles. Make her stop."

"Why the fifty-series are so advanced," said Jane. And looked at Ragi. "And why Ragi is."

"Whatever the hell designation I am," Ragi murmured. "I still don't know."

"Same as us," said Jane. Indicating herself and Sandy. "Same brain. Different body. You're noncombat, so you don't waste all that brain space running what is basically a combat chassis. It takes up about half of Sandy's and my active neurons, all that spatial perception and motor skills. You don't need it, Ragi, being the total pussy that you are. And your uplinks are better, by virtue that you've actually got a brain big enough to run them—with Sandy or me it'd be like trying to power a city block with a hand battery.

But otherwise you're basically a fifty-series GI like the rest of us—me, Sandy, Hafeez. But a noncombat model, which is why you can do wizard tricks in a network, almost like a Talee."

Silence in the Colosseum, save for the whisk brooms of the cleaners, and the distant sound of ancient Rome, floating up beyond the walls.

"Wait wait wait," said Amirah. "No no no, we've done thorough scans on Sandy and Ragi, their brain structure is completely different."

Jane rolled her eyes. "No, it just *grows* differently. That's the point of fifty-series, we're flexible."

"Without the combat chassis," Sandy murmured, eyes wide. It made sense. She stared at Ragi. He looked astonished. "But Ragi can . . . I mean, I can't do what Ragi does on the net, not even close."

Ragi blinked. "Which means that . . ." he stared at Jane. "You say the Talee aren't as advanced as we think? You mean . . . you mean that the most advanced Talee . . . are just fifty-series GIs themselves?"

Jane pursed her lips in mild approval. "Pretty slow for a so-called smart guy, but yeah. Basically. That's what Takewashi did in creating fifty-series. Took the Talee's most advanced synthetic neural tech and ran it on humans. And *you*," she reprimanded Sandy, "never gave him enough credit, because the guy truly *was* a genius. But he couldn't tell you exactly how and why, because he couldn't admit where it all came from. But translating it to human biology, all from scratch, took crazy smarts. I'm not sure anyone else could have done it."

Sandy stared up at the farthest heights of the stadium. Dazed. "So Cai was just a fifty-series too?"

Jane nodded. "All of them. No doubt a few extra bells and whistles, and of course crazy-advanced uplinks and other integrations. But us having their technology really won't change human society *that* much, because we already had their technology. It was us."

"And . . . son of a bitch," said Sandy as the full implication came to her. "It's what I've been saying all along. Talee synthetics don't just have crazy alien skills that we'll never match. They're our *potential*. They're what we *could* become, in time. Not some new, more advanced model. Us."

"There is no more advanced model," Jane affirmed. "More advanced marks, versions of the model, but the model itself is advanced even for Talee.

And you never noticed, because you'd all become used to how advanced fifty-series are, and used to the fact that you still had no real idea why."

"What Sandy argued for intervening in Pantala that first time," Rhian said sombrely. "That GI progression could go in dangerous directions. That it had to be steered carefully."

"Well, I can promise you one thing," said Amirah. "FedInt will not be happy."

"Well, we can't let them know," said Rhian. Looking around, very seriously. "Right?"

"Not from me," Poole muttered. "If they find out you guys could do *that* in a few years, they'd have you killed, and all the rest of us too for good measure."

"We should have heard from Pantala by now," said Amirah, concerned. "If Takewashi was right. It's suspicious that we haven't." She looked at Hafeez. "What was the situation on Pantala last you heard?"

Hafeez considered for a moment. No doubt wondering how much to say. "Negotiations were continuing, between our two sides. If the Talee attacked, they'd have to get through a number of our warships to do it. League and Federation."

"They were docked at Antibe Station?" Sandy asked.

"And near it," Hafeez confirmed.

"Cai took out that station with a VR matrix," said Sandy. "If the ships were all within range, the whole lot could have been taken out by on-station Talee agents without a shot being fired."

"Which would explain why no one's come to warn us," Amirah finished. "And any outer-system recon wouldn't reveal what's happened, the Talee could even be fooling them with fake transmissions, making it sound like business as usual."

"Hell," said Rhian, "we used to do that during the war. Take a station, then broadcast regular ops chatter to fool anyone listening."

"Takewashi said they'd be after other kids like Kiril," Sandy said to Jane. "Other kids that Chancelry did the operation on."

Jane made a face. "There's a lot more on Droze than that," she said. "Whole research centres, devoted to that technology. They might have just nuked it."

"Maybe. But remember, Pantala's where League discovered the Talee's synth tech in the first place. It's our place of origin, from Talee bases abandoned, probably from the last catastrophe. And those bases are presumably still there, Kiet showed me caves, on VR, with evidence of Talee habitation."

"We don't actually know *which* catastrophe," Ragi cautioned. "Cai said the first was thermonuclear, which from Earth's technological timelines would seem to indicate pre-FTL, but not necessarily. Maybe the time gap between the Talee's invention of nuclear weapons and faster-than-light wasn't as big as ours was. Or maybe they had a thermonuclear war very late on the time scale."

"Seems unlikely that they'd have FTL and not use it in a self-inflicted ELE," said Amirah. "FTL is deadly from inception, it makes nuclear weapons look tame."

"Still, Ragi's right to be careful," said Sandy. "And Cai has told us true things while still bending that truth. If those bases were abandoned after the *first* catastrophe, they could be very old. And if the Talee were attempting to destroy all human knowledge of that technology, they'd have to get all those bases. They won't know where all of them are, and after five thousand years they could be very well hidden. They'll need time, to search the whole planet."

"So how do you want to do this?" asked Jane. And everyone looked at Sandy. Sandy thought about it, looking about at the huge, old stadium. Rome had done this kind of thing. Formed factions, which did their own thing, and to hell with central command. It brought the empire crashing down, eventually. Too many emperors, too many generals. Too much unilateral action could pull the Federation apart. But if it had to be done, the price of inaction would be far worse.

"We need ships," she said. "Obviously."

"Captain Reichardt," said Rhian. "Poor guy, he's already sick of us."

"Only thing Federation Fleet's more scared of than League Fleet is hostile Talee. This I know for a fact, they've done all studies on it. And they're not shy about using force."

"Against Talee?" Rhian wondered.

Sandy nodded. "Well, that's our next challenge. Convince them."

"Without Ibrahim?" asked Amirah, worried.

"With him, if possible," said Sandy. "But the fastest way to bog this down is to go through channels. FedInt will hate it. Provisional Grand Council will hate it. A lot of the member worlds will hate it. There'll be a debate, and you know how long that takes, across the Federation, with the Grand Council officially offline until we get a new constitution. We're leaderless right now, there is no decision-making apparatus working. It's up to us."

"Isn't it always," Poole said sourly.

Sandy saw Amirah looking troubled. "Ami? If we had to keep secrets from Ibrahim . . . is that going to be a problem for you?"

Amirah looked up. "Well, yes," she said frankly. "You really don't think he'd join us?"

"Right now he thinks we could have a civil war if we rush off unilaterally like this."

"Could we?" asked Amirah pointedly.

"Maybe," Sandy admitted. "Or we could sit here and let the League commit suicide and take us with it, or let the Talee walk all over us thus inviting future attacks to come. I'm sick of asking Federation permission to do the right thing. This is our fight, us GIs. If the Federation won't support the right thing, what's the use of a Federation anyway?"

She looked at Hafeez. "Next, we'll need guaranteed League help, once we get there."

Hafeez smiled. "I can't do that sitting in my cell."

Sandy awoke as the ward door opened and light spilled in. Uplinks showed her it was just after three in the morning. Full tacnet of the FSA compound showed all security points alert and responding. It was Cai's upgraded system, but even so, she cracked her shoulder, that old injury that still popped as only she knew how; Ibrahim had told her that a similar injury had worked for him. The sensation was familiar enough to convince her.

The silhouette in the doorway was male, squat, bull-necked. Captain Bursteimer. She blinked and hefted her rifle as she rose from the chair in the corner of the ward. On the second bed slept Danya and Kiril, alongside Svetlana. Dodger curled on the floor; Kiril had wanted him on the bed, but the asura liked his personal space and now raised a wary muzzle to peer at the light.

Sandy closed the door behind her and moved several steps away. "Leo! When did you get back?"

"Just now, straight off the shuttle." He looked tired. "Talked to Ibrahim, then came here."

"Ibrahim's still here?"

"Yeah, lots of folks didn't go home." He nodded to the doorway. "How they doing?"

"They're okay. But we can't go home until we're sure there aren't any more Talee infiltrators here, and HQ's the safest place. How did the chase go?"

"Caught up with the surviving ship at DQ-849, where he proceeded to jump somewhere else. We sent local fleet after it and came back here. I hear you're looking for a ride to Pantala?" And to her questioning look, "Togales told me, on the shuttle down a few hours ago."

"You tell Ibrahim?"

"He's not my boss."

"Who is?"

Bursteimer grinned. "Um, well, there's this little old Sikh guy who runs a coffee stall on Nehru Station, I think he's top of the line right now."

"Yeah," Sandy sighed, running a hand through her messy hair. Ever since the Battle of Nehru Station six years ago, Fleet had never really gotten its chain of command figured out. Fleet Captains were autonomous by necessity, and during the war, that autonomy had grown way too large. Nehru Station had been the first big split in Fleet's ranks, Operation Shield the second. Now it was anyone's guess.

"Constitution says it's the Defence Ministry, but the Defence Ministry collaborated with the Office of Intelligence Directorate in implementing Operation Shield, and then the Grand Council was stood down and the consti- tution suspended," said Bursteimer. "Which means it's the Provisional Grand Council, but who the fuck listens to that little prick Ranaprasana?"

"I don't think he's a little prick, I think he's just over his head."

"I didn't ask what you thought," said Bursteimer, smiling. A typical enough response from Fleet. "So that leaves Ibrahim, but lots of Fleet don't like his politics. . . ."

"Yeah, he's been mean to Fleet Captains," Sandy interrupted drily. "They hate that."

"And Fleet HQ is just a bunch of old salts who should have retired years ago and who are supposed to do what the GC says . . . did I mention the GC's been suspended?"

Sandy exhaled and leaned her head back against the wall. Closed her eyes for a moment.

"Hey," said Bursteimer gently. "How are *you* doing?"

"I'm fine."

"You know, I could end up in the infirmary for saying this, but I got this sneaking suspicion you're not actually as tough as you let on."

She looked at him for a moment tiredly. Bursteimer liked her, it was obvious. Probably had a crush on her. He wasn't that attractive, and his manner was usually more irritating than charming, but she'd learned not to disrespect offers of friendship from anyone in her business.

"I don't 'let on' anything," she told him. "It's just me."

"Well, y'know, if you need a shoulder to cry on, mine's available."

"You're a couple of years late," she told him wryly. "I used to do casual sex with equal ranks and superiors. But now I've got kids and I got all respectable."

"Damn," he said. "But you're a good mother. And you put your kids above everything, and that's pretty awesome."

"Kiril got abducted on Droze because of me," she said quietly. "His connection to me made him a target. Now the tech in his head made them all targets. Sometimes I think they'd have been better off on Droze without me."

"Hey." He put a hand on her shoulder. "You're the best thing that's happened to those kids. Droze is a hellhole. You got them out."

"They were so lucky to survive this one. And Talee assassination squads aren't ever going to leave them alone."

"They will," Bursteimer promised. "We'll make them. You need a lift to Pantala? You got one. Reichardt agrees, and we're canvassing others. It'll take a while yet, we have to be subtle, can't talk to anyone who might turn around and tell PGC or FedInt. But hostile Talee are the biggest Fleet nightmare there is, and the war was one giant lesson that deterrence is the only thing that works, again and again, for thirty years."

It was like Sandy suspected. She nodded. "How would you feel about some League Fleet help?"

"Not great, why?"

"Got an ISO senior commander real interested. Share Talee tech, work the attack together."

Bursteimer scratched his unshaven jaw. "I just chased a damn League cruiser across space no League cruiser's got any business being in. Now you want me to buddy up with him?"

"Maybe. Thing is, our ISO boy will need a ride back to the nearest concentration of League Fleet ships, real soon. And real fast."

Bursteimer looked unhappy. "If they don't want us there, you'll be giving them advance warning."

"If Takewashi was right, Talee will be stripping Pantala of all the original source technology that gave the League GIs in the first place. I think that'll be priority over another Federation incursion."

"You're giving them Talee tech," Bursteimer disagreed. "They might not care anymore."

Sandy shook her head. "Our tech is just network tech. Theirs is inception, and potentially the key tech to stopping the League from going insane, the stuff in Kiril's head. There's no comparison."

"Didn't Takewashi have his own stash?"

"And Talee are probably hitting that too. But he was using Pantala to do all the research he wasn't allowed to do at home, like putting it into the heads of kids. So chances are he doesn't have what matters. Pantala's the place."

He thought about it. "Need to have a talk to my fellow captains. Then I'll get back to you."

"You got protection down here?"

That got his attention. He frowned. "Who from?"

"Talee or FedInt, but probably not in that order."

"Right. I'm not down for long, I'll sleep on the shuttle and get some bodyguards."

"Don't leave this HQ without them," Sandy warned. "Are they at Balaji?" He nodded. "Call them out here, someone might have seen you come in and hit you on the way out. Combat flyers only, assume a hostile environment."

"Got it." He looked a little nervous. Fleet Captains weren't much used to ground threats. "Damn. Was safer fighting that fucking cruiser."

Sandy smiled and kissed him on the cheek. "Now go," she said, while he was still getting over his surprise.

"Yes ma'am," he replied, smiling broadly, and left with a jaunt in his step.

"You know it doesn't mean anything?" she called after him. "We don't do romance, it's just a kiss."

"Sure sure sure," he dismissed her, striding merrily away. And burst into song around the corner. Sandy grinned, shaking her head. And opened the ward door, unsurprised to find Danya there, who had obviously listened to the whole thing.

"Aren't you worried someone heard you?" he said, looking up at the corridor ceiling and walls.

"Jammed it," said Sandy, tapping her ear. "You hear everything?"

He nodded. And glanced after Bursteimer. "You like him?"

"Not like that," she reassured him. "Like I said, it's just a kiss." Danya looked unconvinced. "Hey, I like kissing men sometimes. Get used to it."

"You could do better," Danya opined.

"Oh, what would you know," Sandy retorted, and grabbed and kissed him repeatedly as he protested.

CHAPTER NINETEEN

Amirah arrived at the southern gate on foot, before Gandhi Circle, where wide lawns and pavements about the traffic circle made an ideal place for frequent protests to assemble before the Grand Council building and the directly adjoining FSA HQ. The crowd crushing in this morning was ridiculous; surveillance estimated at least a hundred thousand, thronging all the way back up the streets of downtown Montoya, clogging traffic back to the maglev station and beyond.

Before the high steel fence a line of police in riot gear made a wall, backed by vehicles and armoured walkers. She stepped out amongst them now, amidst the yells and chants, and was shown by an officer the way to a police car now on the edge of a swarm of people. There, several senior police negotiated with protest leaders and a crowd of media, all bristling cameras and lights, now turning her way as she approached. They swept forward, blocking her way so that she had to step and shoulder her way through, as the noise assaulted her ears and the beating of drums made her reflexes jump, vision tingeing red as combat reflex descended around her like a veil.

"Agent Togales!" the senior cop shouted above the noise. They all knew her by sight, all the cops and media. She hadn't been a Federation civilian long enough to know if she found it disconcerting or not. "It's getting a bit tense, the protest leaders want a statement!"

"About what?" She was rare for a GI in that she was a good public talker and that normal people didn't confuse her like they did so many of her compatriots. Indeed, she often felt more at home among the "normal" people than she did among her own kind. But big protests like this *did* confuse her, group thinking and group emotion were alien to most GIs, making the organic crowds more machine-like than the synthetics, to her mind.

"About the attack! They're saying it's a cover-up!" Amirah refrained from rolling her eyes. The FSA, like most security organisations, did most things in secret. Everything *was* a cover-up. What did they want her to do about it?

But Ibrahim had told her to come out here and "do something," which was an unnerving amount of faith to have shown a combat GI for doing something other than killing people. She pointed to a journalist by the police car bonnet. "Diggi! Want an interview?"

Digvijay Chaula blinked at her, then pushed around the car to get to conversational range. "An interview? What, before all of them?" Amirah nodded. "You don't just want to read a statement?"

"Yeah, 'cause that won't look at all authoritarian." With cheerful sarcasm. "I have to be seen answering questions—you ask some questions, I'll answer."

"Hey!" said one of the protest leaders. "He's a journalist, not a protestor! Why not talk to an actual protestor?"

"Because you guys suck on camera," Amirah said lightly. "Trust me, I'm doing you a favour." Digvijay leaped into action, uplinked and talking fast to his producers, while whipping out a comb for his hair. "Right, we're going to need some amplification. . . ."

"We've got drones up," said the senior cop, "they do audio. Where do you want to do this?"

Amirah looked around, but there were no platforms, nothing obvious that could be used as a stage. No statues or fountains in the traffic circle, as security codes feared it could give cover to snipers. But over by one of the Grand Council gates was a big police van, three times taller than the cars.

She pointed. "On the roof of that?"

The cops looked. "Uh . . . that'd be a safety code violation."

Amirah gave them an exasperated look. "What's the bigger safety risk—a journalist facing a three-meter fall, or a hundred thousand people getting angry?" The cops looked at each other. "I'll make sure he doesn't fall."

The cops led the way over, riot police making way before them, keeping noisy crowds back. Amirah looked them over as she walked—they didn't look like some rent-a-crowd; there were all ages, a predominance of younger and not-so-wealthy people, but in Tanusha that could be deceptive, lots of folks wore slacks on their days off. A few were a mass of tattoos, crazy hair, and piercings, but those were severely outnumbered, no more numerous than the robed, religious types or other Tanushan protest staples. Many looked mainly curious, straining for a look as she passed, delighted and intense to find themselves this close to the front. Amirah wondered what they actually wanted. Or if they even knew.

The senior cop talked to the others around the van, who made sure the brakes were on, then at Amirah's suggestion opened a door and wound down that window. She leaped straight up to the roof, and then Digvijay climbed to the cabin, got a foot in the open door window, and accepted her hand to pull him up. He quickly straightened his collar, adjusted his tie, and looked distracted as uplink feed came in—Amirah could see it on tacnet, a simple illustration of who was connected to what. If she'd wanted an unfair advantage, she could probably listen to the questions his producers were feeding him before he actually asked them.

From up here she could see the crowd, and the size of it amazed her. All open space before the GC fence was filled with people, with no telling what was road or grass or footpath beneath. Up the feeder roads between the Montoya buildings there was still space to move, and people walking, but still it was crowded. More seemed to be streaming in from the stations. Many of the nearby crowd were exclaiming and pointing at her, recognising her from news feeds, or having the augmented reality feeds identify her on the spot. Some, she realised, were still marvelling at her vertical leap onto the van— effortless for her, and even some straight augments could do it, but the rule with security types was never let anyone see what you had unless you had to. She didn't think it would matter here, and when facing any potential threat, reminding them what she was could be useful, even defusing.

"Hello?" said Digvijay. "Hello?" And suddenly his uplink feed caught his voice, and the seven or so drones hovering over the crowd were booming out his voice. Then silenced, as he reported back to his producers, "Yes, that sounds good, just turn it up one notch more." And to Amirah, "You have the link?"

It was very obvious on her internal vision, short-ranged to only two meters, coming from a booster probably in his pocket. She nodded and made the connection, aware that several sections of the crowd were now chanting different things.

"Tell us the truth!" was the main one, taken up by people all across the circle.

"Feds go home!" was another one, with less volume, but what the hell? People thought this was a Federation versus plucky-little-member-world problem?

"No war on the Talee!" a few others were yelling, not having figured a way to turn that into a catchy chant. Great, so within hours of launching humanity's first recorded alien attack on a human world, those same humans had already formed a pro-Talee lobby group. Damned if we're not the strangest species, Amirah thought, tugging her slightly wild hair into place.

"Hello all!" Digvijay's voice boomed out from multiple locations overhead. Over such a wide area, on multiple speakers, it created a long-stretched echo from the farthest reaches. "My name is Digvijay Chaula, I'm a senior correspondent with Tanusha KBS . . ."

Immediately the crowd started booing over his introduction. Members of the media were not popular, and Amirah had learned that she always came off better in confrontations like this one, because however much people disliked or distrusted the FSA, they disliked or distrusted journalists even more. And so she'd cunningly dragged one up here to hide behind.

"I'm here with Agent Amirah Togales of the Federal Security Agency, and she's offered to let me ask her some questions on your behalf!" Random noise, some cheers, some boos. A crowd this large took on a mood, a personality, all of its own. "Agent Togales, can you give us anything more than you've already said? Was this an attack by the Talee?"

Finally the crowd hushed. Amirah paused for longer, letting them strain for the answer, quietening further. "It was incredibly advanced," she conceded. "Whatever it was, it forcibly puts people into virtual reality, as you've seen. We're putting every technical resource we can onto it right now, we've got experts analysing what they did, and finding ways to stop it from happening again."

"Was it Talee?"

"I can't say." Boos and shouts from the crowd, rising like a wave of sound. Clearly a lot of them already had their own opinion and took anything less than confirmation as evidence of evil government lies. A bottle hurtled from the crowd, very close, and would have struck Digvijay in the face if Amirah hadn't caught it neatly one-handed and tossed it onto the grass behind the van. "I'm not really the best person to be asking," she continued without missing a beat, as the startled reporter tried to process what had just happened, "there are plenty of Tanushan experts who could give you a better answer than me."

Digvijay looked unsteady, as the fear of what had just nearly happened struck him, and cops lashed out through the crowd to grab the bottle thrower. Fortunately, others in the crowd were turning him over, with boos and shoves and pointed fingers. Cops grabbed the thrower and hauled him away. Amirah put a hand on the journalist's arm and gave an encouraging smile. No bottle was going to get past her. Bullets were another matter, but tacnet had the immediate crowd well monitored, and if a longer-range sniper round came in, all Montoya was studded with sensor mikes that would detect the sound and turn it into signal fast enough that she should be able to duck in time. And take Digvijay down with her, though she doubted such a bullet would be for him.

"Well," said Digvijay, steadying himself. "Thank you for that. Don't you think perhaps we should find a safer place to . . ."

"I'm fine right here," Amirah said calmly.

The journalist took another deep breath. "Is there any further danger that you know of?"

"Yes." The crowd hushed again to hear that. "Whoever the attackers are, we can't be sure we got all of them. In fact, I'd tell everyone here to go home for their own safety, but they're probably not going to listen." A disarming smile.

"Do you know of any specific threat to this crowd?"

"No, but the primary targets of this attack were security institutions and the Grand Council. So if you stand in front of them, logically there could be trouble if shooting starts."

"Do you think there's a risk of more shooting?"

"Mr Chaula, at this point I wouldn't like to rule anything in or out. We were in a big fight at SIT just this morning, so it's not impossible, no."

"Stop threatening us!" someone shrieked from farther back. "She's threatening us!" Then boos and yells as others shouted him down.

"Agent Togales, my information says that the FSA and CSA were the primary targets of this . . . this VR matrix that's been attacking people through their uplinks. A number of experts have said that only GIs could carry out such a thing."

"That's possible," said Amirah.

"Were most of the soldiers fighting in the Sadar Institute of Technology also GIs, by any chance?"

"Not all, but a number of them, yes." Which was stretching it, as Detective Sinta had been the only non-synthetic present.

"It just seems that Callay is increasingly at the mercy of synthetics," said Digvijay. "We get attacked by synthetics, we're defended by synthetics, GIs like yourself are occupying most of the high-level security posts . . ."

"Well, that's not completely true," Amirah interrupted, not sure she was liking that line of questions. "The FSA and CSA command posts are all occupied by organics, and . . ."

"It's common knowledge that the FSA's special operations branch is run by Commander Kresnov."

"Right, but special operations is not a core command, it's a special wing. Core command takes a lot of experience, and whatever our capabilities, no GI yet has the experience required for those roles."

"And what happens when you get it?" The crowd were hushed now, the quietest since she'd arrived. She could see tens of thousands of faces watching her. Concerned. Some fearful. Others intrigued. A few, angry. "Commander Kresnov has been here eight years, and she heads special operations. CSA SWAT now has some synthetic SWAT Team commanders; you yourself have only been here a short time, but you're already the FSA's public spokesperson. If the only thing holding you back now is experience, what happens when you get it? Surely *all* our security posts will eventually be held by GIs? I mean, who else could compete with you? You're smart, talented, physically superior. You're collected under pressure, you don't get scared . . . hell, you're even beautiful, all of you. What role is there going to be left for us straights, as I gather you call us, in providing our own security? At what point do we all become passengers in our own society?"

Amirah recalled what Sandy had been saying about the Talee. About synthetic Talee's high position in Talee society. Was that where humans were heading? Was that a good or bad thing? And would others, like those in the crowd before her, launch a war to stop it from happening?

"Couple of things," said Amirah. "First, that's crap that we don't get scared. I get scared. I was scared this morning."

"You were there? At SIT?"

Amirah nodded. "Yes. Second, GIs with command skills aren't as common as you're suggesting. We talk about this a lot amongst ourselves. We agree that most of us probably aren't cut out for command . . . but some are, so sure, you're going to get a fair few of us at senior command levels, especially as new asylum seekers arrive from the League.

"Third, you're drawing a line between us and you. Synthetics and organics. It's also common knowledge that my friend Sandy Kresnov has adopted kids. And several other GIs have gone the same way, while more are thinking about it. I'm considering it myself."

"You are?"

"Definitely. Not anytime soon and when things get much quieter, I hope . . . but one day, sure. Most synthetic people have had organics deciding the course of their lives, for all of their lives. Now that will swing back the other way a little. But it's a pointless distinction anyway because it doesn't really exist—we are you. And you are us. And we got attacked today—we, meaning all of us—and I promise you, we, meaning all of us, are going to do something about it."

Vanessa saw the cheers from the crowd on the cruiser's forward display and shook her head in amazement. "Don't take this the wrong way," she said to Sandy, "'cause I know most people would say that the most amazing GIs in Tanusha are either you or Ragi. But I'd go with Amirah. Look at her. She's young, hasn't grown up with that much social experience really, but she's standing alone before a hostile crowd and gets them eating out of her hand. I've never seen anyone with that knack, straight or synth."

"And it also undercuts her point," Sandy said sombrely from the passenger seat as Vanessa piloted. "We do have an edge. If the numbers keep building up here, we are going to have a huge number of GIs in senior command, eventually. And we do see things differently."

Vanessa made a face. "Making artificial people was always going to cause problems, especially if they're all smart and dangerous like you. That's kinda why the Federation thought it'd be smarter not to do it."

They were flying to see Jane, who was in an FSA strong point isolated from HQ. Sandy didn't like that, but Ibrahim had correctly assessed that Jane was a problem, given the deaths she had caused the last time she was here. Some in the FSA held her accountable, and no matter how useful she'd been here, they resented the idea that GIs were held to a separate moral and legal standard. They'd leak it to someone, and then there'd be trouble. So Jane was elsewhere, and hopefully secret for now, from most of the FSA's own personnel.

"Problem is," said Sandy, "Ami's talking shit and she knows it. League's making another hundred thousand high-des GIs to deal with their internal security problems. They say they're all going to be loyal this time, but how many of them you want to bet will turn up here in a few years, asking for asylum?"

"Probably half," said Vanessa, gazing out at her city. "God knows where we'll put them all."

"If they all want to work security, we won't have enough jobs for them here. They'll have to spread out, other worlds will have to take them."

"See anyone volunteering lately?" Vanessa asked drily. "They still think GIs are the cause of half this mess, they're all quite happy to let Callay take the heat."

"They might be right," said Sandy. Vanessa frowned at her. "Of course, a hundred thousand high-des GIs given special powers to deal with internal instability . . . well, fuck, anything could happen. Given new Talee network tech."

Vanessa gazed at her for a long moment. Then grinned. "That's what I love about you girlfriend, never a dull moment. You don't think League could control them?"

"In this environment?" Sandy snorted. "When I had my awakening, I was isolated. A hundred thousand high-des? With net tech that penetrates the lies and bullshit? My handlers didn't like me watching the wrong movies, the idea that GIs might actually defect to the Federation was unthinkable. Feds were the enemy, they hated GIs, didn't want us to exist. But now there's us gang on Callay, big shots in the FSA and CSA . . . hell, you can't stop smart people from having thoughts. Thoughts like 'why can't I do what I want for a change?'"

"Thoughts like emancipation," said Vanessa. Sandy nodded. "You got any notion whether that'll make the League's situation better or worse?"

"Nope," said Sandy. "But it couldn't be worse. GIs don't get Compulsive Narrative Syndrome. I'm going to give them the power to take charge, if they want. If there's a soft coup in a few years, or a hard one, and the power to make war rests in the hands of League GIs, it should be much safer."

"Of course it would be creating a new autocracy right next door," Vanessa added. "Those don't have great records."

"No longer our problem," Sandy replied with a shrug. "Slave societies don't deserve democracy. Let them reap what they sow, I'm tired of them dumping it on our . . ." Her uplinks blinked, a priority signal. Vanessa got it too and flicked an incoming transmission onto the cruiser's forward display.

"That's coming from the Callayan Parliament." It was a press conference, the local construct showed a dozen media feeds going out live. Sandy jumped to one of them and found a visual of a man in a suit, presumably a politician, talking to journalists upon the steps of the Callayan Parliament. "Who's that?" asked Vanessa.

"Amit Gaur," said Sandy as face-rec told her. "Former Shadow Attorney-General."

"Crazy," Vanessa mused. "Remember the days when we'd know the Shadow Attorney-General of Callay on sight?"

"The world got bigger," said Sandy.

"*. . . come to my attention that the Federal Security Agency has in its custody a high-designation GI responsible for grave crimes in Tanusha, five years ago. In particular, this individual is responsible for the deaths of two Tanushan civilians. . . .*" Sandy refrained from swearing.

"Someone talked," Vanessa observed.

"*. . . demand that the FSA be open and transparent about this individual, and should tell us what they intend to do with her. With the lack of transparency demonstrated by the FSA of late, I think we should all be concerned that this individual should not be allowed to escape Callayan justice, and should be made to answer for her crimes.*"

"You'd think with the former Prime Minister in jail the nationalists would shut up for a while," said Vanessa.

"Jane did commit those crimes," Sandy said quietly. "It's hard to argue with."

"Except that she had the psychological maturity of a vacuum bot at the time." Vanessa peered at Sandy, searching for a reply. "Right?"

Sandy said nothing.

They landed on the big house's rooftop pad. It was HighGate, a very expensive neighbourhood on a slight rise within a river loop. Towers clustered close east and west and farther everywhere else, where visible between lush surrounding trees.

Sandy and Vanessa went downstairs, had their badges scanned by security, and emerged into familiar Tanushan luxury—a huge, tiled floor between columns, with a sunken lounge adjoining a hall and vast kitchen, and windows looking onto a large garden. Within was a pool, where golden fish drifted beneath green lilies.

On a reclining chair by the windows sat Jane, reading a paper book. There was a collar about her neck, with inserts into the back of her head, monitoring uplinks. Sandy knew those collars well. Any disagreeable move from Jane, and a shock would knock her unconscious.

"Who put that on you?" Sandy asked, taking a seat opposite. Vanessa did her customary once-over of the premises, scanning visually and with uplinks. The adjoining rooms contained heavily armed guards, keeping a low profile. Several were GIs—trainees often got shift duty and spent the time studying.

"It's okay," said Jane, lowering the book. She had a red cut across one cheek, smeared with a transparent bandage. She had other shrapnel injuries as well but wore a pair of plain jeans and a shirt that bore the Sadar Institute of Technology logo. Someone's sense of irony, no doubt. "It was either the collar or restraints. This way I get to walk around. I try to remove it, it zaps me." No drugs though, Sandy reflected. GIs would usually be given a muscle relaxant to make them less dangerous. But there were other high-des GIs in the house guard, so even if Jane tried something before the zapper activated, she'd do limited damage. "How's Svetlana?"

"She's going to be okay. A few weeks in hospital, but it's just muscle. She'll barely notice it in a month or two."

"Good," said Jane, nodding to herself. To call it "relief" would be stretching it, Sandy thought. Satisfaction, perhaps. "She's a good kid. Danya and Kiril?"

"Fine. Well, Danya's not sleeping and Kiril's upset . . . mentally I think Svet got off best. It's not good for kids to go through things like that. They shouldn't have to." Her voice tightened, and she swallowed hard.

"But they can get tape, right?"

"Right. Danya doesn't like that either, but even he knows that he has to get sleep. I try to tell him that stress is an injury, like shrapnel. But he's so used to living with stress that he gets stressed at the idea of being without it."

"Makes sense to me," said Jane. "Everything we do and experience has consequences. You try to deny those experiences, you deny who you are. Worse, you lie to yourself and to everyone around you."

"The kids want you to come and live with us," said Sandy. Jane blinked at her. Astonished. "When this is all over."

"And what did you say?"

"I said I wasn't sure if it was a good idea." Mercilessly. Jane wasn't one for flowery sentiment. "I said I didn't know if you were safe. To those around you or to yourself."

Jane looked out the window. Agitated and a little confused. Then looked back, frowning. *"Why* do they want me to live with them?"

"They have this idea that you're family," said Sandy. "I said you were pretty messed up. They said join the club."

A smile tweaked the corner of Jane's mouth. She looked amazed. "They do understand that . . . well, I know I called you 'sis,' but I'm not stupid. GIs don't have family."

"You didn't meet Kiet. Kiet thought we were all family. Brothers and sisters, every one."

"Sounds painfully idealistic."

"You're the one who found religion."

"Yeah, but I don't shove it on others," said Jane. "I have a personal relationship with Allah. It's about me. You may think it's nuts, or your buddy Amirah—I don't care. That's the point, it's mine. I don't go around telling every GI I meet that they all need to read the Koran and follow its teachings, or that they're all my brothers and sisters."

"Do you follow its teachings?" Sandy looked about the vast room. "I don't see a prayer mat."

"Because I don't pray. I'm selective."

"Ah." Sandy repressed a smile. "Nobody really explained this religion thing to you first, did they?"

"Don't give me shit about being selective. You've been at odds with your own command enough times to get yourself shot, in most places. Director Ibrahim must be a very tolerant man."

Sandy gave the ceiling a warning look, then back to Jane. Jane looked unruffled, calm, and faintly amused. And not about to let slip that they were plotting things.

Vanessa appeared behind Sandy, having finished her inspection, and leaned by the big windows, looking Jane over. "Vanessa, Jane," said Sandy. "Jane, Commander Vanessa Rice."

"Second-in-Command of FSA special operations," said Jane. "And your best friend, I know."

"You saw the politicians are after you now?" Vanessa asked.

Jane nodded. "So what happens now? Do you hand me over?"

"No," said Sandy. "You're a security asset. You know important things, and federal security takes precedence over Callayan justice."

"I bet the guy on the feed just now is going to love that," Jane said drily. "And all his friends."

"It's not Callayan justice pushing this thing," Vanessa disagreed. "It's FedInt. They found out you're here—not surprising, they're spies. They were scared of GIs in the FSA getting too much power. Now we've got new Talee technology, that power advantage is about to get serious. They'll set the Supreme Court on us, and Federation public opinion will follow."

"Oh, you've already lost Federation public opinion," Jane said wryly. She scratched at her hair and gazed out the windows. Sandy had somewhere along the way acquired a basic concern for appearance, but Jane lacked even that, always preferring drab, practical, and even scruffy. Like a statement of nonchalance, to show how little she was bothered by anything. That she was above all that stuff. Sandy wondered how much of it was an act, if any. "A Federal Security Agency, based on a world half the Federation's already envious of, now running the Federation single-handedly while the rightful Grand Council sits in limbo. . . ."

"We do not run the Federation," Vanessa said firmly.

"That's a fact," Jane agreed. "Versus strongly held opinions, facts aren't very important. If FedInt makes me the face of the evil synthetic FSA, you might have to let me go. You've got other things to do, you can't sacrifice the FSA's authority defending me."

"If it comes to a trial," said Sandy, "we've got damn good lawyers. You were a different person then, you were made by others to follow orders ruthlessly and without question. . . ."

"You can't standardise that," Jane said calmly. "Laws are about standardising behaviour. I'm a different model of GI. You say I'm responsible for this at this age, but not responsible at *that* age . . . and then other GIs are responsible at that age, but not at *this* age . . . and then where does personal responsibility go? The philosophical cornerstone of criminal law? And how many people in the Federation are by now completely sick and tired of GIs being held to a different moral standard than everyone else?"

"Plenty," Sandy retorted. "But if they're going to judge us collectively as synthetics, then they have to take responsibility collectively as organics for making us in the first place. None of this was our idea. Sure as hell wasn't yours . . . which I told you at the time, if you recall."

Jane smiled faintly. Eyes momentarily distant. Sad. "Yes. I recall. Only dimly, but . . ." she took a deep breath. "And fuck it all if you weren't completely right. About everything. I never thanked you for that. It gave me something to think on, the last six years with Takewashi. After you let me go, when you probably should have killed me. If you hadn't said those things, I wouldn't have chosen what I've chosen since."

"So if they want to bring this to trial," Sandy continued very firmly, "then we can and will get you off. It's not your fucking fault, Jane."

"Yes, it was," Jane murmured. She looked out the window again. "I did it. I didn't have to. If we don't hold people accountable for their actions, there's no hope for society."

"So you'd kill innocent people again?" Sandy challenged.

"No." With a hurt look. Not quite angry. But annoyed. "Of course I wouldn't."

"Hafeez said you'd been Takewashi's assassin."

"Trust me," Jane said drily. "Takewashi had enemies who deserved it. Including some you'd throw me a fucking party for killing, if I told you."

"Will you tell me?"

"One day. I owe Takewashi more discretion, for now."

Ibrahim met them by the HQ front entrance. "Hafeez is gone," he said. With a very suspicious look. "Just disappeared from our cells. The moment one of our agents went in to ask some questions, he vanished from surveillance. It had been a false image all this time."

"Fancy that," said Sandy.

"Bursteimer is gone too," Ibrahim added.

"To orbit?" Vanessa asked the obvious.

"No. He never reached Balaji. He and his Fleet escort disappeared off the grid three kilometres out from HQ."

Sandy stared at him. "Shit . . . that's either Talee or FedInt, I fucking warned him! Are we tracing him? What are we . . . ?"

Ibrahim held up a hand, quite calm. And Sandy was hit by a familiar sensation, confronting Ibrahim—the feeling that she was not at all as in control of the situation as she'd thought. "The thing with Fleet Captains," he explained, "is that while they're cunning as wolves in their natural environment, they're like poor lost sheep on the ground. I had him bugged, something I'm sure even FedInt won't find."

"He's not dead? It wasn't Talee?"

"No. FedInt activated several of their Fleet agents to infiltrate his guard, the very same ones he called from Balaji Spaceport at your request."

"Fuck."

"Very much so," said Ibrahim in the manner of an elder schoolmaster lecturing an unruly pupil. "But as with all such rushed jobs, FedInt has been unable to cover their tracks as they'd have preferred."

"Hang on, hang on," Vanessa interrupted. "Bursteimer and Hafeez went missing *together*?"

Ibrahim looked from one to the other with feigned patience. "You didn't tell her?" he asked Sandy.

Vanessa looked archly at Sandy. "Tell me what?"

"Well, you see," said Ibrahim, "your dear, trusted synthetic friend has decided that only other synthetics can be trusted on these matters. She arranged for Hafeez to escape, with Bursteimer."

"Bursteimer's not synthetic," Sandy said sullenly.

"No," Ibrahim conceded. "Bursteimer was going to take Hafeez somewhere in the League, where they were going to wrangle up some League Fleet ships . . . though Allah knows why they'll listen to Bursteimer after he's just destroyed one of their cruisers."

"They'll listen to Hafeez," Sandy retorted. "He's senior . . . God damn it, you know where they are?"

"Of course I know where they are," Ibrahim said mildly.

Vanessa was still looking at her, not upset but irritated in the way a friend might be at unsurprising yet exasperating behaviour. Sandy opened her mouth to defend herself, then stared again at Ibrahim, eyes narrowing. "You traced them some way that FedInt can't detect? FedInt are spies, how do you . . ."

Because FedInt were very good at detecting bugs and covering their tracks. Unless the trace was an uplink trace, but Bursteimer didn't have that kind of uplink tech, at least not that would work in an urban environment. But Hafeez did. So how could Ibrahim have gotten Hafeez to . . .

"Oh god," she exclaimed as it came to her. "You talked to Hafeez? You *turned* him?"

"Let's not get dramatic," said Ibrahim. "We agreed to cooperate, in this eventuality."

"But if FedInt only moved against Bursteimer, and Hafeez wasn't with him . . ." she rolled her eyes as that came to her as well. "You knew I was going to do this, didn't you?"

Ibrahim gave her a patronising look. "You as good as announced it to me, last we talked. And I do know you rather well."

"And you'd have stopped me if you thought my plan was completely stupid!"

Ibrahim conceded with a nod. "Cassandra, my office is watched rather closely. Hando is somewhat sympathetic to Ranaprasana and has been reporting to him, unsuspecting that I'm onto him. He's not the only one." Sandy remembered Ibrahim warning her that it was more complicated than she knew. "And if you're going to work behind my back, I'm going to work behind yours. I *like* your plan, Cassandra. But it suits me better for the time being to be seen opposing it, inside the FSA and out. And I think your little team probably works better independently, rather than going through me all the time."

Sandy could have hugged him. Mostly, she suspected, Ibrahim had just wanted to see what they'd do. He liked to let independent experts have their head, and the more advanced the network tech became, the less within his comfort zone he felt.

"Sir," said Vanessa, "Shin keeps kidnapping our people. I vote we should do something about it."

"Oh, but you see," said Ibrahim with a very rare glint in his eye, "he did far worse than kidnap one of *our* people. He kidnapped a Fleet Captain. He wouldn't have done it if he'd thought I was entirely in control of my synthetic employees. Appearing to be out of control has its advantages."

"You've told Reichardt?" Sandy gasped.

"And several of his newly arrived friends," Ibrahim confirmed. "They've been coming in since Takewashi's arrival, just in time to hear about the Talee attack and now FedInt's opposition to any response, including the abduction of one of their Captains. They are quite displeased."

Sandy presented her ID at the FITH-Q front gate and waited. It was another warm Tanushan evening, the flicker of intermittent lightning upon distant orange storm clouds. Insects gathered in clusters about street lamps in the nearby park, where locals took an after-work stroll, with no apparent idea what this oddly charming building by the parkside, lost amidst a thicket of native trees, truly was. The gate clicked open, and she walked in, shoes crunching on gravel.

The main door opened as she approached beneath the ornate stone frame and into the atrium, where suited FedInt agents awaited. "Commander," said one respectfully. "What can I do for you?"

"We seem to have misplaced a Fleet Captain," said Sandy. "I heard a whisper he might be here."

The agent smiled. "I'm afraid I wouldn't know anything about that."

"It was a very strong whisper," Sandy insisted. And waited while that was relayed to someone via uplink. Then, after a moment, she was beckoned to follow down the main hall. Into the old-style, high-ceilinged interior, where busy agents at various terminals spared her wary looks, then up the stairs at the back. And finally, to the same room in which Takewashi had been kept when she'd come to visit him here.

In that room, on the same decorative chairs, sat Captain Bursteimer, Chief Shin, and Chairman Ranaprasana. Ranaprasana and Shin rose. Bursteimer did not, looking at her critically. Perhaps covering for a bad case of embarrassment.

"Nice to see there are still *two* gentlemen in this line of work," she told Bursteimer pointedly. "Chief, Chairman. *Captain.*"

"Commander, please join us," said Ranaprasana, coming to take her hand.

He was a small man, grey-haired with a thick Tamil accent and a penetrating squint to his expression. "A drink?"

"Whisky, straight." Which got an odd look, but another agent went to attend to that. This seemed the time to be demonstrating the synthetic invulnerability to hard liquor, among other things. She took a seat on the sofa alongside Bursteimer. "How are you, Burstie?"

"I'm fine, Commander, you?"

"Very well. Take a wrong turn?" Bursteimer took the teasing with relatively good grace.

"The Chief and I were just discussing the alarming new plan we hear that Fleet and the FSA are hatching," said Ranaprasana. "To declare war on an alien race. Is this true?"

"They declared war on us," said Sandy, accepting her drink. "Perhaps you missed it."

"This is unacceptable," said Ranaprasana very firmly. "This kind of thing makes one think that perhaps the people who were implementing Operation Shield had a point."

"We're going to Pantala," Sandy replied, taking a sip. "With a League invitation. We think the Talee have factions. We think one faction has taken Pantala."

"A League matter."

"League invited us."

"From your dungeons?" Ranaprasana scoffed. "You trust the word of an ISO agent?"

"Say," Sandy wondered, "where *is* our ISO friend anyway?"

"He jumped out," said Bursteimer. "When our cruiser's controls were taken. At about five hundred meters."

Sandy shook her head faintly at Shin. "Sloppy."

Shin shrugged. "It's proof enough of what you're up to. Federal Security should consider its position."

"Commander," Ranaprasana said angrily, "the PGC's current primary task is to consider alterations to the Federation constitution in light of recent upheavals. I trust you understand that the position of the FSA itself is in question. The FSA is acting like a loose cannon. New controls can be written into the constitution if necessary."

"You're assuming," Sandy replied, "that a fully functioning Grand Council wouldn't support us."

"Absolutely I'm assuming that!" Ranaprasana retorted. "I think it a certainty."

"And who elected *you*?" She gazed at him pointedly.

The Provisional Grand Council Chairman straightened. "You think my views that unrepresentative? I was appointed on the authority of the member worlds of the Federation."

"And I believe that if the relevant officials of those worlds were to assemble in a security council, like the one we had before Operation Shield trashed everything, those experts would agree with me that the FSA's current actions were the only sensible course. Now this is all hypothetical, because without a functioning democratic system, there is only one unelected tyrant—me, versus another unelected tyrant—you. In the absence of such a system, what are we to do?"

"I'm not about to negotiate this, Commander," the Chairman insisted. "Either the FSA changes course or prepares for a future constitution that negates its power."

"You declaw the Federation just after we've been attacked? Then you're no better than Operation Shield. You saw what we did to Operation Shield."

Ranaprasana's jaw set. "Are you threatening me, Commander?"

"I'm stating facts. Whether you choose to take them as a threat depends entirely on you." From somewhere outside FITH-Q walls, there came a whining noise, getting louder. "Do you gentlemen know *why* democracy was invented? People today seem to think it was about all this cute, touchy-feely stuff about making everyone's voice heard. In actual fact, that had nothing to do with it."

The whining became a keening, louder all the time, and Ranaprasana and Shin looked to the windows in alarm. Bursteimer remained seated, smiling as he recognised the sound.

"Democracy was invented," Sandy continued, "as a dispute-solving mechanism between factions. Without it, the only way to decide the outcome of a dispute was violence. And then the idiot with the biggest axe would win, and idiots with axes often make very poor choices, so democratic institutions were created to transition societies through various disagreements, and decide outcomes, without everyone having to kill each other all the time."

Chief Shin went to the windows and peered out onto the pretty green park next door. Hovering over it, at an altitude of several hundred meters, was a Fleet assault shuttle, the kind of monster that was never allowed to penetrate city skylanes except in extreme emergencies. Engines roared fit to rattle every suburban window for a kilometre, and weapons systems capable of punching holes through space stations now levelled upon the FITH-Q's stone walls. From several lower portals, armoured assault suits were jumping in squads to take up position on the perimeter.

"So here we are," Sandy continued. "With our own domestic dispute-solving mechanism currently out of order. Who do you think will win any given dispute in such a situation?"

Hovering behind Shin's shoulder, Ranaprasana stared at her in horror. Bursteimer smiled and got to his feet. "The person with the biggest axe," he said. "And as axes go . . ." he nodded out the window. "Trust me, it's a beauty."

"What do you think you're doing?" Ranaprasana exclaimed in horror. "This is madness!"

"You abducted a Fleet Captain in time of war," Sandy told him. "In some statutes you'd be lined up and shot."

"Abducted? We're just having a little chat! I assure you I had no intention of . . ."

"He was under FSA protection," Sandy retorted. "You *took* him. Against his will, without consulting us *or* Fleet. We had no idea where he was, for a little while at least. If our Director weren't so damn good at this game, we still might not know now."

"And this isn't a time of war!" Ranaprasana came back, again looking to Shin. Shin remained silent, formulating on uplinks as commotion doubtless broke out throughout the building. Unwilling to support the Chairman, not now. He knew he'd lost this round and would pin the whole thing on Ranaprasana—Shin himself had just been following instructions. Of course. "The FSA does not get to decide when the Federation is at war!"

"Normally you'd be right, but with the GC out of order, we do, and Fleet does. And unlike Operation Shield—this time, Fleet's with us." The FSA hadn't paid enough attention to Fleet the last time, before Operation Shield. Now FedInt and Ranaprasana made the same mistake. When central government broke down, Fleet became the true power in the Federation. They were very poor at making decisions but very good at picking sides once someone else had made them.

"Commander," said Bursteimer, "should we go? Don't want to keep our ride waiting."

CHAPTER TWENTY

Combat jump was different from civilian jump. Once upon a time, as a green Dark Star Lieutenant who felt the need to know everything about the aspects of modern combat that affected her troops, Sandy had looked into faster-than-light physics and the various modalities thereof employed by League Fleet in operations. She'd quickly decided as smart as she was, the space in her brain was far more usefully employed on other matters, because unless you had multiple physics doctorates and dreamed every night in algebra, it was almost incomprehensible.

And so she knew what any other grunt did about FTL—civilian jump was disorienting and occasionally made you sick. But combat jump was painful. She blinked about herself now, head swimming, like awakening from the deepest sleep. Her head wouldn't come clear, and her mouth tasted like acid. A sip of water would be nice, but she had her faceplate down . . . and further disorientation, because combat jump back in the League was not done in full armour like this armour. League armour was basic assault layout, full environment but light, you could unstrap, pop the faceplate, turn your head. This was hopper-armour, FSA-style, and everything was strapped down and immobile, like her own private spaceship.

She blinked on faceplate graphics as her uplinks took time to acquire. Direct feed from *Mekong*, it showed her command feed, which was . . . unusual. In Dark Star, they'd never let her see unfiltered bridge data, but FSA command was different. She blinked, fighting the unaccustomed sensation of double vision. Her muscles ached, old injuries twinging, but she dared not stretch properly in case she damaged the still-inert armour. Vision resolved into . . . a planet. Various ideal approach lanes, outlaid by *Mekong*'s nav comp.

Then came bridge-chatter, a lot of talk about optimum-this, and outlaid-that; even with all her Dark Star experience it was hard to make sense of. But the graphics didn't lie. They were inbound on Pantala, less than fifteen minutes out at present speeds, but they'd start shedding speed soon, before increased proximity to planetary mass made that hazardous. Barely thirty-five minutes with adjusted velocity. Now to begin hunting for defences and trying to make sense of what they were up against, if anything.

Local tacnet established, just her unit. "All marks, this is Snowcat, report in." They called back, one after another—not strictly necessary as their suit schematics and vitals were all available to her, but she preferred to do it audibly, just for the reassurance of human voices. Most advanced combat unit in the Federation they may have been, but very few of them had done a Fleet-supported system assault before.

When they were done, Lieutenant Ndaja called. *"Hello, Snowcat, do you have status?"*

"Hello, Strike One, we're all good." And she relayed that status to Reichardt, who would see it indicate somewhere on his vision. He didn't need the details; he was far too busy—just that little green light to tell him his strike force was ready. Now he just had to deliver it in one piece.

"Okay, boys and girls," she told her team, "looks like we're in and clear. Should be quiet for another few minutes, then it gets interesting."

Approach was the worst. Thirty minutes. You could die any second, though the statistics said it was most likely immediately after arrival (if the enemy had a good ambush set up) or as you neared your destination. They were still alive, so it seemed there was no ambush. And now began a space of time too long to be lively and too frightening to be boring, where the seconds felt like minutes, and the minutes like hours, where at any moment all hell could break loose, or some piece of unseen ordnance or dark obstacle on the approach could kill everyone onboard before you even knew you were dead.

To calm herself she flipped a recording onto her vision, where it played as background, unobtrusive enough to not be distracting. It was the kids, out surfing—she'd tasked a micro-drone to film them a few times, ostensibly so they could watch their best rides together later on. But also, she'd known that when the inevitable foreign mission came, leaving them was going to be hell, and a few still images weren't going to be enough. And so she watched them now, multitasking on several things as she in particular knew how, and smiled at the sight of Danya on a wave, with Svetlana whooping in the background.

The kids were with Rhian. With Svetlana's leg healed enough to let her walk on crutches, Rhian and husband Rakesh had agreed to take their whole family—eight-year-old Salman and baby girls Maria and Sunita—into FSA protective custody. That meant weekly transfers between heavily guarded residences that now, with the latest network tech upgrades, they had a reasonable chance of defending against even Talee. Rakesh had waved away any notion that it was a sacrifice—Salman got along well with the Kresnov kids, and the Kresnov kids were good with the babies, and Danya was practically a third adult anyway. So now it was Rakesh and Rhian, and six kids, and various FSA-appointed security, including several GIs. And it was a stunning gesture, for all Rakesh's protests to the contrary—to knowingly place his entire family in harm's way, given what had nearly happened before, just so Danya, Svetlana, and Kiril wouldn't have to spend these upcoming weeks alone. Even if, as it seemed, the worst of the threat had temporarily passed.

Rhian had of course wanted to come, but that wasn't going to happen with only one eye. Several of Sandy's underground contacts had suggested ways to procure new ones in time, but Sandy had quietly instructed FSA legal to come down very hard on the prospect, when it seemed they might have looked the other way. And so Rhian remained one-eyed and medically unfit for combat duty, much to Sandy's delight. Whatever happened out here, at least Rhian would be okay. And her own kids would have the best possible surrogate parents, and in Rhian, a protector nearly the equal of herself. Surely even trusting Rhian had become a little suspicious at the end, with FSA legal's sudden obstinacy regarding black-market eyes. Sandy didn't care, and she was pretty sure Rakesh didn't either.

Amirah was looking out for them too, at Sandy's insistence. She'd been gearing up to come and do her duty as a high-des combat GI, but Sandy had noticed the atypical lack of smiles, the distraction, the general distress. She'd arranged with Ibrahim for Amirah to stay—she was genuinely becoming too important for FSA command to risk on such operations anyway. Amirah had protested and eventually cried, saying that she didn't want to let anyone down. But was relieved, in the end, when her synthetic comrades had made clear that she'd done enough already and was due to sit one out. Sandy was nearly as delighted at her absence as she was Rhian's and knew most others felt the same.

Ari and Ragi, sadly, she hadn't found a way to leave behind. She opened a direct line to them both, plus young Yogendra, who was one of Ari's friends, an underground net freak with an uncanny knack for the stuff most people found too advanced to handle.

"Guys, you okay?"

"*I'm okay,*" said Ragi. "*Systems functioning, everything looks good.*"

"*Damn that sucks,*" Ari groaned. "*Fucking space travel.*"

"Drink your liquids, get your blood sugar up, then as soon as you can hold it down, eat something."

"*Yogie? Hey, Yogie, if you're gonna be sick, use the damn bag, I'm not cleaning that up.*"

The three civvies were in Engineering, often called B-Bridge, from where technical aspects of the ship were managed in detail. With no hope of making real sense of Talee net technology within the time scales required, Ibrahim had done a most un-dictator-like thing and released it wholesale to the Tanushan underground. Ranaprasana and FedInt had again been horrified, but Sandy thought it a good move regardless—the Talee had used the entire Tanushan network against them, and the vulnerability of civilian infrastructure was as much a problem as that of military and security systems.

The underground would no doubt now start using the technology for nefarious purposes, but as long as the authorities had GIs like Ragi and herself on their side, the new net-tech arms race between legal and illegal users should remain balanced. The Provisional Grand Council's horror stemmed mostly from the massive technological edge this was giving Callay, on top of its existing edge, no matter that the FSA made it available to everyone as fast as starships could bring it to them. But whatever the additional consequences, there was no choice either way—humanity had to catch up fast, and that meant everyone: governments, civilians, cities, and planets.

First to have their systems stripped, shielded, and massively improved were these Fleet ships and all accompanying elements. But that took operators who understood the systems, and that meant the three best that Callay could spare. That they weren't combatants was irrelevant—they just needed to keep everything together once contact with the Talee began. Given the difficulties of hacking ship networks from other ships, at distances where light took many minutes to reach its target, and would Doppler into alternative spectrums due to the variable relative velocities of the combatants, Ragi was relatively confident that network attack would be the least of their problems.

That left the captains to worry about the fact that Talee ships had massively advanced engines and navigation, were nearly impossible for human sensors to detect unless they manoeuvred or fired, and had been observed doing things that twisted the laws of physics to degrees that even the most daring FTL practitioners found baffling. Playing games with them in deep space was not an option. This plan was all attack.

"What's it look like?" Reichardt was asking tersely.

"Can't tell yet. Station's there. Looks intact." That was Antibe Station, where negotiation between League and Federation Fleets had been taking place on and off for the past year.

"Regular station chatter. Sounds normal."

"Put it up," said Reichardt. For a moment, they all listened. It sounded like station chatter anywhere, routine queries about headings, berthing clearances, sequencing. If the entire station had been taken by VR assault, that would mean nothing.

"Traffic plots look normal."

"No sign from Pantala surface. But we're too far out."

"Light-wave will reach them in three," said Reichardt. *"First response in two point four five."*

Vanessa's channel opened. *"Whatcha' think?"* It sounded like Vanessa was chewing gum, sometimes her habit before ops. Tension relief, Sandy supposed.

"We're in the right spot," said Sandy. On the background feed, Svetlana had Kiril on her longboard, the two of them paddling down a small wave together. "Two hard brakes and we're in, farside." Droze was on the other side of the planet, from their current position. The problem with a blind approach, of course, was that they didn't know exactly what they were going to hit yet. Or if the Talee were here at all.

"Would have been nice to do some recon first," Vanessa suggested.

"They'd have spotted it and guessed we were coming. Surprise is better."

"*Yeah.*" Reluctantly. "*Glad you're commanding this one.*" Sandy knew what she meant. Vanessa was a hell of a combat commander, but Fleet assaults were different. The speeds involved, the distances, the sheer scale of everything, including consequences, were unsettling.

"Just like old times," she said easily . . . and was distracted by a new alarm on bridge nav comp.

"*You got that?*"

"*Nav reading! One-forty-nine by twenty-nine! Accelerating!*"

"*What is it?*" Reichardt demanded.

"*Can't be sure, it's . . .*"

"*Pulsing! Boosting for jump!*"

"*That signature's off the scale, that's Talee.*"

"Short-jump," said Reichardt. "*He's seen us, he's heading in to warn the others.*" Sandy guessed what was coming and spoke on her local-only channel once more. "Boys and girls, this is your flight attendant Sandy. Buckle in and swallow hard because we've just been blown. We're gonna short-jump after that scout, he was lying out here silent and we went straight past him."

"*Isn't short-jump this close to a planet kinda dangerous?*" asked Shen.

"Yep," said Sandy nonchalantly. "War's hell."

"*Can you calc it?*" Reichardt was asking Helm.

"*Wait wait . . . running points three and five. . . .*"

"*Scan has the fix.*"

"*Fleet has sync! Fleet has sync, good to go!*"

"*Powered up, systems green.*"

"*Green green, Fleet reports green!*"

"*Helm?*"

"*Wait wait . . . still running . . . got it! Fixed and locked, good to go!*"

"*Fixing the mark,*" said Reichardt, and Sandy saw a new plot appear on their inbound track, like a giant hoop they were about to jump through. "*Mark in five, all hands, short-jump approaching, all hands brace.*" In that bored Texan drawl, like he was ordering pizza. And Sandy's stomach lurched as she recalled that even she didn't like this bit . . .

. . . and it hit, with a force like a ton of water dropped on her head . . . and it should have crushed her, only now she's underwater, floundering, struggling to breathe as that singular instant stretches . . . and stretches . . .

. . . and *wham!* they were back in, and alarms are sounding, and everything felt upside down and woozy. She pulled up her faceplate, feeling every muscle in her arm tensed and rippling, and gasped a lungful of cold assault ship air. Turned her head hard to grasp the drink tube in her lips and took a long gulp into a protesting stomach as scan showed five ships, all in, then three more behind, and several more on a wide flanking pattern, covering for mid-system runners or inbound support both.

"*Station! Station traffic is responding, they've seen us!*"

"*Situation!*" Reichardt demanded, as tense as Sandy had ever heard him. "*Where is that scout?*"

There were ships at station, they were close enough to see that, but no ID. There were anti-orbital defences on Pantala too, put there by humans, but if the Talee had control on the surface they'd have control of them as well. But those weren't going to stop a hard run-in like this and were mostly to deter anyone lingering and raining orbital artillery on those below.

"*Movement at station! Multiple vessels undocking, they're burning!*"

"*Son of a bitch!*" As one of them cycled his jump engines, a flare of energy so close to station it would have destroyed both, had it been a human vessel. "*They're cycling!*"

"*This is Caribbean, fire pattern locked.*" That was Bursteimer, leading that wide group, having short-jumped to catch up with *Mekong*, his transmissions fifteen seconds delayed. Velocity dump was now crucial; only starships had jump engines, and if the assault shuttles were dropped now, they'd take a week to slow down. Given that Pantala's upper atmosphere was six minutes away at this velocity, that wasn't going to work. *Mekong* had to dump down to manageable velocity, but she made herself a big fat target the minute she did so, thus these other attack ships around her, coming in on variable trajectories, making any defenders at station more worried about dodging their ordnance than shooting at *Mekong*.

"*Is that all of them?*" Reichardt asked. Meaning the ships breaking free of station. They were scattering, spinward and outward of planetary orbit, more defensive than hostile.

"*Scan shows four ships on station! One IDs as Murray!*" Which was a

Federation carrier, out here on the extended negotiations that had started last year. *"They're not moving or talking!"*

"Those runners are Talee! Look at them boost up, that's . . . that's too fucking fast!"

"So they've occupied the station," Reichardt surmised. *"Fair bet they've got the surface. Snowcat, this will either be a hot insertion or a cold scouting mission, stand by for dump and release."*

"Snowcat copies," said Sandy. And deactivated her home movies, because if she was glad for anything, it was that her kids weren't here for this.

Again the stomach-churning lurch into hyperspace, but shallower this time, then out, as *Mekong* performed a flip end over end, with three heavy cruisers in support, and hammered on the main engines. Again Sandy's muscles compressed all over, as ten Gs of thrust hit them, and she sucked air with difficulty, vision blurring. It wasn't comfortable for a GI, God knew how the straights coped, augments or not. Actual-velocity approached optimal-velocity, twenty seconds, fifteen seconds . . . tacnet showed that several of her non-synthetic troops were out cold, vitals registering unconsciousness. Vanessa was one of them. And Sandy worried anew at Vanessa's recent augment over-load syndrome, as it had been diagnosed—the doctors had patched it best they could, but there was no guarantee that if physical stress reached a certain level . . .

And scan blinked red alarms, new contacts, but scan on the bridge couldn't say a thing under this much G-stress, could barely force the air from her lungs. Contacts hostile, low angled across the Pantalan atmosphere, and apparently firing. . . .

WHAM! as the grapples cut early, and the assault shuttle was clear of *Mekong*, and Sandy's feed went dead, then new thrust kicked from another direction as the shuttle's own thrusters engaged. This was more gentle, but still fierce at 7G. . . . Sandy's feed came back as the shuttle's own nav comp became independent. And everything abruptly blanked out as *Mekong* cycled up once more—very difficult right above the planet, fire now outgoing with railguns and missiles but carrying little velocity so it wouldn't scare opposing captains into disruptive evasions yet.

One thousand Ks altitude, on a shallow approach but far too fast—if they hit the atmosphere like this they'd burn up like meteors. Even as she watched, the pilot readjusted the approach trajectory to a shallower angle, buying them more time as the engines thundered in a desperate attempt to lose sufficient velocity. A huge flash nearby, someone had been hit, but she couldn't worry about it now, all her ten assault shuttles were intact, it must have been one of the big ships. Just hope none of that incoming fire was aimed at the shuttles. Droze was just under two thousand Ks from their entry point, and reentry would cover most of that . . . this might yet work.

Fleet were engaging, fire going in both directions, and now fire coming from the surface . . . no telling yet who it was aimed at; Sandy decided to assume it was hostile. Unlikely that the Talee would have left human-friendly gunners on the surface. She tuned the Fleet chatter out; she was a ground pounder now, and all her attention had to be on the surface . . . but then, *"New contact, new contact! Three-twenty-eight by thirteen, range point twenty-one!"*

Those were new ships jumping into the system. They broadcast no IDs, so there was no telling whose they were. They *should* have been their League allies, if that plan was working, but if Talee farther out were receiving this light-wave by now, and heading in far faster than news of this attack could head out . . .

If Fleet lost this fight, she and everyone in the assault were going to be stranded down on the surface, with no way off. The possibility of which was, of course, why marines were bred so damn tough since their invention in support of wet navies all those centuries ago.

They hit the atmosphere, and Gs briefly ceased as the shuttles reoriented their shielded bellies and throttled their engines back. It was an intensely vulnerable moment, as it was very hard to dodge during reentry . . . though luckily most ordnance didn't handle well in this midpoint transition between air and no air, so targeting them would be just as hard. Then the Gs came back, worse than ever, ten Gs, now eleven, and everything shaking and banging like some giant had grabbed them for the joy of making them rattle.

It went on for another three minutes before easing off, as active control returned to the pilots, and they hurtled down through the middle atmosphere with flight surfaces reengaging, spreading out across a ten-K formation. Still sixty Ks up and descending fast.

"Entering communications range now," announced the shuttle pilot, and Sandy saw a flicker on the coms shields. Recently familiar patterns, spikes in passive data of a certain structure. Then it faded, finding no purchase.

"That looked like a coms assault," said Sandy. "Let's hope that's the best they can do." If it weren't for their new tech upgrades, they'd be falling out of the sky about now, while dreaming happily (or unhappily) in VR. An eruption of missile contrails followed, from within the haze of the dusty horizon.

"*Made them angry*," said Jane, who was Sandy's wingman for this op. "*They don't like us not falling asleep.*"

"Let's not judge their state of mind," said Sandy. She actually didn't want to think about it at all. These were aliens. She'd never fought aliens before. No one had, at least that they knew of—it was always possible that League had tussled with Talee before and never admitted to it. The existence of Talee was old news; it was nearly two hundred years since the first explorers into this region of space had begun encountering Talee ships keeping a watchful distance. It was one of the longest-running mysteries humans had ever faced, the identities of these mysterious watchers, who refused every offer of friendship and trade. Everyone had hoped that the mystery would not be finally unravelled in circumstances like this.

"*That's coming from Droze*," said the pilot, looking at the incoming missiles. "*Full countermeasures.*"

"*The question now is our tech, or theirs?*" said another pilot.

There was no hope of evasive manoeuvers in huge assault shuttles against missiles that could pluck birds out of the air. But being big had other advantages, and the shuttles packed every countermeasures system yet devised. They engaged now, jamming, active hacking, sensor-blinding, then multiple volleys of antimissile missiles, while lasers and electro-magfire waited for anything that got through, with chaff and flares as final precaution. Sandy registered thirty-plus incoming, but even now several looked to be struggling to acquire. Not Talee tech, then.

They had visuals now, from drones now high above Droze, and Sandy focused on them instead of the missiles. Familiar layouts, city streets and boundaries, the big corporations in the middle, surrounded by high walls and defences, and then the sprawling outer rim, the uninvited settlers who ranged from mildly to extremely poor and desperate. There, on the far eastern border, was Rimtown. Danya, Svetlana, and Kiril's home, where she'd found them, or they'd found her. And if some other stroke of fate had intervened, she'd have missed them, and they'd still be there, and all their lives would be so much different.

"There's ships down in the corporate zone," said Sandy of those visuals, highlighting the dark shapes on the map for others to see. "No apparent street traffic; that's normal under assault. Those ships don't look like any design we've seen."

"*Any coms traffic?*" Vanessa queried the shuttle crews. "*Anything to let us know what's happened?*"

"Look for broadband radio from the perimeter," Sandy added. "Home Guard used the most basic tech to beat the companies. If they've been occupied, one of them might tell us." Assuming Home Guard thought Federation occupation would be preferable to Talee.

"*Looks like scenario C,*" said Captain Singh.

"*That it does,*" said Sandy, as incoming missiles detonated five Ks out, and others spun off as lasers blinded their guidance. Scenario A had been a fast strike, Talee going in and out fast and leaving most intact. In that case, they'd have been long gone. Scenario B had been similar, only more violent, destroying rather than occupying. Scenario C had been occupation, not destruction, relying on Talee network technologies to keep humans subdued for long enough to do a thorough job of searching for what they were after. Of course, Droze presented a problem for them, because only the wealthy, high-tech people in the corporate zone were uplinked. Much of the outer zone was not, especially the younger ones, and that was three quarters and more of the population. On the other hand, Sandy wondered, would that majority care if the corporate zone had been occupied by some mysterious outside force? Would they assume it was League? Or Federation? And would they care what happened to corporate folk at all? She doubted it. The Talee didn't need to subdue the entire population, just the corporates. And the rest of the city probably wouldn't thank her for bringing a strike team down from orbit to solve the corporations' problems and dumping a big pile of ordnance on their heads to do it.

Thirty Ks up, and still no city chatter. "Looks like they're jamming everything," she said, as surviving missiles detonated ahead. "I'll bet they've got much better weapons than these, if we get too close to the corporate zone. We will go deployment by teams, east through north, and advance with maximum speed and cover." She illustrated as she spoke, deployment patterns on tacnet, who went where. "It's not a Federation city, but it is a human city. Let's take it back."

The shuttles began turning, spreading their formation even wider, banking into S-bends to confuse defences and lose altitude. *"Expect heavy defences,"* Vanessa told them, as soldiers did final check on their suits and systems. *"Droze is an armament manufacturer, and the Talee can take over most old-tech human systems by remote. Expect a lot of emplacements used against us, and a lot of remotely operated systems."*

"Snowcat," said a shuttle systems operator, *"counter-bandwidth operational, we're coming into range now."* That was jamming and coms interception. With their new software toys, and a fair idea of what to look for, they might be able to jam whatever Talee signal was used to take control of local human systems.

"Copy that," said Sandy, and slammed her faceplate shut once more, dulling the roar of shuttle engines. Seals hissed and she was airtight. "Marks set for ten K release, all weapons arm."

"If the corporations send remotely controlled tanks into Home Guard zones," Singh sent on private link, *"Home Guard might toast them for us."*

"It's possible," Sandy conceded. "Expect nothing, shoot at anything that shoots at us. That includes Home Guard." She'd run into the Droze anticorporate militia before and wasn't about to do them any favours if they got in her way.

Fifteen K, and the carrier rig holding her suit elevated to forty-five degrees. Suits had to come out sideways; the shuttle heat shielding wouldn't allow it otherwise. Sandy recalled Svetlana asking her when she'd done assault ops before. Well, never in suits like these, save for Pyeongwha. But in the League, she'd done plenty, with lesser armaments. She'd meant to tell Svetlana those stories eventually. Now it occurred to her that she might never have the chance.

Eleven K, and the panels at the end of the launch tube retracted and let in light and a howling gale. The thing that separated this assault from those others, she realised, was that this was the first time she'd really had something to return home to, once it was all over. If she'd died then, she'd have been just another synthetic casualty, a person barely known and barely missed. If she died now, many would mourn, and many would celebrate, and three would mourn most of all. This time, her life mattered, well beyond what she did on the battlefield. And in the skies above a League world, fighting once again to save a League population from invaders, that revelation felt something like a journey brought full circle.

Rails whizzed, and she shot down the tube, then out. She liked this bit, the blessed relief of a view, and escape from the possibility of death while still trapped in the tubes. She liked the next wave of defensive missiles a lot less—suits in free fall lacked the shuttles' defensive layers. But they were a lot more mobile, and she elevated her huge electro-mag rifle to track one at five-K range and put down ranging fire. The rifle plus suit armscomp was accurate out to about three K, even in free fall, and the missile lacked imagination and broke up two Ks out as she shredded its engines.

More missiles came in elsewhere, and more defensive fire, and explosions, spread across this vast stretch of pale blue sky. She ignored it all and looked down . . . and here was Droze, from twenty Ks up, and getting bigger quickly. A big circle, like a fried egg, green and brown in the center, yellow and brown in the outer, all in a sea of yellow-brown sand. About her, other suits were falling—fifty per shuttle, five hundred total, plus ten Trebuchet support launchers and operators, for the bigger stuff the suits couldn't handle. The shuttles peeled away and climbed—further artillery if they needed it, but it took a while to arrive, as shuttles were too important and vulnerable to allow too close to the city center.

Ten K, and she could see traffic on the dusty streets below, between the jumble of boxy concrete buildings that passed for a skyline on Droze. Old factories, blocky residential complexes. Parking yards on vacant blocks. Shanties. Nothing green, nothing wealthy.

"I'm getting an active track," said Lieutenant Terrassi, commander of Green Squad, Golf Company. *"Coming from below, only light."*

"Home Guard," answered Golf Company's commander, Captain Ledo. *"Warning shots, put them in the road."* Magfire answered, and ten Ks below, white-hot rounds blew big holes in the road beside the offending rooftop, rather than dismantling the building and all within it. No return fire followed. With any luck Droze citizens would take the hint, with all the sonic booms and shooting, and go to the most secure parts of their homes. Most Droze citizens had plenty of practise finding those, the past seven years.

Five Ks, and they came under sustained electro-magfire from the corporate zone, itself twenty Ks away plus altitude. It gathered in red clusters, then whipped past, covering the distance in barely four seconds, but only accurate out to three Ks, their odds of hitting anything stationary weren't great, let alone falling at terminal velocity. But they were giving away their positions.

"Those are corporate emplacements," Vanessa judged. *"Probably Mark 82s."* A moment later, tacnet agreed with her and fixed those red dots on the map as M82 tanks. *"So we know they're using local Droze hardware. Stay alert for anything native and Talee."*

That was the real worry, fighting an alien species for the first time. If their weapons were as advanced as their network tech, everyone was in for a nasty surprise at some point. But human weaponry was already pushing the edges of physics, Sandy was doubtful there was very much further that physics would allow.

"Let's hope they are actually this tactically stupid," Jane remarked on private channel, as electro-magfire ripped past, already on its downward arc. *"But it could be a trick."*

"Trick or not, they only have an edge against us while using their own weapons. We know our own weapons far better than they do." Two Ks, and she picked a low concrete rooftop for landing, as tacnet automatically oriented itself to that location, projecting fire-shadows and lines of cover. "All units, fast advance. Stay low, that magfire will get real accurate the closer we get. Evolving situation, stay loose and bring it to the ground as we get closer."

At under one K she decided to hell with the rooftop and kicked thrusters to slow her descent. Then kicked again and blasted forward, still dropping, hurtling over shambolic rooftops and low-tech road traffic, clouds of dust, small fires from garbage piles, small herds of various domestic animals in otherwise abandoned yards. Engine temperatures spiked, hoppers couldn't fly long distances without overheat and burnout, but she gained another kilometre before finally grounding on a dusty road and running through the clouds from her landing. Civilians on the road scattered at the sight of this three-meter-tall armoured suit thumping along the road, cradling a two-meter rifle in its hands. When she'd left Droze a year ago, she would have been quite pleased if she'd never had to return. But if one must return, she supposed, it was far better to do so dressed like this.

Thrusters cooled and she leaped again, keeping low. There wasn't much to hide behind in Droze, all the high-rises were in the corporate zone, and even that wasn't taller than a hundred meters. Red dots began to proliferate on tacnet, drones and flyers mostly, but sensors were indicating emplacements on some of the higher central zone buildings, giving them a good field of fire over the outer city. But they were shooting less frequently now than during the descent. . . . Were the occupiers worried about civilian casualties? Sandy didn't like using the civvie buildings for cover; she didn't mean to use human shields, more that there was simply no other way to attack the city center without getting massacred. And she grounded once more, again running on the road, suit fans howling overtime to rid the excess heat.

The Droze neighbourhoods were getting more concentrated, buildings larger than out on the perimeter. She leapt over several confused vehicles and saw multiple missile launches on tacnet—corporate zone flyers, hovering behind building cover. Nothing was heading her way, so she kept running and saw Jane on tacnet, the next street over, slide for rapid cover behind a concrete facade as an incoming missile struck the upper wall and blew it across the road. Other suits were dodging and covering, some leaping at the last moment, missiles striking cover, others detonating short. Fourteen Ks to the wall, there was nothing for it but to keep advancing as tacnet identified a good spread of return targets.

Sandy selected five and tasked twenty missiles for them. The first twenty soldiers to find a good firing attitude took those shots, it didn't matter which, and the missiles zigzagged away across the urban sprawl.

"Not going to hit anything," Sandy observed, jumping again. "Just want to see the defences." Magfire tore past her as she flew, but meters off course, and erratic. It would get more accurate as they closed, but she was surprised there was no forward-deployed defence. Nothing out here among the civvies, just dusty streets filled with civvie vehicles, alarmed pedestrians, and a few panicked animals. Had the Talee kept out of the civvie zone on purpose? Had they been relying on their network defences to maintain total superiority? Was it really going to be this easy, or were they being lured into a trap?

AMLORAs were now engaging, long-range guided artillery, rising into the sky atop ponderous trails of flame above the city center. FSA Trebuchets answered, grounded now on well-covered land about the perimeter, missiles abruptly tasked with antimissile ops, homing on those incoming AMLORAs. Sandy grounded as the fireworks began, corporate zone defences erupting about her own incoming rounds, and Trebuchets striking AMLORAs in midair over their heads, shriek!crack!wham! as rockets, sonic booms, and explosions all combined, then the ongoing, rumbling echoes off various buildings large enough to catch the sound. Tacnet showed only one of the FSA missiles had gotten through and had blasted a hole in a tower. Two out of twenty AMLORAs had survived, but they were intended for targets both larger and less mobile than hopper suits and had left craters in roads but nothing else. Ten Ks to the wall, and more time consumed. Sandy grounded and leaped again. She hadn't lost a single soldier yet. Surely the other shoe would drop any second.

"Could task the birds to drop heavy stuff on their heads," Vanessa suggested, panting with exertion, no doubt thinking the same thing. *"Could get some of it past their defences."*

"Don't want to play the hand too early," Sandy replied. "Save it till we need it." She landed again as magfire took a nearby rooftop, sending comdishes and concrete showering away. Two more shots hit the opposite wall, clearly aimed at her, so she sheltered for a moment on the cross-street and let the thrusters cool, waiting for that mark to start shooting at something else. Glanced sideways within her helmet as movement showed her something hiding in a basement staircase . . . a young girl, perhaps eight, dirty-haired and frightened. Holding a younger boy down, protecting him . . . her brother? Dear God.

She ran for the neighbouring corner rather than hit the jets right next to them, then blasted up once more. Six Ks, and the streets here weren't as cooperative, zigzagging and stopping short rather than continuing straight, and forcing FSA troops to jump over. More fire, as the defenders concentrated missiles and magfire on smaller numbers of soldiers to increase the chances of hitting. But so well drilled were her soldiers that those under heaviest fire simply took cover, happy to distract the shooters while the targets they *could* hit took the opportunity to advance at maximum speed. Sandy streaked low past an apartment building, saw a row of more, larger buildings ahead, six-storey structures in a row facing the corporate zone, and landed on a low roof behind them. Three Ks, maximum accurate magfire range. Tacnet showed fifty percent of her force within the three-K arc. Seventy percent. Ninety percent.

"Cover and secondary cover!" she directed. "Hit 'em and displace!" She hit a burst of thrusters, rocketed up to the six-storey rooftop, and grounded one foot forward for a good brace. Pumped a round at a flyer, then a building-top emplacement, then jumped back off the building again and behind a neighbour, without seeing her rounds hit.

But tacnet showed what she'd missed—magfire rounds striking home, flyers spinning, nacelles shattered, falling into buildings, exploding. Her own emplacement target atop the building was hit by four rounds in succession, exploding in multiple shrapnel sprays. The remaining flyers wove behind the buildings for cover, but it was too late—more than half of them were gone, and the towertop emplacements were no more.

"Missile defences," Sandy said calmly, and tasked tacnet with those exclusively. More red dots appeared as tacnet cross-referenced multiple visual feeds to spot anything involved in missile defence. Sandy leaped to another building top, and this time remained in place to lay down multiple rounds, not seeing anything left to shoot at her from this angle. All across their front, five hundred FSA mag-rifles poured accurate fire into the outer wall and the tops of buildings behind it, disintegrating com towers, dishes, wall emplacements, and rooftop generators. As they finished, a volley of Trebuchet fire fell into the smoke from on high, and the entire defensive line disappeared in flame and airborne debris.

"All ahead!" They leaped forward toward the smoke, over the remaining rooftops and roads, and grounded just where the neutral zone began before the walls, a dead space of deserted buildings the corporations had declared uninhabitable after the Crash that laid Pantalan civilisation low. Another leap, and full speed across the neutral zone rooftops, powering the thrusters to well overheated as the predictable storm of robotic gunfire came up at them from below. A year ago, Sandy had fought her way through that zone in some of the most hellish fighting of her life. Today, she crossed it in a blur, fire nipping at her heels as robots not meant for aerial defence struggled to find them through narrow gaps, and those with good fields of fire on rooftops were destroyed by magfire, or by missiles that tacnet assigned and fired before the soldiers even thought on it.

And then the corporate zone buildings were rushing up at her, some smoking with floors ablaze, and amongst them . . . "*Hoppers!*" someone yelled, and there was shooting and fast manoeuvring.

Sandy nailed one that raced out well to her right, then cut thrust and fell as several more fired from within the building ahead. She hit thrust again to put her through a sixth-floor window and smashed her way through a partition wall, then down a corridor to the far side of the building. It gave her a view of the zone beyond, more buildings, neat and modern streets, green verges, wealth and technology. And several grounded hoppers by the base of a building, which she shot with her rifle, single rounds punching through that armour like paper. She leaped out and kicked as fire across the zone converged on her, shooting straight upward and spraying missiles from the back rack, as tacnet identified targets too quickly for her to shoot them all. She did her best though, zigging left and right, thrusters screaming for a rest as fire ripped past . . . and then the rest of her team were in, simply bypassing the first enemy hoppers as she had and pouring fire into the next line of defences.

Those defences were too static and poorly positioned. In several seconds, those still alive were falling back fast, pursued by FSA missiles and magfire. Sandy leaped for a new building top . . . and saw AMLORA rounds streaking low . . . *"Airburst!"* someone yelled, then a flurry of airborne explosions, blasting several hoppers from the sky, spinning and crashing to the ground.

But the rest leaped on, like the mating rush of strange, swarming fireflies as Sandy settled on the rooftop and picked off a retreating hopper, then another, then set her sights on the big compounds beyond. This was Chancelry Corporation's section of the corporate zone—the second time she'd taken Chancelry; it had seemed the best bet to attack because it had been worst damaged the last time around, and corporations without as much money as they'd once had might not have repaired it so well. And now, once inside, she knew the way, and where those mysterious grounded ships were located . . .

"Hold!" she commanded, as a new tacnet feed on those ships showed something alarming. They were moving, engines flaring—and this feed was coming from her own circling assault shuttles, well off beyond the Droze perimeter. "Hold and cover, their shuttles are lifting! They're leaving!"

Her troops cut thrust and dropped to the ground or crashed through building windows, seeking cover. The sounds of combat lessened enough to hear the huge, rumbling thrust of shuttle engines from closer to the zone's common center, that space of the zone shared by all corporations, not just one.

"We're not going to stop them from leaving?" Singh asked tersely.

"We might be able to handle them on the ground," said Sandy, "but I'm not taking any chances against their spacecraft. If they want to leave, let them leave."

Because Fleet had had an almighty struggle to drop her team in the right place, and Reichardt had told her endless tales about just how outmatched every Federation starship was against the near-magical Talee vessels. That ship ahead could be packing something very nasty, and the whole point of this exercise was to make them leave.

And then she could see them, angular lifting-body shapes, like nothing she'd seen documented anywhere. Familiar enough to those who knew the aerodynamics involved, but significantly different, in short cuts taken that human designers wouldn't dare. They hovered a moment longer, as the final hoppers leaped their way, landing on the wings, and disappearing inside. Sandy was momentarily surprised, but then asked herself why. It was the alien cliché, that aliens wouldn't have human standards of self-preservation, would all work by some hive mind, would sacrifice themselves pointlessly, instead of risking large vessels in order to save the last few remaining soldiers. Many in the Federation believed the same thing of GIs—the synthetics cliché again. Those who thought they were "normal," liked to believe that they were the only ones who knew and valued individuals.

When the last suit was aboard, the shuttles applied full power and roared skyward, five in total, each about twice the size of the human versions.

"Snowcat to all birds, let them go," said Sandy. "Relay to Fleet, we've got outbound shuttles. I'll bet they'll have inbound Talee cruisers any moment to pick them up. I'd advise letting them go as well."

"Copy Snowcat."

Pillars of orange fire lit the sky as main engines engaged, and the shuttles accelerated toward escape velocity. For another long, several minutes, there was thunder in the sky. And then, slowly, fading to quiet. A stillness lay across the corporate center of Droze, broken only by rising smoke and crackling flames. Sandy had lived a long time for a GI and had seen a lot of strange things. But she had never experienced any moment in her life quite so surreal as that silence.

CHAPTER TWENTY-ONE

Sandy stood by the armoured corpse of a fallen enemy hopper. The armour release wouldn't operate, disabled by the huge magfire hole through the middle, armour melted and blackened into a mass of burnt electrics and blood. But the helmet was off, and within it, head back and mouth open, was a Talee.

A longish face, narrower than humans. Large, wide eyes, now closed. Better peripheral vision, and probably smell, to judge from the prominent nose. Worse hearing, perhaps, with just earholes and little skin flaps. Omnivorous teeth, nothing sharp. A very human-looking tongue. Skin a brown shade under light fuzz . . . but her troops were reporting others had different shades—natural variability or evolved racial difference? A pronounced inverse ridge down the center of the skull, twin brain cases, as all the rumours said. Alien, but not repulsive, not even especially odd-looking, to human eyes. Like just another humanoid species, depicted in one of her kids' animated TV shows. She could imagine such a face smiling, laughing, or frowning, if Talee did any of those things.

And she'd killed him. She did not feel grief—that was reserved for those she loved, person to person. Yet she could rarely recall having felt so sad.

"What the hell were you doing here?" she muttered to the corpse, leaning on her two-meter rifle, still in her suit as they all were.

"Organic," said Jane, taking a knee alongside to look more closely. The suits made squatting impossible. "Probably augmented, but not a synth. Might explain why they can't fight worth shit."

"I've got six organics in my unit," said Lieutenant Rikowski opposite, another GI. "They're all damn good, way better than these guys." Indicating the Talee. "With augments in suits, the synthetic physical advantage is minimal. These guys didn't lose because they were slow."

"No," Sandy agreed. "Their reflexes were fine. They just fought like green rookies. Like they'd never done it before, even in training."

"Technology dependent," Rikowski agreed. "Arrogant dicks, never thought we'd figure a way past their net-tech, and never had a plan B in case we did."

The assault team had five dead, five wounded, all of them in those final, close-range phases when the Talee had finally brought their hoppers into play, then followed it up with airburst AMLORAs to cover their retreat. Sandy had been bracing for thirty percent–plus casualties. Instead, she had one percent.

Talee casualties were forty-six, all of them hopper infantry, and all of them dead. Wounded, in hopper suits, usually only happened from artillery near-misses, and the FSA hadn't been using artillery directly on hoppers. Magfire rarely left survivors, at least not among organics, and the Talee had been in the process of being overrun and overwhelmed, presenting a lot of easy targets. Sandy was nearly relieved she had no prisoners. She didn't want her first face-to-face interaction with an alien race to be her explaining to them why she'd killed all their friends.

"Fuck it," she muttered, and powered her suit back to full mobility. "Put an auto-sentry on each of them in case the civvies come wandering." She looked about at the deserted streets, the empty surrounding high-rise, the manicured street verge gardens, littered with the occasional alien corpse or smoking ordnance crater. "Where the hell are all the civvies, anyway?"

She sealed the faceplate once more, jogged to the middle of the road, and jumped. Cut and landed on top of a hundred-meter high-rise, paused to let the combat-strained jets cool and recharge, then jumped again. To her right now was Chancelry main HQ, an all-too-familiar cluster of low-rise compounds, still scarred from year-old damage she'd participated in inflicting. But her troops said it was empty, that all of the action was over in Dhamsel Corporation Headquarters.

That was across the neutral zone, and she cruised that way, across low-rise suburban streets she recalled fighting her way through on Kiet's ill-judged attempt to rescue the other corporations' high-designation GIs from the certain death that awaited them from lethal experiments. The suburbs looked nicer now than she recalled, bloodstained and horrifying as her memories were. Neat rows of tiled rooves amidst many leafy trees and gardens, it could have been a modest Tanushan neighbourhood. She landed on the rooftop of a ten-storey apartment block, paused again for ten seconds, then jumped again.

In the central zone, she could see where the assault shuttles had landed—on a green belt that half-arced across the northern side, with parks, lakes, and children's playgrounds. The grass was blackened now and imprinted with the marks of huge landing feet. She flew through lingering smoke from smouldering fires and blasted dust, toward Dhamsel compound adjoining.

Dhamsel Headquarters looked much like Chancelry, only undamaged, with shiny glass buildings around common courtyards and paths. She landed in a blast of smoke as tacnet showed her the deployment of soldiers about the compound and a gathering in the main foyer of the central building. She walked that way, past a six-legged AMLORA in the courtyard, immobile once the Talee had abandoned it, like all the other human hardware they'd controlled by remote.

The main foyer doubled as a suit-parking zone, and Sandy shut down her hopper, cracked the forward armour, and climbed out. A soldier directed her to the next floor up, and she unracked her regular rifle from the hopper's back-rack, and walked with Jane to the stairs.

"*We can't find any GIs,*" said Singh as she climbed. "*The GI quarters are empty, so are the cells. No sign of any production facilities either.*" It had never been settled just who was in charge of GI production in Droze, and how it was coordinated. Chancelry Corporation had originated GI technology, had found the initial Talee outposts here on Pantala that led to synthetic replication tech in the first place. But whether Chancelry had *all* of the production facilities, and did all of the medical tests, had never been conclusively proven. Surely not all, because League had required medical testing on a massive scale, given the ticking clock on the neurological disorders the technology was causing in the broader League population. And the other four Droze corporations had all kept sizeable forces of GIs.

"*Check the hospital wards,*" Sandy replied, leaving the stairs and heading down the central hall. "*In Chancelry the top floor were synth-experiments, the bottom floors were organic.*" Chancelry had used their "experiments" as regular security, let them serve to term, then terminated them. Apparently they'd learned a lot. But mostly, they'd learned that the primary generation of neural-synth technology caused flaws when integrated into regular human brains that could not be easily reversed. It would take new tech. And that had been supplied by Renaldo Takewashi, who was still revered in these corridors . . . or in Chancelry corridors, perhaps. The first person to fully decode what they'd found here.

Private Ricardo was guarding a doorway ahead. Through it, Sandy found Vanessa, also in her light armour, sipping coffee someone had made from a still-functioning coffee machine in an adjoining tea room.

"Like some?" Vanessa asked. Several of her other soldiers were also drinking a cup. "It's actually not bad, for synthetic League swill."

"Careful now," said Jane, stretching her stiff neck, "people will think you're talking about me."

Vanessa raised an eyebrow at Sandy. "Was that a joke?"

"She does that sometimes," Sandy explained. And regarded the rest of the office. There were beds in here. Some tables, a few TVs, chairs. Sleeping for fifteen, she counted, squeezed in quite tightly. Sitting on the beds or chairs were various men and women, some in business clothes, others in casuals. They looked worn and scruffy, and very tired, sitting head in hands, hair a-mess. Sandy looked at Vanessa questioningly.

"Prisoners here," Vanessa explained. "Dhamsel Corporation employees. Talee had them VR-locked on and off for weeks, any time they liked. Rounded them up, put them in a central place, didn't let them go home. Interrogated them, we think . . . they're a bit of a mess, not making much sense. At least we can guess from the sleeping arrangements that this whole male-female privacy thing doesn't mean much to Talee."

"Doesn't mean much to GIs either," said Sandy. Vanessa shrugged, conceding. "Guess they didn't need much security to keep them here, the VR-Matrix would know exactly what they're doing any given moment, if anyone tried to escape. . . ."

"Bam," Vanessa agreed. "Straight back under."

"They've got family outside," said Jane. "They didn't return, were kept captive here for weeks . . . so where are the families?"

"All looks deserted," Sandy added. "I think all the civvies here who could probably ran to the other side of the wall. They'll be hiding among the non-corporates. Big fat irony there." She fixed the man seated nearest Vanessa with a stare. "So . . . kept them here for what?"

"Won't give his name," said Vanessa, sipping coffee. "Database has been wiped, and he's not on ours."

"Ours is out of date," said Sandy, taking a knee opposite the man. He looked a wreck, eyes dark and sleepy, suit and shirt mangled and unwashed. The smell wasn't great either . . . though Sandy guessed the office buildings would be quite good for captivity, because of the toilets, showers, and food supplies. "What did they want with you?" she asked him. No reply. She couldn't tell if he was ignoring her or genuinely out of it. "Where's Patana?"

Patana was the CEO of Dhamsel. He'd been the one who sent the kills-witch signal that killed at least a thousand high-des GIs in the confusion of Kiet's failed jailbreak. "Haven't found him yet," said Vanessa. "You know he'd actually be quite useful alive?"

"Sure."

"And he's more likely to help us if he thinks you won't just kill him as soon as he's no further use?"

"I guess." She wasn't about to say any more on the matter, and Vanessa didn't push it. "Are the other corporations like this?"

Vanessa nodded. "Seem to be. Every database is completely blank, and the research labs in Chancelry have been stripped. No sign of any kids like Kiril. But I mean, if that was all they were after, it wouldn't have taken long. So why were they still here?"

"*Could have done more damage than they did,*" Reichardt was telling her on the big displays in the Dhamsel executive offices. "*Did some crazy short-jump reversal to pick up those shuttles from Droze, then left just as fast. League's arrivals scared them too, but they could have hit a lot more of us than they did, if they'd bothered. I think they just wanted out after you beat the crap out of them down there.*"

Sandy nodded, glancing elsewhere in the office, where a search was underway. Desk drawers and shelves were being cleared, any portable devices scanned or taken back to someone who could. Elsewhere, the occasional safe was being cut open, and the network scoured by the Federation's lately-very-superior hacking tools. Anything for clues, no matter how small.

"*You don't look that happy,*" Reichardt observed on the awkward five-second delay that their distance currently made.

"Well, whatever the Talee were doing here, we haven't found it. If it was just Chancelry biotech they had that in the first few hours. But they stayed here weeks, nearly a month."

Again the delay pause. Reichardt was in his captain's chair, studying multiple displays while talking. There was no activity on the bridge behind him, so they were still strapped in on full alert. League Fleet had indeed arrived, a carrier and four cruisers, courtesy of Hafeez and the Federation courier that had dropped him at the nearest known League Fleet base. League's arrival had outflanked and scared off the Talee, but no one knew how long that would last. Now League were inbound, and in typical League style, giving instructions like they owned the place. Which, legally speaking, they did.

"*So what's bugging you?*"

"Talee. I don't take any losses lightly, but getting in here was *easy*. As these things go." On five-second delay she couldn't pause to see that Reichardt was getting her point. "They fought like they'd never done it before. I don't mean just them, I mean we've got some rookies on this mission too, but they did good because of their training. Humans have generations, centuries, millennia of experience at warfare. Green troops can still perform, because they're trained as their ancestors have learned through hard experience.

"But the Talee down here fought like they've never seen war before. Never heard about war, not from their forebears, not from anyone. They had the basic skills but had no idea how to put it all together, like a chef who chucks everything in a bowl and hopes for the best. No sense of sequential thinking, no strategy."

"*Well, they were a lot better than that up here.*" A faint frown, thinking on it. "*But, yeah, I know what you mean. Like I said, they could have done better with what they had. We lost* Vigilant, *but it should have been more, given what they can do.*"

"Arron, their hoppers are *our* technology. I don't mean just inspired by, I mean exact copies. Our techs are looking at them, they say aside from the different saddle shape to accommodate Talee bodies, and some crazy advanced bits and pieces, the basic design philosophy is identical. And they say it doesn't make any sense, because if their technology is that much better, they should have been able to change the design philosophy—that's what better technology does, you put a better engine in a car, suddenly you have the same power for less weight, you can change the shape and layout of everything else accordingly. But Talee haven't done that . . . and these weren't captured suits, they were Talee-made."

Pause. *"You're right, that is weird."*

"You know what it's like?" said Sandy as it occurred to her. "It's like a bunch of teenagers who've watched a war movie and thought that looks like fun, and so decide to build a modern army. And so they look around for some weapons, find something someone else built before, and copy it. No idea of why it all fits together like that, or what it's for, just blind faith that they need weapons, and this is a weapon, so they'll build it."

"So . . . your theory was that organic Talee didn't survive the catastrophe. That synthetic Talee brought them back from extinction, right?"

"Right. So now I'm wondering, what if that was recent? I recall Ari saying that in a total species wipeout, if you had enough birthing tanks and reproductive tech, you could turn a few hundred individuals into millions within the space of a few generations. And from there, millions into billions isn't so hard. Two groups of Talee explains why their tactics suddenly changed, so what if . . . what if the organic Talee aren't here to punish humans at all? What if they're here to punish their own synthetics, and we just got in the way?"

"You're saying . . . you're saying this is some kind of Talee civil war?"

"Dammit, what have you got looking at Pantala right now? Can you see any signs of activity elsewhere on the planet, something the Talee were looking for over the last month?"

"We're looking at everything, Sandy, but planets are big, and this one's magnetism and atmospheric dust are disagreeable with our scanners."

"League maps are better than ours—pull their damn station apart, see if they've got any better maps on Pantalan geography. Whatever they're looking for isn't in Droze, so it must be somewhere else . . . but they had to shut down Droze to access it, because otherwise Droze would have stopped them. I'm betting it's old and somewhere hard to find . . . plenty of blowing sand on this dirtball, over a few thousand years things can disappear real good."

"Sandy, League Fleet's demanding full access to Droze. They say thanks, but they'll take over now, they'll be in position to put a shuttle down in a few hours." Which meant they weren't exactly rushing in and were being careful . . . but in the circumstances, it was fast enough.

"Tell them we have reason to believe there are Talee agents still present here. With our upgrades we're invulnerable for the moment, but League won't be. Tell them if they come down here in force, they'd better bring some comfortable pillows."

A delayed smirk on the screen. *"They won't be pleased."*

"The golden rule of my life," Sandy said sourly, "if League are pleased with me, I'm doing it wrong."

"Let me get this straight, and I want to hear it from you. What do you think we're facing here?"

"I think organic Talee are the rebellious teenagers who got tired of the synthetics running their lives and threw a tantrum. Explains why their fighting style sucks, why they're brash and stupid with foreign relations— they're sticking it to mum and dad and learning the hard way that mum and dad might have had a point. Add to that being terrified of this mental disorder of theirs that Cai described, and I'll bet Cai was right, and they're after that technology most of all before it spreads. But I also don't think Cai was telling the whole truth."

Reichardt exhaled hard as she spoke, the picture breaking into light static as he ran a hand through his hair. *"Well, that's just great. Fleet has this carefully constructed textbook of what Talee are like—they're cautious, they're meticulous, they're clever and rational. And now you tell us that organic Talee are actually none of those things, and that we've been dealing with synthetics all this time. And now the organics are presumably becoming the majority once more, as will always happen with organics because we breed so fast, and that majority are a bunch of petulant, drug-taking, rough-housing school students?"*

"Let's hope that's overstating it."

"What do you think we're looking for on Droze? Some kind of base?"

"Some kind of very old base, or bases. Chancelry discovered Talee outposts here. My own GIs, Kiet's bunch from Pantala, were living in caves the Talee had used a long time ago . . . but there was no technology there, we've gone over all of that before. What we don't know is if this was a base of synthetic Talee or organic. This system is a long way from Talee main space, so it seems it survived their catastrophe, or mostly. This is where the seeds remain that weren't burned in the fire. Seeds that are thousands of years old and hold the key to knowledge that was lost millennia ago. That's what I think the organics are here to find, something that the synths were keeping from them. What and why, I've no idea."

Reichardt pursed his lips, thinking about that. The delay lasted longer than light-speed suggested it should. "*Wow*," he said finally. "*You know, Kresnov, I think I've done pretty well following you around all this time, saving your ass. I mean, I've got to see some pretty far-out stuff.*"

"Find that damn base," Sandy said wryly. "We might not have seen anything yet."

An hour later, Home Guard began lobbing makeshift mortars over the walls. Encouraged by the lack of a more typical devastating response, they started lobbing more and hammering heavy machine gun fire at the visible corporate zone buildings. Doing so under corporate rule would have seen them, and several hundred innocents, immediately incinerated. But now it was playtime for fools.

"Shouldn't we do something to stop that?" Poole asked as they climbed into their hoppers to go attend to the Dhamsel perimeter guard's latest problem. Another explosion echoed, somewhere distant. Then another, nearer.

"Can't shoot them without killing the civvies they're hiding behind," said Sandy. "Let them shoot, it's not like they'll hit anything."

"Dunno about that," said Poole, firing up his power core. "Idiots always get lucky. You think they even know that the last bunch in here were Talee?"

"If all the corporate zone civvies ran into the outer zones to hide, they'll know." She tested feedback, a flex of the arms. "Thing is, they hate Federation nearly as bad as League. They're probably fine with Talee." Outside the building lobby, they fired up thrusters and leaped for the Dhamsel wall.

Below the ten-meter-tall reinforced wall were a series of bunkers and concrete trenches. Sandy and Poole descended by a trench where Lieutenant Duana awaited in his hopper suit, while an unoccupied suit stood nearby.

"Private Tulloch's in the bunker," Duana said with faceplate raised. "The defensive systems are working; they're just not patching into central systems, so we can't control it yet. Tulloch thinks he can do it."

"But you had something?" Sandy asked.

"Yeah." A shell whistled over nearby. "Got a visual myself, didn't tacnet it, it's not tactical. But I thought you'd like to see."

A flicker as Duana's systems patched into hers and an image appeared on her visor display. Zoomed, first-person visual, a bit shaky. It was the far side of the wall, taken from this side, looking down and out. The first several blocks of what had used to be Droze buildings were gone, torn away after the Crash when the corporations had bulldozed a clear space for defence. A hundred meters of kill-zone into which previously anything that wandered unauthorised was dead. Beyond that, deserted buildings, not bulldozed but crawling with killer droids. Those buildings blocked any line-of-sight from the buildings that *were* occupied and provided cover for swarms of easily re-tasked robots that could just as easily fan out as hold the line, if required.

But now, Duana's visual zoomed on the base of one of those buildings by the corner of a main road . . . and she saw them, behind the burned-out wreck of a car. Kids, peering at the walls. Looking both scared and hopeful, and now debating with each other. Even now another one ran over, no more than seven, in dirty old pants and sneakers. Droze street kids, the city had plenty. These ones seemed to have figured out that something had changed, and there might be something on the other side of the wall worth risking everything for.

"Fuck," said Sandy with feeling. "We're sure all the defensive grids are down?"

Duana nodded. "They're safe, but they don't know that. They're taking a hell of a risk."

Sandy shook her head. "No, street kids here are smart. They'll have noticed the defender bots' behaviour changing under the Talee, I don't know if the Talee were still tasking them to shoot at people, but they'll have been different. And now the attack's come through and all the bots are silent, they know the zone's changed hands."

"You think they know it's Federation?" asked Poole. Machine gun fire, from somewhere farther away. Tacnet showed heavy rounds, well out of accurate range, streaking over the perimeter. Accuracy wasn't their goal, just noise. A single missile from her backrack could have silenced them. "You're kind of famous here, you beat Chancelry, took over their HQ. And they'll know Danya, Svet, and Kiril went with you."

Sandy stared at him with dawning desperation.

"Might get a kid dreaming," Poole finished. "And you know kids can dream."

"Fuck," Sandy repeated. She didn't like this at all. "Our protocol is to always inform the civvie population what's happening to them, when possible. I have to tell them the Federal Security Agency has taken the corporate zone for now. But if I tell them that, we'll have street kids and other desperates running for our gates, asking for a ticket to Callay."

"I would," said Duana.

"Yeah, me too. And fucking Home Guard will call them traitors and start shooting them, you watch."

"You think?" With the wide-eyed disbelief that a lot of younger GIs showed for cynical predictions of human behaviour.

"Yeah, I think. Look, we stay quiet for now. Lieutenant, get those kids in here. Don't go looking for more, but if they do show up, get them all in, get them sent back to Dhamsel HQ, find some armoured runabout for transport in case one of these mortars gets lucky. And if Home Guard even *look* like they're gonna shoot at them, you fucking toast them first, got it?"

"Yes, Commander."

"Tickets to Callay are pretty expensive," Poole suggested, looking dubious.

"Federation's rich," Sandy muttered. "If we can afford to carry troops and ammo all the way here, we can afford to carry a few kids back."

"*Commander?*" Tacnet showed it was Williams, farther along the wall. "*Take a look at this.*"

An image appeared: Williams's visual feed. It showed a man, in plain civilian clothes, walking across the bulldozed kill-zone toward the next entry gate along. Behind him, dragged by one hand, was another man, hauled by his collar through the dust. The ease with which the weight was pulled, for so little sacrifice in posture, indicated the walking man was a GI. And his cargo, so unceremoniously hauled, was . . .

"Well," said Poole, viewing the same feed. "Looks like we found Chairman Patana."

Sandy and Poole sealed up and ran, nearly a kilometre along the inner wall, saving their thrusters and not drawing extra attention to that gate. At the gate, more soldiers in hopper armour stood back, while the personnel gate alongside the big vehicle gate was opened. Through it walked the man, dragging the Dhamsel CEO behind him. He dumped Patana and stood calmly before them.

Sandy lifted her faceplate once more and knelt, rifle butt down on the dirt for stability. The GI was African-looking, broad-faced, and handsome. His hair was worn in that series of spikey studs that African hair could attain. She didn't know if that hairstyle had a name. Svetlana would know, being a student of such things. But thinking of Svetlana was a mistake, because suddenly she missed her so badly her eyes watered.

"Who are you?" she asked him.

"Commander Kresnov," the man greeted her, in that very calm, intelligent way only a high-des GI could. Any GI that high-des, and in the Federation, she'd know. That left two options, and if this was a League GI, he'd be ISO, and ISO weren't about to just hand her an asset like Patana. That left one. "I've brought you a gift."

Sandy looked at Patana. A slim, dusky man, half-conscious in a dirty suit, shirt ripped and tie long gone. "I've been given better," she said darkly. "What's the trade?"

The man smiled. It was a wry smile, edged with darkness. "Perhaps I misunderstand the human custom. Is there always a trade with a gift?"

"Among friends and family, no. Among people like us, always. I'm sure Talee are the same."

It was a bold statement, but the Talee-GI inclined his head, not arguing. Biologists had discovered that different life-forms evolving in similar environments ended up following very similar evolutionary paths. Sandy was certain that just as evolution was evolution anywhere in the galaxy, so were politics and power.

"I come to you as a friend. I have no alliance to those who previously occupied the corporate zone. But I think you already know that."

"A friend of ours explained some things to us," Sandy agreed. "He went by the name of Cai. Perhaps amongst his own people he went by a different name."

"Cai is known to us. How does he fare?"

"He died. Defending us and his investment in us." The man's face fell. "He was brave, and we owe him a debt. I owe him personally."

"'Debt' is our custom too. I'm sad to hear he's gone, though he knew it was a dangerous task when he took it. 'Duty,' I believe, is another common concept between us."

"It is," Sandy agreed. She hiked one armoured thumb back toward the Dhamsel HQ. "Your organics are becoming unruly. Can't you control them anymore?"

Surprise in the man's eyes. Then perhaps . . . admiration? Certainly pleasure that she'd reached such a conclusion. "Cai told you?"

"We figured it out." An explosion nearby, a mortar hitting a tower and the crash of falling glass. "Our theory is that organics died in your last catastrophe, and you synthetics brought them back."

A silence as the man regarded her, broken by a rattle of gunfire. Sprawled in the dirt, Patana appeared to wake a little, blinking and coughing, then abruptly slumped into unconsciousness once more. No one felt inclined to check on him. Sandy felt as though the galaxy were holding its breath. This theory had not yet been confirmed. So much hung on the answer.

The Talee-GI exhaled, finally, with a heave of broad shoulders. "And have been regretting it ever since," he admitted.

Sandy and Poole jogged alongside the armoured car carrying Patana and their guest. A mortar hit twenty meters away as they ran, no real threat to armour, but if buildings began to catch fire it would be destruction of evidence, and she had no manpower to spare fighting fires.

"Arvid, let's stop them shooting."

"*Sure,*" came Singh's reply from observation atop a tower roof. "*How? We use magfire against them it'll go straight through them, and five walls behind them, possibly ten. The areas they're shooting from look inhabited.*"

"*Which suggests they know we're Federation,*" Vanessa cut in, "*and they'll use our moral standards against us. Real brave.*"

"Yeah, maybe the next generation of mag rifles we'll have a power reducer, cut the muzzle velocity in half." But she hated too many systems in one weapon—the key to weapon reliability was simplicity, something modern designers forgot too easily. "How about airbursting missiles?"

"*Can't do it with shuttles,*" Singh replied, "*they don't have anything small enough. Backracks might work, but we've never tried it. Could be fatalities, they're not designed for nonlethal purposes.*"

"So long as those fatalities are Home Guard, I'll risk it," said Sandy. "Pick a guinea pig, and if it works do a whole bunch simultaneously. Should shut them up for a while."

She was just arriving back at HQ when Singh, deciding the test shot had worked, launched a full spread of sixteen backrack missiles, zigzagging off toward the perimeter. Soldiers unloaded Patana from the car and carried him inside, while Sandy noted that incoming fire appeared to have stopped.

Inside the main building lobby, Vanessa was in light armour with some others, attending to the rows of opened hopper suits, directing maintenance and rearming. With shuttles down on various HQ pads, spare ammo had been unloaded already, carried by hoppers and placed here for rearming, all without Sandy having to spare it a thought. With senior and junior officers and non-coms like she had, she knew such things would just get done, without her getting in their way.

"Wanna talk to Home Guard?" Vanessa called across the lobby, tapping her headset. Secondary coms were Vanessa's responsibility, and she wouldn't bother Sandy with it if Sandy were otherwise occupied.

Sandy thumped across in full armour. "How long they been calling?"

"Just now." As she watched privates examining the new ammo, checking security tags and serial numbers before loading. "Something about how unfair it is that they can't shoot at us with impunity."

"You do it," said Sandy, lining her armour up with the others, cracking the shell and shutting down. "Then come with us, our new friend's got something to tell us."

"New friend got a name?" asked Vanessa, looking dubiously at the new GI.

"Dara," he said.

"Cute," said Vanessa, flipping channels to talk to whichever indignant Home Guard person was shouting at her.

"Commander," said Dara, meeting Sandy as she stepped from her hopper, "might it not be best to talk without the organics present?" With a look back at Vanessa. "We synthetics have matters to discuss. They require a certain perspective."

Sandy looked at him for a moment, then at Patana, held between two GIs, head lolling. A man who'd commanded the commissioning of thousands of synthetic test subjects, then terminated their short lives for experiments. And then killed upwards of a thousand more via the killswitches built into their brainstems, rather than let them escape to freedom. She couldn't look at him and not see the terrified faces, escapees realising that the vaunted Cassandra Kresnov had no solution and that their great hope of freedom was about to implode and take their lives with it.

"No offence," Sandy told Dara, "but I trust her more than you."

CHAPTER TWENTY-TWO

The office had a view, but window slats were three-quarters drawn in case of a very lucky Home Guard shot. Sandy poured a cup from the water dispenser, and one for Dara, Vanessa, and Jane, whom she'd summoned. Jane had found a baseball cap from somewhere, worn and faded, and wore it under her headset, sitting now with her feet up along the long table.

"What's with the hat?" Sandy asked her quizzically, skimming the cup along the smooth table top toward her.

Jane took it. "Got used to wearing it. Suits me." She sipped. "I'm not as pretty as you lot."

"No," said Sandy, handing Dara his cup. "You're not."

Vanessa entered, carrying fruit she'd found somewhere, one piece for each of them. She tossed with confidence that GIs would catch and took her own seat at the head of the long table. "No idea what they're called," she said around a mouthful of fruit. "Something exotic. Taste good though, and they're on the database for edible foods."

"Thanks, babe," said Sandy, eating. "Thoughtful."

Shrug. "You know me." She glanced at Jane. "This is a fashion statement, huh?"

"Does this look like a fashion to you?" Jane asked drily.

"Don't be embarrassed," Vanessa deadpanned. "When Sandy first arrived on Callay, she might have thought so too."

"Thanks," said Sandy. "What did Home Guard say?"

"Apparently we're not allowed to shoot at them. Only they're allowed to shoot at us. It's some kind of rule." Another bite. "We killed three of them, but jury's out. I think we might have just knocked over a mortar tube while firing and they blew themselves up."

"Any civvies hurt?"

"By us? No way. By them, probably, but they'll blame it on us."

"Of course."

"They said about twenty are dead from our assault, more than that wounded."

Sandy exhaled hard. "Yeah, well, they're probably not kidding on that. There's just no other way to do it. That's their justification for shooting at us?"

Vanessa nodded. "Most of that wasn't us either, it was Talee shooting at us, only they didn't use airbursts at range, only magfire and AMLORA." She glanced at Dara.

"The organics are not sophisticated," he explained. "They've little practise at this."

"We noticed," said Jane.

"They borrowed our weapons tech?" Sandy asked. "From spies amongst us? People like you?"

"You must understand," said Dara, looking down at his cup, "organic Talee are a new civilisation. They've been thriving, but they are isolated. We synthetics brought them into the world, but there remains concern over organic susceptibility to uplink technology. There is a mental condition, it . . ."

"Cai explained it to us," Sandy interrupted. "A drug effect, it creates a narrow-focus mindset, improves linear thinking and processing, maths and data, but at the expense of rationality and context."

"At the expense of self," said Dara. "We call it tokot. Tokot on our home-world are a species of insect. Their workers feed themselves willingly to their young at a certain age for nourishment. It is an effective life-cycle for the hive, at the expense of the individual. Tokot creates such thinking in Talee. It is frightening, yet also seductive."

"And synthetics don't get it," Vanessa finished.

"No. We—synthetic Talee—suspect that synthetic humans will also prove less susceptible to such group thinking among humans. Such as the disorders that we see growing in the region of human space you call the League."

"We've noticed as much," Sandy agreed. Vanessa looked at her warily. "Dara, what were they doing here? What were they searching for? And if you synths are in control of Talee foreign policy, why are the organics suddenly rebelling?"

Her coms blinked before Dara could reply. She put it on speaker. "Kresnov."

Pause for several seconds, then, "*Commander, it's Captain Reichardt.*" She could see that, but Dara didn't have that uplink . . . and with their recent upgrades, might not be able to get it without permission. Maybe. "*Just got a message from Bursteimer, putting it through now.*" Captain Bursteimer had gone off in pursuit of retreating Talee ships, following as they jumped from the system. Now he was another twenty-minutes-light farther out, and this message had been travelling that long.

"*We've been analysing their jump signatures,*" came Bursteimer's voice, crackling with solar static. "*We've seen this pattern before, I don't think they were full charged for jump. I'm ninety percent sure they cut it short, in which case they're just out of the system, possibly regathering. We've seen that before too, and if they've got reinforcements out there, assuming these guys picked up a few smarts from Kresnov's synthetic Talee friends, they'll be back in a few hours, maybe less. We surprised the heck out of them coming in here like that, but Talee ships on inbound assault trajectories aren't anything we can really handle. I'd recommend that Kresnov finds whatever the hell she's looking for down there, and gets the hell out before we cop it in the neck.*"

That transmission cut and was replaced by Reichardt. "*Sandy?*"

"I'm working on it," she said, looking Dara calmly in the eyes. "If you're going to get smashed, retreat, and pull the same stunt on them, don't get shot up on our account. We can take care of ourselves down here, and if the Talee want to come back down and start that ground fight again, let's just say my concern will be limited."

A transmission pause as that went out. Vanessa sipped her water, looking scarcely more bothered than Jane, who was typically unreadable. No one giving anything away in front of their guest.

"*Copy that,*" said Reichardt. "*However, if they've finished with Droze, and have no further use for it, they might just make a large smoking crater out of the corporate zone, which we won't be able to stop if we're not here. Recommend you make plans to head for the hills. Reichardt out.*"

"Doing that too, Kresnov out." She raised eyebrows at Dara.

"Come with me," said Dara, "and I'll show you."

"Show me what?"

"What you're looking for. What *they* are looking for. The thing that defines the struggle of the Talee race, and that might lay clear the future path of yours."

Twenty minutes later, Sandy stood out on the big Dhamsel landing pads alongside one of their assault shuttles, heavy pumps roaring as they struggled to refuel. Loading vehicles rumbled past, taking more ammo to the HQ, and guide lights blinked against the oncoming dark. Jane stood with her in light armour, while Vanessa loomed above them in hopper armour, as were ten others spaced around the pad perimeter, awaiting the vehicle Dara said was incoming. Bereft of sunlight, the air was cooling fast, and the sharpening wind stung with flying sand.

"You realise we don't have any atmospheric radar coverage?" Vanessa shouted at Sandy above the noise. "The network wasn't very good to begin with, but now it's out almost completely, and Fleet say they can't track fast-moving atmospheric vehicles from orbit!"

"I don't think it's an accident that the grid's out," Jane remarked, checking her rifle, wary of the blowing sand. "No way Dara's alone here. And Droze tech isn't upgraded like ours."

"Yeah, well, don't get cocky about those upgrades either," Vanessa retorted. "I doubt they've shown us everything they can do, and we know Cai kept secrets."

Sandy nodded. "We'll be careful."

Tacnet showed something on the edge of visual range, moving very fast. They waited, pleased at least that Home Guard weren't about to drop a shell on their heads, and watched the blip decelerate as it approached.

"Keep Patana alive," said Sandy to Vanessa grimly. "He knows a lot of pieces in the GI research program puzzle I'd like filled in. But that won't matter to some of our GIs if they suspect our debrief and legal process could take years, which it will. He might be useful enough we never get around to executing him. Some of us won't like that."

"Hell, I don't like it," said Vanessa. "But I'll do what I can." Meaning that if one of their own GIs was angry and determined enough, Vanessa wasn't about to stop them with force. Sandy nodded.

"You don't want him dead?" Jane asked Sandy. With that impenetrable stare beneath the brim of her cap.

"Personally? Sure. But 'personally' doesn't come into this. We need to know what the hell League are doing with their GIs and where their medical research program is at. Against that, my desire to blow his head off is insignificant." Jane nodded, looking off beyond the pad, through blowing sand. Sandy frowned at her. "What?"

"I tried rage once. After you nearly killed me, then let me go. I don't think I understood it, at the time. But it felt right, and as I read things, it seemed that rage was appropriate, for a warrior."

"Lots of 'an eye for an eye' in the Koran," Sandy suggested.

Jane shrugged. "Bible too. Most religions. But that's not it. Rage just didn't take, with me. I didn't kill the people I've killed from rage. It was something else."

"What?"

"I don't know. Identity, maybe."

"Hell of a price they paid for your search to find yourself," Vanessa said sourly.

"These Talee too," Jane replied. "That you just killed, because you couldn't handle being left at home with your babies."

Vanessa's expression darkened. Sandy held up a hand to forestall the retort she knew was coming, and Vanessa held her tongue with difficulty. "You're not responsible for how they made you," she told Jane. "GIs can't be held responsible at that age. You were a child, and killing was your only playtime, and blood your sugar rush. Someone else put that in you. It's their fault, not yours."

"Fault, sure. But it's still what I am. What you are. And when they put me on the legal stand, I couldn't put my hand on the book and deny that I love it." From somewhere high in the darkening sky came the shrill of approaching engines. "It's not rage. It's lust."

"There won't be a legal stand," said Sandy. She could see it now, the little black delta-wing. It was razor thin, nearly lost against the sky. "They don't have a case against young GIs, and they know it."

"The law was made for organics, not synthetics," Jane said calmly. "The guilty must be punished, and deterrents established. And I'm certainly guilty." She smiled faintly. "But that's okay. The book loves a martyr too."

The delta-wing approached with a shriek of engines. Tacnet only saw it on visual, radar gave no response, even the corporate zone's electro-mag and multiphase arrays, which would cut through most forms of structural stealth to give at least some signal, found nothing. It didn't look so different from VTOL hypersonics humans used, save for a few more angular lines and low-velocity extensions as it descended. But if you weren't looking straight at it, it was invisible, to human tech at least. Once night fell completely, even the highest-range visuals would be useless beyond a few kilometres range.

"Well, good luck with that," Vanessa murmured, gazing at it. Dara walked onto the big empty pad, and zone scanners detected a faint light pulse, active scanning. Sandy wondered if it was manned. If manned was even a word you could use with aliens.

It landed with a howl of blowing sand, and no visible windshield above the wedge-shaped nose. A door appeared on one black side, a spot of light from inside, and a small stairway dropped to the tarmac. Dara looked back at them, waiting.

"Good luck," said Vanessa. "Most of us have to die before we go to meet our maker."

Sandy smiled at her. "No more them than Takewashi," she said. "Don't screw up my command without me." And she walked, with Jane, toward the angular black craft. She and Vanessa would say no more, pondering on possibilities was bad luck.

They flew for more than an hour, reclined on comfortable seats that became less comfortable in light armour. To judge by the sound, Sandy reckoned they might be flying at somewhat more than the hypersonic standard Mach-6 she was used to. High in the atmosphere, hypersonic vehicles could theoretically travel much faster, but complications of deceleration and heat shielding meant that human designers found Mach-6 the optimum speed. If Talee had found a way to push that out to Mach-10, an hour's travel could put them anywhere on Pantala. At Mach-6, it still covered half the planet.

With no windows, she had no way of telling if they remained on the night side, though she suspected they did. Which suggested a location eastward, against the planet's spin, though as far as she knew, they could be flying in circles to disorient them. Fleet were positioned against predicted incoming attack, and planetary surveillance satellites were down, and besides, were not upgraded to Talee-proof standard. Even if Fleet did have eyes in position to monitor them, it was doubtful they'd see a black hypersonic ship against a dark planet, given the limited view of orbital visuals and the nasty interference the system's magnetics and radiation threw up against other forms of scanning. She and Jane were on their own, and she had no doubt that the Talee intended it precisely that way.

An hour and twenty-one minutes after ascension, they slowed and began a mildly bumpy transition to lower velocities and altitudes. Shortly after, Sandy felt the flight surfaces change, flaps and increased surface area biting the air. Then VTOL, the beginnings of vertical thrust, and a slow descent. This ship needed no runway and could drop into a hole in the ground if required. To judge from the amount of turbulent backwash during the unusually long vertical descent, that was exactly what she judged was happening.

Then a bounce, as wheels touched ground, and the whining decline of the engines. Dara simply waited patiently by the door, as he had been patient through the flight, as Sandy boosted her armour to full mobility once more, checked her weapon, and racked it on her back. Jane saw and copied. Dara made no protest, nor any expression that he thought her insistence on arms bad manners.

"So you've been here the entire time," said Sandy, as they waited for the door. No pilots emerged from the cockpit. Perhaps it was automated. "Living on Pantala under the noses of human settlers, for . . . what is it now? A century plus?"

Dara smiled and said nothing.

"Surveillance tech can be hacked," Jane reasoned. "Even a century ago, people's uplinks weren't nearly as advanced, Talee wouldn't have been able to hack eyes and brains, there was nothing to hack. But I bet they could hack orbital ships and satellites, probably used League's first orbital networks against them. Made them see whatever they wanted them to see."

"And League didn't encourage wide-scale settlement of Pantala, so most of the planet's never really been explored on foot," Sandy added. "Just a lot of aerial and orbital surveillance, looking for Talee outposts. How did they find the first one? Did you miss something, forget to hack them in time?"

Dara shook his head. "We weren't here." Sandy was mildly surprised to get a reply. "We were initially. Two thousand years ago, before the second Catastrophe. Being out here is what saved us. We still don't know exactly why Pantala was settled. We think it was a research base of some kind, but the planet itself is not that remarkable, save for a lot of minerals suitable for manufacturing industries. But it's even farther from main Talee space than it is from the League.

"We think perhaps it was doing something very similar to what League were doing here. Doing research that was politically unsuitable, and frowned upon. We know very little still of the nature of the conflict that destroyed us and have only a rough idea of Talee society at that time. It makes Pantala's nature hard to guess. What we do know is that Pantala was the only location to survive, and its only occupants were synthetic. Everyone else was dead. Billions upon billions of lives. And here, perhaps a few thousand, no more.

"But it was a research base, with many scientific tools and with one ship only, still in orbit. One ship and a pair of shuttles to reach it. No stations; we were not so permanent. So first, the population here decided to boost their numbers. We had insufficient knowledge of organic Talee to resequence their genetic material and grow a new population, but we could make our own kind. And so that is what we did, for a century or more. We grew very good at it, and a number of centres on Pantala specialised in the creation of synthetics."

"Ah," said Jane. It did explain a lot.

Dara nodded. "It takes many resources to make synthetic life, as you know. We bent everything to the task. Our ship made runs back to our worlds and reported the devastation. But we found some salvageable ships and stations there and set about repairing those. With a space foothold above our old worlds, we began spreading our presence, and when planetary conditions allowed, we finally began resettlement. Once there, we had no further use for Pantala. We shifted much of our reproductive capability back, but not all, just in case. That remaining facility was the one that Chancelry Corporation discovered when they arrived here over a century ago."

"And this place?" asked Sandy, nodding to whatever was on the other side of the door.

"This place," said Dara, "we resettled after humans arrived. They had not found it yet, and we did not wish it found. We were foolish to have left Pantala unclaimed and to allow humans to claim it . . . but by the time we found out, several years had passed, and it was already too late. We were not numerous and in no position to wrestle with humanity over a world. So we moved back here and used our technology, as Jane suggests—blinding League with their own technology so they could not find us, nor spot our occasional comings and goings."

The door hummed, then thumped. And cracked open, spilling light and cold air from the outside. Dara went first, down the unfolding stairs and into a dim-lit hangar. Robots trundled on the tarmac, scanning the shuttle exterior, manoeuvring refuel and recharge connections from elevators in the floor. There were several more shuttles and a cavernous stone roof overhead, spotted with small lights. Overhead, a large retractable door, currently closed. The air smelled of landing fumes, and there was no sign of other life.

Sandy and Jane followed Dara, and a small door opened in the wall as they approached. Security systems were not conspicuous. Sandy guessed they hadn't had a lot of visitors.

"What's your power source?" Jane asked as they walked up the narrow corridor.

"Fusion," said Dara. "And various other systems, as you'll see."

"Population?"

"Classified," said Dara, smiling.

A door at the far end opened, this one the first of two—an airlock. They stepped in, and a familiar system scanned them for contaminants. Then it hissed, and Sandy's ears popped a little. She'd been told that pressure differential felt much more profound to organic humans, another weakness she didn't have . . .

. . . and she stepped onto a platform overlooking a cavern. It was enormous, and green, filled with trees. Brilliant green, as huge banks of overhead lights gleamed through filters Sandy didn't recognise and came somewhere close to replicating sunlight. Beneath it were buildings, gleaming with exposed glass and interior gardens, some tall and complex, others low and simple. They lined streets, which in turn ran through small parks, with little flowerbeds that lined paths and verges. She did not recognise any of the plant species. Some equally strange-looking birds flew past, with bright-orange plumage and long tails. Or perhaps they were reptiles, she thought, noting teeth and more scales than feathers on the neck.

On the far side of the enormous cavern, the better part of a kilometre away, water fell in a frothing spray from a stony wall, into a lake amidst trees. The air smelled fresh, far fresher than the usual Droze air outside and scented with plant smells she could not put name to. She hadn't known what to expect . . . a military base, a sterile lab, some berths with bunks for long-term habitat. Nothing like this. This looked like a small, carefully constructed paradise.

"Wow," she said finally. She had to keep her reserve, uncertain yet that she was among friends. But this was impressive, friends or not, and deserved its due. "You built all this up, after you came back? It's recent?"

"Plants and animals from the homeworlds," said Dara. "From the genetic material we'd recovered. Most of those worlds were dead when we returned to them. A few only had surviving insects, feeding on algae and each other. In two thousand years we've done a lot of terraforming and regeneration of species. The homeworld is our greatest triumph. It looks much like this, in parts."

Even Jane looked impressed, mouth open as she gazed across the scene. "It took a long time to get the ecosystems back up again, yeah?"

"Life is quite resilient," said Dara. "We introduced a lot of algaes and bacteria boosters to filter the atmosphere first, then when that grew to a plague we started with the plants, then progressed through the animals. There was a lot of genetic material left, we accumulated libraries of millions of species and cloned them. Homeworld was looking quite green and peaceful within five hundred years. Within a thousand, you'd barely know there was a Catastrophe at all . . . until you saw the urban ruins, reclaimed by the forests and home to animals."

Jane looked a little puzzled. "So Homeworld could sustain large-scale life for a thousand years. And you only brought organic Talee back *recently?*"

Dara gestured for them to walk on. A long, wide stairway descended the cavern's outer wall, with a carved stone balustrade. Its lower steps were lost amidst a thicket of trees.

"It was a matter of great debate," he said as they descended the steps. "Organic Talee destroyed themselves twice. We studied what we'd recovered of their history, their psychology, and concluded there was a grave danger that they'd do it all again. They are not an especially violent species—indeed, what we know of humans tells us that humans have fought vastly more wars, Talee have been historically quite peaceful by comparison. But they do not modernise well. Their psychology is old, rooted in ancient genes that were never designed for uplinks and modern data flows. Lost in these data flows, twice in a few thousand years, they've gone insane and destroyed everything. Some suggested that the Talee race had not actually become extinct but had simply evolved to a new state of being. A synthetic state. Many thought this was a natural state throughout the universe, that organic life would naturally become obsolete, and that synthetic life would replace it."

They descended past the rooftops of buildings, headed for the trees. Some odd little bat-like creatures were hopping on all fours along the balustrades, searching for insects, and disinterested in passing bipeds.

"And a thousand years pass," Jane said with mild disbelief, "or more than a thousand, and you still can't make up your minds on whether to bring organics back. Doesn't sound like much of a debate, it sounds like you'd already made up your minds."

"And then humans came," said Sandy, seeing how the timelines matched up. "Humans took Pantala, and this is like a . . . a special place to you. A holy site, does that translate? The place where Talee survived, the only place. The origin of this phase of Talee life, and your salvation."

"It translates," Dara conceded.

Sandy recalled the statue of the Talee hand that Kiet had shown her on VR, on her first visit to Pantala. Two thousand years old, he'd said. Had it been made by organic Talee, before the Catastrophe? Or by synthetics, just after? A commemoration of disaster . . . or a celebration of survival?

"And we've been recording Talee contact since before Pantala," she continued, "ships out in the deep, watching us . . . but you never thought they'd come here and expand so fast. And there's so many of us, compared to you . . . I know you won't give us numbers, but I don't care how advanced you are—synthetic reproduction takes a lot of time and energy, you could have been spending something like ten percent of your total economy just on making new synthetics. While all organics do is fuck, then wait."

They reached the ground, shady trees over green grass, and a path leading between buildings to a road. "I cannot give you numbers, you're right. But humanity has more than thirty billion. I can tell you we're a lot fewer than that."

"Or you were," Sandy pressed. "Until you brought organics back, once you realised it was the only way to catch up with humanity. And they started breeding, and you used all kinds of reproductive tech to boost it quickly . . . and what, they're in the hundreds of millions already?"

"And rebuilding cities," Dara agreed. "Cities that have not been occupied in millennia. With it comes wealth and industry. Only with organics can the Talee race hope to match the scale of humanity."

"Explains why you've been so cautious with humans all these years," said Jane. "Say, you ever come across an old human story called *The Wizard of Oz?*" Dara shook his head. Sandy stared at Jane in astonishment. "There's a guy in that, he pretends to be this great and powerful wizard who can do all these amazing things, but it turns out he's just a little old guy using tricks to make himself look scary. And here are the Talee, scaring our Fleet Captains with their fancy ships and manoeuvers, being all mysterious and creepy. But it turns out it's just a facade, hiding the fact that you're only a shadow of your former selves."

They emerged onto a main street. It was entirely pedestrian, having no need for large vehicles in such a confined settlement. The surrounding buildings made an irregular podium, surrounding them on all sides like some fancy Tanushan pedestrian shopping mall. Greenery overhung, growing on trellises, and windows of establishments, perhaps eateries. Signs, in fascinating script . . . Sandy flash-froze several images from her vision and fed it direct to storage memory, she'd have to get the writing analysed. And she wondered just how many languages they had . . . or had *once* had, doubtless most of them had died in the Catastrophe, with their speakers.

Waiting for them, to one side, was a group of Talee. Just like that, no great fanfare of interspecies contact, but just like being invited into someone's home, led down the hall, and suddenly there was the family, in their living room, waiting to greet their guests. One of them walked forward, in green and brown clothes that looked more functional, perhaps like a uniform, with obvious pockets. Sandy had only seen dead Talee, and that only recently, yet it struck her once more just how unconfronting those alien features were. A larger lower jaw and thrusting forward, almost like a snout . . . that, with the ear flaps at the top-rear of the longer skull, gave a vaguely dog-like impression. But that impression stopped with the eyes, which were bigger than human eyes, and expressive.

This one was armed, a rifle on his (her?) shoulder, and of a similar size to Sandy and Jane. Dara smiled and gestured to him. "Commander Kresnov, this is Taluq. Taluq, Kresnov-aqaruk-alung." And something else in a flowing tongue that seemed without punctuation, like a whole series of vowels and consonants stumbling over each other.

Taluq made a gesture and replied in the same, then extended a hand to Sandy. Four fingers and a thumb, but elongated, like that statue she'd seen. It seemed a very self-conscious gesture, and Sandy guessed it was not a native one. Talee saw themselves as the advanced species, she realised. Perhaps the superior one. She and Jane were lower, and simpler, perhaps to be condescended to with gestures from that simpler culture.

She took the hand and applied a little pressure. Return pressure came back, slowly building, felt even through the armoured glove's feedback. She smiled in recognition—it was synth-alloy myomer, combat strength.

"Combat synthetics," she said. "You're all combat models."

Dara translated to Taluq. Taluq nodded and said something back. "All of us, yes," Dara translated back. "When you live constantly expecting to be stepped on, it makes sense to have a hard shell."

Sandy smiled. Talee didn't seem to smile with the mouth, but the eyes narrowed a little, in a way that appeared to indicate humour. And the strangest thing about having a conversation with an actual alien instead of just their human-synthetic representatives was that it didn't even feel particularly strange.

Taluq said something else. "That's an interesting set of network barriers you have," Dara translated once more. "Very familiar."

Irony, Sandy thought. Or whatever the Talee called it. "Borrowed it off some friends of yours," Sandy replied. "Jumped our technology forwards fifty years at least. More, once we reverse-engineer more of the uplink and augment hardware that went with it. And your friend Cai helped us as well, for defence."

Taluq made an odd gesture of the head. "Cai thought he would discover the truth about himself, helping humans. Everyone is searching for origins. Us. You. Them."

"Only you're not our originators," said Jane. "*They* are. The organics. Your organics."

Taluq made a face. "They're idiots. The species needs them to grow economic strength, we need industry. And instead they panic over their mental condition and insist we synthetics give them a hand in dealing with humanity. They kill each other, you know. We never do. They impose a death penalty for technologies . . ." Dara paused, searching for the right word.

"Aiwallawai," said Sandy. Dara looked surprised. "Cai told us. Technologies causing the mental condition. Forbidden technologies."

Dara nodded and said something to Taluq, who cocked his head and looked . . . intrigued. Sandy thought. "And then think, in an act of great genius," Dara continued, "to continue that penalty over to humans. Only they don't tell us first. Your friend Takewashi was warned by one of their servant-synthetics, not one of ours, like Cai or Dara. Cai and Dara think for themselves, but our organics' servant-synthetics do not, and pray that you do not discover how this technology is done, to make high-thinking synthetics act like robots." Sandy refrained from glancing at Jane. "We kill them where we find them, but the organics make more.

"If Takewashi had only told *us* of this threat, instead of assuming we were a part of its delivery, we could have taken steps to stop it. Poor Takewashi, he spent his life studying Talee work, yet understood Talee so little. And now your own world has been attacked, and your lives threatened—an act of war upon humanity. Utter madness. We apologise, on behalf of our race. We wish you to know that we do not hold you any ill will for fighting them here. Perhaps you will teach them the lesson that we cannot. But if we are to stop this from spreading further, we must work together, synthetic and synthetic. Your species and ours, together for a common cause. This is the reason I have invited you to join us today."

Halfway through Dara's translation, Taluq raised a finger, the other hand raised to the side of his head. An incoming uplink signal, then. Taluq gazed into empty space for a moment with those big, familiar eyes, then looked at Sandy.

"The organics have relaunched their attack," Dara translated when he spoke again. "It was a short-jump, as your Fleet appears to have anticipated. They are inbound now, we have perhaps half an hour until contact at present velocities. We must hurry."

Taluq led them into a nearby doorway, and they took seats at a long wooden bench in what looked like a restaurant. There were woven mats for wall decoration, and indoor plants, and various bottles of things behind the counter, and smells coming from the kitchen that Sandy had never smelt before . . . and she forced down a wave of frustration that she had no time to explore these fascinating distractions. She sat in the middle of a bench, and Jane, to her surprise, sat farther up the end, allowing several Talee to sit between. A quick glance at Jane's eyes beneath the rim of her cap suggested implacable caution. Jane was not about to fall for emotional appeals for cross-species sisterhood, and Jane smelled trouble, or at least the possibility of trouble. Spreading themselves created possible offensive angles and less defensive vulnerability. She wondered if Talee synthetics had the tactical aptitude to notice, unlike their organic counterparts.

Dara sat on Sandy's right, and Taluq sat opposite, as other Talee filled the benches or stood about to see. This was not first contact for *them*, Sandy knew. They'd been doing recon on humans for a very long time and were familiar with most human things. Doubtless they'd made an academic study of human culture, language, and history for several decades at least, with spies like Cai and Dara to feed them information. And dammit, she wanted to ask them what they thought, what they found interesting, wanted to invite them to Tanusha for a stroll up Ramprakash Road for dinner and a musical, and go to a football game at Subianto Stadium, and see the crowds and flash and glamour and say, "See, we humans are pretty good fun, let's be friends." And then she looked again at Jane up the end of the bench, eyes cool and wary, and reprimanded herself to common sense and caution. Here, she was representing not just the FSA, or Callay, or synthetic humanity; she was representing her entire species. There were no friends or enemies in interplanetary relations, only strategic interests and their satisfaction or compromise.

Sandy began, pointing a finger to the ceiling. "Your organic half. Why are they here?"

Taluq looked around at his comrades as Dara translated. The look of a very intelligent person gathering his thoughts. Deciding how to play it. It immediately put Sandy into cautious mode. These Talee had been hiding under humanity's nose for roughly a century. The organic Talee had acquired their technological arrogance from somewhere, their assumption they could just march into Callay and rough the humans up, and get what they wanted. Did they learn it here, from Taluq and friends?

"Please understand, Commander," Dara translated when Taluq spoke, "organic Talee psychology has shown difficulty adapting to the demands of advanced neurological technology. They killed themselves twice and would be extinct today if not for us. They remain unstable today, as you've seen, and must be controlled. We suspect this is something common to organics everywhere. Observe the League and the death of the moon you call Cresta."

"League used advanced Talee tech in their uplinks without understanding the intergenerational consequences in human brains," Sandy said cautiously. "Federation has avoided the problem, our tech is largely indigenous."

"So was ours, once," said Taluq. He seemed very confident, in the low-key, calm manner of someone utterly in command of the subject. Sandy wondered what he was, exactly. Leader of this outpost? Tech-expert? Human expert? Soldier? All of the above? "It didn't stop the madness of the organics."

"Talee psychology is not human psychology. You've got two brains. The combination of two independently processing neural cores causes complications. We don't have it."

"You deny that synthetic humanity has psychological advantages? Social advantages? Organic humanity has a history of going mad in groups. If Talee experience can teach you anything, it is that neural-synth technology will exacerbate this tendency rather than correct it. And that synthetics are comparatively immune to it, for reasons that have more to do with design and the disconnect of that devastating emotional-feedback loop that passes for conscious reasoning in organics. In that, our best experts agree, Talee and human are alike, both the organics in their unreasonableness, and the logic of the synthetics. That is why I wanted to talk to you, in particular. And Jane, you too, to be based on Cassandra's designation."

Sandy wasn't sure she liked where this was going. Dark possibilities emerged. Dangerous ones. But she was running out of time, as were Fleet, if Reichardt was right about his chances against a Talee strike run. She thought about it for a moment.

"I agree with you," she said finally. "It's been an issue for us in Tanusha for some time. The FSA and CSA acquire synthetic talent, and non-synthetic agencies fall behind. It scares them, that imbalance. I fear for the stability of our institutions if it continues."

She risked a glance at Jane, doubting that Talee could read human expressions of body language that well. A deadpan glance, to make sure Jane understood. She got the same expression back. Jane was ready for anything.

"You will leave them behind," said Taluq. "You know this."

Sandy nodded. "They can't match us, especially with the new tech we just acquired from your organic friends. But I'm less convinced they'll all destroy themselves. We've had so many opportunities to do so, since the creation of atomic weapons six hundred years ago, and FTL a few centuries later. But we're still here, and until we ran into *you*," with a pointed look, "we were doing fine. Don't mistake your problems for ours, my friend. We call you aliens for a reason."

Taluq's face made that humour-expression once more. "Six thousand years of Talee experience suggests otherwise. Your time frame is too small. Humanity's only had what you call high-designation GIs for perhaps forty years. In that short time frame you have transformed the League and are beginning to transform the Federation, in spite of the Federation's stated policy to stop you from even existing. First you dominate their security institutions, forcing other institutions to employ more of you in order to keep up, or to declare war on you to protect themselves, only to be inevitably destroyed by your response.

"But the synthetic advantage is not just strength and force, it is intellect. You and Jane are such dangerous fighters because of your intelligence and its efficient application. Synthetics think better, faster, and harder under pressure, in a high-technology, networked environment most of all. You've seen it. And I'm sure you've seen organics who do the same, but they are few, and their advantage does not grow as your advantage does. In another forty years, synthetic humanity will be even further ahead, and organics will resent it."

"Taluq," said Sandy, holding up a hand. "I feel you're building up to something. I'll ask you again, what are your organics doing here? It seems they're searching for this place," she looked up and around, "or for another like it, if there is one. They've risked civil war among Talee to find whatever they think is here." Her eyes narrowed at him. "Unless you thought to *let* them fight us? That we'd do your dirty work for you? Being so much better at warfare, as you suggest?"

"Commander Kresnov," said Taluq, through Dara. With considered, precise speech. "Do not be too impressed with humanity's martial capabilities. Besting Talee is one thing. Talee and humanity are not all in the galaxy."

Sandy stared at him. For a moment, it was difficult to think. Speculated at, for certain, but there was no way to know further. Humanity had encountered just one nonhuman intelligent species, in several centuries of FTL spacefaring. Talee had been around a lot longer.

"There are others?" she breathed.

Taluq nodded. "Your side of Talee space is our quietest flank. Lately our most alarming, but still our quietest."

Dear fucking god. But the tactical side of her brain refused to shut down with shock. Why did he tell her now? He sought to frame the answer to her persistent question, perhaps guessing that she might not like the answer. Perhaps to scare her into accepting his help.

"You need to think as Talee do," said Dara, as Taluq leaned forward on the table to make his point more directly. "In deep time. If humanity is to survive the perils of its next few thousand years, its synthetics will be its salvation. And you'll need the help of Talee synthetics to do it. You need to be the managers of your organics' destinies. As we now seek to be."

For a brief moment, Sandy battled the sensation of combat mode descending. Her vision reddened, focusing, targeting. "What have you done to them?" she asked quietly. "Before you brought them back?"

"A genetic modification," said Taluq. "A safeguard, for our safety and theirs. It modifies certain mental processes to reduce the effects of the debilitation. It means they are no longer as intelligent as they were, under the influence of drugs and uplinks or not. Sad, but it is an inevitable consequence of Talee psychology that intellect in or out of the state will be impaired."

"They found out, didn't they?" Sandy murmured. Gazing at him, unblinking. "They found out you modified their genome?" She glanced around at the table of watchful alien faces. "That's what you're keeping here? Their original genome, safely out of their reach. Nearly three thousand years and all clean genetic remnants have been corrupted on Talee worlds. They can't know exactly what you've changed unless they can get the original back. And you're keeping it from them."

Taluq nodded slowly, watching her. Impressed, it seemed, that she understood so easily.

"Your genetic technology is advanced enough they could just do their own modifications," Jane interrupted. Her tone was very flat. These days, she was more expressive, emotions engaging more readily. Now, Sandy heard nothing. That meant combat reflex. "Why don't they?"

Taluq made a face. "The psychology is delicate. Modifications need the starting template as a reference point to be sure what they're doing. Already they've attempted what you say and largely made it worse. Even the most advanced technology, you'll discover, finds the greatest difficulty modelling organic neurology with genetic modification. Brains grow chaotically, and organic genetics only controls the variant of chaos; full control that way is near impossible."

"You keep them in the dark about their own genetics," Sandy said quietly, "and again with regard to relations with foreign species, and now they're taking their frustrations out on *us*."

"It is necessary to keep controls on them," Taluq insisted. "They will understand, in time."

"Do you feel very 'in control' right now?" Sandy asked. "You don't look it."

"Commander, I'm offering you an alliance. Talee synthetic and human synthetic, together in partnership. Your own organics killed thousands of your people here, just one year ago. They raise a hundred thousand more for slaughter in a war caused by their own dysfunction. Organic humanity makes a mess, and synthetics suffer trying to clean it up. About time you took control of your own destinies, don't you think? We can help you do that. Not immediately, not alarmingly. But very slowly, at a pace that suits you and not them."

Sandy smiled. "You're going to help us become the master race?"

Taluq nodded as Dara translated it for him. "But you already are. For humanity's own sake, it is necessary. You know this."

It didn't translate, Sandy realised. Master race. Taluq thought it fine. Dear God, she thought. We've been fighting the wrong side. And the incoming Talee organics, racing in from the outer rim, were searching for something that was surely the right of every sentient species, however clumsily pursued.

They were about to hit the Federation Fleet in orbit, her friends amongst them, in search of this thing their synthetic "masters" thought to hide from them, deep underground, on a planet even more remote to Talee than it was to humans.

And perhaps, in some technical sense, Taluq was right. Perhaps his way was smarter, or more efficient, under the circumstances. But it wasn't the human way, or not lately, because humanity had been doing quite well until the League's formation had been mismanaged, itself just the result of an inauspicious discovery here on Pantala, all those years ago. Up until then, humanity had been shedding old divisions and conflicts so that open warfare became exceedingly rare. Absolute divisions made absolute conflict; that was the lesson of human history. If the synthetic-organic divide became an absolute division between humans as it had among Talee, it would become a blood-soaked nightmare that would haunt the species for centuries and possibly end it. Whatever she felt for synthetic emancipation, Sandy knew she could not allow it, at any cost. And she was perhaps a little closer to understanding why the Talee had twice become extinct.

"Dara," she said calmly, turning her gaze on the translator. "You are familiar with the human concept of 'rights'?" A cautious look from Dara. "A moral right. The hypothetical, theoretical concept."

Dara nodded. "I am, yes."

"Does it translate?"

No reply from Dara. And no attempt to translate her question to Taluq. Sandy felt combat reflex descend entirely, a great red wash of slowing time.

"You're talking about violent transition," Sandy said quietly, turning her attention back on Taluq. "I'm trying to avoid it. You're encouraging it."

"The wave rolls in without you," Dara translated Taluq's reply. "The only question is whether you will be on top of it or under it."

Sandy took a deep breath. She could not look at Jane now, lest she give the game away. Jane was no moral paragon. If she did not back her here, there would be no chance. She could only hope that Jane had followed the exchange this far and knew what must come next . . . in the one field of technological superiority they had left.

"In every tale of alien contact told by humans," said Sandy, "there is emphasis upon the need to comprehend alien psychology. The dangers of miscalculation are great. Usually in those tales, it is we humans who are somehow at fault. On this occasion, you are. You misread us, Taluq. This proposal is unacceptable. Partnership, I welcome, but not to wage war on the majority of my species. Give me a different offer, and I'll think again."

"There is no other offer, Commander," came Taluq's reply. "There are only the facts of species evolution and the inevitable superiority of the synthetics. Your choice is whether to accept these facts or to discard them."

"But *you* brought your organics back. You chose to. Why did you need to, if synthetic superiority is absolute? You have every superior advantage except reproduction. But without reproductive superiority, you have nothing, because we'll always be outnumbered."

Taluq made an expression that might have been a smirk. "Reproductive efficiency is for viruses," he said. "Viruses are organic too." Right, thought Sandy. That was your last chance. "Commander, you appear to be having difficulty with these concepts. I advise that you take a moment to think on it."

"No," Sandy said coolly. "Your current actions have put my species in danger. I won't allow it."

Taluq made an expression that might have been a frown. Still Sandy did not sense any great alarm amongst the Talee. "I'm quite sure there is nothing you can do about that, Commander. Our network tech advantage here is quite significant. Your own killswitches, which your wonderful organics built into your brains from inception, are not invulnerable here."

Sandy smiled. "I'll chance it." Quite calmly, she flipped a grenade off her webbing and tossed it under the table toward the far wall, and the room blew up. The explosion blew her backward, already pulling weapons as she rolled on the floor and opened fire on those nearest as they scrambled to recover, then switched to those closer to the blast who'd been scythed sideways and much harder hit. She moved quickly sideways about the room past bodies and shattered furniture as Jane did the same, opening angles past wrecked furniture at point-blank range, not allowing those who recovered fast enough an easy shot. She took three rounds in the armour, and then it was silent, save the ringing in her ears and the slither and groan of those still living.

"Fuck," Jane said succinctly, surveying the carnage of blood and debris through the clouds of dust and smoke. She had a cut on her forehead and several bullet strikes in her armour, but nothing worse. "Arrogant little buggers, aren't they?"

"Weren't going to let us leave either," said Sandy. "Not once we'd seen all this."

"Yeah, I got that."

And Jane went to the doorway, as Sandy checked the bodies, then a burst of fire from the door, incoming and outgoing as Jane engaged. "Three!" she called, coming back in a crouch as bullets splintered the doorframe behind her. "I got one, but more are coming. You want to risk tacnet?"

"I think we'd be pushing our luck, in this place," Sandy suggested, pocketing a couple of interesting-looking network devices. "The whole cave is environmentally controlled, there has to be a central control room. . . ."

"Does there?" Jane shot back. "They're a networked society. . . ."

"And can steal unsecured data too easily. There has to be someplace behind physical barriers where they keep the sensitive stuff."

"There was a bigger tower near the center of town, had laser-com arrays of some kind, that's usually command and control." Jane pointed in the rough direction they had to take—unable to uplink, they'd have to go old-school with verbal and hand signals. "You believe that stuff about killswitches?"

"Yeah, sure. Hey, have you got one? I never asked."

"Big enough to blow my head off. I give us one chance in ten."

Sandy made a face. "Generous," she judged. "Let's go."

"Wait," said Jane, and Sandy paused, hearing shouting from outside. Still no shots coming through the walls—despite their uplink tech, the Talee still seemed unaware that the only people functional in here were human. Like the organic Talee they disdained, the synths seemed not to have fully conceived the uses to which the highest-designation synthetic soldiers might be put in combat. "We're after the organic Talee genome?" Sandy nodded. "What if that's a mistake? They're worse than this lot."

"They're desperate and ignorant," Sandy corrected. "Maybe they'll get better. But it's irrelevant—if we can get it we'll save Reichardt from getting smashed in orbit, if we can tell them we've got it."

"Tell them how? We don't have communications, we don't even know where we are."

"Then we need to take this place over. All of it."

With just two of them. Jane shrugged. "Cool," she said.

They ran upstairs, along a stone-panelled corridor, then past windows overlooking streets, and immediately drew fire. Sandy hit a doorway, kicked a hole in a wall with a thud that brought ceiling panels down, and found herself with more floor-to-ceiling windows overlooking the next street, another building ahead, an unpredictable structure like this one, full of cubist blocks and add-ons—the streets were gridwork, but Talee architects seemed to dislike straight lines. The next room jutted out like a diving platform over the street, so she ran through it and got a run-up, smashed through the window, flew eight meters through the opposite building window, and rolled on floor matting.

Shots behind showed that Jane was covering, and she paused on an angle to minimise her own exposure, covering near streets as Jane jumped . . . a Talee ran up the adjoining road, trying to make the intersection, and Sandy shot him in the neck. Being synthetic, he might survive it or might not—either way, she hated it but had no illusions of what she had come here to do. These Talee synths were fighting for synthetic superiority over organics, while she was opposed to it, and that was that. That this eventuality hadn't occurred to their hosts, either the fighting or that it might go badly for them indicated something increasingly scary about Talee, synthetic or organic. An inflexibility, perhaps a lack of imagination. It fit with a species prone to self-destruction. And, in the surreal slow-motion of combat reflex, she wondered if Cai had been trying to warn her of exactly this from the beginning. He'd been one of the synths, like Dara, but had been unable to discuss this organic-synth division even obliquely. No doubt the likes of Taluq had treated him well, like a brother, as they'd tried to treat her like a sister . . . while condemning many of her best friends, and indeed her children, to sub-humanity and servitude. Had Cai warned them of her proclivities? Would he have warned her, if he hadn't been killed at Sadar Institute, of what Taluq and company's grand plan actually was? So many troubles on both sides caused by ignorance. Perhaps the smartest thing the synth Talee had ever done was to avoid humanity as much as possible. Or perhaps if they hadn't, if they'd thrown themselves into full engagement, with trade, cultural exchange, perhaps even at the level of ordinary citizens beneath the government, better understanding would have been reached, and she wouldn't currently be shooting people she'd much rather have shared a drink with.

Jane crashed through what was left of the window and took the lead, rushing through corridors, while Sandy brought up the rear. They continued like that, moving fast through buildings, changing floors to mix it up for their pursuers, and sometimes changing direction. Talee followed up adjoining streets, not game to rush the buildings, and knowing they'd probably be too late anyway, at the speed the humans were moving. If the Talee had heavy weapons, they didn't appear to want to use them on their own buildings, and within what was essentially a giant underground cavern, there was no airborne surveillance or armament to be seen.

Sandy and Jane's greatest vulnerability was in jumping across roads, but the Talee were having difficulty getting people into good fire positions to hit them in their leaps. At first they put people exposed on the street, but those were quickly shot, so the next took cover farther away but weren't quite high-enough designation to hit a leaping target at sixty-plus meters that was only exposed for a second at most. There were unarmed Talee on the streets now, some running, others ordering or directing—Sandy and Jane only fired on those who were armed and apparently hostile. But the buildings they moved through were clearly residential, with furniture, display screens, and wall art, and a few times they encountered Talee in the buildings, unarmed and frightened, whom they simply ignored.

A hail of bullets announced their approach to the target tower, Sandy immediately skidding for cover behind a support wall as fire kicked over furniture and splintered doorways. Jane covered nearby, then rolled into an adjoining room to peer briefly through a window on a new angle.

"It's a block away!" Jane announced. "They've stacked up the defences." And rolled again as fire came close, punching through walls.

And they'd opened fire too far out, Sandy thought . . . though another two meters and she'd have spotted them anyway. Maybe they were right to try their luck. Suddenly her vision flashed, and she half-flipped into cyberspace, internal visual showing a massive barrier assault . . . but Cai's defences were responsive and kicked in with some fast adaptations that absorbed what was thrown at them and put up new barriers to replace the ones torn down.

"Jane!" she called as her vision cleared. "Jane, you feel that?"

"Yeah, I'm okay. I figure it'll get worse as we get closer. We gonna flank them?"

"You jump over to the next building, we crossfire the defences, draw fire for each other, I think they'll only take the shorter-range shot."

"Gotcha." And Jane rolled, then crawled, then ran as she reached the hall and back the way she'd come, then down some stairs, searching for better cover to get to the next building. Sandy went left, incoming fire seemed random, she didn't think they'd seen her and were just shooting at shadows. A thump told her someone had come down on the roof—counter-manoeuver, she hadn't seen much of that yet. Intense fire from ahead told her someone had spotted Jane's leap and opened up, but her hearing gave her the position down to a meter, and she rolled to a good window angle. Popped up and nailed a head shot, then rolled and scampered away as return fire shredded walls and windows around her. Behind a support wall, she pulled her pistol and aimed it around the corner . . . the targeting sight engaged another fire source in half a second, and she rapidly compressed the trigger, putting five rounds on target, saw another head snap back.

These Talee were fast and deadly, but she could see the lines of possible fire well before they did, and their numerical superiority only gave her more targets. They presumed to use their superior firepower and so weren't taking sufficient cover, looking instead to get the first shot off without realising that exposure only got them killed before they could do so. No one was as fast as her or Jane, not even Talee synthetics, who were theoretically the same designation . . . but not only was she the same technology, she was shaped and advanced by a thirty-year war that the Talee had not gone through. The Talee had all the tech but struggled to put it all together, like a football team filled with star players but no coach and no game plan. They guessed what came next. She *knew*.

Charges blew the ceiling down the hall behind her, and she dropped the first Talee who fell through the hole, then raced low across to the building's far side and dropped another one coming down a corridor as she flashed across it. That brought her to stairs, and she leaped down a floor, then braced against a supporting wall to look diagonally across the street at the defences now facing Jane. Jane's fire opened up on the defences facing her, each of them covered against the targets closest to them, and the Talee lost another four soldiers in a few seconds.

Sandy put three grenades in quick succession into the opposing wall and took a running leap across the road and into the blinding dust and smoke. Crashed into a half-demolished wall and bounced up, moving fast and crouched down the hall and shooting another Talee in a passing doorway who simply wasn't fast enough. She could hear them shouting now, could hear the fear—even a people as heavily uplinked as synthetic Talee resorted to vocals in panic. This was instructive for everyone—Talee synth-tech had been taken by humans, and instead of getting worse, in this one lethal respect it had gotten much, much better. They hadn't realised soldiers could be this dangerous, that warfare against them could be this lopsided, and now came the oldest horror story, the fear of dangerous aliens that no local technology could stop . . . only here the aliens were humans, the most deadly species in all known space.

The defensive block of buildings before the control tower breached. Sandy skipped and ducked down hallways, crashed out another window to bounce across a low roof, then jumped for a higher window as shots hit the wall beside her. The far window now showed the tower, just a low thing, barely twenty floors but with glassy sides and a mid-level garden alcove directly opposite. Sandy took a risk and leaped, and was immediately hit by tracking fire from below, multiple rounds through the right-side armour as she covered her head with one arm and tracked with the other, finding two of them on the street corner and felling both before she fell twisting into the grass and seating on the tower's garden.

She rolled and scrambled back to the edge, scanning as fast as she could for other targets, knowing that exposed like this she couldn't see everything . . . but there was nothing, and Jane came crashing through a nearby window and chose instead to hit a window meters to Sandy's left and disappear within. Sandy pulled back and ran, kicked through a glass door, and slid into a corridor junction, but it was empty. Up the corridor and there in an open-plan office to one side, amidst an odd arrangement of ergonomic chairs and midair displays, Jane was picking herself up awkwardly.

"Jane!" Jane came staggering toward her, armour breached in several places, particularly on her right side. Sandy caught her, but Jane gestured her to move.

"Upstairs," she said breathlessly. "Looks like the control point, laser coms to all points."

Sandy took the stairs, not game to try the elevators when the Talee could commandeer building systems. She leaped up one flight at a time, kicking off walls on the way up with force enough to fracture concrete and bend the steel railings. Smart to booby trap the upper floors, she thought, and paused with two levels to go to take her nearly empty mag off her rifle and throw it a flight ahead. The explosion rocked the stairs, showering all below with debris and blinding smoke. It made perfect cover as she continued, shot the first Talee through the stairwell doors above, flipped another grenade around that corner and went low into the chaos of its explosion.

Moving fast through that chaos she came to new reinforced doors, entrance to a secure room, now with two more bodies at the base. She ramped up her armour's power to max and put a fist into the middle gap. Then she pulled, received fire from the far side, stuck her rifle's grenade launcher into the gap, and fired with the charge set to airburst. Rammed the door the rest of the way open and went in low.

Stairs and a spiral climb. At the top, a 360-degree view of the cavern city, ringed with a bank of displays and chairs. Amidst them, three Talee, all unarmed, all terrified and hiding as best they could. It was impossibly exposed, but being the highest point in the city, no sniper had a view down onto their floor. The cavern walls and ceiling were higher, of course, but those looked mostly smooth . . . save for the lighting setup on the ceiling, which was quite close from here. But sniper line of sight went both ways, and anyone getting up there would find the accuracy at this end was superior. Internal chronometer told her barely five minutes had passed since she and Jane had begun moving this way. Three hundred meters, perhaps eight urban blocks, never reaching street level, through heavy defences, and all without tacnet. She and Jane together were impossibly lethal. No wonder Taluq had not even considered the possibility that she'd turn him down. What could she possibly have in common with organic humanity anyway?

Jane crashed up the stairs behind and hit the base of a display terminal back first, reaching for first aid in her webbing. Blood was seeping through, which was never a good sign with GIs, given how much less they bled.

"Bad?" Sandy asked her, staring across the displays and controls.

"Yep," said Jane, shooting spray foam into the twin holes in her right-side armour to stop the bleeding. "Went straight through." Meaning whatever hit her was very high calibre, to breach both armour and synthetic muscles. Which meant internal injuries. "Can you break into this system?"

Sandy knew it was hopeless even as she looked at it. The three Talee cowering behind terminals weren't going to be any help, not sharing any language. The controls would be similarly alien in language and design.

"I'll have to wireless it," she said. "If I can activate their coms, I can send a signal to Fleet, they can come and find us, get the organic Talee what they're looking for."

"You make uplink contact here, they'll hack you faster than you can blink," Jane retorted.

"Gotta risk it. I've got Cai's protections, I'm the most network-advanced of the two of us. . . ."

"Cai's protections are a patch. They're not going to stand up to Talee systems in their backyard."

"Got a better idea?"

"Yes, I'll do it," said Jane.

"You're not as good at it as me. . . ."

"No, but if they blow my killswitch you'll learn something, possibly you'll even learn enough to avoid them the next time."

"No." A shot went through the tower glass, heavy calibre, spraying them with fragments. "You're not using yourself as bait just because you found religion and want to atone for your sins."

"You give me too much credit," said Jane, popping a painkiller against her wrist and blinking hard against the pupil dilation. "I suggest it because it's the only way to do it."

"Your life's worth as much as mine, Jane!" Sandy almost surprised herself by how much she meant it. She hadn't realised she did mean it until she said it.

Jane smiled crookedly, checking her weapon and her remaining torso rotation with the injury. "Sure," she said. "But Danya, Svetlana, and Kiril make four. Do your maths."

Sandy stared at her with dawning panic. Another round hit a terminal and sent pieces spinning across the control room. Pretty soon someone would decide it was better to destroy this place than risk the humans accessing its coms. "Jane, you can't . . ."

"Just shut up and do it!" Jane snarled with sudden temper. Their eyes met. "Okay, sis?"

Sandy smiled weakly. "Sure, sis." Jane nodded once and closed her eyes. Sandy took a deep breath and felt the rush of external code establish a space around her . . .

. . . and with a snap of sudden pain, the control room disappeared.

She stood in a city. It was an alien city, with nice architecture. Lots of glass and steel and greenery, with cubist spaces and differentiated levels. Like a much larger version of the Pantalan underground city.

The streets were full of Talee. They walked on the sidewalks and sat eating food in a garden square, as road traffic hummed around them and air traffic whined by on overhead skylanes. It was not so different from Tanusha, save that the sun held an orangish tint and washed the tower glass with more red light than her eyes were accustomed to filtering. There were displays that might have been advertising, and lots of strange, scrawling script that changed into shapes and pictures. As though the Talee used a writing script that was conceptually 3D. Intriguing possibility that was. Could it be connected to a dual-brain psychology?

Talee crossed the street about her, and she realised she was standing on a traffic island in the middle of a road. Obviously this was VR. She wondered if Jane were here, or somewhere else, and what the hell was going on. It didn't feel like defensive VR. Defensive VR trapped users in smaller spaces, closed loops that limited external access. Or that limited the ability to kill oneself in VR, which usually broke the trap.

She turned, and on the pavement across the road saw Cai. He wore human clothes, jeans and a jacket, as she'd seen him wear in Tanusha. And he was looking at her.

At a break in the traffic she jogged across the road and stopped before him. "Hi," she said.

"Hello, Cassandra," said Cai quite calmly. "What do you think of the city?"

"Um . . . it's nice. Where are we? The Talee homeworld?"

Cai nodded. "Yes. One of many cities, much like Earth. Billions of people. A little over three thousand years ago, before the second Catastrophe."

Sandy nodded slowly, looking around. "Well, the problem, Cai, is that one of us is dead. Or possibly both. I'm not entirely sure right now."

Cai smiled. "That would be me," he admitted. "I gave you a lot of systems to boost your defences when you finally ran into my people. This is one of those systems."

"Ah," said Sandy. Now it made sense, the rapid engagement of the program, before she could even be sure an uplink had been made. "We're in deep immersion?"

"Yes, time is passing quite slowly. About a ten-to-one ratio, I think, depending on variables. And this version of me is a simulation, of course. But quite a good one, if I do say so myself." He gestured to the streets around them. "This is the best reconstruction my people have of this city, based on what they found when they first landed, having survived by hiding on Pantala."

"How are you running VR?" Sandy asked, as they strolled slowly along the sidewalk. "It takes a massive system to run this."

"Oh, this VR is always loaded on Talee systems somewhere. I happen to know it's loaded on the systems of our Pantalan base. This is a capture program. I've inserted you into our mainframes through this VR."

Sandy blinked at him. "Why? I mean, if we're here, you'd have to know that negotiations between your people and mine haven't gone well."

Cai nodded. "I told them as much. They didn't listen. You see, Cassandra, they really don't respect human opinion as much as they pretend. And psychologically I am certainly human." They edged past some running Talee children, cute and shouting, with big eyes and crazy enthusiasm just like human children. Sandy stared in amazement. "I hoped it wouldn't come to this. And certainly I have sympathy for my people's position against the organics. But I told them that you would not, and they did not believe me. Or they thought that you could be persuaded. Or forced."

"They have no idea what organised violence really looks like, do they?" Sandy said sombrely. "Maybe Talee did once, but today's synthetic Talee are a monoculture. They've no history of warfare, probably they disdain the topic. They understand the technology, but they've no institutional memory of warfare like humans have. They never knew how far out of their depth they were, with us."

Cai nodded. "I tried to warn them of that, too. They thought humans too little advanced to pose a threat. It's snobbery, really. And from what we know of Talee history, Talee have never really fought as much as humans. Which seems a little odd, given it is Talee and not humans that destroyed themselves. Many Talee are in denial about their nature, I fear, even to this day."

"It makes perfect sense to me," said Sandy. "You need training to handle violence. Not all who have that training will use it wisely, but more than those without training. Violence is most destructive when utilised by those who know nothing about it, because they won't know when to stop. Mind you, that might just be me justifying my own existence."

"Humans are frighteningly alien to Talee, Cassandra." They paused at an intersection, where a large park emerged from between the towers. The orange sun shone with a reddish tinge of native leaves, a whole variety of flowers and shapes. "But technology and synthetic snobbery blinded my people to just how alien and frightening. Your internal diversity is staggering. You live in constant internal conflict, violent or nonviolent, and you internalise these conflicts within your institutions. "I tried to warn them. Aiwallawai technologies in human hands frighten Talee, but they failed to appreciate that proposing to elevate synthetic humanity above organic humanity would terrify you just as much. Talee society can tolerate internal divisions and hier-archies without conflict. They may yet manage to convince organic Talee to accept synthetic dominance in some things, once the current disturbance has died down. Everything is rationalised somehow. Humans don't tolerate such things—they fight, and they equalise. Violence rarely seems worth it, to a Talee. Humans think it's always worth it, where freedom or equality are in question."

"You make it sound like a good thing," said Sandy.

Cai made a face. "From my first conscious moment, I hoped to find the answers to who I am. Thanks in part to you, I did find some answers. Humanity's constant conflict creates balance. Talee herd too much in fear of conflict. Add a psychological hitch, aiwallawai, and this imbalance becomes a bubble, which eventually bursts." He gazed up, as a light appeared on the far horizon beyond the towers. "With catastrophic results."

The light grew abruptly brighter, then pierced the sky from upper levels to lower in barely a second. The flash became a wave, orange and red, and white in the inside, expanding at incredible speed. About them, Talee turned to stare and then to scream. Parents gathered up children, while others ran, or embraced, or fell to their knees as though in prayer. Sandy felt her eyes fill with tears. Then the shockwave hit them, and all the world disappeared.

And slowly resolved itself once more. She was standing in a forest, thick with trees and running vines. Strange animals whooped and sang, and birds flittered amongst the branches. But here amidst the trees to her right she could still make out the edge of a building foundation, a raised ridge where a tower had once stood. The same tower, in fact, that she had just been standing beside. Farther to her left, she could see a similar ridge, where the opposing line of buildings had stood. Amidst the leaves and dirt at her feet, the rubber sole of a shoe, impossibly old and torn from several thousand years of wear.

"This is how it looks today," said Cai, standing nearby. "The organics are repopulating some old cities, but not this one. This was a capital, and these ruins are preserved, for study and for heritage. In order to learn from the past, we first must preserve it and observe its consequences."

"You're showing me this as . . . what?" asked Sandy. "A warning?"

"Always a warning," Cai agreed. "How do we handle modernity? Humanity struggled through its various technologies. Industrialisation and modern weapons caused enormous calamities in your twentieth century. Then in later centuries, similar calamities from nano-tech, then bio, and now synthetic replication. Even your political upheavals are technologically driven; new wealth and industries create imbalances, which create political divisions, which can create wars. Beware your new home, Callay, and the power it accrues. Be sure to share it around, or similar divisions will follow."

Sandy nodded. "I know. I've warned of it many times, with GIs in the Federal institutions most of all."

"And one key technology, misused first by Talee, can cause group insanity. Our consciousness is what makes us modern, but our modernity inevitably reworks that very consciousness. Where does that cycle end? Someone must control it, we must rule our technologies, and not let them rule us."

"Cai," said Sandy quite firmly. "You lost. The Talee lost. They had their chance, but they're victims of their own mistakes. I see them now attempting to make similar mistakes with humans. If someone is going to get on top of this problem, it's not going to be the Talee. It'll be us. But we have to be allowed the space to do it on our terms and in our way. We'll bring the Talee along with us if we can, but if not, I won't allow Talee smugness to stand in our way. I have the greatest sympathy for the Talee. I'd like us to be friends. But to be completely honest, I don't see that Talee have anything to be smug *about*." She looked around at the forest.

Cai smiled. "I know. They made a number of synthetic human go-betweens, like me. I've implanted their names and faces in your augmented memory; the files will unlock shortly."

Sandy was surprised. "Really?"

"Interacting with humans, I've come to understand myself. My creators may not see it, but I too think that your way may be best. Had I lived, I may have committed all the way to your cause. But I know that others like me feel the same. Approach them carefully and do not misuse what I give you."

Sandy nodded. "I won't. GIs like that could be our greatest allies."

"And could elevate the fear of Federal Intelligence and their like to yet-unseen highs."

"That's inevitable now, Cai. I'm sorry you won't be there to see it. You'll be remembered."

Another smile. "I appreciate the sentiment . . . only I really don't appreciate the sentiment, because this is only a simulation. But the real Cai would, I'm sure. This program will activate base coms, the Pantalan base is linked into human global networks. A signal will be sent."

"Thank you, Cai, Taluq said others. Other intelligent life." She had no confidence that a simulation program could give her an answer, but she had to ask. "We've only found Talee. Are there others?"

"Five," said Cai. Sandy stared. Unable to think of anything to say. "The locations you should look and the regions of space you should not progress beyond, I've also locked into your memory augments. In the next phase of human expansion, once you move beyond this current calamity, you will encounter them. Three are benign but interesting, one is rather too friendly for their own good, and the last is rather frightening. But you will do your own assessment, in turn. After all, many Talee find humans rather frightening. Now more than ever."

"They should," Sandy agreed. "But only if they screw us around."

Cai inclined his head. "Point well taken. The program has accessed base coms, I'll send that signal now. Good-bye, Cassandra."

"Good-bye, Cai. And thank you."

When League marines burst into the underground city, they found it largely deserted, the Talee population fleeing into deeper catacombs rather than fight the human force that descended upon them. At the base of the central tower, its glass top shattered and burning, they found FSA spec ops Commander Cassandra Kresnov, with a badly wounded but still living high-designation GI whom she called only Jane. In the middle floors of the tower they later found evidence of heavy close-range combat, numerous dead synthetic Talee, and traces of gas where desperate Talee had finally resorted to trying to flush her out by other means.

"Inbound Talee say they got a message from this base too," one of them told her, crouched alongside while other marines began clearing the building. "Say someone told them in their native tongue that Commander Kresnov of the FSA had recovered what they were searching for and was going to give it to them."

Kresnov looked up from the sleeping face of the female GI alongside, as medics attended. "They're looking for their original genome," she said. "We'd better give it to them—we can beat them on the ground, but it'll be a long time until we can match them in space. And I don't fancy being stuck on this dirtball one hour longer than I have to."

CHAPTER
TWENTY-THREE

A year later, the last thing Sandy had expected was that the wedding of a GI, in Tanusha, would be called the "wedding of the year." Maybe if *she* were getting married to someone famous . . . but she'd never in all her life found famous people especially interesting, so there didn't seem much chance of that. But when the glamorous spokesperson for the Federal Security Agency had met big Tanushan movie star Vijay Kulkarni at a charity dinner, wedding arrangements had followed with alarming speed.

Sandy suspected the kids had something to do with it.

She picked her way through the sparkling crowds in the vast gardens to the part that had been left grassy and found a whole bunch of kids running and yelling, playing some game she didn't know the rules of. Svetlana was amongst them, in her baggy orange salwar kameez she'd grown to love since she'd stopped sulking from Sandy telling her she was too young for a sari. And too skinny, damn thing would fall off her with nothing to cling to. And she was being bossy again, shouting at other kids, telling them they were breaking the rules, they couldn't do it like that . . . but that was fine, she was older than most here, and she was organising the littlies, like an umpire running a football game. That was gratifying to see—Svetlana actually giving a damn about other kids whose names weren't Danya or Kiril.

Amongst them ran little Darge, five years old and quite delighted at it all. He looked so healthy now, most unlike the little bundle of rags they'd received off the freighter from Pantala nearly a year ago amongst the thousands of other orphan kids they'd brought back under the standing agreements. That had started an adoption drive like the ones in the immediate aftermath of the war's conclusion, when League had been more sanguine about unloading a few hundred thousand hungry young mouths into Federation arms. This one was much smaller, just five and a half thousand kids, and it had been Rhian cunningly insisting Amirah should come to the hospital where the ones needing treatment were being kept. There she'd struck up a conversation with then-four-year-old Darge and his six-year-old sister Miniya, and they'd talked of little Darge's liver condition and how many more weeks of treatment until it was fixed, and Miniya had cried because everything here was so foreign and she didn't know where she and Darge would end up after he was better . . .

. . . and the next morning Rhian had arrived at sim-training with an evil smile and said that Amirah was filing adoption papers for both of them. A number of GIs had since followed, citing Sandy's and Rhian's example, and promising they'd blame them for every smelly diaper or dinner-time tantrum. Sandy had told them that she, and Rhian in particular, would only laugh.

To one side of the children's games sat Miniya, talking with Kiril. Miniya didn't play very much, suffering from Danya's condition of having borne horrible responsibility far too early in life and struggling with the concept of just having fun. Worse, there had been a third sibling, Leia, who had died of a lung infection two years ago, despite Miniya's attempts to find her medicine, five years old and begging for someone to help her little sister. But now Kiril sat with her beside the garden fishpond rather than play, and talked with her, and Sandy's heart melted all over again at how lucky she was that such a kind and considerate boy had fallen into her life.

"Hey, you two," said Sandy, crouching behind them. "Wha'cha talking about?"

"Mini thinks the big red fish is the prettiest," said Kiril, pointing at the pond. "I think he's the boss fish, he tells all the others what to do."

"Maybe the fish don't have bosses," Sandy suggested. "Maybe they just do what they want."

Miniya shook her head. "No, they don't." With no more explanation, because surely it was obvious.

Sandy sighed. "Mini, your mum wants you. All the girls are getting their hair done up fancy. Would you like your hair done?"

Miniya looked doubtful. She had a big head of hair like her mother, but

African-frizzy rather than Turkish-Caucasus, which was as close as anyone had placed Amirah's ethnic inspiration. "You should get *your* hair done," Kiril suggested.

"I don't have very much to do," said Sandy. She always wrestled with how much decoration she felt comfortable with at events like this, but she was actually quite enjoying the salwar kameez pants and loose top, mostly because she could move in them. And she could keep a pistol strapped to her thigh without anyone noticing, which in a Western-style dress would have been awkward. "But I'm going to get my hands done with henna, and I know Svetlana will too. . . ."

Mentioning Svetlana was usually enough, and Miniya nodded. "I want some henna."

"I said I wanted some henna too," said Kiril, taking mock offence, "but they said it's only for girls! It's not fair."

Sandy laughed and held out her hands for them to take. They walked back into the party, which was a moderate-sized do for a Tanushan movie star wedding—only about eight hundred people crowded into an enormous mansion with huge rear gardens. And scandalously, it was only going to last a weekend, rather than the entire week some of the bigger weddings took. Sandy had heard some rumours at the budget—about six times her annual salary, and she wasn't paid peanuts anymore either. For months Amirah's work colleagues had been teasing her, interrupting her media briefings with fake magazine articles about hot GIs who married for money.

Sandy led the kids past several food stops set up on the patio around the pool, where chefs made finger food on barbeques to be carried by waiters amongst the crowds who mingled in the din of conversation, laughter, and music. There was a live band playing Indofunk inside, and they pressed through dancers and dodged elaborate decorations and people ferrying armfuls of drinks to their friends, before they finally reached the end of a huge lounge where gold and red silk drapes had been hung from the ceiling to make a separate space.

They went through the flap and inside found a cacophony of female conversation and laughter. In the middle of it was Amirah, looking obscenely pretty in a wedding sari and all the jewellery, her hands decorated with henna up to the elbows as someone else put final touches to her hair. She saw Miniya and held out her arms, and Miniya ran to her with a grin.

"Quick quick!" someone shouted, pointing at Kiril. "The height test!"

"Oh, he's not too big already!" Sandy protested. "Don't tell me that! I want him to be small and cuddly forever!"

As Vanessa came up in her own salwar kameez and an embroidered vest and stood beside Kiril. "Nope, not over my waist yet!" she opined, standing on her tiptoes and ignoring that Kiril was now somewhat taller than her waist, as others laughed.

"Doesn't count on you!" someone told her.

"Oh, ignore them, Kiril," Vanessa told him, "you're not too big yet, you come and sit with me."

They went, and Sandy observed the crazy scene—the bride's side of the family, which was funny, of course, because the bride was a GI. And so female friends and colleagues piled into the girl-zone, making it full of synthetic female warriors more accustomed to armour and combat boots, but now bedazzling in every colour imaginable. Several henna artists moved among them, decorating hands, while several guests who actually knew about these things attended to hair and makeup. Rhian was here, little Maria on one arm playing with some bangles, and Raylee Sinta, somehow managing to look better than even women who'd been designed in laboratories. Radha Ibrahim was also there, the boss's wife injecting some much-needed age and wisdom, Amirah having become something of a daughter to them both these past years. And Sandy's old friends Anita and Pushpa, the net-tech geniuses who were friends with all GIs with their unconditional help to all new asylum cases.

Sandy talked with Bec and Taylia, both high-des GIs and FSA squad commanders who had never attended any wedding before, let alone something this size, and seemed to regard it as something between a game and a practical joke. Crazy just what large percentage of Callayan-based elite soldiers were now female, Sandy reflected—when she'd first arrived here it had been rare, with Vanessa practically the only female grunt of any rank. Now the female GIs were just everywhere, and both FSA and CSA had never had so many local girls just out of school applying, apparently inspired by all these unexpected role models. Sandy still wasn't sure that adopting synthetics as role models was the wisest thing for straights, but on the social level, to say nothing of the emotional one, it was kind of nice.

Ari pushed through the drapes, looking very flash in a black kurta that came down to his knees, and was met with shouts of "Height test!" Lila, who was newly promoted section commander, proceeded to carry out the height test by forcing Ari to his knees and face-to-face with her bare midsection, to hoots and hollers from the rest, until Raylee broke it up with mock offence. Then Danya came in behind, and Sandy grabbed him before any more lewd females could take advantage of him, with a warning finger at any who might dare. Fifteen and handsome, he was nearly as tall as her now, and he observed this mad cluster of femininity with wry bemusement mixed with predictable interest. Many of the GIs had opted for sexy two-piece numbers that were theoretically fitting with the Indian theme, but only in fantasy movies.

"Like what you see?" Sandy asked in his ear, arms about his shoulders from behind and grinning.

"Um, yeah, maybe. S'not bad out there either," he said, jerking a thumb out the drapes. "Ari's been showing me around."

"Oh, he has, has he?" said Raylee with a deadly stare.

"Nah, no," Danya came to the rescue. "He's been good, Ray, relax."

"See?" said Ari, pointing. "Thanks, buddy."

"Don't want blood on my conscience," said Danya, tapping his head. As Raylee dragged Ari away for some closer attention.

"So you bring that girl Sandy was telling me about?" Vanessa asked Danya, suffering the indignity of having to look up at him these days . . . but she was used to that.

Danya made a face. "Nuh." A glance sideways at Sandy, chin over his shoulder. "And Sandy shouldn't gossip."

"Aw, poor boyyy," said Sandy, and ruffled his hair.

"So what's up with the girl?" Vanessa pressed. "Not hot enough for you?"

"See, now you've got Vanessa asking questions," Danya accused Sandy. "And she's like a pit bull with smaller teeth."

"Not a good kisser?" Vanessa continued. "Smells like an old cabbage, what?" She clicked her fingers. "Won't go down, will she?"

"Vanessa," Sandy said sternly, as Danya cracked a grin.

"Doesn't compare to any of Sandy's friends," Danya said diplomatically.

"Ah!" said Vanessa, very impressed. "Holy shit, Sandy, he's getting smooth."

"Tell me about it," said Sandy. It was nearly alarming how fast he was growing up, matching verbal jousts with the likes of Vanessa on questions that just a year ago would have turned him red.

"So what is it really?" Vanessa repeated mercilessly.

Danya exhaled hard in defeat. "Girls my age are boring," he said. "You name it, she's not into it, won't try it, never heard of it. And don't even start with the sexual innuendo."

"Nah, shit, you're right," Vanessa agreed, munching a prawn cocktail she snagged from a passing female waiter. "I was dull as mud that age. Sandy was . . . hell, Sandy's *still* that age, right?"

"Not quite," said Sandy.

"Anyway, we get more interesting, thank god for all of us. And if you wanted a girl to learn the ropes with, free of emotional entanglements, plenty of hot GIs here." Indicating the room before them.

"Hey, I've been getting requests," said Sandy. "Or offers, you know—hey, if you want someone you can trust to show your boy a few things before all the nasty girls get to him . . ."

"Um, okay," said Danya, freeing himself from her, "I'm now officially uncomfortable having my Mum and her best friend discuss this like I'm not even here. . . ."

"But if you do make a move," Vanessa added with evil mischief, "you'll keep us in the loop, right?"

"Sure," Danya deadpanned, "oh, Sandy, nearly forgot, Ambassador Quan's looking for you. Where's Svet, out back?"

"Yeah, looking after Darge, she promised Ami she would." Danya nodded and ducked out.

"I shouldn't," said Vanessa with a grin, eating the rest of the prawn. "But he's too adorable when he's embarrassed."

"Gotta go," said Sandy. "League Ambassadors are calling."

"Hey!" called Amirah as Sandy made to leave, from where she and two others were addressing the difficult task of braiding Miniya's hair. "Sandy, where are you going, are you working? There's no working at my wedding!"

"Oh, that's sweet," Sandy teased her for the crowd. "Look, everyone, Ami still thinks there's a distinction between her home life and her work life, isn't she cute?"

"Don't you get all matronly on me!" Amirah called after her as she left. "You're only twenty-five years old!"

"Which is twice as old as you," Rhian retorted on Sandy's behalf. "You shouldn't be allowed to have sex yet, what's with all this marriage business anyway?"

It was a running joke among Tanushan GIs, especially in the light of Jane's ongoing civil trial. The "world of their own" brigade were protesting fervently at Jane's defence team's arguing that GIs should be held to a separate moral standard. Jane bore the same moral burden for having killed those Tanushan civilians seven years ago as any legal adult did, they said. Sure, Sandy and Amirah had replied whenever the media asked—the same way GIs aren't allowed to drink alcohol until eighteen, or have sex until sixteen, or operate vehicles until fourteen, or have uplinks before eighteen, or make decisions without a parent or guardian present before sixteen, right? It was self-evidently preposterous to argue that GIs and straights should be treated the same, when GIs were fully formed and legal adults from anywhere between three and six years depending on their designation and developmental method. They had "adult" physical and technical capabilities from an age when human children were still wetting the bed, but nothing close to full mental maturity—especially when, as in Jane's case, that psychological development had been achieved dangerously early by taking crude and nasty shortcuts.

GIs already had waivers from all the usual age restrictions in Tanusha, be it for sex, alcohol, uplinks, or anything. Everyone knew that "age," as measured for organics, meant almost nothing for GIs, as physical maturity did not equal mental maturity, and the ability to question one's early programming for most arrived late, and for some not at all. The responsibility for murder conducted under the influence of that programming, logically, rested upon the people who programmed her. Oh, well, Sandy thought as she pushed through the dancing, shouting crowds to find Ambassador Quan, this was the fate of synthetics in an organic-predominant society—another day, another legal test case.

She found the Ambassador talking to Phillippe, who was holding little Rupa and talking about violin concertos, of which the League's latest

Federation Ambassador was a big fan. Sandy waved to the baby and got a cheesy grin back.

"Hello, cheeky girl! Where's Sylvan?"

"Oh, you know that one," said Phillippe, "straight to bed after feeding. But this one loves a party, don't you?"

Immediately a woman came and tugged on his arm. "Phillippe, your other little bundle is awake and bawling."

Phillippe sighed. "Should have kept my mouth shut, shouldn't I?"

"Oh, here, I'll take her," said Sandy, removing the baby from his arms. "You go see to the troublesome male child."

"And how's Vanessa, well?" Phillippe asked sarcastically.

"Baby-free and wonderful," said Sandy.

"Must be nice," said Phillippe, and left for the creche on the second floor.

"He wasn't complaining when his cousin got married last month and Vanessa juggled two babies all night," Sandy remarked to the Ambassador, wiping a little drool from Rupa's chin. "Although come to think of it, that was me and Ami, actually." And she smiled at Quan properly for the first time and extended a free hand. "Hello, Ambassador! Enjoying the party?"

"Quite so, yes," said Quan. He was a tall, elegant man, and probably a bit too cultured for an event like this. But everyone who was anyone in Tanushan and Callayan security was here, from Fleet to Intel to the relevant politicians Federal and local, so he could hardly pass up the opportunity. "And how is young Kiril?"

Kiril was of great interest to all senior League officials after the Federation had agreed to share what it had of the aiwallawai tech in his head. League had replicated and farmed it out at rapid speed, with massive upgrades conducted for the general population whether they liked it or not. Many had refused, understandably cynical of League Gov intentions, but plenty were by now aware that the crazy increase in political violence was not just a "thing," and the brain scans that proved it were widely available on the nets. Enough had agreed on the upgrades to mitigate the existing crisis to the point that no more moons or planets had lately been destroyed, though they weren't out of the woods yet.

Among other calamities someone *had* nuked a small city on Fortune, killing forty thousand, and on Far Reach a cult had famously burned themselves alive atop a city skyscraper in full view of cameras because they were convinced beings from an alternate dimension would welcome them as gods when they "crossed over." Upgrade dissenters had been silenced perhaps more by that event than by the nuking, because the nuke had been PRIDE and its usual separatist nonsense, while the cult was . . . well, unthinkable in the rational, scientific League. The sight of a hundred and twenty people, families with children among them, writhing in that towertop inferno of flammable liquids, had convinced most that something was going badly astray. And now, every League official involved in the upgrades was demanding weekly updates on the health and progress of little Kiril Kresnov on Callay, as he'd had these uplinks for the best part of two years now and was further along than any other subject. Pantalan corporation records suggested several other kids had been similarly upgraded as Takewashi had suggested but had disappeared after the Talee invasion. Whatever recent agreements with the Talee, Sandy wasn't about to forgive that any time soon.

"I took Kiril scuba diving last week in VR," Sandy told the Ambassador. "There's a terrific sim program of the Outer Luzian Shelf, it's got some of the best diving anywhere in the Federation. I'd love to go there for real, but I've never had the time. But the sensory input for underwater swimming in VR is very different from anything Kiril's had before, and he was fine, all the parameters were good, the doctors were very pleased."

Rupa took interest in the Ambassador's tie. Sandy broke all protocol and gave it to her. Quan was at pains to look amused. "I'm very pleased to hear that. He's a very special boy for all humanity."

"Oh, you've got millions of test cases now," Sandy said dismissively. "He's only a year ahead, it's not so much."

"Yes, but League are only upgrading adults, not children. Kiril remains the only child in human space with next-generation uplinks, and that makes him special."

"Well, that's not *actually* what makes him special," said his mother. "Besides, with the new stuff that's coming out now in the underground, Kiril's tech will be obsolete pretty soon."

That was the stuff that had leaked as a result of the Talee attack. Predictably some supposedly secret data on Talee-GI uplink tech had leaked to the Tanushan underground, who were now releasing unstable and dangerous versions on the black market to anyone crazy enough to volunteer as a guinea pig. And so began the new disruptive phase of human uplink technology, and Sandy had few hopes that this one wouldn't have all the challenges of the last, and more. Just hopefully it wouldn't promise mass annihilation.

They were interrupted by a slight commotion in the surrounding crowd, a lot of people pointing and looking, which resolved itself into none other than Shejali Myalinamani herself—better known to the people of the Federation as Mya, and as of last month the newly elected Chair of the Federation Grand Council. From that election she was the holder of by far the largest electoral mandate in human history—somewhere approaching nineteen billion people. Her term would be six years, calamities not forthcoming, and she was by all accounts a big fan of Vijay Kulkarni, who had travelled all the way to Earth to make two movies in India, which had gone on to become Federation-wide hits.

"Commander," she said with a broad smile, taking Sandy's free hand past the baby in a well-practised two-handed clasp. "Good to see you. And this gorgeous little girl . . . hello!" Rupa grinned at the leader of the Federation and grasped her finger. "Are you minding her for someone, or did you succumb to the new adoption drive and take another for yourself?"

"Oh, no," said Sandy. "This is FSA Commander Rice's daughter. Babies are fun, but who am I kidding, I've got the most responsible fifteen-year-old son ever, and if I took a really *little* kid, poor Danya would end up looking after her all the time, my hours being what they are. I couldn't do that to him." And as she'd initially feared, being her child could be very dangerous. She still felt awfully guilty when she thought about it and had to remind herself that she'd had no other choice, and that her kids' lives would have been much worse, and possibly ended by now, if she hadn't adopted them. But if she'd had a baby to care for during the last episode with the Talee . . . it made her shudder to think of it.

"And Ambassador Quan," said Maya, "nice to see the Commander and yourself on speaking terms."

"We have a deep common interest in the Commander's youngest boy," said Quan. "I've assured her many times that his safety and well-being is now a top League strategic priority. If he needs anything from us at all, we will grant it as a matter of state importance."

"Gratifying," said Sandy, with restrained enthusiasm. Mya was a handsome, strong-featured woman who'd been first a successful businesswoman, then an Indian politician, and had somehow emerged as the choice of the largest centrist faction to the new, democratically elected Grand Council. She had a preference for "neutral" fashion, rather than the saris of many Indian politicians, and struck most people as a sensible if slightly bland candidate. Inoffensive and easy to manipulate, some cynics suggested—just how the factions liked them. Sandy wasn't so sure. "Nice to see you've got time for a wedding."

"Well, I could hardly miss this one," said Mya, "they're calling this the wedding of the decade."

"I used to fear that politics in Tanusha was becoming too much like show business," Sandy conceded. "Now I'm convinced of it."

Mya laughed. "I read Ibrahim's little internal memo about the dangers of a directly elected Grand Council. Word in the corridors is that a lot of it came from you."

Sandy raised her eyebrows, neither admitting nor denying. "And what did you think?"

"I admit it has its dangers. And he, or you, are obviously right about the problems of strategic lag, trying to get institutional feedback from outer worlds in time to make coordinated decisions, without risking long-term alienation. But after all that's happened, don't you think that having a council full of people elected only by politicians, not by the public at large, is even more dangerous? Given how unaccountable and self-interested those people have proven to be in times of crisis?"

"Probably," Sandy admitted. "But politics has this nasty habit of dividing the issue, then polarizing each side. Just because the old system was bad doesn't mean the new one will be good. I saw a lot of irrational exuberance in the election, and I guess that's understandable given the sheer scale of it . . . but irrational exuberance in politics usually comes back to bite you. Especially here."

"There's a lot of truth in that," the Grand Council Chair conceded. "But as you'll appreciate, it's my job to make this thing work, so I'll keep my cup half full for the time being."

"And plenty of others will be trying to take that cup and drink it for you."

The three of them talked until Svetlana dashed up and tugged on her arm. "Sandy Sandy! The Director's telling stories!"

"Yeah, um, Svet? This is the leader of the entire Federation, Chairwoman Myalinamani."

"Oh, hi," Svetlana amended.

"Hello, Svetlana," said Mya. "I've heard so much about you. How is your leg?"

"Oh . . . it's fine, not even a scar. But Sandy!" as Svetlana returned her attention to her mother. "You *love* the Director's stories, come and listen to one with me! Please?"

"Director Ibrahim tells children's stories?" asked Mya, astonished.

"It's one of his less advertised talents," said Sandy, trying to keep a dignified posture as Svetlana dragged on one arm. "I'm sorry, it's a rare highlight for them. . . ."

"No, of course! I'd join you if I could, but I told my advisors I'm here to work, so I'd better work."

"I gave up trying to separate work and family when Kiril became a League strategic asset," said Sandy in retreat. "I'll see you again before you leave, I'm sure."

They returned to the girl-zone first and took Kiril from Vanessa's care by swapping him for Rupa, bringing a new round of cooing from all the women. Then Sandy and Svetlana sat on the grass in the huge garden beneath a lovely old tree, with the music and laughter pounding the background as Director Ibrahim took off his shoes, sat cross-legged on a low garden wall, and told about thirty kids and a handful of adults a story. It was about three brothers who journeyed across Persia and India in old and enchanted times, full of wizards and monsters and flying carpets, on their way to rescue their sister who had been kidnapped by an evil Khan. He told it well, and Sandy thought she had never seen him looking quite so much at home—before a bunch of mesmerised children in the garden nightlight, a man of authority and power, but kind and wise. Sandy sat with Kiril and Svetlana leaning on each arm, and Danya alongside, and lost herself for the better part of an hour, until good had triumphed and family had been reunited.

And then the children left, chasing rumours of cake, with Sandy calling after them, "Kids, say thank you to Uncle Shan!" Which they dutifully did before rushing off, and Sandy sat at his side on the wall.

"Thank you," she said. "That was lovely."

"An old author," he said, "centuries dead. Passed down through our family, I know that tale backward. It is a part of the reason I sought this profession."

"To fight evil Khans for justice?"

Her boss smiled. "Exactly."

"How we doing on that score?"

"Not so bad, I think. If only the enemy had more evil and less pathos. That would be easier."

"Wouldn't it always." He could have been talking about the Talee or the League, it applied to both. "But I think the pathetic have begun to accept that they *are* pathetic. That's the first step."

Ibrahim nodded. "Jane is not here?"

Sandy shook her head. "She's free, but . . ." She sighed. "She's not much for company at the moment."

"I hear good things," said Ibrahim with measured confidence. "Of her chances, from people who should know."

"You mean Radha." Ibrahim's wife was not defending Jane; that might have looked improper given Jane's links to Sandy, and thus to the Ibrahims. But Radha was as respected as any lawyer in Tanusha and knew all the inside gossip.

"Good things," Ibrahim repeated. "And as a legal precedent, much needed."

"That means League will be held responsible for a lot. They won't like it."

"Good," said Ibrahim with an edge of dark satisfaction. "You told me once that if you weren't upsetting the League, you weren't doing it right. In this case I agree." He put his hand on hers. "Jane will be well. You worry too much."

Sandy hung her head. "I'm still not even sure how much I like her. She's aggravating."

Ibrahim shrugged. "Same in any family."

Sandy looked at him and smiled. "Kiril still won't accept that the dog's not actually a dog."

"Dodger?"

She nodded. "He tries to teach Dodger to fetch, and Dodger just looks at him like he's nuts. Asura don't fetch, they stalk."

"But he's safe?"

"Oh, yeah, he's safe enough. They're hierarchical, he knows I'm boss. I just keep an eye on him with visitors."

"You know wild asura have killed people on Emerald?"

"Like I said," said Sandy. "A close eye. But we have an understanding. He's safe when he knows where he stands in the group."

"Still a wild animal though, however FedInt trained him."

"I know. Oh, and you should smell the poo!"

"I should *not* smell the poo," Ibrahim corrected.

"Unbelievable. The kids have to clean it. I tell them I'll soak up high explosive for them, but I won't touch the poo."

Ibrahim looked amused. "I believe you're becoming finicky."

"Finicky, huh." She thought about it. "I can live with that."

"I have it on good authority," said Ibrahim, as a new din of drums and trumpets started out the front of the house, "that we have a Talee guest here tonight."

Sandy nodded. "I hear that too. We're keeping an eye on him as well."

"You know who it is?"

"We think so. Someone sympathetic, as Cai said . . . or Cai's implant program, anyway. We're fairly sure the synth-Talee don't want him here, but he came anyway."

Ibrahim nodded slowly. "Work carefully with that. Now I hear the org-Talee are working on human-infiltration GIs of similar type—thinkers, not drones. Like Cai. So soon enough we might have Talee-made GIs from both factions fighting it out in Tanusha."

Sandy sighed. "Great. But inevitable, I suppose. We're not vulnerable to them now, or not anywhere near *as* vulnerable, and we get stronger every year. I'm more worried about internal upheavals from all this new tech than I am about Talee, it's going to shake up a lot."

"Inevitable, as you say," said Ibrahim. A faint smile. "It's Tanusha."

"Yes. Yes, it is. Keep us all employed, I guess."

"You've read the proposals to make our own synthetic Talee and spy on them like they spy on us?"

"Over my dead body," Sandy said grimly.

Ibrahim nodded. "Mine too," he said. The racket out the front grew even louder, and people in the garden and at the back of the house began leaving to check on it.

"It's a great, great thing you did," said Ibrahim. Sandy looked at him in surprise. "You were presented with a vision of ideological purity. A world where GIs would be respected and feared. Where you would become masters of your own destiny. You've fought for such a thing all your life, and yet you threw it away, out of concern for us. Your oppressors."

Sandy smiled. "You're not my oppressor. My kids aren't. Vanessa isn't. People are individuals, not groups. We either live together as such, or we abandon any hope of civilisation."

"You could have used synth-tee cooperation to force synthetic emancipation in the League."

"And League would have resisted even more strongly and fought back, and a lot more people would be dead, synthetic and organic. Look at it now—the battle's a long way from won, but League owe me. They owe all us synthetics, big time. We'll translate that into political power, you watch, and when all the new GIs keeping the peace over there in the next ten years begin to come of age psychologically . . . it'll change. One way or the other, it'll change. I think the League leaders are starting to know it, too. We'll make it come faster if we can convince them that emancipation can be peaceful and not another bloody war."

A blare of trumpets out the front, and some fireworks popping and echoing off towers near and far. "I think this means the groom has arrived," said Ibrahim, getting slowly to his feet. He gave Sandy a hand up, despite the silliness of expecting she'd need it. Sandy smiled and accepted.

"I suppose we must," she sighed. "I'm not sure I see the attraction, to be honest. But Ami's an odd girl and she deserves to be happy."

"I give it five years at most," Ibrahim said drily, and Sandy laughed. "Vijay is a very egotistical man and Ami will tire of him eventually. But Radha disagrees. He is very good to her and the children, I must admit."

"Grumpy grandpa doesn't want to see his little girl get hitched," said Sandy, taking his arm. "Shall we?"

"Oh, and Cassandra," Ibrahim added as they walked arm in arm toward the house, "speaking of grumpy grandpas, I don't want to be the one to put limits on the new freedoms our female GIs are discovering so joyously . . . but do you think at future events you might encourage them to put on just a *few* more clothes? It's a wedding, not a brothel."

Out the front, crowds of guests had gathered at the end of the big driveway through the gardens and trees. The groom's procession wound its way in from the road, leaving behind swarms of media and cameras that had followed it this far. Guards kept them out while admitting proper guests, with some confusion as to who was what, while the rest danced and beat drums and blew trumpets, an entire marching band keeping up a hammering rhythm, while others shot firecrackers skywards and hover drones recorded the whole thing for posterity.

Vijay Kulkarni rode a white horse above them all, decked in gold and red, with a gold turban. Word was he'd wanted an elephant, but Tanushan officials had only grudgingly allowed them to close down several streets for the procession and were *not* in a mood to grant permissions for an elephant, even if the zoo could spare a trained one. He rode proudly, waving to everyone above a sea of dancing, garland presenting, and petal throwing. . . . Sandy supposed there was a lot of custom to it all, but it just looked like confusion to her. But a fun confusion, the kind she'd always enjoyed.

She found the kids, Kiril on Danya's back so he could see over the crowds, and Svetlana jumped on hers, and they watched the arrival together, manoeuvring onto the grass at one side for more space and a better view. Amidst the trees something made her turn her head . . . and she saw a dark figure nearby, alone and watching. Familiar.

Sandy put Svetlana down and walked across. The woman wore sensible salwar kameez, nothing fancy, with a fashionable little hat with a veil that came down across her eyes. But before she reached her, Sandy knew who it was.

"Jane?"

"Hey, sis," said Jane. "Nice party?" She looked awkward in these civvie clothes. *Feminine* clothes, for the first time since Sandy had known her. It wasn't her style. To be loud, to be seen. To be companionable. She had the weight of a new, legal morality hanging above her head like an axe prepared to drop and didn't feel like company at the best of times . . . yet here she was. God knew how she'd gotten in.

"It is what you make of it," said Sandy with a smile. "The groom's an ass, and there's too much work and politics . . . but my friends and family are here. All of them, now."

Jane smiled back, a little awkwardly. "The food any good?"

"You see what this costs? It's *amazing*."

Jane took a deep breath. "Guess it couldn't hurt. For a while at least."

"Auntie Jane!" yelled Kiril and came running to hug her. Then Svetlana, then Danya, progressively more restrained but no less heartfelt. Jane picked up Kiril and put an arm around Svetlana, and they all walked together back into the colourful crowd.

ABOUT THE AUTHOR

Joel Shepherd is the author of five previous novels in the Cassandra Kresnov series—*Crossover, Breakaway, Killswitch, 23 Years on Fire,* and *Operation Shield*—and four previous novels in the Trial of Blood and Steel series—*Sasha, Petrodor, Tracato,* and *Haven.* He is currently midway through a doctoral program in International Relations, and has also studied film and television, interned on Capitol Hill in Washington, and traveled widely in Asia.

© Impact Image, South Australia